How She Died

Other Houghton Mifflin
Literary Fellowship Awards

To E. P. O'Donnell for *Green Margins*
To Dorothy Baker for *Young Man with a Horn*
To Robert Penn Warren for *Night Rider*
To Joseph Wechsberg for *Looking for a Bluebird*
To Ann Petry for *The Street*
To Elizabeth Bishop for *North & South*
To Anthony West for *The Vintage*
To Arthur Mizener for *The Far Side of Paradise*
To Madison A. Cooper, Jr., for *Sironia, Texas*
To Charles Bracelen Flood for *Love Is a Bridge*
To Milton Lott for *The Last Hunt*
To Eugene Burdick for *The Ninth Wave*
To Philip Roth for *Goodbye Columbus*
To William Brammer for *The Gay Place*
To Clancy Sigal for *Going Away*
To Ellen Douglas for *A Family's Affairs*
To John Stewart Carter for *Full Fathom Five*
To Margaret Walker for *Jubilee*
To Berry Morgan for *Pursuit*
To Robert Stone for *A Hall of Mirrors*
To Willie Morris for *North Toward Home*
To Georgia McKinley for *Follow the Running Grass*
To Elizabeth Cullinan for *House of Gold*
To Edward Hannibal for *Chocolate Days, Popsicle Weeks*

A *Houghton Mifflin*
——*Literary Fellowship Award Novel*

How She Died

by Helen Yglesias

Houghton Mifflin Company
Boston

The quotations on page 139 are taken from
Revelation 21:4 and *The Moment of Cubism* by
John Berger, Pantheon Books, page 4.

Chapter 1 appeared originally in *The New Yorker*
under the title "Semi-Private."

Second Printing w

Library of Congress Catalog Card Number: 76–173778
ISBN: 0–395–13529–X
Printed in the United States of America

For Jose

How She Died

1 ———

BEYOND MY BED, opposite me, a contraption of weights, raised heaps, ropes (they had figured in my nightmares) materialized into a traction device. After long study, I discerned the head of an old woman raised on a mountain of pillows past the elevated legs; her face distorted with painful sleep was surrounded by a wild halo of yellow-gray hair. I considered it very clever of them to string her body like a hammock between those elevated legs and head. And what trickery have they thought up for me? Something. Something I remembered being insistently shouted at me in the recovery room: precancerous tissue. A bright little flame licked away at the edge of remembering. It lit up and charred as it burned, so that I remembered and forgot, remembered and forgot, in split instants. They took off my breast. No. They took off my breast. No. I fell asleep.

When I woke again, a pretty, middle-aged woman stood in the center of the ward fussing with a clear plastic bag filled with an extraordinarily bright orange liquid. It looked evil. From the bag a narrow tube disappeared under her blue nylon matching gown and robe. Her hair had been teased and rinsed into a bouffant hairdo of an alarming shade of blue. She was fussing with a metal clip attached to the tube. It was not because I recognized the liquid as urine that I started to vomit. I retched into a metal container at the side of my bed so automatically that I knew I had been vomiting before. If the breast was really gone, it had no business hurting, but my sudden movement had started another fire there. The woman with the urine bag called, "Nurse, nurse, that poor child is throwing up again." How foolish. Vomiting was nothing. The fires! Put out the fires!

The nurse came immediately, carried away the container and returned with a warm, soapy washcloth which she passed like a blessing over my face and hands. I saw her young, flawless skin. The brown brows and brown eyelines which made her eyes a fawn's were perfectly drawn. The brilliant blond hair must have been dyed, and she had suntanned all the parts of her luscious figure which were visible against the prim white uniform.

"Feeling better? Sure thing. You have it licked."

I said, "Have I been saying a lot of — dumb things?"

She fixed my pillow and straightened my covers. "Now you don't think all I have to do is listen to what you say, do you?"

"Should I have all this pain?"

She said that if I was in *great* pain I could have an injection because it was long enough after the anesthesia, but since I was still a little sleepy and nauseous perhaps it would be better to wait a bit. I tried to determine what *great* pain was and told her that I'd wait. Then I asked her if my husband was here and she told me that he would be coming back at two-thirty. After she left I realized that I didn't know what time it was and had no idea how long it would be before Matt would be coming. This made me violently angry with him and I started to cry. I stopped immediately because she was back at my bedside with iced ginger ale which she induced me to sip through one of those impossible bent plastic straws. I did and vomited again, but not much. She urged me to keep sipping the ginger ale a bit at a time and I did. I kept sinking in and rising out of that muddy sleep, but each time I emerged I had a clearer sense of being in a particular place, until finally I really knew where I was.

Precancerous tissue. I had never heard of that before. Like coming attractions. Next week cancer of the lung. Someone must have said it to me. Dr. Altman must have said it in his loud fast voice, yes, in that crazy baker's outfit they wear when they operate. Was it in the operating room? Didn't I remember Matt there too, with lying frightened eyes, holding my hand in his trembling one. It couldn't have been the operating room. It must have been the recovery room, after they had done it. They never ask the patient. The patient is anesthetized on the operating table, cut open. They call in the husband. "We think it best to remove this precancerous breast. Since this is your hunk of meat, do we have your permission, husband?" And Matt? No-decision-Matt? "Why, you know best, doctors, whatever you say, whatever is best for you, less trouble" — smiling his eager-to-please, handsome smile. "Yes, yes, yes, cut off her head, anything."

As if I had rung a bell, the pretty nurse came in with an injection for me.

"I'm not in *great* pain now either," I said. "I don't want to go to sleep again."

"It's time now," she said. "You won't get sleepy. It will make you more comfortable."

I expected her to give the injection badly, but she was deft and I hardly felt it. It did make me more comfortable and very quickly. It had the unexpected result of allowing me a straightforward view of the landscape burning in my head. I will die of cancer at 28, leaving my little boy and my newborn baby girl and invalid mother in the hands of a scared and childish man who will run right out and get himself a beautiful two-breasted new wife to replace me. To *replace* me? She will spoil all my work. She will put my mother in a home and mess up my children's lives and allow Matt to slip into his worst self. No. She will adore him and do whatever he wishes and rear the children perfectly and bake her own bread. He will be happy for the first time. No. I will be fine. I will finish all the work of my life. They have removed all the precancerous tissue and I will be well. Matt will love me with only one breast. He will be here soon. He will look into my eyes with steady love. We will have a real *Ladies' Home Journal* scene. All the bitterness between us will evaporate like magic.

The old woman had been unstrung from her weights and ropes and was lumbering out of bed, groaning exaggeratedly with each movement. She wrapped herself in a printed quilted robe and called out to see if I was feeling better now. I said yes. Upright, she was thick and short, her face a broad, healthy-colored field flowering her lively blue eyes, all of it surrounded by the wild halo of yellow-gray hair. She had a man's deep voice. "Such a shame, a young girl like you to be in a hospital so sick. It's not right. But now it's all over and you'll be fine and healthy again. Tell me, what do you have, what's wrong with you? What did they cut you out?"

"A tumor," I said.

She shook her head. "Where — in the breast?"

I nodded, trying not to show her how I hated our conversation.

"Where else? That's how it is with us women. But listen to Mama. A tumor in the breast is nothing as long as it's benign. So you see it's nothing." She came close to my bed, carrying with her messy appearance a clean baby smell of talcum and clothes dried in the sun. "They said it's benign?" Waiting, a held concern in her bright blue eyes.

I said yes and closed my eyes against the thought of my mother and the smell of my children in this old stranger.

"That's right, darling, rest, rest," she said. "Now it's all over, soon you'll eat a little something and feel stronger. Meanwhile, rest." I squinted, watching her labor her way from me to Blue-Rinse to whom she again observed that she hated to see a young girl like me in the hospital. "Especially on Friday. She should be home enjoying the weekend with her husband. Such a nice-looking girl. You're married?" She turned back to ask. I nodded. "Hospitals! They take your wedding ring away, you can't tell who's married, who's not married. A wedding ring is bad when you're on the operating table, what it does to you God knows, but they take it away from you, rings, a watch, even false teeth, thank God you don't know from that. False teeth I can see, you could swallow them, God forbid, but a wedding ring! You're suddenly going to bite off one of your own fingers and swallow a gold ring with diamond chips?"

I laughed and she responded with a surprisingly merry laugh in an upper register where her voice belonged.

"Never mind, you're all right. I see you didn't forget how to laugh. Next weekend you'll be home enjoying with your husband. And maybe you have children?"

"Two," I said.

"Look at that. These days babies have babies. She's a baby herself."

"Some baby," I said. "I'm twenty-eight."

"I wish I were twenty-eight again," said Blue-Rinse.

"So what would you do with it? The same thing you did before, so what's the use to do it over." She turned back to me. "The girl in the bed next to you, she's not here this minute, they're changing the bandages from her eye, she's your age and she has five children. Of course, she's Catholic, not that there's anything wrong you should be Catholic but in her case it's not the best in the world because that's why she's sick with her eyes, the babies eat up something in her eyes that it's making her blind and still she has to have the babies because that's her religion. I don't say religion is wrong but in her case it's not so good. One operation last year, one operation this year, one operation next year, who knows if she'll ever see good again. The doctors say maybe yes, but you and I know how it is with doctors, with them everything is fine, because does it hurt them? No, it hurts you and me and them it puts money in the pocket, but God bless them they do their best." Groaning and talking, she had made her way to a bathroom at the end of the ward. She left the door slightly open and the sound of her urinating was like a waterfall.

Manipulating the plastic bag and disappearing tube with fussy daintiness, Blue-Rinse came close to my bed. Mouthing her words soundlessly, she said, "Good soul. Good soul. Talks too much. Don't mind her."

Did I imagine it or did she smell foul?

In the same soundless speech she said, "Poor soul. Two stone-deaf children." She used her free hand to hold up two fingers and pointed in dramatic pantomime to her ears.

I said, "What?" but when she went through the same procedure, I was sorry to have asked. I thought she must be mad. Or myself? Had I gone mad? I tried to sit up, and speaking normally now in her prissy voice she said, "Oh, no, dear, you'd better not do that without the nurse," and rang the bell at my bed.

But the nurse did not come and I must have slid again into a twisting half-sleep of nightmare, where I struggled with two teen-age girl friends I hadn't seen in years. They hung at the window to my left and scolded me for unspeakable crimes. I argued shrilly, engulfed in a hot, sticky weakness, protesting, pushing against the amorphous accusations, accusing them in turn of having no business being here. It was Matt who should be indicting me. For lying. For talking divorce when what I wanted was the world changed. For having gotten pregnant twice when he didn't want me to once. For all the agony of our life in bed. And out.

Forcing myself awake, I recognized the two meager lengths of printed material at the window as my friends. What a remarkable likeness! The fall of the fabric from the valance to the sill re-created the slope of the girls' shoulders into their long slender arms. And how clever of the drapes to make the comparison. I had never noticed that their bodies were shaped alike. The long line of their waists too. Very elegant. Why had I lost touch with them? How sad my lost friends looked hanging there! I felt my eyes dribbling unwilled tears. I brushed them aside with my right hand, thought of my left side with loathing, and burned with thirst. I groped for the ginger ale and knocked a glass over.

"Don't worry about it, dear." That was Blue-Rinse, who still seemed to be hovering at my bed.

"I'm thirsty," I said. "I'm not worrying about it." My speech was thick and angry. The sound of it surprised me. "Where is that bell for the nurse?" I groped a little, afraid to stretch.

"It's all right. Here they come, hurrying along right this minute." It was the young woman in the bed alongside mine. I couldn't see her because it meant turning my body and I was afraid to, but her words had the pleasant upward-ending turn of the New York Irish.

The nurse came almost immediately. With her came attendants and rattling lunch wagons, all the cheerful clamor I had found so enjoyable when I had had my babies in the same hospital, but which was now unbearable. It was the same pretty nurse and she asked me whether I would like to try to eat some lunch by myself or have the attendant help me.

"I'm terribly thirsty," I said.

"Perfect lunch for thirst," she said with maddening good cheer. "Soup, tea and Jell-O. Toast if you like." She rolled up my bed. "Comfy? Little more?"

They had placed the tray within my reach on my right side, the whole side, so I supposed it was all right for me to stretch at least with my right arm. "Little higher," I said, and felt better with my head raised.

The nurse washed my face again with a warm, soapy cloth. When she searched for my comb in the drawer of the side table, I could see her name pinned to the pocket of her uniform. MISS JOAN BERNARDINO, R.N. She smelt delicious. Everything was very nice about her. Matt will be crazy about her. Two breasts too. She knew exactly how to comb my short hair and brought a few light hairs across my forehead the way I do myself with her long cool fingers.

"There!" she said. "As good as new."

I exhausted myself trying to eat and after finishing the soup, I gave up. The bustle in the room had quieted to the serious matter of eating. Now that my bed was cranked up and I was turned to the right I could see the young woman alongside me. She was being fed by a Negro attendant who could have been 19 or 50, it was impossible for me to tell. Though a bulging bandage covered the girl's left eye, she was obviously very pretty. Her hair was dark and softly arranged around her face. Her skin was marvelously fresh-looking. She sat upright in her bed, her mouth opening and closing daintily on the spoon. Her lips, cut with exquisite precision, were perfectly lipsticked.

"Did Miss Bernardino put your lipstick on?" I asked her. "I'll get her to do mine before my husband visits."

Her head swiveled toward me on her long neck in a deliberate, proud movement, the bandaged eye looking directly at me. "No," she said. "I did it myself."

The attendant feeding her burst into a ringing, mocking laugh. "Lady, you're the one who said it. Not me. But I'm telling you, I've been holding back saying it. I've been feeding that pretty mouth lunch and supper now for three days, thinking to myself, so how come I'm sitting here feeding that pretty mouth with lipstick on it so perfect? How come she can put her lipstick on so perfect but she gotta be fed like a baby?"

"Don't be foolish," the old woman said, but not sharply. "You think she likes to be fed? Not even babies like to be fed; they can't wait to pick up a piece of cheese or meat or bread in their little fingers."

"Now that is one thing I really am, foolish. Foolish, foolish." The Negro woman laughed. "But I was just saying she certainly knows how to put her lipstick on real good." She went on feeding as she talked. "The doctor orders to feed her, the nurse says to me, 'Wilson, go feed seven-o-one her lunch,' I feed her. But I just wondering, just like this lady here who asked the question, how come she can do one thing and not the other."

"It's a different thing," the young woman with the eye bandage said very sweetly.

"That's not what I meant," I said peevishly to the attendant.

After the next mouthful, the young woman said she wouldn't have any more, thank you, just the coffee, please. The attendant held the cup to her lips. She sipped one, two, three times, swallowing with difficulty in between. Then she thanked the attendant again.

"That all you going to eat?" the attendant said.

"Oh, I've had more than enough, thank you," the young woman said.

"Sure, now? I don't want to be hearing from them how I'm not feeding you good now." She laughed her mocking laugh again.

The girl didn't answer her, but rested her head, still upright, on the pillow behind it as if the bulge's weight had dragged it back. Her lips shaped a permanent smile on her uptilted face.

When the Negro woman left with the tray, Blue-Rinse said, "I don't know what's wrong with those people. She didn't have to say all that. It's just that they hate any extra work. Hate to work, those people. You'd think they'd be happy to have such a nice clean job."

"Don't say 'those people,' " the old woman said. "A person is a person. Not — 'those people.' All people have good and bad ones."

"It was my fault," I said. "I started it."

"The Jews know what it means to be called 'those people,' " the old woman said.

"Please!" Blue-Rinse said. "You can't compare the two! What a comparison. Why, those people are as anti-Semitic as they come."

"I didn't know you were Jewish too," the old lady said, turning to Blue-Rinse with new interest. "You talk so fancy I'd never know. These days you can't tell who's who anyway. They go to college, they all come out talking the same way. Mumble jumble, you can't understand a word."

"The thing is," the blinded young woman said, "I like to keep doing things for myself. I like to keep after myself and help myself as much as I can. After all I have five youngsters at home. If I can manage at home, I'm all right. My big girl helps a lot, she's eleven."

"God bless her," the old woman said.

"I surely don't feel right if I don't keep after my personal appearance," the young woman said. "I learned to do a lot of things by feel. I can put make-up on by feel, even eye make-up. Not mascara though. My daughter puts that on for me. I can put my hair up in rollers and comb it out just by feel. After all, a woman has hair to do something with, to look nice in the sight of man and God, and I try to do my best. I'm bringing up my girls the same way. I can't understand these women who just let their hair lie around their faces any old way."

"Five girls?" Blue-Rinse asked.

"Oh, glory be, no! The two youngest are boys. Three girls. My husband was getting kind of desperate after the first three. But he's real proud of them; they're real little women. I'm trying to bring them up right. I teach them it isn't nice to walk around in rollers like so many of their friends do. You see them everywhere, don't you now, in the supermarkets, even in the subways going down to work, my husband tells me. Some of my closest friends do it. It's a disgrace. I set my girls an example. I get up every morning at six o'clock and put rollers in my hair for an hour. I never go to bed in rollers or with sticky cream on my face. Men hate that. Just that hour in the morning and by the time my husband wakes up at seven, I have it combed out silky and pretty. Once a week I wash it in the afternoon, put in the rollers, and by the time my husband comes home from work, it's all combed out silky and pretty."

"I could never manage without the beauty parlor at least every ten days. I can just stretch it ten days," Blue-Rinse said.

"Oh, it's a sin to waste money in the beauty parlor with all these new products they're putting out. And the hand dryers and all," the young woman said. I was mesmerized by her talk. Because of the way her voice lilted, it was so musically, poetically pleasant to listen to her.

"Silky and pretty." The old woman labored out of bed as she talked. "So what's the big deal to be so silky and pretty? You need another baby? Just what you need — another baby. I lived a whole life without rollers and without beauty parlors, but I know nowadays it's different, so we won't argue." She stopped at the foot of the young woman's bed. "And how does your husband support so many children and all these operations? He has a business?"

"He's with Consolidated." Her pretty lips closed on the name with ultimate satisfaction. "And of course there's all the benefits, sick and hospital, you know."

"Also a big deal," the old woman said. "If he clears a hundred fifty dollars a week it's good already. Don't be so busy with the silky and pretty. See better that you don't have any more babies. You're a baby yourself. Take care on yourself. Tell your doctor. Or the priest who comes to you every morning. He looks like a very nice young fellow. It can't be like people say. Every religion is reasonable. In my religion if you're a sick person you don't fast on Yom Kippur. It must be some arrangement like that for you in your religion. You want Mama should ask him for you?"

Patchy streaks of color spread on the young woman's cheeks. It made me think of flowers and of steak also, of a delicious piece of rare meat. She put her head back on the pillow as she had before with the painted smile uptilted and said, "No, thank you, Mama. My priest and my doctors know all about it." She brought her head upright again. "My eye surgeon is a wonderful man and he's doing what he can. He's Jewish, too. He's very funny, always kidding around. I have this habit, whatever happens I always say God knows best. Last time I said that to him he said, 'Well, He'd damn well better, because *we* sure don't.'" She blushed again in that healthy streaky way.

"That's not nice of him to say, even if he is a surgeon," the old woman said. "It's all right to say such words I guess, but not about God."

"I'm sure he didn't say it because he's Jewish," Blue-Rinse said.

"I'll tell you another thing," the old woman said. "God helps those who help themselves. I've had plenty troubles in my life. You think I put it all on God? When my children were born deaf, I didn't thank God and I didn't curse Him. After I realized with the first (she was four already, it took me so long to realize) something's wrong, *something is wrong,* I went and I did. I found doctors first. Nothing to help. Nothing. So I found a school. People helped, sure, but if I didn't try, could I make it so that from that poor child a real person could grow? At least give the baby a chance. And the same with my third child when he was born deaf. Did I waste time arguing with God, why He made one child normal and two deaf? And to me — *two?* — one wasn't enough? Life is too short to argue. Life is too short to understand God altogether, especially nowadays. I went and did and tried again, only this time I didn't wait so long. So my son hasn't found happiness yet like my daughter but please God one day he'll meet a nice deaf girl, she doesn't have to be Jewish, and together they'll make a life like my daughter and her husband. They should live and be well with their two perfectly normal children together." She continued to the bathroom. "I don't know what it is with me, the medicine or the food, that I have to pass water all the time. I'm sick and tired from the bathroom already."

"Where there's life there's hope," Blue-Rinse said. "When they told me that they had done a colostomy on me, I said to myself, I'd rather be dead. But later I told myself, where there's life there's hope. What else can I do?" Why did her hopeful resignation make her voice sound so querulous? "What an awful, dirty thing to have when I've always been so fussy about my person. When my girl friends come to my apartment, they tease me about it. 'Don't touch! Don't touch! You know how fussy Anne is.' And I am. I am very, very fussy. And I'm supposed to learn how to clean this awful thing by myself. I don't know how I'm ever going to get used to it. And this!" She gave the tube of the urine bag, hanging near her side, a furious little pull. "Am I going to be trailing this gorgeous object around the rest of my life? How long does it take to clear up a bladder infection anyway? I've been here for weeks. They cure one thing and make you sick with another."

"It's a shame," the young woman said.

"And then in a few months I'll have to have another operation. They say. To put back the normal evacuation channel," Blue-Rinse said.

"Sure and you'll be as good as new again," the young woman said.

"You know," the old woman said on her way back from the bathroom, "before you, I never heard from such a thing. Whoever heard of it, you cut a hole in a person's side to go to the bathroom in."

"Oh, please don't talk about it," Blue-Rinse almost screamed.

In the silence that fell over the room I decided that we were all dying. Buddies at death's door. But they weren't the buddies I would have chosen. Especially Blue-Rinse. That blue-haired ladylike creature with the evacuation hole in her side and the orange urine was turning the place into a nightmare. And they were all wasting my time. I had to think about the spot I was in, how to get out of it and whose fault it was. That was important. Find out who's to blame. Put it all down on paper. *Organize this thing.* Analyze it.

I was too tired to do anything but put my head back to rest. With my head in that unnatural position I frightened myself. Borrowing her gesture, I pulled upright, but the gesture tugged like an enchantment, straining my head back and shaping my lips into the faint smile hers held constantly. Good, I will escape myself. I froze my face into the borrowed mask of a beautiful young woman cheerfully going blind for man and God.

In that uncomfortable position I fell asleep for one of those short naps which feel like a long, solid sleep, and when I opened my eyes on my two doctors standing near my bed I was completely refreshed.

"That's the girl. Best way to sleep, elevated. How are you? Feeling good? Fine." My surgeon's loud fast voice infuriated me. "Your chart is great. Keep up the good work. Don't use your left arm, we don't want those sutures to tear; do anything else you want. Been out of bed yet? We need you out of bed, it's twenty-four hours since your operation. The nurse will help you to the bathroom, you'll *shmear* a little make-up on, you'll feel better for it. What do you say there, Dr. Guerrero" — he drew Bob into his frenetic activity — "doesn't she look great?"

Bob followed unwillingly. He only nodded and pinched my toe through the covers. But before his eyes blinked away from mine I had caught something unmistakably terrifying drowning in his soft brown eyes. I really *am* going to die, I thought, as if it had not occurred to me before. The information shone out of his eyes, a live *thing* swimming in his eyes.

I missed a lot of what Dr. Altman was rattling on about trying to see if I could find that thing in his eyes too. But they're very different, their eyes of course are different. Bob's are brilliantly soft and expressive, but also Bob is my friend as well as my doctor and it wouldn't be just another happening, all in the day's work to him, as these things are to all doctors. But still I felt that if it were true, it would show in Dr. Altman's eyes too and I wanted to catch it there, or rather I wanted to be sure it wasn't there at all; or both at the same time. I have often had this reaction to sensing a hidden fact, sleuthing it out. Even if it was unpleasant and damaging, I would feel pressed to prove that it exists. I feel it as a pain in my head. It will flit in a glance from one face to another, a real flying thing that I must catch in my hand. Even if it's something I hate to hear I'm glad when I'm proved right and someone comes out and says it plainly. But when I started to chase after this one, I started to run away from it too and the pain in my head became intolerable. I made a great effort to speak like myself and cut through Dr. Altman's talk.

"Isn't it nice that he's so cheerful," I said to Bob.

"Dr. Guerrero is cheerful too," Dr. Altman said. "Right, Guerrero?"

Bob nodded again.

"What's the matter?" Dr. Altman said to me. "Are you worried about something? You worry too much."

"I'm morbid," I said.

He laughed as if I had delivered the punch line of a comic routine, and then lowered his voice. "Listen, you've got nothing to worry about. Everything's out. You're absolutely clean. We have to watch you of course. We'll do a little deep therapy as a precaution and that's it."

He looked to Bob for help, but Bob was staring at my bed covers.

"That doesn't make sense," I said. "Why therapy? If there's nothing left? You mean radium?"

"Bob and I were talking about cobalt. We think cobalt."

"I won't do it," I said. "I don't want to. If everything's all right why do I need cobalt?"

"So Bob and I can sleep nights." He laughed, again disproportionately.

"Why you?" And then like a child, I kept repeating. "I'm not going to take it. I don't want to."

A roughness hardened the edge of Dr. Altman's good cheer. "Don't be silly now. You be a good girl now. You'll do what you have to do. It's a routine procedure."

"Aren't you supposed to be worrying about how I sleep?" I said, furiously. "And what's this about tearing the sutures. Can't you even sew?"

He turned to Bob with an angry gesture which also asked for help. Bob smiled. "You know we can't do anything right, Mary." He reached for my right hand and felt it between his two warm hands, examining the fingers, pressing the nails lightly. "Are you cold? You seem a little cold." He looked into my eyes with such tenderness that I became very frightened again.

"I'm all right," I said. "I'm not cold."

"You weren't the one who spoke to me, were you?" I asked Bob.

"Spoke where? What?" Dr. Altman said.

"After the operation, somewhere in a room. Who told me all about it. Precancerous tissue. So much out only as a precaution. Was I dreaming?"

The look of tenderness on Bob's face had become so strained it made him appear foolish.

"That's right. That's right." Dr. Altman was all cheerful bustle again. "That's just what I'm saying. Sure I spoke to you. Everything is fine. Listen, do me a favor. Don't think so much. Concentrate on getting well and home to your babies. We'll talk about the rest some other time. Talk it over with Bob here. I have another patient on the floor. I'll see you tomorrow. Want something to help you sleep tonight? I ordered it for you."

He was walking away as he talked — out the ward door and gone like a trick. In the silence that followed, the old woman elaborated a fantastically long, embroidered sigh and turned over in bed. I started by laughing at the sound with Bob but found myself crying in a strange strangled way I never had before. I tried to overcome my sobbing or hide myself from Bob. But he didn't allow it. He pulled the curtains all around the bed, shutting us away from the rest of the ward, at least visually. My head was down and as I cried I felt his hands stroking my hair.

"It's too much," he said. "It's too much."

When I stopped crying, I kept my face turned aside. I'm not one of those women who imagine they look charming in tears. In a few seconds I was able to say in an almost normal voice, "What's too much?"

"This. For you," he said. "Right after having the baby. And with your mother. And all your activities." His voice trailed as if he meant to say more.

"And the war and the elections. What else? All the trouble Matt and I are having?" I added.

"You know I don't believe in that trouble," he said.

"What do you believe?"

"About you and Matt?"

"About anything. About precancerous tissue."

"They say if you make it through the first eight years, you have it made."

"After the operation? Eight years? Does it take so long?"

"Oh, no. I meant the first eight years of marriage."

"Oh for God's sake."

He said, "I don't blame you for being angry with me. I feel to blame."

"What? For all of it?" I laughed.

"For not insisting that you go to another surgeon during the pregnancy."

"But you did."

"But you didn't go. I should have insisted that you go."

"No. I didn't go. Because it was all the same to Matt whether I lost the baby or took the risk."

"That's not fair to him. Altman assured him there was no risk."

"He was wrong, wasn't he?"

"Altman?"

There was a silence between us in which I felt one of those

things growing, a certainty which in a moment would be made palpable between us.

"Was Matt with you and Dr. Altman last night?"

"I wasn't with them," he said. "I was delivering a baby." He said it as if it had been on a newspaper-covered kitchen table in the South Bronx and the baby had died, but I didn't pursue that.

"When did you find out?"

"Right afterward. Matt called me and we were together the rest of the night."

"What did you talk about?"

He made a vague gesture. "You know."

"Does he feel to blame, too?" I asked.

"He shouldn't. These were medical decisions."

"So I'm really in trouble," I said, taking a deep breath. I would dive in.

He looked startled but recovered with a falsely blank look. "You'll be fine now."

"What have we been talking about then?"

"That we could have saved the breast."

"Oh," I said. I felt desperately lost. I had been exhilarated up to that point, as if at any moment I would break the surface of a sea in which distances would be clear at last. "I see," I said. "Yes. What a shame. Because they're really nice things to have two of."

I heard Matt's footsteps before he thrust the bed curtains aside. "What kind of therapy do you call this?" he said. He looked, laughing, at Bob, not at me.

Bob pulled the curtain open all the way around. "As a matter of fact I must see another patient."

"Don't go," Matt said. Brilliant with nervous urgency, his black eyes maintained a constant movement over and about my face, like a hummingbird approaching a flower. He grabbed Bob around the shoulders with both arms. "Where are you going? I just got here. I want to talk to you."

"I'll be back," Bob said, "as soon as I'm through with this patient. Shouldn't take me more than ten minutes or so."

Matt seemed to have become jointed to Bob at the shoulders. He walked halfway across the ward, stuck to him in that absurd fashion while I iced up with anger. He came unstuck suddenly, wheeled about and walked back to me almost jauntily, nodding to the others in the room, his eyes flitting wildly. I stared fixedly into his face, a silent bird watcher. Still and black as death, drowning in fear, his eyes looked directly into mine for an instant and spun off erratically as he reached my bed. He gave me a light kiss on the forehead and in a voice that strained to be trivial, he said, "Well, baby, are you still going to divorce me?"

2 ———

I KNEW THAT MARY was going into the hospital for the removal of a tumor in the breast. As a matter of fact, I had taken care of Mark when she and Matt had seen the surgeon the first time, about the third month of the pregnancy. They had returned to my house to pick Mark up, apparently pleased that Dr. Altman felt nothing had to be done about it, though there was a current running between them which was a clear indication to me that they must be in the middle of one of their long, killing quarrels. I paid no attention to any side vibrations because I wanted to be relieved about Mary for entirely selfish reasons. At that time, after having presumably sailed through my own troubles with the separation from Harry in great shape, everything began to be impossibly hard for me. I couldn't use any extra tensions. I was already up to here with my own life.

When Mary had the baby, I missed seeing her in the hospital. I had just started on this job as a secretary to one of the big brains in a public relations firm. That outfit was a real zoo and I spent each day eating myself alive trying to make it in that world, so that I had just enough energy to pull through the day, get home to my three boys in time for their supper, homework supervision, music practice, baths and all that junk, and flop into bed out like a light. They get maternity cases home from the hospital so fast these days that Mary seemed to be out before she was in. I did manage to send a paper mobile as a gift for the baby; and I snatched a twenty-minute visit with Mary one evening on my way home from work. It wasn't much of a visit. Even though Mary had a firm grip of control, the house was in utter confusion. Mark had a cold and kept close to Mary's side, whining away in a nasal monologue. Mary's mother, Bella, kept wandering in and out of the room, in the belief that she was being of assistance, trembling and babbling incomprehensibly. And there was a party or something merry going on in the apartment across the hall and Mary's noisy little dachsie kept rushing to the closed door, barking furiously and sniffing like a bloodhound. Matt had been delayed at the office and they were all impatiently waiting for him to get home so that they could get dinner out of the way. In the midst of all this, Mary seemed radiantly transfixed on her new little daughter, a tiny little nothing. I used to go into a trance myself over newborns, whatever they looked like, until I had my third and then I was turned off completely. Babies are okay, I haven't got anything against them. I'm not for abandoning them on the hillside or any of that stuff, but I just seem to have passed through the stage of internal stirrings at the sight of any infant. I had to make an effort to understand Mary's fascination with her child. And I wanted more of her for myself, for our own friendship. I was glad to leave quickly. Mary had told me during the visit that she would be going into the hospital for a day or two to have the tumor removed now that the baby was out safe, but I must have blocked off the information. When I got a hysterical phone call from Matt's sister, it stunned me.

She opened up with, "Jean! Jean! Our Mary is fighting for her life!"

I had always shared Mary's distaste for Gloria. I asked her coldly, "What does that mean? What's the matter?"

"They give her six months. A year if she's lucky." I said nothing and she rushed on. "She doesn't know what she has. Matt is trying to spare her whatever she can be spared. We must be very careful what we say when we see her. Her last days must be spent in peace. I'm taking the children to Long Island with me. Mark loves it with my girls and the yard and the big house. I can't take the dog though. I can't stand that dog. Oh poor Matt, how my poor brother is suffering for her."

"Is it cancer?" I knew that it must be.

"Oh, please don't use that word. I can't bear it. Yes. It is. That's what they found. A terrible form of it. It gallops. Because of the pregnancy. Six months to a year at most. Matt wants only you and me to know. We musn't tell anybody else. To protect her. For her sake, we must be on our guard when we see her."

"You sound like a soap opera. Do people really say these things?"

Her silence was full of shock at my response. I quickly added, "I mean the doctors. Do they really talk that way?"

She rallied. "That's nothing, Jean. They told Matt that it's spreading like wildfire. They removed the breast. But it's too late. It's too late." She broke out into sobs.

I asked Gloria to please excuse me. "I can't talk here at the office." Then I asked if I could reach Matt at home. She sobbed, "Poor Matt. Poor Matt. And two children on his hands." I said good-bye and hung up.

I went out to the booth in the lobby of the building where I wouldn't be overheard, but I couldn't bring myself to call him. I imagined Matt responding to the call in his teasing, bright social manner. But of course he wouldn't be his usual self, and I couldn't imagine what other self he would be. If the thought of speaking to him was so frightening, how would I ever be able to see Mary? Before I got myself any more worked up I dialed their home number. It rang for a while — six or seven times — and I was about to give up when someone said something unintelligible. I recognized Bella's garbled speech and then she must have dropped the phone from her nerveless hands because I heard it clattering and banging. I said, "Hello, hello," several times to no good purpose when Mark's sweet little voice said, "Hi." Then he said, "Mommie? Is this Mommie?" Little kids on the telephone are a nuisance, but when I heard Mark I started to cry.

"It's Jean, Mark," I said. "Is Daddy there?"

"No," he said. "Mommie's in the hospital having something fixed up."

"I know," I said. "Who's home with you, Mark?"

"Grandma and the baby," he said. "She's crying. And you know what? She makes in her clothes not just once in a while like an accident. She *always* makes in her clothes."

"Who else is there, Mark?"

"You," he said. I could hear voices, the furious barking of Shtrudel and then the click of the phone.

I went back to my desk and concentrated on my work, a long memorandum from my boss to the top idea man outlining a new approach to determine whether the campaign for a coffee product had the right appeal. He had dictated the original memo two weeks ago and I had since typed it with its varied changes a dozen times and was thoroughly sick of it, but he needed the latest version for an eleven o'clock conference and I pushed myself to finish it. I still had four pages to go, larded with handwritten insertions. At the top of a clean page I typed, "The thrust of our inquiry must be to the heart of the matter. Has the ultrasophisticated approach had its day? Is the public saturated with camp black humor and sex? Are they ready to quit swinging, and come down to earth? We must boldly put the question: IS NOW THE TIME FOR SIMPLICITY?" The phone on my desk rang. It was Matt, with a strange, hoarse voice.

"Can you meet me, Jean?"

"Right now?"

"Did Gloria explain everything?"

"She called a little while ago."

"Can you meet me?"

"I can't get out this minute."

"Okay. How about twelve? Will you meet me at twelve? I'll come down to your office."

"Matt. Is it really as bad as Gloria said?"

"They say it's as bad as it can be. They'll try everything. But short of a miracle they don't hope that anything will stop it." His voice suddenly cleared and he had given me the worst information in his usual strong, lively voice.

"Shouldn't you be at your apartment, Matt?"

"Gloria's there. She's taking the kids to her place on Long Island. I'll meet you at twelve in front of your building."

I decided not to worry him about my telephone call. Gloria had probably just slipped out for a minute. I said yes and gave him the address. Then I tore into the rest of the typing, not thinking of what I was working on, not thinking of anything really, my head filled with a mist of amazement and horror.

It was this feeling that I expressed to Matt later, when we were having lunch. "It's that old, old thing that everybody feels. I know that these things happen. But to us? Not to us."

He was black with tiredness and the need of a shave and a

good wash to get the city dirt off his face. He had been up straight through the night since the operation the day before, talking, talking endlessly to Bob and to Gloria and now to me. He couldn't stop. He hardly had any voice left. Matt was always full of talk, that's his great charm, stories and inventions for all occasions, opinions and comments about everything, theater, vitamins, politics, music, urban renewal, cookery, business, anything — all of it amusing, original and bathed in his special lighthearted view. This was different. "You don't know Mary. None of you know her. You don't know what will happen to her. I'm terrified. Bob blames himself. He thought all along it was a risk. But he deferred to Altman as the expert. I never thought about it. When we went to Altman and he said why disturb the pregnancy, I never gave it another thought. He was so sure it was nothing, that little lump. I'm afraid to face her. You don't know what she's like. They have no right to tell me so much. Altman is a lunatic. You should have heard him. He seemed to *enjoy* outlining to me all the possible horrors in store for her. For him, it's interesting shoptalk. He painted the details so vividly that when I left the hospital I puked all over the street. But it didn't help. I'm sick. I can't get this sick feeling out."

He was eating an enormous serving of lasagna and my reaction must have been plain on my face because he halted for a moment, smiled a bitter, artificial smile and added, "That's me. Comes twelve o'clock, I'm hungry and eat lunch no matter what." He went on talking and eating, investing both with such nervous energy that just watching and listening exhausted me. I had led him to a quiet place in a brownstone on 58th Street that's never badly crowded, where I knew we could talk. The waitresses were teen-aged dance, drama and art students, real delicious little morsels in mini dresses and flying manes of hair. Matt didn't miss a movement of their bodies as they passed back and forth. They had to do a lot of that; they were very inefficient waitresses. It was an odd thing to discover about him at such a time. I had never noticed that he was a girl-watcher. When I came back to what he was saying, it was about Mary. "I'm an idiot without her. It comes from letting her do my thinking for me."

"Come on," I said. "You know you don't."

"Yes," he said, "I do. I use her as a guide. Ever since we met everything has been measured for me by what she thinks. But I can't do that with this. I can't discuss this with her. We can't even quarrel about it. I've been going crazy trying to prepare myself to watch out, act natural, don't give her a clue."

"It was the doctors' decision?"

"What, to remove the breast? Yes, and they were ready to do more, take out all kinds of glands, God knows, I didn't even know what they were talking about anymore. It was too horrible. And what I couldn't understand was why do all this if it's hopeless, why not leave her alone? And I make the decisions? What the fuck do I know?"

I said, "No, I meant about her not knowing."

He came to a full stop and for the first time seemed to concentrate all his energy on one thing. His eyes frightened me. I don't like Matt's kind of eyes, in spite of his being so handsome. I always think of eyes as the way into people, but his have a hard brilliant black surface that bounces you right off. Even then, the misery in them warned me to keep off, as if his emotion held more anger than grief. "They asked me whether in my opinion she was a stable or unstable individual. The idea was that even if there were any doubt, it would be better not to tell her. Altman felt so guilty about his original mistake that he called in a psychiatrist to consult. I don't know what *he* was supposed to know about it. Altman wanted Bob too, but we couldn't reach him then. He was delivering a baby. So the shrink and I talked. Altman had already told him a bit about Bella and prison and the Shaeffers and the Committee and I filled in a lot of stuff. I hated talking about it. I realized how much I detest that whole background of Mary's. He kept saying, you're describing a very strong personality to me, don't you agree? Until I said outright that I didn't, that I felt that Mary is only strong when she's in control, but that she can't float, she can't go with what's happening, good or bad. She has to create what's happening, be doing it, herself. So he came up very strongly against telling her the truth. I warned them she wouldn't be easy to tell lies to. They said they would handle it. Altman went in with me then. She was completely dopey. I was terribly frightened. I hardly heard what Altman was telling her. General reassuring stuff. Like she was going to be fine. I didn't feel right while we were doing it. It didn't have the feeling of saving her; it felt more like killing her. Did we do wrong?"

I said that I didn't know.

"Has she been telling you that we've been having a lot of trouble?" I made a vague gesture. "Things aren't good between us. When I think of Mary I feel all wrong, I feel guilty of some terrible act that I can't comprehend. I would do anything for her but I can't do anything right so there's no use doing anything. Is there?"

I said that I didn't know.

"You don't really know her, Jean. She seems great to you, to all of you, but she's a lost soul most of the time." I shook my head, no, but he said, "She is. She is. And when she's like that she beats at me, at herself, at her life. I didn't know what

this would do to her. I had to protect her, didn't I?" He
pushed his coffee mug aside and cupped his dirty face in his
dirty hands, smearing the soot under his tormented rubbing.
When he looked up and smiled, his normally charming smile
had been transformed into a deathly parody — white teeth
gleaming, surrounded by dirt, and his eyes so strained that the
whites showed below the dilated black pupils. "I can't see her
alone, Jean. Please come with me. You have to come with
me. She'll want you anyway. I know she will."

"Will they let me up? And how about the Committee
people? Won't they all be there?"

"No. Nobody's told any of them yet. I want to keep them
out as long as possible. We'll wait until visiting hours at two-
thirty." He placed his hand over mine. "I feel it, Jean. What
you're doing for me." I was chilled and the warmth of his
touch started something moving in me. Matt had always attracted me. He would most women, especially if he wanted
to, and used his lost dog appeal. I took him straight to my
apartment. The woman who cleans for me one half-day a
week was just about to leave. Viola has been with me a long
time and knows all my friends. And she had worked for Mary
from time to time. I even paid her myself a couple of times
because Mary has this thing about living like the working class
and doing her own garbagy dirty work; but after the babies,
and twice when Mary was so involved with political work that
the house had practically run away with itself, Viola had done
some ironing and scrubbing and waxing floors at Mary's.
Viola always interested herself in people's ailments and she
remembered that Mary was going into the hospital. When
she saw us she assumed there was trouble and immediately
reassured Matt. "The Lord takes care of His good children,"
she said in her deep South accent. "Miss Mary is one of the

Lord's children. He will protect her." Matt stood, smiling an awful, painful smile into Viola's little round black face, suffused with sweetness and unhappiness. "Thank you," he said in a strangled voice, "thank you." Viola said, "I'm praying for her, Mr. Matt." She called us Miss Mary and Miss Jean and Mr. Matt as a way out of using our first names — a form we insisted on. It was all pretty silly. Like also insisting that she eat with us. She'd sit down with me and the three boys at the dining table if we were alone but as soon as someone else walked in, she'd melt away into the kitchen and finish her meal there. I didn't care about that nonsense anymore anyway, though some years back before the black community really got going I had been sold on it. It was Mary's mother who had stressed all those forms with Mary, and Mary believed in Bella's beliefs and I believed in Mary's.

I gave Matt shaving stuff and a towel and when he came out of the bathroom he looked like himself. "Very thoughtful of you to keep shaving materials on hand," he said.

"Don't you know that women shave their legs and armpits?"

"Not my generation," he said. "It's against their religion. How about you? Is that how you do it, with shaving cream and after-shaving lotion?" He was smiling at me provocatively.

I laughed. "I stock that stuff for you. And a couple of other strays."

"In a way we're in the same bag," Matt said.

"Are we?"

"Yes. We'll both be alone."

My first reaction was pleasure; the conversation was surely some kind of invitation. Then I became appalled at his having finished Mary off.

He laughed at the bourbon and ginger ale I had mixed for him and took a long drink. "It's good," he said. "Almost as good as orange soda, my real favorite." He took another long drink. "How do you afford it — bourbon, this whole set-up?" He included the makeshift comfort of my living room in his gesture, as if it were luxury. It looked good at the moment — clean and sunny and warm. "Do you earn enough to carry it all?"

"No," I said. "Harry pays the rent and utilities. My lawyers are trying for more. Meanwhile I stick him with doctor, dentist, clothing, camp, music lessons, anything I can get out of him. Let's not talk about it. I'm up to my ears in debt. I accept all money gifts or loans offered. But don't you ever lend me any money. I'm a bad risk."

"Who has money to lend?"

"You will. Soon. You're on your way."

"That sounds as if Mary hasn't convinced you that the greatest blow dealt the international working class in this decade is my becoming an architect."

"I don't go along with all of Mary's *mishagos*," I said.

"So you think I'm going to be a success?"

"Yes. Oh yes," I said.

He laughed with delight. "What a beautiful word. *Yes.* Mary never says it. She's the great qualifier. She would have said" — and he mimicked Mary's "wise" voice — " 'Why must you think in terms of "success," Matt?' " Suddenly, he seemed almost physically to lose his bearings. He looked around wildly and shouted, "What's the matter with us? What are we talking about?"

I fixed another drink for him and he swallowed more than half at once. I realized that he didn't know what he was drinking or eating or talking about. He was whirling helplessly. Anybody could have led him anywhere at that moment. I promised myself to protect him. Even from me.

"It's impossible to believe now here with you, isn't it? I can't believe it. It isn't happening. Mary mutilated, and suffering and dying. She won't let it happen. She's very strong, you know."

I didn't remind him of his inconsistency.

"Shall I tell you something else?" He laughed a quivering laugh. "A whole part of me is relieved. And excited at the possibility of getting out. Of all of it. How's that? Confessions of your best friend's husband."

"I'm not listening to what you say," I said. "Talk. Talk."

"Grab my two kids and run. Let Shtrudel take care of Bella and Bella take care of Shtrudel and the Committee makes three. A sweet neat solution."

"And Mary?" I said.

"You said, talk, talk," he reminded me.

"Who's taking care of them now, Bella and Shtrudel?"

"A neighbor comes in and prepares Bella's meals and helps feed and wash and dress her. A kid in the apartment house walks the dog. Mary arranged all that before she went in. But now . . ."

"Don't worry," I said. "Ride with it. One thing at a time."

He was looking at me, with something warm and speculative in his eyes. "You know I haven't had a friendly conversation with a girl in so long, I don't know what to do about it."

"It's the liquor," I said. "And my advanced age. Strong stuff."

He shook his head. "No. It's the woman. I don't know what it is with us. What's wrong."

"Wrong with us?"

"Me and Mary. There's blood all over the walls the minute we're together."

We walked part of the way toward the hospital. Matt was still very talkative, but three drinks had slowed him down a bit and had deflected his talk toward his work. He was telling me that he was attracted to city planning, and to writing about architecture, with perhaps a base of university teaching — for the security. I wasn't listening closely to the details; but I was entering wholly into the country of his being, matching his long stride step for step, my arm entwined in his and hugging his side, and comfort flowing out of me into him. I felt beautiful, happy, good — walking with him along ugly uptown Broadway. There's nothing I enjoy more than giving a man what he wants when the taking and the giving is moving right. That's the way I begin with a man. Later that warmth gets all mixed up with bad other things because men don't seem to understand how love is passed back and forth between lovers and how important it is to keep the feeling from sinking into the ground. Perhaps with someone as young as Matt it would be possible to keep love airy and filled with light. It wasn't that I had forgotten Mary. But the Mary we were on our way to see didn't seem to be my Mary at all but some new person locked away in a tragedy and horror that didn't have much to do with me. This character who was to be protected by plot and lies from a terrible truth seemed a stranger to me. Just before entering the main door I tried to force the two Marys to merge in my mind, but that produced only panic. The hospital smell did the rest. I couldn't face her yet. I told Matt that he really should go in alone.

"She'll want to be alone with you. For a few minutes at least. I'll join you very soon."

He listened to me. The liquor had made him braver.

I found a ladies' room next to the bank of elevators. It was a mess, a small, two-cubicle one crowded with people and littered with paper towels on a partially flooded floor. I walked out and made my way through the connecting buildings to an adjoining private pavilion. I know the medical center well because I had worked there when the children were younger and I needed to be close to home for lunches, emergencies, illnesses and all that, so I knew just where to locate a good ladies' room. I have a thing about ladies' rooms. I can pinpoint the best ones half around the world. There was only one other woman in the quiet lavatory I found, and she soon left. I took my time, pulled all my make-up out to redo my face. It surprised me, looking so bright and pleasant. I felt that it was showing no sense of propriety, sticking to its customary light prettiness at a time like this. After I had my teeth straightened and the dark mustache removed from my upper lip I became a very pretty woman. I don't know why this made so much difference, but it did — and letting my straight hair alone, wearing it smoothed sideways and upward into a fat crown on the top of my head. I have a miserable, low forehead but my eyes are liquid and flirty, with naturally thick, curling lashes, and since I was taught how to shape my lips properly I have a beautiful mouth, especially with straight teeth. Anyway everybody says I'm very pretty and I am, monotonously so, every day in the week, not like Mary who's beautiful but very changeable and who can look pitiful, dreary, even ugly at times. I tried to imagine her face at that moment, Matt entering, her greeting. I couldn't. But while I was retouching my lips with a lipstick brush (my face didn't need much because of the very thorough twenty-minute basic job I do every morning) I remembered the grotesque mouth

Mary makes when she applies lipstick to the inside of her lower lip. I thought how that gesture would die with her. Is this what I would remember with pain — such stupid losses? Mary was in a semiprivate ward on the fourteenth floor. That was probably at Bob's insistence. Mary would have chosen the clinic, to be with "the people." I didn't go for that self-denial part of her. "She's pushing for a saint," Matt had said once about her at a party, and I laughed aloud even though I knew that Mary would feel demeaned by the quip. I don't know what ghastly change I had expected to find, but it was an immense relief to see her looking like herself, propped up in bed, whatever they had done to her decently covered by a hospital gown. She was smiling at something going on in the lively conversation around her bed. Matt needn't have worried about being alone with her. The whole crowd was there. I headed for her outstretched hand, hardly greeting anybody though I was being welcomed with gushing effusion. Particularly the elderly couple, the Shaeffers, went in for their usual song and dance. "Look how beautiful," she said, kissing me. "You never look a day older." And her husband, "Quite to the contrary. She only knows how to get younger and prettier" — accompanied by a big, wet kiss. "Ugh," I said, "I hate wet kisses," wiping it off dramatically, but smiling as if I really liked it. Then I was at Mary's side. Her intelligent eyes, cloudy gray today, were swimming in tears. When I kissed her she clung to me, her fingers closing on my arm in a grasp desperate enough to hurt. That and the tears were not like her.

"Be careful of me," she said. "I'm fragile. I come apart if you poke me."

"You look terrific to me. I expected to find you flat on your back."

"Isn't she?" Bob said. "Isn't she terrific?"

There were visitors in the ward for other patients, though not as many as around Mary, and in one corner there was some sort of strange din — guttural, loud sounds and extravagant gestures and laughter. Most of the room was watching us. It was easy to see why. The Committee people are quite a crew — all styles, ages, shapes, accents, colors, and each in his way whatever he is up to the hilt. Add me and Matt, handsome enough to make our living by our looks, and that ward had a free show going. When Paula swept in, her shining blond hair done in a smooth cone, wearing the dull orange wool cape she had brought back from Spain, there was a furious nurse in her wake. Everybody but Matt and the Shaeffers had sneaked up through connecting hospitals.

"Four visitors only," the nurse scolded. "The rest of you without visitors' passes must leave immediately. I should think you'd have some consideration for the patient if not for our hospital rules."

Paula had closed in with Mary for a quick visit before she was put out and Mary was being amusing in a very low voice about the assorted characters sharing the ward with her. It began to seem like a regular Mary-type gathering.

Matt looked very flushed and was helping the nurse urge the crowd out. "Who told them all?" he whispered, as he passed me, his eyes hard and accusing. I lifted my shoulders and shook my head. I seized that moment to tell him that I was going, that I had to get back to the office, but he said that I mustn't leave and without discussing it further asked the Shaeffers to please give me their passes. "Of course," Stella Shaeffer said in her weepy voice, "I'm more than happy to. After all, you're so close, you're more like sisters than friends. Of course I'll be glad to give you my pass. After all, she surely wants to see you more than she wants an old lady like me." I thanked her and told Matt that I had better do something about informing my office. I went out to the corridor to look for a telephone booth.

I told my boss that during lunch I had vomited and gone right home. "I guess it's one of those stomach viruses," I said.

He whined, "Jean, you can't do this to me. The conference was a holocaust and I'm redoing that approach right now and have to have it first thing in the morning. The old man has called a breakfast meeting at his place in Great Neck. What am I going to do?"

"Sarah will do it for you," I said.

"No, I can't stand her, Jean. I've just about had it with you, you know. If it's not your kids' stomachs it's your stomach. Or your period. Or the plumbing. Or open school week. You know this isn't some kind of temporary, part-time job you contracted for here."

"Oh, for God's sake," I said. "I thought you liked my work."

"I love it when you do it. Come on, you've got to get back here."

I said, "All right. I'll rest for another hour and then come down to finish. I'll just work right along, however long it takes."

"Jean, sweetheart, baby, I'll make it up to you, I promise," he said, and I hung up.

Bob and Matt were in the corridor. They seemed to be quarreling. Matt looked even more flushed and furious than earlier.

"Don't you see that it doesn't make any difference?" Bob was saying in a patiently reasonable voice.

"They're going to tire her. They're wearing her out. You

can order them to stop coming. You're her doctor, aren't you, and the head of that committee?"

"I'm not the head of any committee," Bob said. "What's the matter with you, Matt? So what if it makes her tired? If it pleases her, what's the difference?"

"What's the difference? What's the difference?" Matt mimicked Bob's soft voice cruelly. "I'm not going to have her overrun with organization people. Understand? Or me. I'm telling you that straight. I'm not putting up with any of it."

"Mary's perfectly capable of telling us if she's tired. None of us want to harm her, you know." Bob walked away rapidly, but he turned back and began again. "I know this is a very difficult period for you, Matt, and I want you to know that we . . ."

But Matt stopped him. "I'll kick you in the balls if you make sententious speeches at me, you old fart."

Bob was speechless. I took Matt's arm and led him to a little terrace at the end of the corridor. "Time for a cigarette," I said.

He offered me one and though I don't smoke, I took it. I didn't want to refuse him anything at that moment. The terrace was bare, covered with soot, and totally enclosed by a fine mesh of heavy steel. To keep the patients from killing themselves? Through the mesh, the sun danced a brilliant jig on the river. It shone on little leftover bits of greenery sticking above the crossing pattern of the highways and on the long, graceful bridge playing across the water like an ingenious toy with moving parts. I fussed with my cigarette. Matt smoked, staring in blank fury into the wire mesh. He looked like a little boy, slightly cross-eyed because of the screen and inarticulately sullen.

"What am I supposed to do now?" he said. "Give up everything? Give up my life to making life a heaven on earth for her for the next six months? I have work to do. I should be downtown right this minute. And those people and their whole scene make me sick. They always did and they always will. Who told them?" He put his fist against the steel screen and his head against his fist and groaned.

"Mary," he moaned into his fist. "Mary."

I felt entirely alone. It was foolish of me to have thought I could comfort him. Or help Mary. Or anyone. Anyway I had a million other things to do. I told the back of his head that I had to return to the office and left Matt standing there. He probably hadn't heard me because he didn't respond.

I walked back through the corridor to say good-bye to Mary and met Paula on her way out. Paula began to cry and cling to me, and I loosed myself quickly, saying that I wanted to get back to Mary. "How can you be so calm?" she said. I couldn't tell whether she was admiring or criticizing me. "Please call me, I must talk to you," she said, and I waved and nodded in agreement as I walked into the ward.

Mary grasped my arm as she had before when I told her that I would have to leave for the office in a few minutes.

"No, please, you must stay."

I said that I would for a while and she asked me what had happened to Matt.

"He's having a cigarette," I said.

"It's all right to smoke here," she said, indicating her own cigarettes and ashtray on the table. "I'll have to tell him." She smiled. "Cancer is only the foremost enemy when profits are not involved." I didn't feel like being politicized and I turned away toward a commotion going on in one corner of the ward. Mary asked me to lower her bed and I cranked it down until she told me to stop. All Mary's energy seemed to have leaked out. With her face shut away from me she asked in a very low voice if I knew that they had removed a breast. For a second, I was all confusion. How much was I supposed to know? Then I said that I knew.

"It feels funny," she said.

I said that I imagined it would. I tried to think of something hopeful to say, but I had never been a liar with Mary and I didn't know how to begin. Instead I said that it was good of Gloria to be taking the kids to Long Island.

"You know what that fool said to me?" She became animated and turned her face to me fully. "She said that it shouldn't bother me as much as it might other women because I had never had much breast to begin with. Then she proceeded to list breastless celebrities, especially ones with beautiful big bubbies. Roll call of the one-breasted famous. What a revelation! I don't know where she amassed this data. Like those people who can tell you everybody who's really Jewish. Or fags."

"She's a fool," I said. "Never listen to fools." But what I was seeing was Mary's body before it was mutilated. I saw her pregnant because that was the way I had last seen her naked. I saw her standing in her tiny bathroom with a towel across her shoulders. I saw the slope rising from under her firm, small breasts with rosy, prominent nipples. Under the bulge of the baby, her shapely legs seemed miscast — too chorus girly. What did she look like now? I saw her stomach smoothed, narrow hips, one rosy-nippled breast and on the other side scars, stitches, blood, bandages, flatness. Which side?

"I'm getting those kids back to my apartment, fast," Mary was saying. "I don't know why it couldn't have been left the way I had it set up to begin with. I have to talk to Matt about that. Before she ruins my kids." Her face was contorted with anger and her eyes were dramatically narrowed in a way I had never seen before. "And Matt! You know how he greeted me? 'Well, baby, how about that divorce now?'"

"He was joking," I said.

"Yeah. A real ha, ha, funny joke." Her eyes were still narrowed in a strange, ugly way until they flooded with tears and opened up like Mary's again.

One of the visitors of the noisy group at the end of the room came toward us offering chocolates, making unintelligible guttural and nasal sounds. There was something charming in his disarming assumption that this speech could be understood. He was a tall, thick man with a large, flushed face and wonderfully open, blue eyes. We refused by shaking our heads and smiling.

"Take, take, darlings. It's my son, he came to visit me." The old lady he had been visiting called to us from her bed in a man's voice. To make up for her son's muteness? "Don't be afraid to speak. He reads your lips. He understands every word."

I took a candy and said, "Thank you very much. I love chocolates," using a formal tone as if I were addressing a non-English speaking foreigner. He responded with some crazy-sounding noises which were pleasantries, I guessed, and went on to the other people in the room, his mother's deep voice accompanying him, introducing and encouraging communication.

"She's your sister?" the old lady called to Mary.

"Practically," Mary said. "She's a very dear friend."

"You look like sisters," the old lady said. "And you're married, too?"

I said, "Yes," and let it go at that.

Mary whispered, "She's looking for a wife for that son. Watch out."

"I could do worse," I said, and meant it. I observed him offering the candy to a woman trailing some kind of hot water bottle from her body. "At least he might be grateful."

"Is that what you're looking for — gratitude?"

"How do I know what I'm looking for?"

"And this is my daughter and her husband." The old woman indicated another handsome pair, who greeted us with the same pleasant-unpleasant noises while the old lady clued them in with her finger movements.

"What's going on?" I asked Mary.

"Isn't it strange" — she spoke very low, her eyes fixed on them gravely — "what people survive — to go on to live the most ordinary lives."

"What happened? Were they all in a concentration camp or something?"

"Nothing happened," Mary said. "It's just nothing. Accidents of chance. And failures of medicine."

She put her head back and closed her eyes in a fake way that was so unlike her. "Everybody in this room is dying."

I managed a cliché. "Everybody is. We all start to die as soon as we're born."

She opened her eyes and the look she directed at me was so straight and honest it frightened me. "Are you going to be a fool too? I was counting on you at least."

"You can always count on me to be a fool," I said lamely.

I was experiencing difficulty containing the mix of feelings which began to boil in me — fear, embarrassment, grief, pity, relief, and identification so acute it made my skin tight and my breast ache, and most troublesome, there was an alien cold anger at her cornering me. I waited for what she would say next, trying to return blankness to her searching gaze, and we acted out a stupid staring-down game for a couple of seconds. Then, horribly, her face broke up in a child's grimace and she cried. She reached out for me, clutching my hands, and between sobs, blubbered my name and whispered desperate hissing words which I couldn't catch. I felt a helpless impatience and wanted to run. She stopped as suddenly as she had started and asked me to pull the curtains.

"I'm not myself," she said, speaking with difficulty. "I can't control myself."

"Well, that's perfectly natural." I was glad to channel my impatience toward safety. "Good Lord. You always demand so much of yourself. Nobody expects you to act like Joan of Arc."

Again that straight, searching look. "Am I going to be all right, Jean? I'm not in trouble, am I?"

She was so obviously looking for reassurance that I let it gush out automatically. I spoke so fast that I didn't know what I was saying and didn't give myself time to think. When Matt stuck his head around the curtain, I had her spellbound; she was hanging on my invented medical assurances as if they made sense. Her face crumpled at Matt's approach and when he put his arms about her, she sobbed. I said that I really did have to go back to the office and almost ran from them. They were clinging to each other, and the vision I carried away to think about while I typed my boss's approach once more was of Matt's face, tortured with the effort to keep himself from crying, pleading with me to stay.

3 ———————

I CALLED TERRY from the office and told him to open a can of soup and ravioli for himself and his brothers, but he started a hullabaloo about eating at a Chinese restaurant and Paul got on the extension and helped him. Terry said he still had his birthday money and would use that if I promised to pay it back, and of course I said yes, but that they weren't to spend more than seven dollars plus tip and to be sure to order barbecued spareribs for Elliot because that was the only thing he would eat. "I'm quite aware of that, Jean," Terry said in that snotty way he's developed lately.

I'm not one of those mothers with illusions about child rearing. I admit to total disorganization. I just go along coping with whatever comes up trying not to hurt them or myself too much in the process. I had a parcel of theories once — who didn't? — between Freud, Gesell and Spock you'd have to have been an Australian aborigine not to. But after everything turned out such a ridiculous fizzle between me and their father I lost all my pretensions to wisdom. I lost my taste too for anyone who claims to know anything about plotting out human life. My boys know all they need to about my system. What it all boils down to for them is that I start out saying no and end up saying yes.

At any rate I had avoided coming home to the mess the kitchen would have been if they hadn't eaten out. When I arrived after eight all was peaceful, Elliot watching television on the floor, Paul doing his homework at the table with one eye on the TV and Terry in his room with the door closed, practicing the Mozart sonata he had been working on for weeks now. I tore out of my clothes and into the shower and into a big, comfy granny nightgown with my hair brushed out down my back and made myself a cup of tea in the kitchen. I didn't feel like eating. The two younger ones were on the phone with their father in a sort of relay system. It irritated me that he kept up all this useless contact by phone and letter and little meaningless visits. If he needed them so badly why hadn't he stayed with me and taken care of them? Not that I wanted him. I guess what I really wished was for him to disappear quietly and stop complicating my life.

Harry asked to speak to me and began some nastiness about Elliot being upset because I wasn't home very much these days. Didn't I seriously think that I owed it to the children, especially a little boy of six, to stay home once in a while?

"Okay, buddy," I said. "Are you ready to carry this household so I can be at home all day? Any time you say."

"Come on," he said, "let's not put too much strain on our credibility now. Nobody works till this hour in this enlightened age. You don't expect me to believe the line of crap you hand out to my boys."

I saw on our children's faces the sick shame and fear our quarreling created. Paul had a way of opening his mouth and taking in short gasps of air like a dying fish whenever we had a fight. I said to myself, drop dead, and aloud to Harry, "Excuse me, the water's boiling," and hung up. He called right back, of course, but Terry had come out of his room and I asked him to please answer the phone and if it was his father to tell him to discuss the matter with the lawyers. Terry dutifully repeated in a deadpan voice, "Jean says to please take up any questions with your lawyers, Dad." Then Terry listened for a long time (while I drank my tea), his dark face getting almost purple and his beautiful curly lashes batting away at his stormy eyes. He looks so much like me and is so beautiful to look at, I find endless satisfaction in looking. When I finished my tea, I said in a loud, cheerful voice, "Tell your father it's time for bed now." Terry made a furious gesture with his hand and turned his back on me.

Elliot asked me if he could have a snack and I said no, it was after nine, time for bed, and what was he upset about anyway. Why couldn't it have waited until I got home? He said it wasn't anything and I said well it must have been something. He said that it was about singing a song in his class play and while I made him a peanut butter and jelly sandwich and a glass of chocolate milk, he filled in the details of how he had accidentally told the teacher that he knew how to sing "Where Have All the Flowers Gone?" and that she asked him to sing it and that he did and now she wanted him to sing it in the class play in front of the whole class and in front of Miss Janus' class too. "That's bad?" I said. "Yes, yes," he said, bursting into tears. "That's Billy Harris' class."

I gave him his snack and he stopped crying and devoted himself to his sandwich. "Is that what you were talking to your father about? And what about Billy Harris?" I really couldn't make head nor tail of this tragedy.

He said, "I told Dad all about it."

"And what did the big brain suggest?"

If I hadn't been so tired I would have kept myself from saying that. Elliot had a desperate look again and Paul began to gasp. "You mean Dad? Nothing," Elliot said. "I just told Dad that I had spareribs for supper in the Chinese restaurant and Dad asked me where you were and I said that I didn't know." "Why did you say you didn't know?" I yelled. "Because I didn't know," he yelled back. "You knew perfectly well I was working at the office." "I did not," he said, and began to cry again. He pushed away the half-finished sandwich and drink. "I thought you said I couldn't have a snack. I don't want it if you don't want me to have it." In a fury, I grabbed it and had almost shoved it in the garbage when Paul said, "Please, Mom, can I have it? Instead?"

So I forced myself to simmer down. I told Elliot that of course I wanted him to have his snack and I made another of the same for Paul while Elliot and I continued an endless unconvincing discussion about his mysterious problem. It was Paul who finally settled the matter by telling Elliot there wasn't a thing he could do about it. "School plays are just like any other schoolwork, spelling or math or special projects. You don't stand a chance. You haven't any choice. You have to do it. No matter what you say, they won't let you off. The thing is never let them know that you can do anything." Terry had finished his telephone conversation and though he didn't join us at the kitchen table, he stood nearby, using the top of the refrigerator as his table for a snack of sliced white sandwich bread which he was dunking into a glass of Coca-Cola. His face was closed and angry. He remained that way while I tidied up and as I was leaving the kitchen he asked in a tight voice if he could please have the seven dollars and eighty-two cents he had spent on supper. His coldness clenched my heart, and when I settled into bed with the *New York Times* I found that despair had come along as my mate. I turned the pages of the paper mechanically, unable to read. The house was quiet except for Terry's radio, tuned to the droning foolery of WBAI. Paul and Elliot seemed to have gone straight to sleep. I gave myself up to staring into space, my eyes welling with tears intended for Mary, but splashing over my own arid life, when Terry opened his door and stood, one hand looped on the lintel of my bedroom doorway, looking at me.

"I'm sorry, Mom," he said. He called me Mom when he liked me. It was the other way around with Paul; Paul used Jean when he was feeling especially friendly.

"What for?" I said, forcing my voice into brightness.

"I don't know," he said. "You don't look happy. I guess we're a lot of trouble to you."

I said with more passion than I usually allow myself to show, "Terry, don't be crazy. You're the best thing in my life, you three." Then I told him about Mary so that he would understand why I was upset. He listened with an expression of distaste and when I finished said, "Man, that's tough luck."

After a little silence he asked if I had heard him practicing. I said, "Not really."

"Do you think I could be a great pianist, Mom?"

I said that I wasn't a proper judge but that it seemed to me if someone was going to become a great virtuoso it showed up very early.

"Would you mind if I stopped taking lessons then?"

"Not if you want to," I said. "But if it gives you pleasure that's good enough, you know. Why don't you think about it first?"

"It's not good enough," he said.

"Do you think everybody should be great at whatever they do?" I asked.

"Yes, I do," he said. "I think it would be a big improvement if everybody stopped doing things in a mediocre way. If everybody only did what they were great at."

I didn't ask him what he thought that would be for me or for him, because I didn't want to hear the answer at that moment. His coming to talk to me in a friendly spirit had so relieved my heavy feeling that I was sure I would be able to sleep. We said good night and I asked him to switch off the overhead light. I put out the lamplight and thought I would drop right off. Instead I began to think. Think is the wrong word for the dipping, darting, useless activity which seizes me when I'm upset. It's more like driving one of those carnival cars. I bumped into Mary — and Matt — the minute I closed my eyes, dodged them, bumped into my anger at myself for having involved Terry in my arguments with his father, dodged it, decided that I really should take Mary's children into my house, plus her mother, plus her dog (my kids would love the dog at least), started again with Matt, thought of his hands, his mouth, the way he tore up matchbooks while he talked, dodged that, bumped into Terry and his absolute music standards, dodged, bumped, dodged until I put the lamp back on and went back to the *Times*. I read for a while, my eyes burning with fatigue and put the light out to try again. The whole thing started then with Elliot. Was it all going to be too much for him and was he going to turn into one of those messy kids who lean on an analyst forever because of divorced parents? What did it mean that he didn't want to sing in front of his class? Shit. Think of Mary. Oh, Mary. What can I do for you? Tell me what to do for you.

What I did was to get up, pour a jigger of brandy with a little water and take it back to bed with me. I could see a crack of light under Terry's door and hear the sound of his radio's talk program. It was after eleven, but I closed my door to protect myself from marching in and telling him to go to sleep. Tomorrow was Saturday anyway, even if they did have to be up early to meet their father. I sipped the drink and read the women's page, including all the recipes. One turned out to be great — artichoke stuffed with bread crumbs, herbs, garlic and olive oil, and baked in the oven. I was dreamily planning having someone I really wanted to cook it for come to dinner tomorrow, when I realized the man I had in mind was Matt. The phone rang at that moment. I was sure it would be Matt, but it was Joanna, apologizing for calling so late.

"Did I wake you?"

I said, "Yes," hoping that would end the conversation right there. "Can I call you first thing in the morning? When I know what I'm saying? I've had a terrible day and took something to help me sleep." I was ready to say anything to avoid a conversation with Joanna at that moment.

"You said you would call me," she said. "I've been waiting all this time. That's why I'm calling so late."

I said, "I'm sorry."

She said, "Well, when will you call me?"

"In the morning. First thing."

When she rang off, I thought about her and felt guilty. She was the first friend I made in New York. I was on my first job in a typing pool for a drug firm and Joanna was sitting at the next typewriter. I was fresh out of an Altoona high school and Joanna was Jewish and a Communist and older and she seemed to know everything and I thought her dazzling and exotic. After I had met a lot of other exotic New Yorkers, she fell into place for me. Joanna was a member of the Communist Party, USA, and still is, which hardly anybody is anymore. It was a big revelation to me, being intimate with a real live

Communist Party member. Joanna was so sensible and thrifty and she was such a whiz at the typewriter and got such a bang out of being a first-class drudge. Nothing to do with wild-eyed revolution. She wasn't good-looking. Her face had no definition, so that all you noticed was heavy-lensed glasses and dry, wiry hair. She had a good figure that didn't go with the rest of her. Everything she wore cost a lot and was tasteful in a deadly fashion, but she never made any kind of a splash to look at.

It wasn't long before I realized that all the information she supplied me was just a repetition of articles from socialist newspapers and pamphlets and magazines that I could have read myself. It began to irritate me that she acted as my teacher and was always straightening me out about everything under the sun. But inertia kept us close. Family close — not real close. All her talk consisted of topics. She kept the things that really matter to herself. I didn't care. I babbled all my troubles right out anyway. Her life consisted of petitions, meetings, raffles, demonstrations and talk, talk, talk, all fairly mild stuff. I never felt that she was covering anything up. She wasn't attractive enough to be having an interesting secret life — political or personal.

Yet there must have been some hanky-panky between her and the boss she began to work for, soon after we met. He was an old man then, but lived on for almost twenty years. Then he left her the townhouse he had been using as his place of business and enough money to convert it into apartments. At least that's what she did with the money. She used one apartment and rented the rest and didn't have to work anymore.

In the beginning, Harry resented her, then he got used to her and ended liking her a lot. He never minded her spending weekends with us in Forest Hills. If we had a date, he'd try to include her, but she would be equally happy staying home with the kids, teaching them yoga or leather tooling or playing Monopoly or cards with them. The kids tolerated her, like a kind of aunt. When Harry and I separated, Joanna made us a formal speech, declaring her neutrality. She wished to continue her friendship with both parties. I don't know whether Harry was seeing her, but she was in and out of my house all the time, half driving me up the wall and the other half saving me from desperate loneliness. If it was annoying, it was also soothing to have her arrive at the house with new mattress pads for the kids' beds ("these are the best kind, the pad won't ride or twist under the sheet") or a great-smelling Spanish soap without a trace of detergent, or a fine English tea, or a new game for Elliot we all played, or spouting information on phosphates and the secret war in Laos and the best way to wash wool sweaters and clean marble surfaces, or unloading a dozen different petitions demanding the release of Greek political prisoners or the end to killing baby seals, and spilling all the latest gossip about the political crowd. There were moments when my heart sank at opening the door to her ring, and days when I blessed her as the only adult I could really count on for help.

Joanna's thing was to be good — with a heavy hand — and I'm afraid I was one of her prime targets. Mary was another. But with Mary it was all mixed up with her political life with the Committee. Mary had been eleven years old when Bella was sentenced to thirty years and only eight when the case was initiated. I don't know what would have happened to her without the Shaeffers and Joanna — all the Committee people. I owed meeting Mary to Joanna. Joanna worked at involving me in the Committee to rope me into political activism, but I was too wound up in being Harry's wife and my kids' mother and a Forest Hills lady, though I did throw a couple of fund-raising events.

Joanna told me a lot about the Committee but never the real inside stories, so I don't understand everything about it, any more than I understood the legal intricacies of Bella's case. I accepted Joanna's version that Bella was framed. The trials of the fifties were different from political trials now, more scary and hush-hush, complicated by the legal people, and by the Communist Party behaving as if it were slightly to the left of the Democratic Party and had never heard of overthrowing a capitalist power by force and violence. If Joanna was a typical member, that seemed very likely. Harry had believed that the Party bungled the politics of Bella's case and that the defense lawyers bungled the legal end. It all seemed ghostly and unreal and creepy and to fade into history even as it happened, especially when the Rosenbergs were electrocuted. It wasn't until I met Bella years later that I made the connection between history and her living body. The protest action wasn't started until Bella was sentenced to life imprisonment. It was Bob who started the Free Isabelle Vance Moody Committee, with the Shaeffers and Joanna. They were very successful at raising money and at rousing foreign protest, even if they got nowhere with the case itself. The money raised was used to take care of Mary, as well as for the endless legal appeals. Mary was only a kid but she would say a couple of words at the meetings or just be around for people to see so that they'd be moved to help. But the courts stepped in with an injunction against the Committee for misusing a minor, or some such charge. They threatened to claim custody of Mary, so Bella gave her up to the Shaeffers for legal adoption, but it was really the Committee that adopted her.

Then, out of the blue, a couple of Trotskyist lawyers on their own came up with a legal gimmick that got Bella's sentence reduced from life to thirty years. That was before the Khrushchev revelations on Stalinism. When that burst over the Party here, the repercussions almost tore the Committee apart. Another scandal followed that one. The Committee treasurer was a young financial wizard who was managing a variety of Party funds. He had invested the Committee money in a little electronics company that boomed because it got into missile hardware and Mary got wind of it in the late fifties. We were friends then, though she was ten years younger than I and still at college. Her disgust was beautiful. She blew everything wide open and cut herself free of financial ties with the Committee. She didn't stop living with the Shaeffers or quarrel with Bob or Joanna or any of the others who had been taking care of her. They all insisted that they hadn't known what the treasurer was about, and perhaps they hadn't. She went out into politics, too, testing the injunction. She did everything — student organization, civil rights, poor people's organizing, peace work and then militant antiwar civil disobedience acts. Nobody got on her tail but the reporters. They'd make a little story about anything she was doing, always describing her as the daughter of convicted atom bomb spy Isabelle Vance Moody, now serving a thirty-year, etc., etc. Then she pulled back from political action and wrote a lot of poetry and married a young man nobody knew — Matt. I had never discussed much of this with Matt but I knew he hadn't bargained for what he got. Bella was released long before her sentence was fully served. She was very ill and that was given out as the reason for her release. But Mary felt it had more to do with the state of the country and the strength of the protest movement now. Though the Committee was only one of many here, it was powerful abroad, since her case had been linked to the Rosenbergs'. The name of Isabelle Vance Moody was as well known in political circles in Milan or Istanbul as it was in Stella Shaeffer's kitchen. Mary also thought that it was because of an article Bella wrote, while she could still write, which called the Communist Party and her original defense team reformist liars and elitists. Mary's theory was that between the illness and the defection, they counted on Bella only adding confusion to the left, so why not let her out? Especially since a pardon would defuse the worldwide protest movement and make the administration look good.

So Bella came home, wrecked, to Mary and to Matt — and to the swarming of the handful of Committee members who had been too close to the case for too long to give it up. And like everything else in Matt and Mary's life, it was ambiguous whether Matt and Mary themselves wanted the Committee totally out. I had overheard at least one quarrel in which it was Matt who argued that they needed the Committee money, that they couldn't manage with Bella without it. It was also Matt who was likely to throw a fit of annoyance at Stella's presence or Joanna's if they came around too often.

I could have talked it all over with him right then, because the phone rang and this time it was Matt, but he hadn't called to talk on the phone. He wanted to come up.

"Did I wake you?" he said. "I'm going out of my mind."

"I wasn't asleep."

"The house is spooked without Mary and the kids. I slept for a while. Then Bella started walking around and bumping into things and woke me. I was afraid she might fall. I tried to help her go to the bathroom but she wouldn't let me and she managed somehow. The whole thing unnerved me and I couldn't go back to sleep. Then Shtrudel started this weird whining. I got the creeps. Dog howls. Master dies miles away. It occurred to me that maybe the kid hadn't walked him properly so I got dressed and took him out. That was it. Poor Shtrudel ran around watering and shitting like crazy. I have to get a better dog walker."

"She's worse, Matt, isn't she?" I said.

He said, "Jean, can I come up right now? I need to be with someone."

I said yes, of course. The upstairs doorbell rang so soon after that I didn't see how it could be he, but when I looked through the peephole, it was, and I let him in after opening all the locks. Terry emerged from his room to see what was going on but I called to him that it was all right it was just Matt. He greeted Matt with an embarrassed gesture and went right back into his room. I was in my nightgown and bare feet which I hadn't given a thought to until Matt looked at me. All our crowd kiss in greeting, and the way Matt noticed me, hesitated, and finally *didn't* kiss me became a self-conscious provocation. The house was cold and he suggested that I get back into bed. I walked ahead of him, down the narrow hall, my body coming alive under the clinging gown and myself very aware of my movements, of my hair streaming down my back and the flat sound of my bare feet on the wooden floor. He sat in his coat on the little rocker in my bedroom. I pulled the covers up to my neck but continued to shiver.

"Something bad happened to Mary?" I asked him.

He was arranging his cigarettes and matches and searching for an ashtray and just shook his head.

"God, you scared me," I said. "When you called I thought she had died."

"That's not the way it works. So fast. Not this thing. I'm sorry," he added. "It didn't occur to me. I didn't mean to frighten you. I just had to be with someone."

"Aren't you going to take off your coat?"

"I'm cold," he said. "I will when I warm up."

"How'd you get here so quickly?"

"I was already here," he said, smiling. "I called from the subway station."

"How'd you get in downstairs?"

"It was open."

"Damn super," I said. "Always forgetting to lock up."

"The subway was acting out a Metropolitan Opera chorus version of itself," he said. "Drunks, prostitutes, male and female, puking addicts and dreamy ones, tiny Puerto Rican kids being hauled home by their tiny little parents, mad old men, packs of running kids. I rated it overdone, overcostumed, overacted."

"Friday night," I said. "Bad night for the subway."

"Why is that?"

"Pay day and despair. Might as well splurge it all on liquor, drugs, sex, whatever. Add some money to the usual constant debris, and that's it."

He laughed. "Have you made a study of this or did you just make it up?"

"It's a well-known sociological fact. *Everybody* knows it."

I had stopped shivering under the warm covers and permitted myself a luxurious yawn. Matt said, "Poor girl, you're sleepy."

I said, "Aren't you?"

"I'm impotent, you know," he answered.

That woke me up. "What's that, a recommendation?"

He got out of his coat and resettled himself in the rocker with a new cigarette. "Is that why your marriage went — sex troubles?"

"My marriage didn't 'went.' Harry left me."

"Because of sex?"

"Because I'm an idiot. You see, he put through this long-distance call to my hotel in Florida and it didn't get through until five in the morning. He had sent me there to rest when Elliot was four months old. We were both supposed to go but at the last moment a case came up and he couldn't leave. I wasn't eager to go because I don't like to do things alone but I was up to here with everything — including him — so bored and trapped." I remembered myself heavy with Elliot, dragging myself about the three-story house in Forest Hills, pushing myself to survive a pregnancy that seemed interminable, suffocating within an overwhelming lethargy, as if I had become the fetus and the pregnancy had enclosed me. I longed for a daughter, a small, lithe creature who would grow up to be my friend. Elliot was born ten pounds eleven ounces. It exhausted me to lift him. I even hated him a little for being male. Now there would be four men to do for. A holiday was supposed to make all that look good to me again. "I met a couple of Harry's colleagues there," I told Matt. "It was some kind of legal conference. Most of the men had brought their wives but I had a ball with the few who hadn't. Real fun. The last night one of his friends came back to my room with me. We had a very nice time and fell asleep afterward in that yummy double bed with a view of the sea. Harry called at about five in the morning to say he was taking a six-thirty plane and would be in Miami for breakfast. I was so befuddled I asked him if he would like to talk to his friend and that goon was so befuddled he actually said hello to Harry before we all came to."

Matt burst out laughing. I shushed him. "And then?"

"By the time I came home he had left me, shut off all the charge accounts, put that stupid announcement in the papers, and he was threatening to prove me a degenerate and to sue for the kids. But the charge wouldn't stick. After all he was up against another lawyer with a family and a reputation to protect. He'll never make it stick though he's dangled some pretty scary possibilities in my face. My lawyers mounted a counteroffensive, charged him with desertion. They're fighting it out in the courts, a bunch of lawyers are going to get rich and I'm struggling along."

"What can he threaten you with?"

I turned on my side toward him, my head propped on my arm, and looked into his eyes, bright with curiosity. "Okay," I said, "let me tell you. Fun and games in the suburbs. You know about that, my child, don't you? We had a thing with our closest friends when we lived in Forest Hills. Three of us and Harry watching. That's the way he liked it, but when all that happened he said he was going to bring those poor shnooks into court to prove — you know . . ." I trailed off because he looked shocked and avidly eager in a breathy mix that bothered me.

"And now you're divorced?"

"No. Legal separation. Harry can ease that into a divorce any time he wants to with the new laws. Meanwhile he's still fighting with me and as long as it isn't settled he can keep on fighting and I guess that's what he wants."

"He really doesn't want to give you up, does he?"

"Oh, who cares?" I said, sickened by the conversation.

"He's a nut," Matt said. "I always thought he was. He should have made your life miserable and hung on to you. You're too good to let loose."

I laughed. "He's not vicious like you. Just stupid." I warmed up to the explanation. "He really is stupid, Matt. I never would have harmed Harry. I was working for his success like crazy, you know that. And I would have put up with him forever and ever, been bored with him forever and ever and gone on doing whatever was best for him and the kids forever and ever and he threw all that away as if it was nothing. For what? He kept saying, 'It's a symptom. It's the handwriting on the wall.' He did the whole thing up in his mind like Anna Karenina or Emma Bovary. I've never been all that romantic about myself, but there he was casting me as the wife who cheats, enjoys, and drives the husband mad. And I didn't have a rag of a man to fall back on. I hardly knew that guy, Harry's friend."

"It doesn't make sense," Matt said. "How about that other stuff? Didn't that figure?"

"What other stuff?" I knew what he meant.

"You know. Why was that acceptable?"

"I can't explain it," I said. "We were younger; that was about ten years ago. I really don't know, I can't explain it."

"Did you ever tell any of this to Mary?"

"Of course not," I said. "I've never told it to anybody except my lawyers because they keep after you so. It's worse than confession. They make you tell them all. They say so that they won't be surprised in court, but I think it's because they have nasty tastes. I don't know why I told *you*."

"You're responding to the priest in me," he said, smiling. His eyes were still lit with avid curiosity. "What's it like, three at a time, is it better?"

"That's the general idea," I said, and added, "Four. You forgot Harry, watching."

"I can't imagine it," Matt said. "And you make it all sound so careless."

"I'm beginning to see why you're impotent." He flushed, and though I had meant to be cruel, I was immediately sorry. It's odd about sensuality. It seems to exist purely in the body but there's a whole other set of nerve endings involved. "It's funny," I said, "but in the end we ended up a traditional couple. We got rid of the other two one night. Of our friends, the man was sweet and tender and his wife was one of those 'suffer me to love you, oh please suffer me to give you pleasure' nuts. And she was all torn up about which body she loved more, mine or her husband's. Finally I just wanted to be alone with that sweet tenderness that he had. We pushed her out of the bed and both of them, his wife and Harry, out of the room, locked the door and went on by ourselves. It was the best time we had, even though we could hear her screaming and raging in the living room. Harry didn't rage then, but he threw a fit at me later. That ended it. They moved away soon after and we never saw them again."

I could see him trying to take it all in. "And love? I thought women insisted on love with sex. Women like you."

"I don't know what you mean," I said.

"You know. Liberated women. Like you and Mary."

"Wouldn't that be a dirty trick!" I said. "Anyway don't confuse us. There's nothing liberated about me. I think."

He was studying my face with interest. "I can't understand

you and Mary being so close. You're so different. You don't
go in for absolute judgments the way Mary does."

"Wait, wait," I said.

"I always thought that you and Mary told each other everything. That's why I thought you knew about me."

"No," I said. "I knew that you were having a bad time, the
two of you, especially during the pregnancy. But I just assumed that meant you were having other girls."

His eyes slid away from mine. He put out his cigarette and
thrust his trembling hands between his knees. He looked des-
olated, crouched in the rocker, staring into the corner of the
room.

"Oh, for heaven's sake," I said without thinking. "Take
your clothes off and get into bed with me. At least you'll be
warm." He was out of his clothes and in his underwear so
quickly, it was like a comic routine, except that he looked
stunning throughout. Only at the end in his white T-shirt and
madras shorts, the unexpected thinness of his long legs, covered with silky black hairs, and something childish about the
way he held them, slightly pigeon-toed, made him look frail
and pitiful. He was cold to touch when I took him in my
arms. It was awkward. He is much taller than I am, and very
broad at the shoulders and a good part of his legs must have
been hanging over the edge of the bed. But he got up again at
once, took off his underthings, put out the light, all in a busi-
nesslike way, and arranged me alongside him with his arms
under and around me and his lips at my breast. He stroked
my back and twined his legs around me. His flesh rose and
hardened immediately.

"Some impotence," I said. And then, "Just a minute. I
have to get up." I lit the lamp.

I went into the bathroom to put in my diaphragm, the same old one I had gotten before Harry and I were married. I've never swung over to the current methods. In a way, I'm bothered every time I use it. I don't feel that way about my flesh. Isn't that always renewing itself? But the diaphragm is just a stale, used object.

I was troubled too that I was doing this with the kids in the house, a thing I had never done before and had promised myself not to, ever. Terry's light was out and the radio was quiet. His door was shut tight and I closed my bedroom door carefully. Matt was flat on the bed staring at the ceiling with a look too dark and terrible to decipher. He had the covers pulled up to his neck.

"Don't think," I said, and turned off the light and slid in under the covers.

He was on top of me at once. So quickly that there wasn't time to respond, he had entered me, having raised my bulky granny nightgown to my neck where it puffed out over my face. He came at once and sweat seemed to spray out of every pore of his body, bathing me as well as him. It was one of the worst lays I had ever had but I felt very good lying under his sweat and his sweet release. It was like a quick dash into the sea. He fell asleep immediately and I eased him off me, covering us both well, because the drying sweat was chilling, and then I must have fallen asleep myself.

The alarm woke me at seven-thirty. The kids had to make an 8:15 train to spend the weekend with their father. Matt was gone. I searched for traces of his visit, other than my own sticky body, as I went through the routine of getting the kids off. They had trouble getting out the door and the open locks left by Matt remained the only sign I was to find. Was it this that depressed me? After my boys departed, and the breakfast dishes were done, and a shower had washed away the smell of our odd union, and the bedspread covered the place, I set to work on my face and hair without pleasure in my good looks. What had entered my head as if no one had ever thought it before was that life was meaningless. It really is meaningless, I thought, carefully applying my eyeliner. There's no other explanation.

4 ——————

EARLY IN THE MORNING of the day I left the hospital, something went wrong with Blue-Rinse's bladder bag contraption and it spilled urine all over the floor. Attendants arrived fairly soon to mop it clean, but I fled the ward as if from a plague, as if escaping that room and its inhabitants might guarantee immunity from some dark, medieval curse. The nurses let me wait in a visitors' lounge for Jean, who was coming to take me home. I looked forward to home as a shelter where I would regain myself, the whole self that I had brought so carelessly to the hospital with such assurance of all my strengths.

But I continued to feel strange, even at home. Gloria had brought the children back and I tried to establish the apolitical life I had promised myself for Bella and Matt. I tried, without hurting them, to avoid my friends from the Committee and their offers of help. I hoped to build an ordinary, human life where Matt and I could reach each other, where Bella would be safe and the children nurtured. But my intent seemed just beyond each day's reach. Tomorrow, I thought at the end of each electric day, tomorrow, I'll begin that good life, when I'm stronger and through with the treatments.

I would suddenly lose my bearings. I had understood that I

would have to stop breast feeding, however the surgery turned out, but it seemed to be a shock I hadn't absorbed because I would forget and bare my breast to feed my baby daughter, sometimes even the mutilated one. I couldn't remember the baby's name and bewildered Matt by calling him at the office to ask this question. My mother shuffling into the living room with her hands trembling before her and her hair in disarray frightened me. Who could that woman be? Once, dozing on the couch, startled by Bella's appearance, I thought I was back in the hospital with the old mother of the deaf children. After such incidents, I would take the baby in my arms and hug Mark close to my side and sit on the couch waiting for Matt to come home, schooling myself with the words, "Here, here is your reality, in these children and in Matt."

When I wasn't languishing and weepy, and finding the smallest chore too much for me, I was bursting with fierce energy and couldn't find enough to do. I had taken to waking very early in the morning. A terrible noise would wake me, as if a metal sheet had been banged with a hammer, a sound that lived in my head or in my dreams. Nobody else heard it. In some way I connected it with lying alongside Matt in our double bed. I could feel Matt's loathing even when he was asleep, I could feel him cringing in his sleep at the thought of touching me. But all I could think of was — touch. I was on fire with need, as if we had just begun, as if we were in the midst of making love for the first times. Matt was impotent, as he had been all through the pregnancy, but I couldn't let him be, and at the end I forced him to use his hands. Our sex had become a kind of murder; I thought we might both die of it.

During the day I dreamt of us restored as friends and good lovers. Every night we reopened the battle wounds. Away from him, I puzzled about us, brooding anxiously over incidents in our past, yearning for solutions and hopeful that it would be made right. I tried to sift through and clarify my emotions by writing them down and I took to spending part of each day when the baby was asleep and Mark at nursery school organizing my ideas about love and marriage. But as soon as Matt and I came together every evening all I could read in his face was dread and flight, and the sight made me hate him.

One night I woke to that terrible clanging noise, with the conviction that Matt had whispered in my ear. "It's cancer," I had heard him say. "You're dying." The room was still. Matt's breathing sounded as if he were asleep but I felt that he was faking it. His body was turned away from me to the wall, curled as close to the edge of the bed as possible. I switched on the light and leaned across him to see his eyes. They were shut and I was sure that he was pretending to be asleep. I fixed my eyes on him with great intensity, saying to myself, "You die, you, you," and he opened his eyes and yelled out, "What is it?"

I said, "Sh. You'll wake the children."

"What's the matter?" He spoke more quietly. "Are you all right?"

"You spoke to me," I said. "You said something to me, but I didn't hear it. What did you say?"

I was sure that his bewilderment was pretense. "No, I didn't. Or perhaps in my sleep. What did I say?"

But he wasn't going to trick me that way and I said, "I don't know." We didn't go back to sleep but we didn't speak any further. He read. I got up and made the baby's formula and ran the diapers through the washing machine and did some ironing.

Our apartment was hateful to me, the six dark little rooms

and particularly Matt's clever devices to utilize the tiny space. One afternoon I tore down the dressing table he had designed and built for handling the infant and I bought an ugly bathinette to replace it. My mother stood in the doorway, trembling and babbling at me to stop as I ripped it out of the wall. I felt very strong and powerful and the noise of the table coming apart sounded beautiful to me as I razed it. I wanted to do the same to the candy store on the corner when the woman who owns it talked to me about my operation and offered advice about the best place in the neighborhood for a foam rubber breast. I wanted to pull the whole place down on her head.

When Matt came home we fought about it. I accused him of telling her in order to humiliate me and in his lying way he insisted that he hadn't spoken to her.

"Why don't you ask some of your sacred Committee people if they told her? They're so fucking busy with your condition they're turning it into a new national cause. They were probably in there asking for a donation. Ask pop-eyed Joanna."

His cruelty left me speechless. He knew how hard I was trying to keep Committee people away, and that I had refused to accept any more Committee money. When I got my breath I screamed that he was jealous of the fact that there were people around me who considered that I added up to more than a pile of shit. I called him a pig and a bourgeois elitist. He was helping me get Mark ready for bed, pinning a double diaper on him, because of the bed-wetting, and Mark shouted, "Daddy, you stuck me, on purpose," and began to cry uncontrollably. I pulled Mark away from Matt to soothe him and Matt slammed out of the house.

While I put Mark to bed, finished clearing up the supper things and settled my mother for the night, my head was racing with ways to punish Matt, to keep him out for good. We were all better off without him. It was then that I first thought of changing the lock on the door of the apartment, but I didn't do anything about it because it was too late. Instead I called Jean and told her the whole story. Then I called Joanna. Finally I called Bob and told him that Matt was going to pieces, going crazy or something, and that he had deliberately stuck Mark with a large safety pin because he was angry with me. Bob asked if I would like him to drop by. I said, "No, better not," and he said that he would be by tomorrow to see Mother. Bob and Jean were the only friends I was seeing regularly, Bob because he was our doctor and Jean because I wanted to see her.

I was impatient for Matt to come home so that we could continue our fight. In the quiet apartment, with the children and Mother asleep, I paced up and down the narrow hall, daydreaming what I would say to him. I would tell him there was nothing to do but separate, as we had been discussing before the operation, that nothing was changed, that nothing would ever change him, that he had no desire to change. Though I didn't shape his response into words, implicit in my scenario was his reassurance that his love and devotion were greater than ever. But it got very late and he didn't return.

I became dulled with disappointment and my high expectations gave way to an amorphous and sickly anxiety. It was a relief when the baby woke. I changed her and kept her in my arms while I heated her bottle. After I fed her I couldn't bring myself to put her away from me, as if we were still bodily attached. With great difficulty I climbed into her crib with her and curled up to fit in the confined space, the baby buried in my body. For one flashing second, I thought, "What are you doing?" but it was quickly gone. I cuddled the baby for

comfort and cried to myself and then I must have fallen
asleep.

I startled awake. There were hissing noises and cries and a
hovering shape. I didn't know where I was. Matt whispered,
"Mary, what are you doing in here?" The baby was howling.
My cramped, chilled body felt like a hollow filled with wind.
Matt lifted the baby to his shoulder where she quieted immediately. He reached out toward me, "Let me help you out of
there." In the faint light of the room I could see his face contorted with horror, his black eyes dilated with the inevitable
fear he felt whenever he looked at me. I screamed, "Get away
from me. Let me alone," and he backed away toward Mark's
bed where Mark slept as if nothing was happening. For a second, I thought I was in the hospital in a labor crib. Then I
recalled climbing in with the baby but I could no longer understand why I had done it. I had great trouble getting out,
but I did and ran to my bed and pulled the covers over me. I
didn't want to speak to Matt. I didn't want to discuss what I
was doing in there. It frightened me now and I didn't want to
think about it.

I was being given the cobalt treatment in a hospital in the
Bronx. Dr. Altman said it had the best department in the
field. The next morning I went there as usual, by subway
down to 145th Street, going with the morning rush and then
crossing over to the uptown Bronx side for an almost empty
train to the last stop. I couldn't read. I sat, enclosed in a
violent torpor, automatically doing what I had been told to
do. A Negro came into the car at Yankee Stadium and
slumped into the first seat near the door. I noticed him because of the smell. He had urinated in his clothes and vomited on himself, but above the wreck of his filthy, torn,
stiffened outfit of makeshift bits of clothing, his head, fallen

back against the subway window, was beautiful and dignified. He was black, with fine Caucasian features, though with some prominence in the sculptured lips, and his wooly hair was silvery white and cropped close to his well-shaped head. He opened his eyes while I was studying him. Except for their blackness, his eyes resembled mine. They were very large, octagonal shaped and with the kind of prominent eyeball which swivels freely in the socket, like a lamp. The look he gave me was full of direct, liberating anger. He stumbled out of his seat, lurching down the car. It was almost empty of passengers. Two high school boys, working at their books, sat on one side; on the other a third was asleep with his incredibly long legs stretched over his book bag and across the aisle. The Negro fell over the long legs of the boy and the others laughed, though all three rushed to help him up. Lying there, he yelled, "Don't you touch me. Fuck it. Fuck it. Fuck you long-legged white boys full of vitamins. Don't you laugh at me, motherfuckers. So long as you have the same asshole pointing down to God's earth, you're no better than me." They retreated from him, their natural good color heightened by embarrassment. I guessed because there were women in the car. Myself, and another down at the far end. She began to scream, "Get a cop. We're coming to the station. There's supposed to be one at every station," and when we pulled into the station, she stuck her head out the door, yelling, "Police, police!" When nobody responded, she dashed out, between the closing doors, and as we rolled away I saw her running toward the change booth, her high fake-fur Russian hat wobbling on her head. The two boys packed their books and slung their green book bags over their shoulders and started to move toward the connecting car doors. The third picked up his plastic briefcase with a school name on it and joined them.

They all wore good desert boots, corduroy jeans, hooded car coats, as if uniform dress were required. Sprawled on the floor of the car, the Negro had been yelling throughout, cursing them and the woman, but now he went on to something else. "Don't you start talking to me about the vote now," he proceeded in a quietly reasonable voice. "All that vote shit doesn't bring one bean in the house. Talk about a hundred-and-fifty-dollar-a-week job. That's the kind of talk I want to hear. None of that vote shit. I've been voting for twenty years. Started out pissing in my drawers, ending up in the same condition." And he did, filling the car with the smell of fresh urine. The boys held the door for me, looking at me urgently, straddling the swaying cars, but I surprised myself by saying, "No, I'll stay here with him."

The Negro laughed at that and propped himself up against the center post. Urine flowed across the floor into a corner as the train tilted. "You better run, little lady, run with the rest of them. It stinks here. You hanging around for my stink?" He laughed so hard that he exhausted himself. He slumped sideward and fixed me with a steady stare conveying an angry urgent intelligence. I concentrated on receiving the message he was sending; that was why I had stayed. The light of his eyes connected with an inner light and fire in my brain. I was powerfully surrounded and bathed in this light, but I felt weak too, as if I might faint or scream uncontrollably. Then it all flashed into focus. I knew that we were one, he and I. And I knew that all the senseless fragments of my selves had coalesced at that moment into a perfect crystal unity. When the police boarded at the next station and shoved and drove him out of the car it was as if I had been taken with him, cast out of the society. I had gone with him, but he also stayed within me, riding on.

At the hospital I gave them my body for their humiliations and tortures but I withheld my mind. It lived its own life, protected and kindled by that extraordinary light spreading from that new center of my brain. I had asked the technicians about the burns the cobalt was causing and they had turned me over to two doctors. They studied my x rays and said some gobbledygook to me and then spoke only to each other. A middle-aged secretary entered with her glasses hanging around her neck on one of those gadgets. A whole new discussion began about some error on a table of organization which they needed for an imminent conference. I was perched on the edge of the table, naked to the waist, and one of the doctors continued to hold my arm as if I were a sheaf of papers or a pen he had forgotten to put down. I shook him off, put my clothes on in the dressing room and walked out. I wasn't ever going to come back.

Outside, I noticed the weather for the first time. It was a cold, gray day, not a good day for a long walk, but I cut around the cemetery with the vague notion that Bronx Park was somewhere in that direction. My anger felt good, something like happiness. I walked rapidly, almost without effort, for a long time. At one point I climbed to a height which circled a reservoir and I must have covered it many times, my thoughts like lightning, correcting, adjusting, planning for the people everywhere. All the dreary work of Committee meetings and canvassing and reports, all the failures, all the half-mad efforts at actions and exhortations and the heartbreaking quarreling among ourselves was culminating in this moment of conviction that it all had to be that way and now, *now*, it was gloriously going to start to really move. I passed only a few mothers with baby carriages, all bundled up against the cold. I didn't speak to anybody. When I came down into the streets

I was in totally unfamiliar territory, an area of garages and odd stores for plumbing supplies and upholstery. One storefront had a sign in the window saying HELP WANTED.

I went right in and asked for the job. It was a mimeograph, photo-offset and Xerox press. They hired me to type stencils, do paste-ups and to proofread, when I said I could do all those things, though in fact I couldn't do any of them except type and not on stencils. The owners were two long-jawed sad-faced brothers. They were hiring me, they explained, because their sister had been doing that part of the work but they were always fighting and she had quit the day before which she did repeatedly. The idea that they could really replace her seemed to be very exciting to them. The place was miserable — small, dark and dirty, though it had a tangy smell of ink and paper and a light back room overlooking a pleasant little yard. They said I could bring my lunch and make coffee on the burner. The salary was $95 a week. The taller of the two sad-faced brothers asked if I could begin work immediately and I said that I could after I had had some lunch and made some calls. The smaller one methodically put on a hat and coat and scarf and came outside with me to show me that "down two blocks turn to your right and walk three blocks, there's a little candy store on the corner that has a luncheonette service, you can eat there and make your calls. At least, nobody ever died of eating there that I know of." I waved and walked off but he called me back, "Miss, we don't even know your name." So I returned to the store and wrote my name and telephone number and address and he gave me one of their cards

AY-WON PRINTING PRESS

A. SHEROWITZ & SONS

NO JOB TOO SMALL

with an address and telephone number in the corner. I saw that I was way up in the east 200s.

The luncheonette was a narrow store with a counter and two little sticky-surfaced tables in a corner opposite a telephone booth. I ordered a bacon and tomato sandwich on toast and coffee from the owner behind the counter. He must have had that illness that distorts the features into an animal's, and when he came out from behind the counter later, I saw that he had a bad limp too. Together, the long hanging lip and the loping walk made him thoroughly animallike, but a gentle, patient beast of some kind. He argued that he had nice fresh chopped liver, why didn't I have that instead on a good piece of rye bread? I agreed and he served it with a delicious dill pickle and a little paper cup of cole slaw. After I finished I used the washroom. I had started to menstruate, but I had some Tampax in my bag. I looked ugly and distraught in the dirty mirror and I couldn't understand why the sad brothers had hired me. When I came out, because the booth was right there, I decided to call my mother and tell her everything about the Negro and the job. Matt answered the phone, and I asked to speak to Bella. I called her Bella instead of Mother and disguised my voice so that he wouldn't know who I was, but he said, "Is it you, Mary? Are you all right?"

I said that I wanted to speak to Bella, please.

"We've been worried sick. I came home from the office. Where are you? There's no formula for the baby and the hospital said you left hours ago. Are you all right?

I said that I wanted to speak to Bella and when he went on again about where the fuck was I, I hung up. I was trembling. I needed desperately to tell someone of the important decisions I was making. I called Jean at her office and they told me that she had gone home ill, but when I called her house there was no answer. I couldn't remember Bob's office number. I looked up Dr. Guerrero in the Manhattan telephone book, lying in a dirty heap of papers on the floor of the booth. His secretary answered and said that he was with a patient. I almost rang off but when she asked me who was calling and I told her, she said, "Oh, please hold on, will you?" as if it were very urgent, and in a second Bob was on the phone.

Before he could say anything, I said, "Bob I've had the most wonderful morning. I understand everything now. I see through all the mistakes and how to correct them. We must get together and organize along entirely different lines. I know I can lead us to a new beginning. I've been working it out all morning. We've been too exclusive. We've cut off our base. We have to include those who stink, who piss on their clothes and vomit on themselves, the poorest of the poor, the sick and the dying. You understand, don't you?"

"Yes," Bob said. "Where are you now, Mary? Are you at home?"

"I'm in a luncheonette run by a patient animal. He's beautiful. He has delicious chopped liver. I can't talk anymore now. I just got a job and have to go back to work."

"Mary," he said. "Please wait a minute. I must see you immediately. Can I meet you and talk this all over? Tell me where you are and I'll come right there to meet you."

"I don't know exactly," I said, delighted with his response. "Somewhere in the Bronx, in the east two hundreds. But we'll get together tonight. If you could get in touch with Joanna and tell her to get a couple of key people together. And you and me and my mother. Bella would be invaluable. I know I'm on the right track to a real revolutionary movement."

"Right," he said, "right. But it's very important that we get

together first. Mary, will you do this for me, will you please
stay there and wait for me? Don't do anything, just stay there
and wait for me?"

"What's the matter with you?" He was not normally so
excitable.

"Nothing," he said. "I think you and I ought to get together first, before the others. Couldn't you just sit there and
wait until I arrive? It shouldn't take more than half an hour,
wherever it is."

"Sure," I said.

"And will you ask the luncheonette man to please speak to
me? I need the exact address."

"Sure," I said.

When I turned around the proprietor was looking at me
oddly. I asked him if he would please speak to my friend on
the telephone, that he needed to know exactly where I was.
He moved to the phone in his strange, loping, bent-over, almost four-footed walk and said, "Hello," in a very wary tone.
He kept one eye on me, dumb-beast fashion, as he talked. He
didn't say much more than, "Yes, Doctor. No, Doctor. Yes,
Doctor." Bob spoke to him for a long time. Then I heard him
transmitting elaborate directions, West Side Highway, Bronx
Expressway, exit Eastchester Road, etc., etc., and after a few
more yes, Doctor, no, Doctors, he hung up.

We had a good talk and the time went so quickly that it
seemed only a few minutes had gone by when Bob came in the
door. It was something of a shock to see him there. The
luncheonette had become a self-contained world for me, the
little store in the strange neighborhood, where everybody
knew each other and customers were intimate friends of the
store owner. Herman and I became very close too. I was in-

terested in everything about him and eager for him to know
about me too. I could hardly wait for him to finish a sentence
so that I could go on talking. We had gotten onto the subject
of New York City. He understood me when I described how I
imagined New York as it had been before it was settled by
Europeans, a green jewel in its surrounding waters. "Do you
know, Herman, even now you can take a subway going in any
direction and end up at a magnificent body of water, any direction at all? Do you realize that, that you can ride the subway and bang, there's the Atlantic right there at the end of the
line, or the Hudson meeting the Harlem?" He understood exactly what I meant. He had traveled a good deal in his work
and told me about the beautiful settings of cities like San
Francisco and Barcelona — on the sea, with the mountains
behind.

"My mother's brother died in Spain, fighting," I lied. He
nodded sympathetically, but I didn't think he understood
about that. "I'm going to go there one day and see Barcelona.
I want to go everywhere. Do you know I've never traveled? I
want to see every street in New York, too, and all the paths in
all the parks. Do you know Crotona Park in the Bronx? It's
beautiful and hardly anybody knows about it. Do you know
Inwood Park? And Prospect? I'd like to spend a year just
walking all over the city. Why shouldn't I do that? Maybe I
could live with you and your family while I'm working for the
Sherowitzes." We had already discussed all that and he had
told me that he and his wife rented a room now that their two
children were no longer at home.

He said, "Well, you never can tell."

I rushed to explain to him that the most important thing
for me at that moment was to change my life, catch hold of it

and control it, and that the way to start was by getting a job and living on my own. I didn't tell him about the children because I didn't want to think about them then.

He agreed that I should do what I thought best. Then, after a customer left and we were alone, he said, "Excuse me, I couldn't help overhearing your conversation and I was wondering about that revolutionary movement you mentioned — with your mother?"

I studied his gross, kindly face, considering whether he could be trusted. "Did you ever hear of Isabelle Vance Moody?"

"Sure," he said. "She's a very well-known Communist. Isn't she in jail?"

"She was released, after fourteen years."

"Is that so?" he said.

Something wary in his response started anger moving in me again. "They had to release her. The Committee worked very hard at it, and worldwide opinion was against them."

"She was a very good-looking woman," he said. "You must take after her."

I didn't respond to that part of his remark, but I asked him if he had ever seen her and if he had been in sympathy with my mother's cause. He was looking down at the counter which he was scrubbing carefully. "Well, I don't know too much about it. I was a trade union man myself before I got sick. Ten years in the Merchant Marine. I heard her once at an NMU meeting. She really could steam things up. She had a big reputation as an organizer. Is she still such a good speaker?"

I was telling him about Bella's Parkinson's disease when Bob came in. I don't think I had ever seen Bob looking more upset, not even at meetings when others were being particularly stupid. He led me in an unfamiliar courtly manner to the car but didn't get in himself. He said that he needed cigarettes, but he took so long returning that I followed him and found him pressing what looked like a ten- or twenty-dollar bill on Herman, who was resisting. "Listen, Doctor," Herman was saying, "I haven't gone so far that I have to be paid to be a human being."

"Oh, I forgot to pay for my lunch," I said, but Herman refused that too, saying that it had been more like a visit anyway.

"You forgot to say good-bye, that's what you forgot," he said, and looked at me reproachfully. "But I forgive you." And his poor misshapen, pendulous lips formed a monstrous smile. I kissed him on the cheek. He smelled like a man, and not the enchanted beast I had been conjuring. When a pulse started in his throat, I felt ashamed and hurried out.

Bob sat down in the car behind the wheel and I said what I was thinking. "We're unspeakably cruel to each other. At bottom, where all the important things lie, we never touch."

He looked at me in alarm. "You mean — us?"

"Everybody," I said, "people, humanity."

I saw his soft brown eyes water before he turned away.

We had been driving for a while before I asked him where we were going. I had been talking rapidly, telling him about the day's events and especially about the Negro on the subway, but I couldn't convey its special message, the story was coming out wrong. Bob seemed abstracted, not really listening. I wanted only to feel pure love toward Bob but instead I was becoming agitated. When he said that he was taking me home, little tongues of hatred darted up around me.

I said, "You haven't been listening to me. I'm never going home. I have a job and I'm going to live with Herman and his wife and start a new life. My old life is dead, don't you understand that?"

He was maneuvering in the traffic, entering some highway and not paying any attention to me. I said, very fiercely, "Stop the car this minute. I'm getting out," and I put my hand on the door handle. I had no intention of opening the door. I knew very well that it was dangerous. Cars were streaming past. He screamed at me, "Don't touch the door. We'll go anywhere you like."

More calmly, after a few seconds, he said, "Where would you like to go, Mary?"

I said that it didn't matter to me, it was he who had wanted to talk right away. "I should get back to Sherowitz and Sons, eventually." I had no idea of the time, but I thought it would be okay with them if I took another hour or so to discuss things with Bob.

Bob said, "There's a nice place nearby to have a drink and talk."

We were traveling smoothly at an easy pace in the right lane of a parkway. He put his hand over mine on the car seat. His hand was warm and meant to be a comfort. "Don't get so mad at me. I'm with you, sweetheart. I know what you're going through." He turned toward me and his eyes filled with tears again. Hatred shook me. I looked out of the window at the thin, brown pencil lines of the wintry trees and the occasional patches of snow or frost. I let my anger run with the car. When I was quieter, I said, "I'm going to get a car and a license, first thing. It's good for me to keep moving."

He said, "What do you want to discuss first, Mary, your personal plans or the plans for the new movement?" as if he were interviewing me. He drew a deep, gasping breath at the end of his question.

I said, "What's the matter with you? Nobody acts like themselves anymore."

He said, "It's because we're worried about you."

I laughed, furious again. "Worry about yourselves. Are you in such good shape? You're a nervous wreck. So is Matt. Look around you, look around at our crowd, at anybody, at anything. Don't worry about me. I'm in better shape than most things are in this world."

He said, "You're angry again. I'm sorry." He took one of those deep breaths.

"You're a fool," I said. "Matt's right to despise you. You know that he despises you," I said with careful deliberation, staring into his face. I felt my own face burning.

"I don't think that he does," he said.

"He says that you're in love with me and that you won't do anything about it."

"Yes," he said. "But I'm going to do something about it now."

"Like what?" I made the question sound derisive.

"Ply you with liquor at a country restaurant," he said, and managed a weak smile.

"Very funny." I was choking with anger. "You middle-aged swingers are not to be believed." I felt that he was making fun of me. Who would want to touch me now? Not even good, old, kind Bob.

He pulled into a rest area to get gas and to phone his office. I went to the ladies' room. It was very clean and empty and the radiator hissed gently. I changed the Tampax and when I washed my hands in a sink before a mirror, my face shocked me. It looked pinched, bluish, yet very red, especially the nose, and my eyes stared angrily. I heard myself say aloud, "Whose face are you?" and clearly heard the silent response,

"The dying face." There was some soap in a dish and I scrubbed away. A lot of the pinched look was washed away with the city soot accumulated on my long walk. From my bag I spread out all the make-up Jean had bought me and taught me how to use, and scolded me regularly for not using on my face daily as she did. I applied everything, white under the eyes, eyeliner, panstick, three kinds of shadow, mascara, a touch of rouge, two shades of lipstick. While I was carefully applying mascara, a woman entered and said, "Your boy friend asked me to find out if you're all right. Are you?" I asked her to say that I would be finished in a few more minutes. But I fussed a long time with my hair; it had flattened under the knitted hood I was wearing. I brushed it and fluffed it and wet the bangs a little to place them. My heart was banging as if something crucial hung on the results of my efforts. Finished, I couldn't tell whether I looked pretty or ridiculously painted but at least I didn't look anything like that girl who had come in with me. That pinched, red-nosed, failing creature. I studied myself and found the side view excellent, and I turned up the collar of my fake fur and walked out. Bob started when he saw me.

"Well, well, well," he said. "What have we here?"

"Is it too much?"

"It's great," he said. "You're beautiful. Let's go."

The restaurant we drove to stood on a height above an enormous shopping center. The entrance was ugly, but the building extended toward the trees beyond and the table to which we were led overlooked a small, natural waterfall. Once inside, it was possible to forget the parking lot spreading like a disease outside. There was a fire in the fake Colonial fireplace. The place was very quiet, almost empty. The piped music was tuned very low. Bob ordered drinks and a dish of cold shrimp and clams on the half-shell. Surrounded by props, I put myself onstage, held my head erect and swiveled my eyes so that Bob or anyone else who happened to be watching me could see how fine they were, and I smiled with the seductive lips I had drawn with the lip brush, as I talked. Bob seemed fascinated by me, if not by what I was saying. He listened, nodding and interjecting a question now and then. He grew weary and apprehensive toward the end, but by that time I had wearied myself and I was very drunk. I had had three martinis.

I had explained my new plan. I had presented it in detailed particulars, but in a rush and without orderly organization. We would dissolve all separate existing movements on the left, ending all the nonsense of divisions and probing forays into disparate sectors of the people. We would start at the source with a call for the immediate formation of Communist communities, here, in the heart of the country. The Committee's job would be to institute an intensive study of a given number of recommended sites in the search for the proper location in which to found the first colony. (He questioned this and I admitted I knew nothing of this aspect. But it was obviously no problem. Maine, for example, contained vast stretches of wilderness. There was unsettled acreage in the West and in Canada, and there was also the possibility of reclaiming depressed areas, such as Appalachia.) We would then issue a call for 40,000 young people, under twenty, and 5000 adults, over twenty-five to any age, to join the first colony. The Committee would make a determination not only on the site but on the best economic activity for that site. However, each community must be planned to include agricultural and industrial works so that each had the capacity to be self-sustaining. The community would quickly create its own spontaneous culture and the educational facilities suited to its structure. Money would not exist, and personal possessions would be limited to basic needs. Temporary living quarters would consist of barracks for single people, small double cottages for couples. A "couple" consisted of two people who had filed a request to be so designated. Such people were granted "couple's rights" and no questions asked. Under a simple free-choice system, children old enough to choose decided whether they preferred to live with their "couple" or with other children in special children's houses. Infants lived with a "mother" or a "couple" or in an infant's house, on the decision of the mother, or the father, or both. Specially trained people would care for infants and children apart from their couples, but psychoanalytic approaches were not to be tolerated, nor any of the "gross nonsense taught in the ed courses," I said.

He interrupted here. "You mean then to dissolve the traditional family structure?"

"Of course," I said. "That's certainly been proved unworkable."

All the necessities of life would be provided by the community and as many as possible produced by it, clothing, food (dispensed at community cafeterias, on the job, in the fields, at schools), building materials, medicine and medical services, etc. What was produced would pay for what had to be bought. The community would arise in the wilderness just as the first settlements of the early colonists did, one group erecting the structures which would house the people, while others farmed the land, fished the streams and tended the livestock to feed them. Later the more complicated industrial and educational units would be developed. There would be no organized militia, no police; the entire population would be the defense force and there would be no weapons other than the bodies of the people. No existing laws of the country would be broken and therefore the community would be invulnerable to attack. All colonists would work and study in equal parts down to the children and all the way up to the community elders. There would be no stratified group of leaders or teachers but a constantly flowing pool of expert, knowledgeable minds and bodies to attend to the problems they were best suited to solve, the way a plumber is called to fix a leak, a doctor to fix a broken leg, an architect to design an edifice. Work must consist of equal parts of manual and intellectual labor for everybody in the colony, including the children. "The children must not be left to founder through endless aimless years of play and idiotic schooling," I said.

"Those early colonies were heavily funded, you know," Bob said.

"Right." And I told him that would be the Committee's first task, to determine the minimum capital necessary to start the community moving and to initiate a crash fund-raising drive. "Why, if we just pulled out all the money now tied up in defending the movement in court, we'd probably have enough," I said. I went on. All left organizations would be invited to participate, all humanist and antiwar groups, all concerned with altering the path of the abysmal actions we were engaging in as a nation. All ideological differences would be wiped away and we would all be able to work together. "One success will lead to another. One good community will spark the creation of ten more. We will colonize our own country back into sanity. Do you see?"

Bob said, "I take it that you're not thinking in terms of a small utopian farm. Something more ambitious. Did you have Cuba's Isle of Pines experiment in mind?" He spoke very stiffly as if he were interviewing me again. That irritated me. "Perhaps some of the details might match," I said. "But don't you see that the overriding philosophy is different? Cuba's solutions are political ones, based on force and power." I had never been there but I understood the situation well enough from my reading. "Mine start at the source of society, the family structure, the virtual enslavement of women and the use of power in personal human relations. Don't you see that you must take power, coercion, economic bullying out of the human situation first? Communists have always advanced the notion that seizing the economy automatically creates a human social order, but it hasn't of course and it won't, not if Russia produces till doomsday, not if socialism outproduces the rest of the world, as long as the same rotten power relationships are maintained — man to man and woman and child."

He took one of those long breaths. "That's really quite an ambitious plan, Mary."

"Yes," I said. "But you see it, don't you? How simple and perfect. It will take time and patience but soon there will be far-ranging changes. The life will be drained out of the cities, the power plants, the war industries, the jails, the hospitals, the ghettos, until they collapse of inner emptiness. All the real life will be in the communities. The communities will have drawn everything to them, don't you see?"

He nodded and took my hands in his. "Don't you think you might be taking on too much right now? A new job, a big change in your personal life and a huge political task?"

"*What* political task?" I demanded. I began to feel furiously impatient with his attitude. "That's exactly what I want to keep out of this. Politics. Even Matt would understand

me better than you have. That's exactly what I've been trying
to explain, to convince you of, that we must remove human
affairs from the effects of politics. Why can't you understand
me?"

He rubbed my hands, examining them closely as he had
when he visited me in the hospital, bending the fingers back at
the tips. He had his head down and I had the sense that he
was crying. When he looked up his eyes shone moistly but he
was smiling, and he said, "I don't think there's anybody in the
world I understand better."

It sounded, as he said it, like an old-fashioned declaration of
love, but I chose to hear it as an insult. "Am I so simple,
then?"

"No, you're very complicated. But I love you, and all your
complications unroll before me like an open book."

I said mockingly, "You-know-me-better-than-I-know-myself
bullshit." But when he didn't respond and kept smiling with
that foolish moist look in his eyes, I lost all my good, powerful
feeling and became permeated with a nostalgic sadness. Perhaps it was the cold blue color that the air had taken on seen
through the window behind his head, or too much to drink,
but I felt that I would weep in a moment.

"You don't have to keep saying you love me, just because I
teased you before." I said it with difficulty.

"I love you, Mary Moody Schwartz," he said with the same
half-weeping smile, "even if you do have a very funny name."

"Whatever happens I'm dropping the Schwartz. Ridiculous custom, changing your name when you marry."

"Mary Moody is still pretty funny," he said.

"It's Mary Vance Moody, and I don't know how we got
into this stupid conversation."

"That's the way love talk is," he said.

"You don't love me," I said. "It's just that I'm in trouble and that's what you think love is. It's not."

"What isn't it?"

"Helping someone when they're in trouble. You don't even know what you love about me. You don't know me at all."

"I know that you're a beautiful person."

"Yech," I said. "What does that mean?"

"You're beautiful because you're young," he said.

Very angry now, I told him that was a bad reason to love someone.

He called for the check and said, "Let's go home, Mary. Let's try to straighten out some of these things. With Matt. And you must be very tired; you were up early for your treatment and will have to be again tomorrow."

"I'm not taking any more treatments and I'm not discussing anything with Matt. There's something wrong with Matt. Do you know that he deliberately stuck a pin into Mark's flesh just because he was angry with me? That's evil. A man who could do that is capable of anything." I remembered the strange way Matt had lifted his elbow to jam the pin in and was trying to describe this to Bob when I realized that I had told him about it on the phone the night before. "I told you all about it," I said. "What are you doing, humoring me or something?"

"Yes, if humoring you means I wish you well." He started that irritating kneading of my fingers again. "I wish you were at peace."

I had a vision of myself laid out. I began to cry uncontrollably. Though I was conscious of being in a public place which was now full of diners, I couldn't stop. A part of me didn't want to cover up and was even enjoying the concept of an audience, onlookers at a drama, wondering who is that pretty girl with that older man, what's the matter with her? Bob put on my coat and led me past the people, muffling my head in his shoulder. He left me in the car in the parking lot and ran back to pay the check. We were on a rise overlooking the masses of parked and crawling cars. Crowds of shoppers surged through the carefully planned mazes of the shopping center. The scene contributed to my grief in some way I couldn't untangle. I couldn't bear the sight of activity against the intensely blue, lonely sky, darkening into night. I cried luxuriously, letting myself go in the enclosed cave of the car, sobbing aloud, rolling my head from side to side and banging my fist against the seat. When Bob let himself in on the driver's side, he said, "Sh, sh," and took me in his arms. He kissed me on the hair and on my wet eyes and tried to kiss me on the mouth. He smelt of liquor and middle age. I was dismayed to feel nothing but self-pity at his embrace. I murmured, "You're so good, Bob, you're really good. Not like Matt. There's something weak and evil in Matt." I was crying uncontrollably again. "And I love him. I love him. And he can't bear me, he can't bear to touch me and it will never be fixed, it will never be right again."

Bob put me aside then and started the car. I didn't care. I went on sobbing and crying out dramatically, "Help me, Bob, please help me," throwing my hand appealingly at Bob's chest and rocking my head from side to side. One part of me was disgusted and helpless before my actions, but the part that liked the idea of an audience thought it wasn't bad.

5 ————

I SLEPT A LITTLE in the car. When we arrived at the apartment, I went directly to my bedroom and changed into a black velour top with a portrait collar that Jean had given me. The house was full of people and I wanted to keep myself onstage. Hamlet in that top. I put a heavy silver chain belt on my narrow hips and after touching up my make-up and cleaning up the smeared mascara, I went out into our small living room. What was going on was like a combination party and Committee meeting, with Jean and Matt and Joanna and the Shaeffers and Paula and her boy friend and Bob. Someone had brought sandwiches from the delicatessen and there were Scotch and beer and Danish pastries and a big pot of coffee laid out on the sideboard. I took some Scotch. Bob tried to stop me, offering me a sandwich and potato salad and cole slaw on a paper plate, and urging me to swallow a little green capsule.

I said, "No," to all that, and when he persisted I pushed him away so violently that the plate tipped and spilled on the floor. I had hardly glanced at Matt, though the whole show was for him, but it was obvious he was in one of his black despair moods. I kept laughing in a bold and silly way, insisting on wiping up the mess myself. Shtrudel waddled out of his warm spot behind the radiator and wolfed it down. He even gulped down the capsule, whatever it was. That was terribly funny to me and I sprawled back on the floor, propped up on my elbows with my head back, laughing artificially. My mother came to the door of the living room, everything about her trembling violently and unable to get out a single intelligible sound. Jean led her back to the bedroom. Matt stood over me, very tall and straight, with a beautifully tender expression on his face, all the more so because it was so rare with him. He cupped his hand on the crown of my head; warmth poured from his finger tips into my hair roots. "Okay, shorty," he said. "You come sit near me." He lifted me up and placed me on the ottoman of his chair and began playfully to feed me bits from his plate. I was happy, but a little contemptuous of him. Obviously he liked me silly, made up, costumed. Now I knew how to keep him. I flirted as if we were newly met, enjoying it all enormously, when I remembered the children and was overcome with panic. I had hardly thought of them all day and had the sudden fantasy that I had switched them out of existence. I showed my fear to Matt, as if he had caused it. "Where's Mark and the baby?"

"It's all right," he said. "They're asleep. Jean put them to sleep."

I had to go see for myself. The baby was asleep in the crib but Mark was lying in his bed with his eyes wide open. He barely greeted me. Perhaps he had just that moment awakened. I kissed him and he stared at me very solemnly. The night-light cast an unhappy gloom over the spare pieces of furniture and the bare neatness of the room. I thought of the comfortable messiness of Jean's house and wondered that she had managed to keep this room as I did.

I whispered, "Did you have a nice day?"

He shook his head, more dismissing the question than answering it.

"Are you sleepy? Did you just wake up?"

He didn't answer that either. He said, "The company's making a lot of noise." I cuddled him a bit and after an initial yielding, he pulled himself back and said, "I want to ask a question." I told him to go ahead. He was so grave that I was sure it was going to be about sex, but it was the other one. "What happens when you're dead, Mommie, tell me again." I went into my usual number about nothing really dies, all matter turns into other matter and is reborn as something new. "But after you're in the ground, do you come out again a little baby?" I said no, that you would come out again as grass and trees and leaves. He said that he would rather come out as a little baby boy again. I didn't say anything. After a while I got up, covered the baby and was about to go out of the room, when he said, "After I'm dead, you know what, Mommie? My penis is going to grow into a flower."

As soon as I returned to the living room I took center stage, adorning myself with Mark's poetry as if it were my invention. But the telling miscarried. I thought of him awake, staring at the ceiling, listening to me repeat what he had said and hearing the exclamations and the laughter. Mama Shaeffer said, "So young, and he already knows what's what." And Joanna went into a fit of admiration, her thick-lensed glasses misting up. "The beauty of a child's mind. What an exquisite metaphor. The genius that resides in a child!" and on and on. I could almost see the good feeling draining out of Matt. He was all blackness again, and I began to feel depressed myself.

Bella reappeared in the same state as earlier and Jean went to her side, but I was sure that my mother wanted me and I led her down the narrow hall to her tiny room and helped her to bed. She clung to me, very agitated, but unmistakably indicating that she had something to tell me. I waited out her struggle to recapture what small center of her responses still existed. Since her release I often found myself waiting for a signal, studying this frail wreck for a sign of the extraordinary organizer, the beautiful Communist woman victim who had become the symbol of a worldwide protest movement. Only the diamond-shaped fierce blue eyes had some resemblance to the vibrant face that had been reproduced on the posters. But this time I allowed myself a surge of spiteful anger. I thought of holding her quivering hands firmly in mine and telling her, "You cheated me of everything and came home to collapse on my hands." That might stop her trembling.

I must have communicated with her through the walls of our bodies because she did stop trembling enough to tell me a garbled story of a man calling to see why a Miss Moody hadn't reported for work. She was frightened. She was sure they were after her again. I had almost forgotten the Sherowitz brothers, or that I had used the name Moody with them. The day had been so long and complicated that pieces of its events seemed to have happened to someone else, or if to me then weeks ago. I reassured Bella and kissed her and took the time to brush out her matted hair, to make up for my earlier terrible thought. But when I left her I was chilled with fear, and went straight to Bob with my apprehension.

"Those people called," I whispered. "The Sherowitzes. I used my own name. I'm worried about it. I gave them my address and telephone number, everything. And Herman. I told him too much. I told him all about Bella. And about my own plans. They can put everything together now. They can make all those connections."

Bob looked unhappy. He squeezed his lips together and

rubbed his eyes with one hand. "What did they want?" he said.

"I think they wanted to know why I hadn't come to work."

Bob said, "See, that's nothing. Please don't worry about anything. There's nothing to be concerned about. There's no reason to be." And again he began urging that damned capsule on me.

Matt got up and joined us in the corner of the room. "What about that weird call," he said. "I couldn't figure it at all. They kept asking for Miss Moody but it couldn't have been Bella they wanted. They called twice. What's that all about?"

"It's a private matter," I said to him coldly, but as I turned back to speak to Bob I caught Bob gesturing as if he would explain it all to Matt later. I screamed at Bob that if he broke security and dared to mention a word of what I had confidentially told him, I would throw him out. I heard myself screaming, ". . . if I have to get a cop to do it, you fucking son of a bitch," and couldn't believe it was my voice.

The room had become unnaturally stilled. My friends were frightened by me, but no more than I was of them. I had explosively penetrated to a core of betrayal and cowardice in each. I knew that they would strike no blows for me. I opened my mouth to tell them this plainly but instead I found myself yelling into Papa Shaeffer's open-mouthed consternation, "And I'm sick of you New York Jews. I've had enough of your cowardice, your false gentleness, your phony ideals. When all you really care about is security and money. You do, you do. All you're good for is money, anyway. Well, I don't need you. Stay away from me." There were clanging noises in my head and hideous billowing colors. Paula's Negro boy friend was smiling, and hitting his fist into the palm of his other hand. I clamped my hand over my mouth and shut my eyes tight.

I felt disconnected. When I opened my eyes I was on the couch. Everyone seemed to have left me and Matt, except Bob and Jean. At some point, I realized that Jean was clearing the supper debris from the living room and I helped her. In the kitchen I saw that she was running a laundry through the machine, and that she had prepared the formula. I kissed her and clung to her, but when I looked steadily into her charming eyes, she slid her gaze away. I thought she might be angry with me because I had walked away from my responsibilities, leaving them for her to pick up. I said, "Are you angry with me?"

She said, "Mary, baby, will you please go inside and lie down on the couch and stop having dumb ideas. You mustn't be so hard on yourself."

She was so natural and impatient with me that she made me feel like myself for a minute. In the living room, Matt and Bob were gloomy and ill at ease. I said, "Okay, let's get down to business and talk." But I was exhausted and asked if they minded my lying down on the couch while we talked. Matt tossed over a couple of pillows. "Put these under your head," he said. I knew from his tone that he was suppressing intense hostility, but the pillows had absorbed it from his touch and they flung themselves at me viciously. I dropped them to the floor. Jean entered as Bob began to speak. She sat on a stiff-backed chair, stroking her lovely crossed legs, and widening and narrowing her eyes as she listened. She does that when she's nervous or bored.

"I guess there are some very important matters between us which should be clarified," Bob said.

As soon as he said that, I got very upset and excited. This

wasn't going to be like one of those committee meetings where other people decided what happened to my life. "No," I said. "Let me speak first." I had no idea what I was going to say but I wanted to control the conversation.

I launched into a general discussion of marriage and of what it ought to be. Phrases and ideas leapt up, dressed in the same words I had used when I was working them out on paper. ". . . a free concourse of two equal people who choose each other freely to live with, to work with, to love, to build a new set of relationships founded on friendship as well as passion. This presupposes high ideals such as I had brought to our marriage. But Matt brought none of this. That's the crux of the trouble. But Matt can't help it." I got up and paced the room. "Everything is against him. His middle-class Jewish background is against him. Look at his mother and the rest of his family. No wonder he hates women. Look at his sisters. Look at his brothers. How soft and dependent they are, just exactly in the same way that you are, Matt. While you all act so big and domineering. The other side of the coin. Face it. It's true," I said, turning to Jean. "He wants to lean on me, to have me carry all the weight, and he wants to dominate me. Is that fair? He doesn't understand the meaning of equality and doesn't want to learn. He doesn't understand the difference between a woman like Bella and a woman like his mother. He doesn't see the difference between a woman like me and a woman like Gloria. Or that cream puff on the Coast that he can't keep his hands off. He tries to force me behind their silly masks. I'm me. Me. I can't bear any more of this ugliness. I can't bear any more of this degradation of my ideals. I can't bear any more disillusionment. Do you know why he married me? Because I was pregnant and he thought he had to. Brought up the way he was, what else could he feel?"

"No," Matt said. "That's why you married me. You asked me to marry you, remember?" There was a tight little smile on his lips. Fighting with Matt was always invigorating to me, even if it was painful, and now everything was heightened because there was an audience.

"I was too young," I said. "I didn't know what I was doing. I thought my life was over."

"Call that high ideals?" he said.

"Don't do that, Matt," Bob said to him.

"Oh, fuck all this shit," Matt said, and closed the door that led to the bedroom hallway. "Better not let Mark hear her ranting."

"There. There," I said dramatically. "There's his ugly essence. Let him be himself before you. Let him be his irrational self. Do you know that he stuck Mark with a big safety pin? That he lifted his arm like this . . ." — I showed them the strange, evil way that he had bent his elbow — ". . . and stuck it in as hard as he could. Like that." I showed them that too. "Matt needs help. Nobody knows that better than I do. He's sick. He's very disturbed. He can't help it and I don't blame him for any of these weaknesses. He's had to contend with too much. But the first thing we must discuss is for Matt to get help."

"Okay," Matt said. "Let's make that number one on the agenda." He groaned, and covered his face with his long, slender fingers. I wanted to capture them, cover them with kisses or bite the knuckles, and the oddity of my reaction at that moment stopped my speech.

"Look," Bob said, in the pause. "Maybe this is the moment

to make something clear. About me. Though you're probably all aware of it."

"No," I said. "I haven't finished. There's more. So that you'll understand. Do you know what his parents gave us for a wedding present? A gross of condoms. He must have told them about the pregnancy and the abortion after we got married. He must have. Why else would they have sent a gross of condoms? Hideous things. That's the kind of people he comes from. And he didn't even use them. He used silk, my slip, a handkerchief, his underwear, anything so that our flesh wouldn't touch. He never let our flesh touch. That's because he's a homosexual. These are the things he can't help and must get help to overcome. Hatred and weakness is consuming him. Do you know what he does? When I'm asleep? He makes a loud metallic noise to wake me. He whispers in my ear that I have cancer and that I'm dying. I can't put up with these things anymore."

Jean said, "We must stop this. Isn't there some way to stop this, Bob?"

Bob put out a hand to check my walking back and forth. His touch was cold and sweaty and I saw that his face was beaded with perspiration, though the room didn't seem too warm. He said, "Mary, sweetheart, this isn't getting us anywhere. Can't we try to discuss this constructively?"

Matt said in a dead, mocking voice, "You have something constructive in mind?"

Bob took one of those long, trembling breaths. "I just wanted to make this clear, though I guess you pretty well know it anyway. If Matt and Mary" — he directed his statement to Jean as if she were some kind of arbitrator — "if Matt and Mary are really through, if they've come to the end of their relationship and of its possibilities, I think that it's important for both of them to know, very openly, that is for me to state very openly how I feel." He sucked in his breath again. "I would like to marry Mary. And take care of her. Of course, that would include Bella and the children."

"Wow!" Matt said. "Big news. Big, big news. You forgot Shtrudel."

I screamed my humiliation at Bob. "Why are you making a fool of me and of yourself? 'That would include the children.' What do you think you're negotiating here? Marry Bella if you need a helpless creature to tend." I guess I meant to hit him but Matt placed himself between us. He held me and said, "Mary, don't," with a gentle, firm urgency that stopped me. I don't know which one of us was trembling more. He asked Jean and Bob to please go, said everybody was overtired and that we could talk about all this another time, there was only danger in continuing.

Jean said, "Are you sure you can manage?"

"Manage what?" I asked, and Matt waved her away.

They left quickly. Matt held me in his arms on the couch and wouldn't even let them kiss me good night.

Bob gave Matt a capsule for me before he left. "Try to get her to take this," he said.

"He's obsessed with those capsules," I said to Matt, and he laughed.

Matt sheltered me on the couch, but whatever warmth and moisture had spilled over from his initial intent, gradually dried and turned cold. Nothing blossomed. I began to cry. He suffered my crying on his chest for as long as he could bear it. Then he said, "Let me help you to bed." I expected him to come to bed with me but he didn't. He placed the capsule and a glass of water nearby. "Take it, if you want to. It will help you sleep."

"It's you I want, not that fucking capsule," I said. But he walked out, murmuring something about finishing some work.

After a while I got up and found him standing at his drawing board in his little study. Was he as beautiful as I saw him, his back, slightly bent, held in a perfect tension of relaxed grace and concentrated control, his dark forearms resting on the upslanting board, strong against the romantic folds of his rolled-back white shirt sleeves? Or did I glamorize Matt to tinsel up my own life? See the handsome man I have caught. See how successful I have been.

But that wasn't the way it had been. We had been in the same Shakespeare class, talked a bit, and one soft spring day met accidentally on campus. I noticed how his eyes changed when he saw me. Just before we parted for separate classes, he said, "Let's do something together this afternoon." "What?" I said. "Anything," he said. "I don't care." He had a cruddy room in an apartment he shared with a couple of other fellows because his family lived out on the Island. We made love any time we could. I remembered us parting at a subway station after an afternoon in his room. We were going off in different directions for some reason, but he waited until my train pulled away, looking at me seriously through the glass, until we started to move, when he placed his palm over the window — a caress for me to carry away with me. I didn't care, I even liked it, that he wasn't interested in politics; I was in a state of revulsion against activism then.

I said, "Aren't you coming to bed?"

He said, "I'm sorry, honey, I really must finish this. I haven't had a chance to work on it all day." He lit a cigarette, sucking and exhaling smoke in the handsome, masculine manner glorified by the TV ads. Marlboro Country. He was submerged in a self-concern that men arrogate for their work, ig-

noring me, my rage and my grief as if they and I belonged to
an understrata of life that confused and disgusted him. "Kick
that garbage in the sewer. Clear the decks for important stuff
like my work," was what his back was saying to me.

I said, "You don't love me, Matt."

He didn't raise his head or look at me. His face tightened
into a grimace. "Listen," he said. "I'm not going to have one
of those conversations now. I have to finish this."

I said, "I'm not putting up with you anymore. You'd better
put your work aside. We have important things to discuss.
I'm leaving you. I have a job. It's all set."

"Whatever makes you happy," he said.

"Makes you happy, you mean," I said, like a child.

I returned to our bedroom in a fit of anger so intense I
couldn't contain it. I slammed things around and moved the
chest in front of the door to keep Matt out. The senselessness
of what I was doing struck me. He didn't want to come in. I
moved the furniture back. I would change the lock on the
door tomorrow and keep him out entirely. I was unable to rest
in bed. I got up again and worked at my notes on marriage, on
the communities and how they would function, and I started
some new notes on how to cure cancer by a diet of clams and
white wine.

6 ———

Bob called me at my office early the next morning. We had hardly spoken to each other when we left Matt and Mary the night before, quitting their place as if we were fleeing a burning building. He had offered me a lift home, but I begged off, taking as my excuse the fact that his car was parked way over near the Harlem River. I caught a Broadway bus, glad to get away from him and any discussion of the harrowing evening we had just spent. His call was to ask me to attend a Committee meeting at Paula's house the following night.

I said, "Why? My presence isn't worth the space I use up at a meeting."

He said that he'd like to explain first why he wanted me there — and Matt too — and that he had already arranged with Matt to meet for a drink after work, and that he hoped I would be able to make it too. Bob sounded dispirited and tired. I agreed and jotted down the name and location of the bar. The kids were having supper with Harry anyway and Matt and I had been planning to spend the evening together.

The call so unnerved me that I asked my boss if I could take a break. He said, "Suddenly, you ask?" The coffee shop in the building was still crowded with breakfast people, so I took a container of coffee back upstairs to a little office supply room and locked the door from the inside and sipped and brooded, perched up on a high stool. The only thing I could figure was that someone had found out about me and Matt and had taken the information to the Committee for action. What action seemed inconceivable to me, but in a minute I had dreamed up a criticism/self-criticism session with me and Matt as the stars. I could just see me denouncing myself as a bourgeois, decadent slob and then summing up in tearful gratitude for having been straightened out. The prospect of how Matt might react to such a scene was both frightening and amusing. From there, I slipped into a delicious daydream about Matt. I could feel a foolish smile clinging to my mouth and before I left the little sanctuary, I blotted my lips against each other to wipe it off, but the pressure of my lips against each other brought with it the pressure of Matt on my skin, like a wave of heat. How difficult to explain to others what had come to shimmering life between us — or to protect it from them — especially from those concerned with Mary. Those concerned with Mary. As if we were not.

Bob was into the conversation before our drinks reached the table. It wasn't anything to do with me and Matt. It was about Mary heading into what he was calling "a schizophrenic episode." Both words frightened me.

I said, "Can you become schizophrenic overnight, for God's sake? Mary's always been remarkably sane. Saner than anybody. Wiser. She's upset. With what's happened to her, she's got to be upset. That isn't crazy."

"Where were you last night? Weren't you listening?" Bob looked more harassed than the night before — even ill. His skin was gray and his eyes were bloodshot and watering. "I'm talking about delusions, visions, paranoia. Of course there's cause. That's why I think it may be an incident which will flare and dwindle, if we handle it properly."

Matt said, "She is crazy. I know she's crazy. But I keep right on reacting to her as if she were normal."

Our drinks came. Bob was having only ginger ale because he said his stomach was upset. His hand shook as he raised his glass. We were in a very crowded midtown bar; the city roared outside, background to an almost deafening inside din.

I hardly heard Bob say, "I can't let her spend her last days in torment."

But I heard Matt clearly enough. "Are we going back to the idiocy of last night?"

Bob said, "I don't know what last night meant to you. Do you want Mary to die in an institution?"

"I don't want her to die at all," Matt said. "If you fucking geniuses hadn't made so many mistakes, we wouldn't be sitting here having this unbelievable discussion. About Mary. What's the purpose of still another discussion? If it's more of that number you were doing last night, I don't want to hear it. It's between you and Mary."

Bob said, "What an arrogant bastard you are. You need to grow up a little."

I was afraid that Matt was going to hit him, and I said quickly, "What did you want with me, Bob?" and asked Matt for another drink, to keep him busy.

What Bob wanted with me was so startling that I missed some of the details, though I got the general plan. He was suggesting that I quit my job and be paid by the Committee for keeping an eye on Mary and taking care of her. Nothing menial. Mostly to be with her, on call, in constant touch with Bob and a psychiatrist, if we could get her to one. I was to be there whenever Matt wasn't. Then Bob outlined a complicated plot for luring her into the hospital for the remainder of the cobalt treatments.

"But if it's all no use?" I said. "Isn't it just a cruelty? It bothers her so much."

"It would be criminal not to try everything," Bob said. "We don't know why remissions occur. And they do all the time. Even if that doesn't happen, maybe her life can be extended. She's precious. Every day she spends on earth is one more better day for the world." He spoke defensively, as if we were going to deny his statement and that he hated us for that. "Okay," he said, "we made mistakes, all of us. Not telling her the truth may have been the biggest mistake of all. Anyway that's what the psychiatrists think now. They think the downward spiral may be stopped if she's told the truth now."

"She wouldn't believe it if she didn't want to," Matt said. "She's too smart for that." He threw a mutilated matchbook into the ashtray. "Are you suggesting that I tell her? Because I can't. I'm not telling her the truth."

Bob didn't look at him. "You'd be the last person I'd ask to do that," he said.

"Me?" I said, afraid.

Bob looked impatient. "No. That's the whole point about the hospital. So that she can be told in a controlled situation. By a psychiatrist. And then go on with the treatments under the same sort of control. What I would say to Mary is that we need to have some more tests. But there won't really be any tests. Then a professional can manage the business of telling her what she has and what it requires in the way of treatment and suggest that she can stay on for them. Maybe the whole destructive process can be stopped."

"Is that true?" Matt said. "Is that really possible?"

Bob said, "It's always possible. That's why we have to try."

"I don't really understand what you want me to do," I said.

"She needs to be watched all the time now," Bob said.

"Are you going to put her in a psychiatric hospital?" I said. "I don't want to help you do that."

Bob said, "That's exactly what I'm trying to avoid. The best thing would be a private room in the pavilion. The psychiatrist could visit her in her room. I have a very good man in mind. Sensible and sensitive. She could be taken down for the daily cobalt treatment and brought back to her room. Flowers. Visitors. A view of the river. As pleasant an environment as we can manage and still control it. You could be a great help, especially the preliminary work. She's very fond of you and she respects you for some reason."

"That's going to be expensive," Matt said.

"Let me worry about the money," Bob said. "There's still plenty of Committee money left."

"What about Bella?" Matt said.

"What about her?"

"That situation is out of hand. Are you making plans for a home or something? Things are bad enough right now, but if Mary goes back into the hospital, who's going to deal with Bella's problems?"

"You can't wait, can you?" Bob said.

"It's easy enough for you," Matt said. "You're not living with it."

Bob turned to me as if he were crossing Matt off his list. "Will you think about it, Jean, about taking on this assignment, if I can get the Committee to agree? I'm going to put in for two hundred dollars a week for you. And expenses —

because you're going to have to be available around the clock and you'll need extra help at home. Do you have a car?"

I said, "No."

"But you drive?"

"Sure."

"Are you going to do it?" Matt said. Strangely, I read his expression as eager that I should.

I said to Bob, "How soon must I let you know?"

"Tomorrow," he said. "As early in the day as possible. So that I can present it to the Committee in the evening. Because she should be watched every minute now."

"Why?" I said.

"Because she's a danger to herself and to the children. Even to Bella."

"Never," Matt said. "You don't understand Mary. She'd never kill herself or the children or her mother." He rubbed his eye hard and laughed. "It's me she'll kill."

Bob said, "You're incredible."

"But Mary doesn't want any part of Committee money," I said. "Isn't that right?"

"Yes," Bob said. "But she won't know." He got up to go, and picked up the bill.

"I'll take care of the check," Matt said.

"No," Bob said. "I invited you." He offered me a lift uptown, but I told him that I was meeting a friend nearby. His eyes flicked over to Matt. "You, Matt?"

Matt was a bad liar. He fumbled his cigarette and, looking for it in the folds of his jacket, said, "Thanks, but I'm heading back to the office. I have some work to finish."

"Is Mary alone then?" Bob said.

"Some friends are dropping by, and I should be home by nine or nine-thirty."

I said, "All we seem to be doing is getting in deeper with more elaborate lies. Like how am I going to explain being free to spend all my time with her? She'll think that awfully queer."

"It can all be worked out," Bob said. "We'll talk about it again, once we've agreed in principle. After we've cleared the money end with the Committee." But he looked exhausted and hopeless.

Matt repeated, "Agreed in principle. Here comes another fuck-up."

I said, "It bothers me, Bob. Getting into somebody else's life so deeply. It's hers. It belongs to her."

"She has a right to kill herself or her children?" Bob said. He was standing in the aisle, struggling into his topcoat, jostled by waiters and the thickening cocktail hour crowd.

I said, "God, I don't know."

Bob said, "Well, I do. You lean back on that high-minded philosophic guff, but what it comes down to is sitting around on your ass and letting things go to hell."

"You think I don't want to help?"

"That's right," he said.

"That's not so," I said. "I just don't want to meddle and do harm."

"We're talking about Mary," Bob said. "She's in danger. Maybe we can help save her life. At the least, maybe we can insure her dying with dignity." He stopped struggling with his coat and threw it over his arm.

"Who knows what that is?" I said. "Maybe all we should do for her is to show our real feelings. Put down our heads and weep. And stop thrashing around doing things."

Matt put his head in his hands. "I have a terrible pain in my eye," he said.

"Take some aspirin," Bob said.

I fished around in my bag and found a little pillbox of Bufferin and offered it to Matt. "No," he said. "It's going away."

"You talk as if it were possible to live without responsibility for each other," Bob said. "If your philosophy prevailed, the world would come to a dead stop."

"Maybe it should," I said.

"Bring your own world to an end," Bob said. "I'm old-fashioned enough to still have hope for mine." He put a tip on the table. "Let me know what you decide," he said, and walked down the crowded, narrow path between the tables. His jacket had wrinkled up, exposing his broad, tired, middle-aged backside, cringing in the wide seat of his trousers.

We left right after he did. We were lucky to find an empty taxi directly outside the bar, and crawled crosstown and uptown in nauseating jerks of speed and smelly halts. It had begun to rain and all the undulating neon was multipled in the sheen of the wet streets. I had a blinding headache. Matt was busy inside himself, staring away from me out his window, smoking a cigarette whose smell was killing me. I put my head back on the car seat and covered my face with my arm. My coat smelled better than anything else around. The cabby asked if it was okay to go through the park and Matt said, "Yes, fine." I took my arm away from my face and found him looking at me.

"What's the matter?" he said.

"I have a bad headache," I said.

"Would you rather I didn't come home with you?" he said.

"God, no," I said. "That would give me the biggest headache of all."

He smiled and put his cigarette out the window on my side

and stayed leaning over me, looking into my eyes, and slowly bringing his mouth to mine as we entered the park. For a second it was sickeningly unpleasant, the smell of the liquor and the sour taste of his tobacco breath almost gagged me, but his tongue made it all sweet at once. We savored each other, tongue, teeth, lips, breath and spit. At the apartment, we went straight to my bed.

What is it — about explaining love? Why is it so impossible to grab logically, even for oneself, if not for others? Among the studies, articles, papers, dissertations (I hardly knew what to make of them) that Mary had begun to mail to me almost every day now, was one which tried to cut away the garbagy sentimental stuff surrounding love and discover, if it existed, a core of emotional truth or need, or appetite, even. She went all around the subject of what she called "monogamous romantic love." Her paper more or less concluded that love was a fraud, a necessary glue to stick the nuclear family together, developed along with the economic and social organization of bourgeois society. Love for an individual was no more related to true consciousness than was love of country; both were superstructures, decorative embellishments to the ugly base of nationalism and free enterprise and the loss of earlier forms of social organization. If society were set up so that all individuals — men, women, children — had equal importance, love as we pretend to know and honor it would cease to exist. Joinings would be fluid, natural and guiltless, and there would be as little emotional value attached to sexuality in any form as to hunger or thirst.

It wasn't a mad paper or even a very original one, given the concepts flying around these days. In fact, it was studded with quotations — from Engels to Bettelheim. I studied it more carefully than the others arriving in my mailbox daily because

I was trying to understand myself and my feeling for Matt. But however interesting the ideas and arguments, her paper didn't touch the spot I was trying to understand. It just didn't seem to have anything to do with it.

That was later anyway. What was happening at the moment was that I was being fueled and floated away on a substance — love? — that I had never experienced before. A lot of it seemed to have to do with Matt's beautiful, smooth penis. (I couldn't figure the impotence bit; there wasn't a sign of it.) But other males I had known had smooth penises, that functioned just as pleasingly as his did. It didn't seem to have much to do with knowing about techniques, or getting over hang-ups, or putting your tongue anywhere or hanging from the rafters or any of that stuff. And we had so many different kinds of times in bed, so many different kinds of joy and joinings, that it was foolish to talk about big, special orgasms as if that was all it was about. It was more like some new extraordinary invention was being made between us, growing in that tiny space which persists even through the fierce, final union. I. Me. You. You. In all the tiny spaces between, between our casual touching and our casual conversation, along the indifferent telephone wires that carried our silliest talks. It lived so palpably that I felt it would take only the proper instrument to see it, touch it. It existed even when we were apart. I had no word for it but love, and in some ways it resembled what I felt for my boys and for Mary (I recognize that I run the risk of being misunderstood, bringing her in at this moment), but with them, my love, or whatever it was, ran up toward them, and sometimes something ran down toward me from them, while with Matt *I* and *You* ran together and toward each other in lovely minglings and explosions so that when *I* and *You* separated, we were different and the sparks had created this other distinct thing, this new invention I've been talking about.

That's the way it was with us, that's the way it became between us after that disappointing but oddly pleasurable first lay, when Matt began to come to my bed regularly. Even the day before had been beautiful. He had called me to come up to help him with the children during the time when nobody knew where Mary was. I quit the office without asking, while my boss was at a meeting, and left a note on his desk saying that I was feeling ill and had gone to the doctor and home. I figured that if I was fired I could always get another stupid job. Until Bob called and told us that Mary had telephoned him from a luncheonette in the Bronx and that he was going up to get her, we were sick with worry, but even during that time it was beautiful between us. And later, when we knew that she was tended, if not entirely safe, sharing the relief became itself another way of making love. In the afternoon, after everything was tidied and Bella was resting in her bed, the baby asleep in her crib, and there were still fifty minutes before it was time to pick Mark up at nursery school, I suggested to Matt that he lie down on the living room couch and rest. He asked me to come sit near him and I did and stroked his temples and forehead. He took my hands after a few minutes and kissed them on each nail and in every joint and circled the wrists and we began to kiss each other on the eyes and hair and ear lobes and then with our mouths fully until it became unbearable. We went into his tiny workroom, which had an inside latch on the door, and there on the floor, pinned between the cabinets and bookcases, loved each other.

In the evening, Joanna and the others came and Joanna and Matt went out to get the delicatessen supper while I read to Mark and bathed Katy and stuffed cereal into her mouth, which she dribbled right out. Stella Shaeffer took care of Bella. Matt came into the kitchen and stood watching while Mark babbled away at me and I handled the baby.

"How natural you are with them," he said.

"Who do you think raised my three kids?" I said, surprised.

"That wouldn't keep you from being icky with them," he said, and that was the first time that it came into my head to hope that he would stay with me afterward. Perhaps I wasn't just a device to help him get through this bad time. Perhaps he hadn't chosen me for bad reasons only, because I loved Mary and because I was ten years older than he and he could use me without suffering too heavily from a bad conscience.

Our meetings were usually harder for him than for me to arrange, because by one of those strokes of good luck that don't often come my way Harry had met a girl he was crazy about and she had moved in with him. He had the kids visiting with them almost every weekend and I had Friday evening, all day Saturday and part of Sunday to be free for Matt. Lately, Harry and his girl also stayed in the city Tuesday nights and took the boys out to a Chinese restaurant or a delicatessen. Matt and I had until eight-thirty before they would be returning. Though we were hungry afterward, Matt didn't want to waste time eating anything elaborate, so I fixed some sandwiches and we ate them in bed, talking nonsense. He got up then and dressed and said he needed to work at that job he hadn't finished at the office.

"I planned it," he said. "It's something I want to do. Work in the same room, while you sleep."

"I'm not sleepy," I said. "And there's no surface for you to work on."

"Look, baby," he said, "you solve your problem, I'll solve mine."

I snuggled into the covers, turned toward him and watched him take out of his case a sketch pad, a pen, a handsome brass-trimmed ruler and some loose sheets of graph paper. He settled them on his knee and looked at them intently. From time to time, he added a line or did something else. Sometimes he just stared outward, his eyes full of calculation and activity, looking in my direction, but not seeing me. Once he did see me, and smiled, full of deeply pleased content, and went back to his work. I fell asleep and awoke to him kissing me by rubbing his lips against mine in a soft sensuous gesture which opened me to him utterly.

"Now you're my true woman," he said. "By the ancient laws of the Hebrew fathers."

"You're kidding," I said.

"He who works in the presence of his sleeping woman works well. According to the laws of Moses, Isaac and the State of New York," he said.

"You know that I'm a daughter of Israel," I said.

He looked startled. "You mean you're not a Pennsylvania Polack?"

"In my heart, yes," I said. "But I converted when I married Harry."

"Are you making this up as you go along?"

"No. I really am. I really did. It was the price I had to pay to marry into a good Jewish family. I liked doing it. It was fun. I like seders, Chanukah, bar mitzvahs. That's good stuff. My mother was very pleased that I had latched on to a religion, any old religion. I hadn't been a very good Catholic."

"What does she think now?"

"Nothing. She's dead."

"You really did? Instruction from a rabbi and mikveh and all?"

"I really did."

He seemed marvelously delighted. "You're going to have to tell me all about that when we have time. I like that you did that. Mary wouldn't have done that for me."

"Of course not," I said. "And she's right. She thinks principles mean something."

"That's funny," he said. "That means that your kids are Jewish and mine aren't. The mother is the determining factor."

"Think of that!" I said. And then, I asked him what he thought I should do. "Shall I do what Bob asked? Will it bother you? Will it make you uncomfortable?"

"You mean because of us?"

I nodded.

He said, "Does it make you uncomfortable?"

I said, "No. I can't explain it. I love her. And I love you. I don't connect the two things. Is that crazy?"

But of course I did connect the two things — in a secret place hidden from concerns with having an affair with my best friend's husband, while she was fatally ill, in a well so deep that all of it flowed together into a different, other source.

"You never said that before," he said.

"What?"

"Do you really love me?"

I laughed. "You're an absolute egomaniac. All subjects return to you. Come on, tell me what to do."

"I guess I'd like you to do it," he said. "I'd feel better if I knew you were in charge."

"I don't know about that 'in charge' bit. I'm probably going to be a dupe of the Committee."

"My beautiful, beautiful dupe," he said.

He was playing with me, entwining his arms in mine and

interlacing the fingers of our hands, when a big open diaper pin fell out of his jacket pocket on my bare breast.

"Stabbed!" I laughed. "The diaper pin killer strikes again."

He wasn't laughing. He had picked it off my breast gingerly. It was one of those big-headed pink plastic safety pins made specially for newborns. He searched the pocket from which it had fallen and brought out a small white note, neatly folded. His face changed as he read it. He passed it to me. It was a single line of type:

TO REMIND YOU OF YOUR CAPABILITIES

"What's that?"

"Mary," he said. "I stab babies. Remember?"

I couldn't make any sense of it, and before I had really considered my words I found myself saying, "Matt, please don't blame yourself. People do crazy things when they're angry."

He looked at me searchingly, and then spoke with difficulty, as if he were forcing his speech. "Are you talking about me or about Mary doing crazy things?"

I said, "I just meant, you know, about sticking Mark with the pin when you and Mary were quarreling."

His black eyes hardened and shifted so that the whites showed under the pupils. "You believed that," he said in that strained speech. "You believe that version."

I wanted to take back the whole conversation, but I nodded, because I did believe it.

He said, "What else do you buy of that stuff she talks?"

I said, "I don't care about it, Matt. I love you. I don't care what you say or do with Mary."

I had sat up and was trying to embrace him, but he pushed me away violently with the flat of one hand and the rough woolen sleeve of his arm. It felt like a very harsh gesture against my bare skin.

"That's disgusting," he said.

"What?" I said.

"What you just said."

We stared at each other with suddenly no place to meet.

He said, "I want to know. What else do you believe of those things she was saying last night?"

I said, "Matt, don't. You have to go so soon. Please let's not talk about it anymore. Let's leave it for another time."

"No," he said. "You think my family sent us a gross of condoms for a wedding present? That I wake her in the middle of the night whispering in her ear that she's dying of cancer? That I have never let our skins touch? Or that shitty, sick innuendo about my kid sister?"

"You're not responsible for your whole family," I said, like an idiot.

The downstairs bell rang. He started to pack the papers he had been working on. I scrambled around, putting on a body stocking, some pants and a top. Matt had his coat on and was almost at the door when I caught up with him, running in my bare feet.

"I'll believe anything you tell me to, Matt. If you tell me those things aren't so, don't you know I'll believe you?"

He said, "I'm not telling you a thing. Figure it out for yourself. Why don't you check it all out with Mary?"

"But I don't care about it," I yelled. "I care about you and me."

"I don't know which one of you is worse," he said. "Supermoral and amoral. And between the two of you, total annihilation."

I said, "What are you talking about?" but he just went out the door.

I heard voices down the hall greeting Matt. Harry and his girl had brought the boys upstairs, a cordiality I could have well done without. Leaving the front door open for them, I ran to the bathroom and turned the lock.

My ridiculous face looked merely flushed and prettier. I tied my hair back with trembling hands, then held them against the cool washbasin edge to steady them. For all its airiness, I guess I had been counting on our precious invention to be indestructible. But it wasn't, obviously.

7

PAULA WHITE lived in one of the great old apartment houses in the eighties. The lobby, painted gilt, blue and white in a 1930s movie version of a Renaissance palace had dirtied to city-soot brown, gray and yellow. There were baroque angels hanging on the wall of the elevator landing which opened directly into her penthouse apartment, and a delicate, slender, untortured Christ carved in wood — Spanish perhaps, or Portuguese — and a poster of Ché, not the much produced romantic one in which his eyes, saddened and tired, look off into an uncertain future, but one I had never seen, with a fat cigar in his mouth and lively, roguish eyes sliding off to the side. The Oriental rugs started in the hallway and continued thickly through the apartment. The door was open. The living room was already crowded. There seemed to be about fifty people, many more than I had been prepared to see there. I hung my coat in a huge walk-in closet decorated with oversized posters of Cardinal Spellman and Mick Jagger, facing each other in amusing juxtaposition. Or seriously co-existing? Paula's cleverest effects were often accidental. She had a flair for turning her ignorance and the bits and pieces of chic information she had picked up from her truly brilliant husband into startling witticisms. But Paula would have drawn followers no matter how she was. That she was clever and attractive was an added fillip. All the White family money had ended in her hands when her husband died. It was she who now administered the foundation he had set up to finance left scholarship projects, or new groups, or publications, or anything that seemed worth pushing along. Leonard White died soon after I met them, but I had seen enough to feel he wasn't the kind of mind fools could suck up to. Paula was something else. She seemed so obviously manipulable, that she drew a swarm of operators. Whether they got what they wanted was another matter.

The meeting hadn't begun. Everybody was standing around in clumps, drinking and talking. The largest group was gathered about Matt. I hadn't expected him to be there and certainly not ebulliently ruling a roost. He had put on his party voice, ringing with life.

"Why not get the City Center Ballet to lead all antifare-rise demonstrations? They leap over the turnstiles and the rest of us follow. That will carry the middle classes. The working class will carry itself."

An elegantly dressed, very tiny, middle-aged man said, "You're joking, Matt. But we can't joke about it. It would be a tragedy for workers and the regular subway user in the city. Another subway fare rise is unthinkable." He used a tiny hand to stroke his thick, curly sideburns. His close-fitting jacket was a rich, deep purple velvet.

"Like the last one," Matt said. "I give us two more unthinkable events to come to pass in the city and we're dead."

"And they will. They will," Paula said. She was in crocheted white pants and a top down to the floor, with long slits up the sides, the whole lacy confection in constant floating movement around her. She kissed me with silvery lips; her hair and face were done in a deathlike black and white mask.

Matt saw me and nodded. I read his greeting as coldness and anger. It stabbed me and I turned away to find Mary to give her the copies of the paper I had managed to Xerox. She was at the opposite end of the living room, standing next to an incredible Biedermeier grand piano on which a life-sized papier-mâché sculpture of a woman lolled. Mary looked serene and simple in a black skirt and sweater, but when she turned her eyes on me, they were suffused with hysterical excitement. She didn't kiss me. I started to explain that her report was so long that I hadn't been able to run off more than the two copies, but she took the papers from me as if she didn't know what I was talking about, almost as if she didn't know who I was, and dropped them on top of a bunch of other material on the piano. I had gone to considerable trouble to make those copies of her twenty-one-page report, and I was annoyed that they ended up doing nothing all evening but sitting on the piano. She had called me at seven in the morning, just before my alram rang, to ask me if I could make the copies, and I had even gone to her house to pick up the original. It was bad getting to work from her house, local all the way, and jammed with little Puerto Rican clothing workers jabbering away without a pause in shrill Spanish, unable to reach the straps and falling all over each other and everybody else at every jerk of the train. But too sweet to get mad at.

With all that I managed to read Mary's outline on my way downtown. It was a fascinating account of a plan to set up Communist communities now in the United States. This was one of the documents later used to prove her insane, but if Mary's plan was insane, what about moon landings? Or Cortez in Mexico? Or heart transplants? I don't mean by that that I thought Mary's plan workable. Not that I'm anyone to judge. After all, television works by some mechanism which will never be clear to me, doesn't it? If it comes to that, there isn't much about the real, big world that does appear to me to be reasonably workable. Compared with current inept organizations of society that go right on functioning as if they were workable, Mary's vision was a model of order and humanitarian efficiency. What was mad was to imagine that it would be allowed to happen.

She read her paper to the gathering after Bob's general political introduction, which was the regulation boring anti-imperialist line without a single original twist of phrase. He hadn't greeted me, but he had called me earlier to warn me that something had gone wrong and that the meeting wouldn't be just Isabelle Vance Moody Committee people.

"I don't know what the hell it's going to be," he said. "Mary's been on the phone all day asking people to attend, even people she was in the hospital with."

"I thought Mary wouldn't be there, or even know about it."

"Somebody screwed it up. Paula, I think. She was under the impression that Mary knew. Even Bella wanted to come. Mary thinks it's a meeting to get her communes going."

"Is there any point in my going?" I had already told him I would take on the assignment if the Committee said yes.

"We'll get together somehow, just the few of us who should, and settle the question concerning you. If I knew what to expect I'd be more explicit, but I haven't any idea where this thing has taken off to."

I went for that, and to deliver Mary's copies. But she was using another copy to read from. As soon as she began, the kind of listening changed. I was watching Matt and he looked astounded. He hadn't had any foretaste of her report, apparently, and he was following her intently, with a warring mix of responses clearly showing on his face — admiration, skepticism, intellectual interest, pride and yes, love. He took a little pad from his jacket pocket and jotted down notes while she read.

She had already gone through the material which called for abandoning current modes of struggle and turning the combined energy of all dissenting groups toward pulling out of this society and forming the new one now in the heart of the mother country, and she was in the thick of particulars of her scheme — how much money would need to be raised, possible sites, industries to be established, etc. — when the first interruption occurred.

A heavy-set woman rose, muttering unintelligibly, and made preparations to leave in a noisy confusion. She rearranged some packages in a Lord & Taylor shopping bag, and after some trouble locating her clothing in the big closet, she put on her boots, fur coat, fur hat and long deep-green Mexican wool scarf and blundered about looking for the entrance to the elevator. I had no idea who she was. Bob was gesturing to me, and I interpreted that as a request from him to help her, so I got up and led her out to the elevator foyer.

She said, "Thank you, darling. I'm sorry to be a trouble."

I said, "Not at all. I'm sorry you have to leave."

"To tell you the truth," she whispered, "I don't know what I'm doing here altogether. My friend Sadie mentioned to me that she got a call from a wonderful young friend of hers that money was needed for a worthy cause. Sadie knows her friend Runya. I'm always ready with whatever I can afford to give for a worthy cause. She suggested that I come because she couldn't. She can hardly walk, my poor friend. But to tell you the truth, I can't understand a word that very intelligent young lady is saying, not so much the words, but what they all add up to, so I may as well leave. I'm glad you got up though because it gives me the opportunity to make a contribution, however small. So here," she said, thrusting a ten-dollar bill in my hand. "I hope it will be a little help. I like to do my part."

I didn't know what to do about that, and tried to get her to take it back, but all that brought on was a cry of "Don't worry about a receipt. I never worry about receipts," as the elevator door closed on her. I stuck the bill in my suit jacket pocket and went back to my seat.

She was a charming little old lady, with clever, slanting Lenin eyes. She must have had some other reason for leaving; she didn't look stupid. I would have liked to learn all about her. That had been happening to me lately — wanting to know everything about strangers, at once. Instead of the meeting, what would have really pleased me would have been for everyone to tell his story, all around the room, one by one, like a Russian novel. The girl sitting next to Matt — how would her life come out, if she began, "I was born in 19——— in the town of_____"?

One of a group of young black men and women, sitting apart in a bay of the room formed by three handsome full-length windows, stood up and requested the floor. The woman's commotion had hardly affected Mary's reading — only a slight push for more clarity and volume in her voice and one commanding sweep of the gathering with her enormous eyes to demand — and get — silence. But when the young black rose, she lowered the paper to the piano and fully turned her face to him in a formal, courteous manner. Her eyes were lowered in a self-humbling, serious, agreeable expression which somehow looked honest on her. He was saying that as spokesman for his brothers and sisters, he was making the announcement that they were leaving in a body because what they certainly didn't need was to stay there to be told what to do by whites.

"No personal offense to you," he added with a princely bow of his head at Mary.

Mary nodded continuously throughout the short statement, interjecting, "I understand," in the pauses, and she maintained a respectful silence as they filed out. Others copied Mary and tried to fix the same sort of face on the blacks' retreating, marvelously costumed backs. But the attempt mostly looked ludicrously phony.

Mary returned to her paper and read on for a bit, but another young black rose. "First," he said, gathering us together with an expressive, holding gesture of his hand, "first, I mean to explain why I am interrupting you again, Sister Mary Moody Schwartz." Impossible to mimic his accent, especially the way he lifted the words "Sister Mary Moody" and then both dropped and raised his voice on the last one-syllable name "Schwartz" to render it helplessly derided and contemptible. I glanced at Matt. If he was uncomfortable it could have been because of his situation, sunk in the center of an oversized down couch, his long legs trapped sideways by a coffee table whose glass top protected a gouache drawing of Paula White's head. Paula herself was seated at Matt's left, and on his right was a girl in a severe military-style mauve leather suit (the skirt ended at the torso where soft suede boots began). Her face was made up in a pale shade of green with a lot of creamy white around the eyes. The Shaeffers were squeezed in next to her, sitting primly at the edge of the

couch, their snowy white heads and bright pink faces looking comically alike, sweetly and gravely turned toward the
speaker.

"I cannot allow you to continue, Sister Mary," the young
black said, "without making it very plain . . ."

An older black man cut in. He had the kind of deep bass
that vibrated in the chair I was sitting on. "I can't allow *you*
to continue, friend," he said. "The discussion will take place
later."

There were yells of "Let him speak," and "No discussion
now," and a tall blond young man stood up and rattled off
something I couldn't hear against the general din. Bob was
trying to establish some order, but Mary took things in hand
herself and insisted that the young black be allowed to finish.

"I want to make it very plain," he began again. He was
angry and it had the effect of slowing down his speech and
making him repeat himself. "Very plain that because we are
staying, because some of us have elected to stay, it does not
signify what you may think — you know what I mean. It does
not signify *any* endorsement of *what* you are saying. And it
does *not* signify any repudiation of our brothers and sisters
who elected to leave. I don't speak here *just* for myself. I
speak for *myself*, I'm telling you, but . . . I also speak for
those black brothers and sisters still present here in this re-
gard."

"Don't speak for me, brother. I'd appreciate it." It was the
older man again.

Around the younger man were three beautiful black girls
and a boy who looked no more than fifteen. It was then I
realized that the speaker was Paula's latest boy friend and that
I had met him at Matt and Mary's the other evening.

"Now, you listen," he said. "We here have the highest re-
gard for Sister Mary personally and that is the *major* — the
primary — I would say the *only* reason that we are staying.
But —" He paused for solemn emphasis, and someone
yelled, "Cut the discussion. The discussion is later."

"But," he repeated, "we want it made very plain to this as-
sembled gathering that we fully endorse and wholeheartedly
concur in the action our brothers and sisters chose in walking
out and . . ." He paused again, very meaningfully. All was
quiet. "I mean we want it plainly understood that in fact
symbolically speaking, those of us who are staying also walked
out — fully partaking of their action to the degree that we
could and yet remain here."

"Now . . ." He held another significant pause, raising a
commanding hand warningly to stop Mary, who was nodding
and saying, "I understand." He had a round face with very
large melting black eyes made cunning by being almost lidless,
and a voice capable of such infinite varieties of tone and nu-
ance that it gave to everything he said an impressive and startling cast. "I want to add only one small addition. We reserve the right to speak later, you know what I mean, we are
declaring our right to speak later on the very important matters, the many, many very important points being raised here
tonight by Sister Mary, including the interesting fact that she
has not yet made one reference to blacks in her entire paper.
We will speak after us sisters and brothers have conferred between us because we do not speak" — he shook his bushy
head in very solemn assurance — "you know what I mean, we
do not speak as individuals here, that is something we *never*
do, but when we speak out we are speaking out as the repre-
sentatives of our people and that's the way we're going to

speak tonight when we speak." He sat down to long-lasting applause from his group and uncertain, scattered applause from the rest of the room.

Mary started to read again, but stopped after a little bit. Hesitantly, in a manner unlike her usual persuasive self, she said, "Perhaps I should take a moment to explain that if this outline of a plan for new societies in the heart of the mother country seems to slight the question of our time, that is racism, racist savagery, that's because I'm just taking it for granted that you understand the outline presupposes a common understanding and acceptance of the primacy of the question. That's what it's all about. About people." She kept slipping into jargon. "The plan is projected for all but without presuming to be a blueprint for any section of the people. In calling this meeting, I . . ." She paused, lost herself, hurried on over another interruption of "What about pot? What about drugs?"

"This is just a preliminary discussion of the plan. We don't constitute any kind of organization ourselves, we're not looking to co-opt any other organization or groups of activists. The plan should be looked upon as a tentative program for unified and positive action, as a possible way out of our desperate present impasse."

"Who the fuck is 'we' this time?" a young man called out. He was a long-legged, sprawling, curly-haired blond in a turtleneck Scandinavian-type sweater so heavy that it seemed to me he should have fainted wearing it in that overheated room. "Who's here? No workers, no people, no street people, no revolutionaries. We're not talking to anybody here. It's nothing but bullshit with martinis."

Across the room, an agitated, very thin young man pleaded for order. "It's very unfair to the speaker," he said. "All these

interruptions. I think she should be allowed to continue reading her very interesting paper without all these interruptions
from special interest groups. We're in on the birth of a very
exciting idea and I think we should have a little more humil-
ity." With a girlish movement of his head he tossed away the
long straight black hair that swung over his face. He had a
long fattish nose and terribly sad, drooping black eyes. He was
wearing skin-tight blue jeans and a see-through embroidered
peasant blouse. A heavy silver chain was looped across his tiny
hips.

"Who are you?" Mary said to him, and then to the room,
"Who is he?" She had turned fierce and frantic. "Who is he?
Who asked him here? Who are all these people? That
woman who left, who was she? Who asked her here? Who
asked you to come here?"

"It's okay, Mary," the girl in the leather outfit called out.
"He's my hairdresser. He's a good kid."

There was some laughter in the room, but I don't think it
reached Mary. She continued to look about fiercely, melodramatically. "Who are *you*?" she said to the girl in leather. "I
don't know you."

There was more laughter, but it stopped when Mary began
to shout. "There's been enough playing. Enough of your kind
of playing around. Enough mistakes. No more mistakes."
She couldn't seem to stop. "Damn you all. Listen to me. No
more mistakes. No more mistakes."

Bob was calling to Matt and Matt was trying to work himself loose from his pinned-in spot. The moment lengthened
interminably as time stretches itself at a peak of catastrophe.
Bob and Matt reached her simultaneously, but it was Matt
who led her away and Bob who stayed to pull together what
was left of the evening.

Everything that followed was very fast, in contrast. Bob kept shouting for order, but there was a general melee going on. The older black man was arguing incoherently with Paula's boy friend. "But who's getting out on those barricades, brother, you? Talk, talk, talk, that's all you're all about. You're full of violent talk, but when it comes to action, that's another matter. Who gets it in the neck? My people. Not you fiery orators carrying on about guns, guns, guns. Plain working people get shot up in Harlem, in Newark, in Detroit, in every ghetto across the country."

Paula's boy friend was laughing. "You want to know what you are, man? You are the epitome of nigger mentality. In short, you are a Knee-grow. You don't understand what it is to be a man, to stand up and protect our people. I say power to our people and what you are saying is slavery and starvation for our people. What you are saying is genocide for our people."

"Talk, talk, talk," the older man said in his deep bass. "Comes the action, baby, you're up against guns, water hoses, tear gas, bayonets, helicopters, chemicals, and if all that fails you'll be dragged legal through the courts. Are you crazy?"

The older man's wife stood at his side listening, saying nothing, but she would smile when the young black spoke and eye her husband skeptically when he answered. I thought I had met them before, perhaps at Joanna's. Joanna dislodged herself from a quarreling knot in another corner of the room and joined me. Almost crying, she seized my hand. In her agitation, she twisted it painfully without realizing it. She said, "This is terrible. This is awful."

"Well, don't break my arm," I said.

Joanna had triggered something in the girl in the mauve

leather suit, standing next to me. She climbed on a chair, waved her arms as if she were blessing us and called out, "It's beautiful. It's beautiful."

Paula joined us. "This is so good. I'm so glad it's happening in my living room. It frees people. It clears the air."

People were moving around the room, and had started to pour drinks for themselves from the bar. Someone offered me a Scotch and soda. I took a sip but then left it on a marble-topped side table. Bob must have given up, because he was no longer at the head of the room, in front of the grand piano. Someone else was, a man with elaborate sideburns and vivid blue corduroy pants. He seemed to be enlisting volunteers to start Mary's community at his aunt's estate in Bar Harbor, while the tall fellow in the turtleneck sweater struggled with him and yelled at him, and at the room in general.

Papa Shaeffer was walking up and down, one hand raised high, his pink face upturned and his beautiful white hair shining like a saint's, calling out to nobody, "Please, my dear friends, may I have the floor for a word of explanation? I want a word. I want a word." In his Russian accent, the effect was ludicrous and I burst out laughing.

Joanna said, "Are you going crazy?" I had no idea that she had been hugging my side as I went about the room looking for Bob. I wanted to tell him that I was going home, but when I found him, he asked me to please meet him and some others in the lobby, that he was arranging for us to go on someplace else and settle our business.

Joanna and I left together. She was very agitated, about Mary, and about how the meeting had fallen apart, and about Bob being angry with her.

"Why you?" I said.

"It's all my fault," she said. "I told Mary when I shouldn't have." But she rallied, sitting on a bench in the gilt, blue and white lobby, waiting for the others to join us.

"Nobody explained it to me properly. How was I supposed to know? I'm just going to tell that to Bob. I don't care how mad he is."

She was whispering — it must have been the size of the lobby that made whispering seem the only proper form of communication. That, or declaiming. The white pillars soared two stories high above us to the blue and gold ceiling, and across the expanse of the marble-floored space I saw us reflected in a huge ornate mirror. Wrapped up for winter, we looked like two dowdy middle-aged ladies. I took the woolen scarf off my head and straightened up.

I asked Joanna about the older Negro couple and she told me that I had met them before.

"Cora and Chuck Spalding. You remember. He used to be a member of the City Council. Before the war."

When Joanna said, "Before the war," she meant before World War II, and I didn't remember, of course.

"Is he a politician, then?" I said.

"Oh, no," she said. "He's a cabinetmaker."

"How'd he get into the City Council?"

"He was a Communist Party councilman. I mean elected on the CP ticket. But he's not in the Party now, and he's not active in politics. Not anymore."

Then she said, "Why are you asking about them?"

"Just curious," I said.

She said defensively, "It was perfectly okay for them to be there. They're Committee members."

They were with Bob when he joined us. So were the Shaeffers, looking disheveled, as if they had been pummeled.

There was another couple I didn't know, and a tall, handsome older woman with magnificent red hair, who looked familiar. She turned out to be Jennifer Torrington, a Catholic Socialist who had been running for office without success as long as I could remember.

A light, wet, penetrating fall of snow had begun. We went to a chic bar nearby, close to Lincoln Center. It had a quiet back room with large round tables. The bar's Irish coffee was very good and I promptly ordered one when Bob asked me what I would have. Bob looked like the Shaeffers, as if he had been in a fight which had left him slightly dazed.

For a while, the talk was all about the meeting. They were all so outraged or appalled in one way or another by the turn it had taken, they couldn't stop rehashing it. The couple I didn't know seemed to be the editors of some little radical paper. They kept referring to the paper, to articles in it and to writers who had appeared in it, but if you didn't know anything about it, as with me, it was impossible to follow their comments. The only ones who didn't speak were me and Cora Spalding. But she listened more intelligently than I did. I could tell by watching her eyes.

Bob kept trying to steer the talk where he wanted it, but they were confused and clung to the notion that they had been called together to act on the question of Mary's communities. He began by hinting that Mary's plan was more a symptom of the illness than a political objective, but they went right on attacking it or each other. Finally, Bob came right out and said that Mary was breaking down, or had already done so, and putting aside all diplomacy he made his proposition about me very directly. There was a short space of silence in which I thought they were going to turn the suggestion down. Then Stella Shaeffer plugged for it and for me. Joanna was silent and I felt her resentment that it wasn't she who had been asked, and that she hadn't known about it earlier. But she didn't object and she voted along with the rest to hire me at $200 a week plus expenses for as long as I was needed.

Once the affair was settled, I found myself almost faint with apprehension. What was I doing? It was mostly because Matt had said that I should that I had decided to take this strange assignment. But that was before our quarrel. Left to myself, beyond his urging, all my instinct was against it. It was too meddling for my taste.

I felt that I had lost Matt, if not for good, then for real in the way that mattered most to me. Because if our love or whatever it was was going to become difficult, if all its taste and clarity was going to become strained through misunderstanding and threat and fear, who needed it? And if everything ended between me and Matt, it would be sickening to be seeing him constantly while I was tending Mary.

There was also the little matter of my ambivalence toward the group itself. Or any group. I hated meetings, organizations, joint decisions, hammering out ideas. At best, the most I could muster for such activity was a numbing boredom. At worst, I became stupidly cynical, arrogant and negative. Nothing suggested would work. Everything proposed was stupid. Too much was forever being dropped out of sight to keep theories intact. Social activists might be better human beings than I could ever be, but I was convinced it was because they were dumber, more gullible and naive and false about human experience. I was contemptuous, and in a way, envious, of their innocent and lofty point of view that there was something useful and active to be done about every situation, even this one, Mary's. It was the thought of Mary, alone, that kept me from reneging on the whole deal right that moment, sitting at the table in an agony of impatience to be free of them all. Because Mary was different. Wrenched out of her life and her perception of the world, her politics came on to me as a natural and unselfish way of being and of acting to make the world better. Even when I thought her ideas wrong, I never thought of her self as false. I could put my faith in a leader like Mary — if there were any. I could even see myself falling in with her plans. If that little group could have seen into my head, that's what they would have found. That I would have done anything for Mary. As a matter of fact, they could have asked, and I would have done what they wanted for nothing and then scrounged around to keep me and the boys and the house going, somehow.

8

I GAVE NOTICE the next morning. My hysterical boss, halted on his way to a conference upstairs, insisted that I stay two weeks while he found a substitute. I called Bob to tell him that.

Bob said, "That's impossible. You don't seem to understand the urgency of the situation. I'm beginning to wonder if maybe we haven't gotten the wrong person for this assignment. What's the matter with you? Tell him you're leaving. Don't worry about forfeiting your severance. We'll make it up to you."

"Listen, Bob," I said. "I didn't go looking for this set-up and if it's going to be like this I want out right now. And who's got any severance anyway? I've been here less than a year."

He honeyed his voice professionally. "Hey, hey, I didn't know you were touchy. I'm sorry. Okay? But, sweetheart, you don't owe them anything. Just walk out. It's a question of priorities."

I said, "I'll think about it," and hung up in a rage against myself for having agreed to put myself under orders from Bob. Was he going to worry about me later when I needed a new job and couldn't get a reference?

When the mail was distributed, among all the junk for my boss was a fat envelope for me, marked PERSONAL, containing a group of communications from Mary. One was a twelve-page typewritten paper, with a scrawled note attached: "Jean, ten to twenty copies of this, please. Thanks. Mary." I put that aside to read later. There was another scrawled handwritten message on a sheet of white paper. " 'And there shall be no more death, neither sorrow, nor crying' " — or " 'lying,' " it was hard to decipher which — " 'neither shall there be any more pain: for the former things are passed away.' " And another yellow sheet with a message typed in caps, in red, with the lines justified, forming a square on the center of the page:

IF THE WORD REVOLUTION IS USED
SERIOUSLY AND NOT MERELY AS AN
EPITHET FOR THIS SEASON'S NOV-
ELTIES, IT IMPLIES A PROCESS.
NO REVOLUTION IS SIMPLY THE
RESULT OF PERSONAL ORIGINALITY.
THE MAXIMUM THAT SUCH ORIGI-
NALITY CAN ACHIEVE IS MADNESS:
MADNESS IS REVOLUTIONARY FREE-
DOM CONFINED TO THE SELF.

After I had opened all the mail and pinned past correspondence together and made my notes on whatever I knew my boss needed to be filled in on and had deposited the collection on his desk, I went down the carpeted corridor to the coffee wagon and brought a container back to my desk to drink while I read the long paper by Mary. It described a sure cure for cancer through purification of mind and body by way of white wine, clams and music. I read, skimming sentences:

We are a total instrument. Our flesh cannot rot without the mind disintegrating. Every vibration of sound, touch, taste makes its way through flesh, nerves, sense to the whole system. The clam, a primeval tissue produced in the sea, as is all living matter, enters the system through the walls of the stomach to regenerate tissue rotting from man-made poisons . . . Wine is the conduit which carries the cure through the poisoned blood stream . . . Music opens the nerves . . . The music must be loud, as loud as the ears can bear it. The wine must be served in a paper-thin glass — GLASS — so that the accumulation of life-giving properties of the sun's rays are best preserved. Hold the glass against the light and the wine will turn yellow, the sun unlocked to be swallowed whole . . . Rolling the head and slowly rotating the torso to the music is good and will distribute the cure evenly. Sing, sing with the music . . . Do not wait for cancer to strike to follow this regimen. Eat no other foods or drink. Avoid idle conversation. Start your children on this course immediately as a preventive measure. If the child is too young to manipulate his body, place his head lower than his torso. This will allow the head to roll freely. Stroking the genitals is good . . ."

I put the paper aside and called Bob again. He answered the phone himself.

I said, "Mary sent me some very peculiar stuff to Xerox."

He said, "Is it the clam cure for cancer?"

I said, "Yes, that and some others."

He said that he had received the clam cure. "She's asked me to present it to the medical profession. In whatever manner I think best." He laughed, but his voice was heavy and dispirited. He excused himself and was gone from the phone for a while. I could hear him in the background talking to a patient in a loud bantering voice.

When he came back, I said, "Bob, I'm quitting right now."

He said, "Christ! We really need you. What am I going to do now?"

I said, "No, no. I mean here. Quitting here. Tell me what you want me to do."

He said, "Oh. Good girl." His voice became lively and authoritative. "Go straight to Mary's and just stay with her, no matter what happens. Call me if you need me. I've already spoken to her about going into the hospital for more tests, so if she brings it up, you know where to throw your weight. Don't bring it up yourself. She got terribly angry with me."

I said, "Is that all?"

He said, "The main thing is to be sure she doesn't do any harm, to herself or the children. That's your real function. Do you have any money?"

"About twenty dollars. What would I need money for?"

"I don't know. All kinds of things. I'll get to you somehow today and give you enough money so that you can operate. I'd like you to have a car. I'll arrange all that. You just get up to Mary's and stay with her. Take a cab," he said. "We'll make it up to you."

I was immediately angry with him again, or if not with him, then with the situation and my ambiguous role in it. Money made it all worse. I typed a note for my boss, still at his conference. I hadn't given him a real reason for quitting earlier, but just said that it was because of personal pressures. I made up a half-lie:

I'm sorry but much as I would like to stay the two weeks, I can't. My sister is gravely ill and I'm needed at her side. I must leave now. Everything is done that needs to be done. The morning mail is under this note. Again, I'm sorry. Jean.

I carried the note into his office and placed it on top of the other correspondence and checked his calendar to make sure the incompetent didn't miss an appointment. There was a luncheon date listed and I took a red pen and circled it so that he'd notice it and saw directly underneath a light-penciled reminder around the three o'clock line, "Good place for whips," with an address in the east thirties. That was startling. But maybe the word was "slips." Or maybe he kept horses. I gathered all my junk from the desk and the closet, packed it in a Bloomingdale's shopping bag and left without a word to anybody.

I did take a cab and wondered what I would tell Mary as the driver connived his way crosstown and uptown through a mess of delivery trucks, buses and cars. But when I got there and she answered the bell, it felt so natural to be with her that I more or less told her the truth.

"I quit my job," I said, "and came to celebrate with you."

There were whole stretches in the day we spent together which were smooth, pleasant, quite without self-consciousness. Then there would be a sudden fit of railing against Matt. I heard again the story of the condoms, of his homosexuality, the implication of incest, his fear of letting their skins touch and the pin-sticking episode, dramatized as before. Her rages were sickening but compellingly convincing. It was as though one were to deny that vomit was real because it was disgusting. I found myself shaking with the conviction that Matt was the evil person she was conjuring and that there was something wrong with me in responding to him as I had. At the same time, I heard her out avidly, with excitement, wanting him terribly to come to me again. I didn't argue with her or try to stop her in her ranting. Afterward, she would lapse into a hostile silence, even more frightening than the talk. Her eyes narrowed and darted about the room melodramatically, at one point with such exaggeration that I thought she must be kidding me — putting it all on. Then, in between, the return to the quiet normalcy of her routine as an efficient housewife, loving to little Katy and to Bella, and sometimes even affectionate to me, though she kept a constant watch on me.

I babied her a bit. I fixed a crabmeat salad for lunch which we ate leisurely while Katy and Bella were napping. There was no sign of the clam, wine, music cure. In the afternoon, I trimmed and washed and set her hair with a couple of curlers to give a little body to the top. She looked lovely when I combed it out, though she thought the whole thing silly. At about four-thirty, I dragged Shtrudel out at the end of a leash into a sleety rain, and I picked Mark up at a friend's house where he had gone to play after nursery school. Matt called to tell Mary he was leaving the office. She asked him to pick up a cake if he'd like some for dessert. The tone she used in speaking to him surprised me. It was gently and friendly. I got ready to leave about a quarter to six. I wanted to avoid seeing Matt there, in that house, before Mary.

Mary walked me down the hall, the baby resting against her flat hip. She said, "Bob's bugging me about going into the hospital for some tests." She looked at me searchingly.

I said, "Oh," in what I hoped was a neutral voice.

"Something to do with finding out why the cobalt was bothering me, so that I can finish the treatments." Again, the searching look.

I nodded.

She said, "I don't know what to think."

I said, "It sounds reasonable."

"Reasonable! From the people who made one mistake after another? What's reasonable about it?"

I said, "I don't know, Mary. I just trust Bob more."

She said, "So do I. Why do we?" And then, "Maybe I'll do it."

I called Bob from the corner drugstore to report. He sounded weary, but his voice took on life with the new information. "That's good," he said. "That's very good. Stay with her until Matt gets there."

I didn't tell him that I wasn't going to do that.

He said, "I'm due at the hospital for a delivery. With luck it will be fast. I have to see you this evening. What can we arrange?"

I told him that I was staying home and he said that he would call me later.

I stopped at a gourmet delicatessen near my house and blew what was left of my money on cooked food: shrimp, noodle soup, chicken, farfel with mushrooms, French bread flown in from Paris — slightly stale — cucumber salad and a big Spanish melon. The boys and I feasted. We ate in the kitchen and the feeling was good until Terry and Paul got into a nasty little fight about helping with the dishes. Their quarreling snapped a nerve and I ran howling to my room, where I closed the door and gave myself up to sobbing. It was all over in minutes and I got up and washed my face and went back to the kitchen to reassure the boys. In a spasm of contrition, they had finished cleaning the kitchen so well and so quickly that we got past the bad moment by turning it into a joke.

I gave them a brief run-down on Mary and my new situation. "She has a very bad illness," I said, "and the shock has affected her mentally. So I won't be working on my other job anymore but I'll be spending most of my time with her to keep her safe. I might have to be away from home a little more than usual but I'll try to have someone here to take over. I know I can count on your understanding and cooperation. And anyway it won't be for very long, maybe just a couple of months."

"More than usual!" Paul said. "You're out all the time now."

Elliot said, "Where are we going to get any money? Will Dad give it to us?"

"No baby sitters," Terry said. "I don't want any baby sitters around here. I can make hot dogs and baked beans."

Paul said, "Is she crazy? How does she act? Are you scared to be with her?"

"Don't be silly," I said. "She's just like herself. Only depressed."

"Oh, sure," Paul said. "I know about that."

"So why do you have to be with her to keep her safe?" Elliot said. "Is someone after her?"

"People like that commit suicide," Terry said.

"What's that?" Elliot asked.

"Kill herself, shmuck," Paul said.

"Wow!" Elliot's eyes opened. "Does she have a gun?"

I told them to get going on their homework.

The laundry and cleaning had been delivered earlier in the evening, and I was putting away the fresh linens when Terry came and stood beside me, swinging the closet door back and forth, his presence heavy with a painful desire to communicate.

"Jean," he said, "could I be having a mental breakdown?" He lifted his heavily lashed lids for an instant and I got a quick glimpse of terror and despair in his eyes.

"I didn't know you weren't feeling well," I said.

"Oh, I'm feeling fine," he said. "It's nothing like that."

"What's it like then?"

He moved the door back and forth.

"Don't do that," I said.

"Why?" he said. "Why shouldn't I do that?"

"So do it."

"Like that," he said. "That makes me very upset. And everything else. I hate everything I'm supposed to do. I have to push myself to do everything."

"School, too?" He was a whiz-bang student, top of the class, class president every other year, student council, student patrol, milk brigade, newspaper editor, big man on junior high campus, a real gung-ho kid. "Come on, you know you love school."

"Man, I can't even *talk* to you. School is the biggest drag of all. As soon as I walk in and smell it, I feel like vomiting."

I said nothing.

"Mom," he said. "I can't stand to get up in the morning. You know?"

I knew. I remembered the feeling of waking up in the crumbling little bedroom I shared with my sister when I was thirteen. I could remember the despair and hopelessness weighting my body like blocks of ice. I remembered the enormous effort it took to get myself to school. I was failing something. Typing. Or biology.

"If you feel that way tomorrow, why don't you stay home?" I felt funny about that suggestion.

"I'm afraid of that," he said. "I'm scared of starting that.

You have to keep control of yourself or everything could just go . . ." and he ended with a really remarkable noise, like an engine running down and then blowing up. "One of my friends stays home and watches television all the time. In his bedroom. He won't even see any of us. He won't even talk to us on the phone. Maybe that will happen to me."

"Come on," I said. "You know it won't. You're smarter than that."

"Jeff's a lot smarter than I am. He's practically a genius. He's a great poet."

"You mean Jeff Halley?"

He nodded.

"Is hiding in his room, watching television? When did this start? How long has it been going on?"

"Couple of months," he said. He gave the door a sharp whack. "He's not *hiding*. You don't understand. He's closed himself away."

"Really!" I said.

He mimicked me. " 'Really!' Man, what a reaction!"

I said, inspired, "Terry, are you in some sort of trouble at school?"

"What particular trouble would you like me to be in?" He had assumed a sophisticated manner meant to put me down. "Drugs? Sex? Revolution? A crime syndicate, maybe?"

"If you're going to act stupid," I said.

"First I'm smart, then I'm stupid," he said. "Would you like to make up your mind?"

Underneath his attempt to be arrogant, I thought I sensed the small-boy tears pushing. I shoved the rest of the linens in the closet and put my arm around his waist. "Let's go into my room and talk this over quietly. Okay?"

He pulled away from me in outrage. "No," he yelled.

"That's not going to work. You're just trying to break me down. I know your tactics. Now you'll try love and kindness." He turned away into his room, slamming the door behind him.

If I had let myself go at that moment, I would have stormed in and hit him, or thrown myself down on my knees for a round of "Hail, Mary, full of grace . . ." — automatically doing what my mother would do when my sister and I turned bitchy against her. It was either that or stormy tirades about how our trampiness would end with our becoming whores. And dying of syphilis and tuberculosis. One of my Polish friends really did become a whore after she came to New York. I visited her as soon as I arrived myself. She had a nice little apartment in the west fifties, with a cunning little kitchenette built up on a balcony and when I asked her what she was working at, she said, "Oh, I thought you knew. I'm doing pretty well. I'm lucky. The man who sets them up for me is a good guy." She seemed placid and unchanged from her high school days, though maybe not so high spirited. She was a lot cleaner than she used to be, especially her hair. She was always catching lice back in school. It was odd seeing her in that life after all the years of hellfire and brimstone warnings from my mother. Her occupation seemed so natural and human. A young man rang the bell while I was there, and I left. He was just an ordinary young man. I couldn't work up a quiver of horror at the thought of what they were going to do. My other close Altoona high school friend became a nun, but I never visited her or had any contact with her after we both left the town. Maybe the convent would have seemed a natural solution to me too.

Ginny was an Italian girl. She had a beautiful face, but a big, sloppy body. She loved to eat and I loved to eat too when

I was with her. We cut school together. We would meet near a disused railroad embankment and she always had something fresh from the bakery with her, like hot, dripping chocolate éclairs. That was a delicious thing to eat before eight in the morning. By eight-thirty, we would backtrack to her house, where everybody had left for work. We spent the day in idleness, gossiping about our classmates, fantasizing our futures, swapping myths about sex, love and men, and eating all day long. But after a couple of successful adventures in cutting, we were surprised by her mother, coming home unexpectedly from an emergency tooth pulling. Her face was swollen — and livid with hysterical anger against Ginny. She ignored me as if I didn't exist. She told Ginny that she would end up a whore, exactly as my mother would say to me and did that evening because I was sewing a blouse for myself with a deep V neck. Did they go to some sort of mother's school? Was that what Terry was asking himself about me?

My mother never discovered my hooky playing. The school had accepted my forged notes without question. Ginny and I stopped cutting school, but it had made a bond between us. Once when my sister was spending the night with a girl friend, Ginny slept with me. The bed was small for such a fat girl and me, and Ginny sighed and groaned a lot, tossing about, complaining that she couldn't sleep. I offered her some aspirin, but she said, "No, no," and pulled my head to her lips, whispering, "Let's pretend that we're lovers. First, I'll be the man, then you will, okay?" I whispered, "Okay. But I don't know what to do." She sucked at my breast and stroked and licked until I was frantically aroused. Frightened that my mother would hear, I tried to push her away, but insistently and skillfully she persisted and brought me to an astounding climax. I never took my turn. I didn't want to touch her thick flesh and pendulous breasts and the thing where it all happened. She lay alongside me crying until she fell asleep. I stayed awake for a long time — wondering, excited, sad, and displeased with myself. After that, I did it to myself, when I could find the privacy, but I stayed away from Ginny.

I tried to imagine a similar situation that Terry might be suffering through. Though what today's equivalent might be escaped me, since anything seemed to be permissible and "beautiful" to the kids now. And were they wrong? Why couldn't I have responded to Ginny? Instead, I forced myself to "fall in love" with the first boy who had the sense to get me down on the ground, after a Pulaski Day picnic and a lot of beer had made us both brave. I could hardly remember anything about him except his flat cheekbones and light blue eyes which turned hot when he looked at me.

I was about to knock on Terry's door and try again when Bob called. He asked me to meet him at a midtown restaurant. I tried to persuade him to come to the apartment, because I didn't want to go out again. I was tired. But Bob hadn't had his dinner yet and he insisted. I got out of the jeans I had put on when I came home and into a decent-looking pantsuit. The boys were upset about my leaving and I saw that it had been a mistake to have told them about Mary. It was impossible to figure. It was supposed to be good to tell them the truth, but when I did, look what happened. I assured them that I wouldn't be gone more than an hour.

But I had to take the bus down because all my money was gone and when I got to the restaurant Bob had finished his dinner and was drinking a green liqueur and feeling expansive and talkative and I never got back to the apartment until after midnight. By that time, the house was dark and quiet.

I drank chartreuse with Bob and listened to him. He was

talking about Mary when she was little and about Bella when she was young and about Mary's father, Matthew Moody.

"Muttel was ugly," Bob said. "He looked like a frog, but dames were crazy about him."

"Did they call him Muttel because he was ugly?"

Bob laughed. "Muttel was a Russian Jew. Matthew Moody's real name was Moshe Moteliansky, called Muttel by everybody. He changed his name when he became CIO regional organizer for Ohio, Pennsylvania and a piece of New York state. But he never shook his nickname. He had more energy than any man I ever knew. And guts. Nothing frightened him. He got chased out of the Tri City area by company thugs who were out to kill him, but he managed to stay a few miles ahead of them in his new Pontiac. He brought Bella back to New York on that trip. A beautiful, delicate-looking girl with big blue eyes and a peaches-and-cream complexion and soft, curly brown hair, with the constitution of a horse. She had a beautiful figure and she wore beautiful clothes. She came from a solid family with plenty of money. Her father was a local banker. Her mother was some kind of Presbyterian missionary. In no time, Bella could outtalk, outorganize everybody around, including Muttel."

"Did he resent that?"

"Not one bit. He wasn't a man whose self-confidence was easily shaken. They worked together all the time. Whenever she spoke — she was a glorious speaker, really glorious — it was hard to believe that such eloquence was emanating from that slender, glamorous girl. He liked to hear her. He would listen with his frog's grin, very proud of her."

"But you weren't around then, were you?"

"Sure," he said. "Sure I was."

"Weren't you too young?"

"For what?" he said. "I was younger than Muttel. But Bella and I are exactly the same age. It's her illness that makes her seem older. I was an educational director of the Party." He paused, smiling, nostalgia bringing moistness to his eyes. "Those were wonderful times," he said. "People were different then. Maybe we made mistakes, but we didn't make the major mistake they're making now, of going along with no theory and no guidelines. We believed in something. Something positive. We had a goal. We were working for the happiness of all mankind. The New Left blames us now for the ills of the whole world, but we were a force then. We stood for something. And we had our influence. We changed things."

"You're not complimenting yourself on the state of the world, are you?"

I guess I had sounded derisive, because he said, "I don't want to talk about it. I don't think you have the background for such a discussion."

"You don't need more of a background than having lived in this world since the Second World War."

"You were a baby then. You couldn't begin to understand what the thirties and forties were all about."

"I wasn't," I said. "And what about the fifties and sixties? And what about the Soviet Union right now?"

"What about it?" he said, furious, and then making a face as if he had indigestion. "I don't want to talk about it."

He called the waiter for another round of drinks. "Let's get on with our business," he said.

"Why don't you want to talk about it?" I persisted. "Don't you think I'm worth convincing?"

"Everybody's worth convincing," he said. "Anybody is worth winning over, if he's going to go out and act on his con-

victions. Are you going to go out and act on your convic-
tions?" His smile was nervous and cruel.

"You've apparently already answered that question for
yourself," I said.

"The answer is so obvious," he said.

I said coldly, "Maybe we'd better get on with our business."

He put his hand over mine. "I didn't mean to insult you,
Jean."

"I'm not sure of that," I said.

"Believe me, I had no such intention." He put the slightest
pressure on the back of my hand with his warm palm. "But
what's the point in kidding ourselves? Know thyself. I don't
kid myself that women are constantly falling head over heels
in love with me, do I?"

I took my hand away.

"To know one's limitations," he said. "That's the essence
of maturity. There have to be some advantages in growing
older, and that's one, coming to an understanding with oneself. That's one thing I very much admire about Joanna. She
knows her limitations and accepts them. A worthwhile trait."

Joanna and Bob! Well, well. I thought that was just crazy
enough to be right.

He smiled a liquidy smile at me and reached out for my
hand again. I put my elbows on the table and propped up my
chin with both hands and smiled at him. If he was flirting, it
was automatic on my part to flirt back. "You're not really
mad at me, are you?" he said.

I shook my head, smiling, and turned the conversation back
to Bella's father. "What happened to Muttel?"

"He died of a heart attack in nineteen forty-three. Just before Mary was born. Overwork. He never stopped. I never

knew such a man for work. And every evening, something else to do." He stopped. "Does this interest you? Shall I tell you about him?"

"Very much," I said.

"It was part of his union and party work, but they turned it into fun. Dances. Shows. I think they were responsible for more productions of *Waiting for Lefty* than any production company. Picnics, forums, Marxist study circles, Russian war relief, and on the side they practically built the IWO single-handed in their area."

"What was that?"

"What?" he said.

"The IWO," I said.

"See." He smiled. "You were too young. The International Workers Order."

"Sounds heavy," I said.

"It was a fraternal benefit society. On ethnic lines. Very sound idea." He paused, dreaming backward into another time. "They were so full of life," he said.

"Who are they?" I asked.

"Bella and Muttel. He was even a good dancer. He was at least fifteen years older than Bella but he could stay in there and lindy hop with her all evening. They did everything together. They went to the Soviet Union for a leadership course together."

"Did she stop when he died?"

"Nothing stopped Bella but the FBI. She was heartbroken when he died, but nothing could stop her. She had the kind of faith that doesn't exist anymore. Faith in the people."

"Were you in love with her?"

"Who wasn't?" he said. "But I didn't stand a chance. There was nobody but Muttel."

"You like remembering that time," I said.

"It was another world. I wish I had it back."

"Not all of it," I said. "You can't want that. There were horrible things happening."

"All of it," he said fiercely. "It was my youth."

"No," I said. "You can't. You can't be sentimental about concentration camps and Hitler and purges and socialism going all wrong."

His face grew dark and mottled. "That's your excuse," he said. "You use that as your excuse to sit back and do nothing. But I'm not talking about that. I'm talking about how it felt inside to live through that time. It was a time when it was possible to think of living a good life, a dedicated life, of thinking like a Jean Christophe, or of becoming a Dr. Norman Bethune, and not feel like a fool for harboring such hopes.

"That's the trouble with the current generation," he went on, after a pause. "Their disgust is healthy. Okay. But they throw everything out with it. They have no goals, no organization, no theory. And they're stubborn and stupid. They don't even have the good sense to listen to the people who know, who have had some experience, who could help them."

"They think you failed," I said.

"Well, we didn't," he said. "Our goals were different. We had a hand in every major reform granted by society. And even if we failed by their lights, studying failure is very valuable. Any scientist will tell you that. Why the failure? That's of the essence."

"Not to them," I said. "Everything that's happened is too disgusting. History is too disgusting. I can see why they want to throw everything out and make it all new."

"And you call me sentimental!" he said. "That's just dreaming."

"Then what do you think of Mary?"

"Mary's sick," he said. "Please, let's not talk politics." He made that indigestion face again, and belched a little before ordering another chartreuse for each of us. But he began again after a sip.

"You don't know what you're talking about. You don't know what we went through. Can you understand what Bella went through? All of us in one way or another? You know how many sets of Little Lenin Libraries I have stuck up in the storage closets of my mother's apartment because people were afraid to keep them in their bookcases? You think I'd be more of a hero if I shit all over my past, like so many ex-Party people do? Not me. I'm out now. I don't think they're a force anymore. I don't think that's where the impetus will come from. Not from that direction anymore. But I'm not going to crap all over what I was and what I did. Nobody works the way we worked, always together, pulling for a common goal, a world of peace and plenty for all mankind. Whatever mistakes there were, and, between us, I'll admit there were plenty — our position on the Negro was enough to hang us right there — but those mistakes were *our* mistakes. It's *our* business to discuss, not some ignorant Yippie kid's business." There were unhealthy-looking streaks of red down his heavy cheeks and his liquid-eyes were bloodshot, from the liqueur perhaps.

I said, "Don't get upset."

"Upset!" he said. "Listen, I never played their game. I have my integrity. I could name names. Colleagues who were right there alongside me in the Party and in the professional units, but they don't want to be reminded of that now when they're riding the good-time jet. Suddenly they're for peace. They're against the war, because it's safe and fashionable.

Were they out there on the streets with the Stockholm Peace
Petition when it was worth your life to try it? During Korea?
You can be contemptuous of Joanna because she stays in the
Party. Okay. I don't agree ideologically. I have my differences, but I give her credit for loyalty and for courage. She
was on the street with the Stockholm Peace Petition when
what is now called the silent majority would come after you
swinging their over-the-shoulder bags to kill and the cops
would arrest you for littering if you complained. I know what
it's all about. I was poor. They're all rich now. On the Jewish
side *and* the Cuban side, except for the few who stayed with
Fidel. But we were all poor then. I worked as a busboy and
waiter all through school, and my mother was chained to the
machine and my father was nothing but a glorified dishwasher, whatever fancy title they gave him in that kitchen.
Salad chef! I'm not going to let that end up on Park Avenue,
making a fortune out of hysterectomies. Or allergies."

I grabbed for a cooler topic. "Is that really true about hysterectomies? That they're not necessary?"

"Greatly exaggerated," he said. "Most doctors are very decent human beings. It's the system that's wrong. Let's not
blame it all on the individual doctor." Then he went into a
long bit about socialized medicine, free abortion, preventive
medicine and some other stuff, but I had stopped listening.
The liquor had numbed me somewhat. The big, shabby restaurant felt more plush than when I had walked in and its
clattering confusion more hushed. The liquor was softening
my vision. And my responses. I wanted to be with someone
who meant something to me. Matt. Why couldn't my life
shape up decently?

I told Bob, when he paused, that I had to get back home,

but he asked me to stop by his office with him for the car keys. Before he paid the check, he gave me two hundred dollars in twenty-dollar bills.

"Keep an account of all expenses," he said, "and we'll reimburse you. Be liberal about everything. Don't worry about money. There's plenty. The two hundred is for you — that's salary. And you don't have to report it either. Be a little extra there for you."

His office wasn't the seedy place I had been expecting. It was in a big West End Avenue apartment house, up a couple of stone steps into a private entrance, carpeted and wallpapered. Framed Ingres prints (originals?) on the walls. A Spanish table with a single piece of Spanish pottery. Inside, the same quiet tone repeated in the small waiting room. He lit lamps as we went. Then, into the spacious office — his consulting room. Impressive Spanish desk. Paneled walls. Abstract paintings, perhaps by a friend. Oriental rug, bookcases, leather armchairs, fresh dark red roses. I didn't notice the oversized leather couch until later, after we had had another drink, a Cuban brandy, and he had given me the keys, the registration, and directions about picking up the car at a garage.

"I sometimes sleep here," he said, and with a flick of his arm, as if he were acting out a TV commercial, he had transformed the couch into a double bed.

Did he really mean to try that, after all the putting down, beginning with his statement the other night that Mary was fond of me and respected me *for some reason?* It seemed so. Though he hadn't said anything, the plea was urgent in his bloodshot eyes and strained breathing. I was revolted.

I wanted to hurt him, demean him in some way before re-

fusing him. I said, with harsh gaiety, "What, no pillows? I
like it with pillows."

But he took my comment straight. "Yes, yes," he said, and
brought out of a closet two down pillows in fresh pillow slips.
His cleaning woman was certainly kept amused. Or perhaps
his medical secretary? His relief and pleasure in what he took
for acceptance made him laugh and giggle like a boy. He sank
back against the pillows he had placed on the bed. The sultan
and the new concubine.

I said, "No time to waste. I have to get back to my kid-
dies," and took my suit jacket off and let down my hair. He
lay back, breathing hard, a cringing voluptuous shame in his
eyes. Under my jacket I was wearing only a sheer body stocking. "They sag a bit," I said, following his eyes. "But then,
I'm almost forty."

"You're beautiful," he said. "Exquisite." His eyes watered.
I turned away. I don't know what he thought I was going to
do, but he said, "Don't, don't. Let me look at you more the
way you are."

I said, "I can't believe it. What about all that pure love for
Mary?"

Tears, again, and a hand flung across his face. "I'm a very
weak man," he murmured. "But it doesn't matter. That's a
lost cause. She loves her young husband."

"Me too," I said.

He either didn't hear me or, more likely, was totally without
interest in what I felt.

"Now, sweetheart," he said, gesturing to his swollen crotch.
"Now take the devil out. He's banging to get out. He can't
wait to get into you."

I yelled, "You're incredible. What do you think I am? You

don't think anything of me and you expect to screw me? For what? What am I supposed to get out of it? Ecstasy? Because I'm such a slob, the worse you treat me, whatever you think of me, the more my tongue hangs out?" I meant to go on, but his pleasure stopped me. His eyes were squeezed shut and tears were rolling down his cheeks. He writhed on the bed. Were there also whips in the closet that held the down pillows?

"I'm an awful human being," he moaned. "Awful. Awful."

I sat down on the bed. "I can't win," I said.

He pulled me against him, slobbering into my breasts, moaning and crying, "You're beautiful. You're exquisite. I said all those things because you're too beautiful for me. I was afraid. I was afraid. I was afraid you would turn from me in disgust, my honey girl . . ." — he was getting my clothes off as he spoke in that new rasping voice — "beautiful bits of honey, swollen grapes, let me kiss, let me, let me, let me drink from you, let me feed from you, let me suck your honey, let me, let me . . ."

He talked throughout, reaching really extraordinary verbal heights at the end. The strangest thing of all was that through the resistant coldness of my sense of myself, my body responded to his sensual rapture and deliberately slowed and heightened climax as it never had before. I had reason enough to be depressed on the way home, but the strongest sickness with myself came from the knowledge that I would yield to him again, if he wanted me to.

9 ———————

Bob called me first thing in the morning, even before the boys left for school. In passing, in a voice charged with fake, hot intimacy, he said, "I hope you slept as well as I did, sweetheart," and rushed on to say that I must get to Mary immediately, that she had called him at six-thirty in the morning, crying hysterically, whispering that Matt had put something in her food to keep her awake.

I found Mary calm and the house organized into its usual antiseptic order. Matt had taken Mark to nursery school on his way to work. The baby was asleep. Bella was sitting in a chair in the living room, her blue eyes staring about wildly. She was neatly dressed and her hair had been combed. Mary was in blue jeans, but she seemed to have put on false eyelashes or enough mascara to create the same effect. She didn't question my being there, which was an immense relief. I was running out of lies. She said, "For a cup of coffee, will you walk Shtrudel for me? I have a million things to do before the baby sitter comes."

"Where are you going?" I asked casually.

"I have to do something," she said. "At a demonstration."

I said, "Do you mind if I go with you?"

Her back was toward me. She was filling a kettle at the

kitchen sink. Her voice was icy. "Why?" she said, and then, more friendly, "It's instant, okay?"

I said, "Don't bother with coffee. You're too busy. I thought it was made. Instant's fine, but I don't want to delay you."

She had put the gas on under the kettle and turned to me fully, her eyes ridiculously crafty in their dramatic heavy make-up. "Are you a liar?" she said in the icy voice.

"Of course," I said lightly. "Isn't everybody these days?" And then, because I couldn't bear any more pretense: "Mary, it's just that I want to be sure you're all right."

"What does that mean?" she said in the icy voice.

I looked directly into her eyes. "You know what it means."

"I don't," she said. "Tell me." She busied herself fixing the instant coffee. I said nothing. "There are millions of people in trouble all over the world. Go find one of them — or a dozen."

"I don't know them," I said. "It's you I care about. Even if I'm of no use to you, I can't stay away from you while you're feeling this way."

"What way?"

I said, "You know."

Within the frivolous fringe of lashes, her eyes were hard with hatred. "I know all about you, Jean," she said. "I know what your assignment is."

I shook my head. "It's only that I care about you. Don't think anything else."

Her look stayed level, hard, full of hate. I felt bereft of the Mary who had been my darling friend. At the same time I was suffocated by my guilty involvement in the life of the hostile stranger facing me. I cried, dropping my face into my hands, trying to stop the tears I was ashamed of. But they had a miraculous effect and touched her in a way I could not have deliberately calculated. She put her head against mine and cried too.

Clinging to me, between sobs, she whispered, "Will you help me, Jean, really, will you, no matter how dangerous it turns out to be? You don't know what I'm going through. It's horrible. The lies, the plots, I don't know who to turn to anymore. I don't even know about you. Only Bella, only Bella is trustworthy. If only Bella were well. If only she could help me."

"Trust me," I said.

She pulled herself back and looked at me with such wild entreaty that I felt my heart would crack. Her face was streaming with tears. Either the make-up was waterproof or the eyelashes were false, because the tears were doing no damage, as if she were an actress onstage. "You must tell me, you must tell me who the man with the camera is. You know all about him. You know you do. You know that he's downstairs this minute waiting for me to come out of the house. You must tell me, Jean, you must."

I shook my head. "I don't know."

"Jean, please, please," she whispered dramatically. "Oh, please. Don't do this to me."

I said, "Shall I go ahead, and see if he's there?"

She stared, transfixed. "Would you do that? Would you? Even though you know what the camera is?"

"What is it?" I said.

"You know it's a gun."

"I'll walk Shtrudel and see if anybody's hanging around," I said.

The day was bright and unusually warm. The streets were alive with activity. I found myself studying every passer-by as carefully as if I were as paranoid as Mary. Why not? In New York City, to expect sudden death, one way or another, was a sensible notion, not a lunatic one. Shtrudel's frenzied study of every smelly object in the gutters gave me an excuse to look about as carefully as if Mary's fears made sense.

When I got back I reported that there was nobody suspicious-looking outside. She said, "He knew enough to take cover," but she seemed relieved. While I was out she had changed into a black maxiskirt and sweater and high, shiny black boots. Bella's friend arrived and Mary gave her instructions about the baby's schedule. Then she added a long, red tweed cape to her outfit. It was very flamboyant for Mary.

"When did you get those?" I asked.

She swung about affectedly. "Do you like it?"

"You look marvelous," I said, and in a hopped-up way, she did.

She left the house with unconcern, as if the man with the camera had never been discussed. We were heading for the subway but on an impulse I mentioned that Harry had given me the use of a car for a while. She was delighted with the thought of a car, but it immediately worked out badly. The car gave her the notion that we could go anywhere and do the thousand disorganized things buzzing around in her head. She had a friend in White Plains she hadn't seen in months. We'd visit her before the demonstration. But before that, we had to pick up some leaflets in Washington Heights. And the Cloisters would be so beautiful in the sudden, warm weather, we would drive around there a bit but without getting out of the car or going inside. And since it was such a beautiful day, we surely had time for a drive into the country and lunch at a country inn before the demonstration. I said yes to everything, except the friend in White Plains.

Going up to Washington Heights wasn't anything of a problem because most of the traffic was going the other way, but I had an uneasy half-hour, sitting in the car, double-parked on a dismal street lined with look-alike gray apartment buildings, hearing nothing but the whine of garbage trucks eating up the refuse dumped in with great crashes of sound by two young black men and an older white man, while I tried to figure out which building Mary had disappeared into, and didn't seem to be ever coming out of.

When she did come out, she had a bunch of leaflets in her arms. They were wrapped in brown paper. The top one was exposed. I read it when we reached the Cloisters and pulled into an overlook on the Hudson where the river widened northward into a majestic stream that had no connection with the struggling city behind us. The top half of the flyer was a slogan in heavy black lettering:

TOWARD THE VIOLENCE OF NONVIOLENCE
AND THE NONVIOLENCE OF VIOLENCE!

"What are these?" I asked Mary.

She told me that she had written the leaflet and had had a thousand copies mimeographed at her own expense because it was so urgent to get this message to the people. She pointed to a particular paragraph and asked me to read it aloud. I read:

> But when we say "Power to the People" we must always incorporate Mao's question, "Who are the People? And who are the friends of the people?"

She said, "Do you see how important that is?"

I said, "Oh, Mary, I'm just a slob, politically, don't ask me.

I don't know anything." Then I asked, "What are you going to do with them?"

"I'm getting them distributed at the Panther rally," she said. She placed the bundle on the back seat and I threw my long woolen scarf on top. I don't know why I wanted to make them less conspicuous. Not because I believed in Mary's man with the camera, certainly. But if the leaflets were another sign of her madness, it made me feel better to hide them.

She seemed to have forgotten all her urgent business. "Let's just drive somewhere," she said.

But she became morose and silent as we drove across the bridge and up the parkway on the west side of the river.

"Why does it all look so dead?" she complained, as if the landscape had set out to spite her by its appearance.

"It's resting until spring," I said.

"I don't like it," she said. "The trees are like skeletons." She put her head back and closed her extravagantly lashed lids. When she opened them, she had gone down into the obsessive circle of her despair. She began again on the Matt atrocities and either the repetition or the closed heat in the car made me feel faint and nauseous. I tried to deflect her by putting the radio on, but she turned it off immediately. She told me of their latest quarrel in great detail. It had been about putting Bella in a home. I tried changing the subject, but there was no getting her off that track, and I ended by nodding silently and feeling again that strange sexual excitement about Matt. She wound up in a rage against everything that had conspired to wreck Bella's life, which was exactly as she was seeing it, as a conspiracy involving everything and everybody.

"Matt thinks Bella was guilty," she said. "He really thinks she *was* a Soviet spy. He makes excuses for her having become one. He says he can understand what led her astray. Can you imagine such political naiveté?"

I said, "I guess a lot of people believed that. There really are spies on both sides, so they think, why not?"

"But can't he see how ridiculous the charges were? And that she couldn't possibly have known anything about the atomic bomb?"

"But she wasn't charged with any knowledge. Just with making contacts, and carrying things back and forth."

She said, "Why are you defending them? Why are you finding excuses for the terrible ideas of those days?"

I said, "I'm not. I don't believe it. I'm just saying that I can understand why other people might."

"We're not talking about other people," she raged at me. "We're talking about Matt. My husband."

I thought how foolish it was of me to be arguing with her. What if she did something violent to me or to herself at that moment while we were going eighty miles an hour? But she turned away and stared angrily out of the window.

When she turned back, it was with her sly look. "I know all about you and your precious understanding of Matt."

"What's that?" I said.

She said nothing but continued to watch me with narrowed eyes. I kept my eyes steadily on the road.

"Are you hungry?" I said. "Shall we start looking for a good place to eat?"

"I fixed up a date for you," she said.

"How about that!" I said, but I was in a kind of terror. "What about lunch?"

"I'd like lunch," she said. "Aren't you interested in your date?"

"Sure," I said.

"Because there's nobody special in your life right now, right?"

I said, "The usual shlemiels. You know."

"I don't know how you stand it," she said. "Being alone. But I admire you for it. That's the way I'm going to live — on my own."

I was maneuvering off the parkway to a route where we might find a restaurant. I said, "There are advantages to being on one's own, though there are lots of times when I can't think what they are."

"You're not on your own," she said with sudden contempt. "You let Harry go on supporting you. I won't allow that when I leave Matt."

"How about this place?" I indicated a sign coming up on the road. Neither one of us could see the restaurant itself, but she said, "I don't like it."

I kept going.

She said, "I arranged a date for you with Sadie's son."

I was so relieved that it had nothing to do with Matt that I laughed out loud. "Who's Sadie? Not to mention her son."

"You met them at the hospital," she said. "You remember. The man who offered us chocolates."

"How about that place?" I said, indicating a billboard advertising a seafood restaurant.

"That looks good," she said, and I set my right-turn indicator. When we drew up at the parking lot, she put her hand on my arm to keep me in the car, and looked directly into my eyes. She brought her face so close to mine that I lost focus. "Aren't you pleased about your date?"

"I don't remember meeting anybody at . . ." I began, and then remembered the deaf mute son of the old woman with the deep voice. "You didn't," I said. "I don't believe it."

"Yes, I did," she said, and smiled. Her face was still very close to mine and it seemed distorted with cruelty. I understood how people came to believe in witches from the poor crazed women who actually thought they were. I understood too how Matt could go on fighting with her, madly digging into this alien for the Mary who existed somewhere inside, chasing the real shadow that flitted in and out of this other real creature.

In the restaurant, busy eating fried clams, she seemed to become herself again. Remembering her cure, I ordered the same dish and white wine for both of us. Perhaps under the glow of the wine, the date looked funny to me, and I laughed aloud.

Mary said, "What's funny?"

"My date," I said, and almost choked. "How does he know when he's reached me? I can see that I'd know. When the phone rings and I say, 'Hello,' and nobody answers I know that's my date."

She said, "That's not funny. Why do people think it's funny to be deaf?"

I stopped my laughter. "Well, how did you set it up? Is his mother coming along?"

She gave me a grave, reproachful look. "He'll be at your door to take you to dinner Saturday night at seven-thirty."

Furious, I said, "I'm busy Saturday night."

"No, you're not," she said, and called the waiter for another glass of wine. "I asked you yesterday. Before I made the arrangement with Sadie."

"How do you know he wants this date any more than I do? Maybe you're being nasty to both of us, instead of just to me."

She looked stricken. "Nasty?" I turned away from the look

in her eyes. I felt miserable. I was making such a mess of my assignment. "You said yourself you could do worse," she said. "And I knew he liked you immediately from Sadie. He told her he loved you at first sight. Why not? You're so pretty. And I said yes to Sadie because of you, because I was counting on you, on your compassion. But you're talking like a shit now. All you can see is his handicap instead of his humanity. His wound. And you turn even that into a joke."

I couldn't seem to stop. "You should have fixed him up with Joanna."

"You call me nasty," she said.

"What's wrong with that idea?" I said.

"The way you meant it." And then, "I thought you wanted to change your life. That's what you've been saying — that you've had it with one empty relationship after another . . ."

"So you set up my big chance," I said, smiling. "I thank you kindly."

Her eyes narrowed. "You hate me," she said, "you're not my friend," and she seemed to turn completely inward on herself. Her face became like an animal's, like a fox face, and with the eyelashes, like a Disney fox face. Her lips quivered with self-pity and her eyes turned in to condemn herself. "There's something wrong with me," she said.

In a panic, I tried to undo my blunders. I reached out to grab her hand, but she pulled it away. "I'm sorry," I said. "I was just being silly, trying to be funny." But she stayed closed away through the rest of our lunch, saying nothing except, "There's something wrong with me. There's something very wrong with me," two or three times.

Almost as soon as we got back in the car, she fell asleep. It was a relief. She had become an unbearably oppressive presence. And I couldn't count on myself, either.

I didn't know where to take her for the demonstration so I stalled coming back to the city, taking the old slow roads which run through all the little towns. She woke on the bridge into the city, more like herself again, but very agitated about being late for the mobilization. She told me we needed to get to the Mall in Central Park. Traffic was heavy on the bridge and I took the lower deck which mixed me up and I found myself in the Bronx and by the time we made the west side of the park, she was frantic. When I stopped for a light, she opened the door and dashed out, saying, "Park it somewhere and meet me at the Mall." I could have killed myself for having taken the car.

I kept her in sight for a few minutes, but at the next crosstown street, the crowd was too thick, a wilder-looking crowd than the peace kids, giving off an aura of exuberant, confident happiness, as if happiness were a natural element, like vapor rising from frost as the sun warms. I drove into a side street, looking for a parking space, and spent almost an hour circling in the maze of run-down, partly spruced-up west-side streets and finally drove the car uptown a bit to Bob's garage. I took a cab back to the park.

When I left the car, I snatched my woolen scarf from the back seat and thought about bringing the leaflets she had forgotten. But I was glad to leave them. I turned them face down on the floor in the back. By the time I reached the park, the demonstration had begun to move out, a pseudoragged army as far ahead as I could see. Mary might have been anywhere, up there already past me, or back here with the line of march waiting to move on. The thing to do was to get ahead so that I could scan the marchers as they came by, but I had no idea of the line of march. Mary had said something about Queens. Queens? How were they going to get to Queens?

I tried to find somebody in charge. There were a couple of kids holding bullhorns, using them to direct the crowds. Each had a red rag tied around his head. But I couldn't get to them, and I wasn't sure if the red Indian band was a sign of authority in other kids running around, or just a general style. One boy rushing past looked familiar and I stopped him, shouting, "Hi, you probably don't remember me, I'm a friend of Mary's. Have you seen her?" on the chance that he belonged to her somewhere.

He said, "My God, you're here too. It's fantastic. We never expected anything like this. It's a whole new thing." He grabbed his head as if his pleasure was agonizing. "My aunt Stella is up ahead, right there." He waved his arm vaguely into the crowd. "People like you," he said. "I can't believe it. Joining with third world people. It's fantastic." He clutched at his wild hair again. I remembered Stella's nephew as a little kid. I thought of him as being Terry's age, though he was obviously older. He was bearded, reeking of perspiration through his old army jacket. Under the red band, his open, babyish blue eyes were stunned with delight.

I said, "Do you know the line of march?"

"Over the bridge. Over the bridge," with another vague wave of his arm. A tiny girl flew up, grabbed him, tearing him urgently away. She was all hair, flying scarf, her poncho fringes bouncing, covered with ragged banners as if she were a post.

I plunged into the crowd to try to find Stella, and found her with the dignified Negro woman who was a member of the Committee, the wife of the man who had been quarreling with Paula's boy friend. Stella said, "Jean, what a pleasure to see you here," and continued with an elaborate introduction of her dear friend, Cora Spalding, though we both tried to tell her we had met. Cora Spalding had a wonderful accepting smile for all that.

I explained to them about losing Mary. They hadn't seen her and I ran ahead, leaving word with them to hold her if they found her. Cora called out that Joanna and Paula were up ahead, maybe they had seen her. If Joanna was here, that meant the Communist Party was backing the demonstration. I couldn't understand that. I would have thought it was too militant for them.

I kept ahead of the marchers' pace, running along the sidewalk and crossing intersections while the marchers were held back for traffic, trying to scan the lines, to distinguish her red cape in a crowd very partial to red, until I got a stitch in my side, a pain I hadn't experienced since I was a little kid. I leaned against a lamppost and rested. The demonstrators filled one half of the broad avenue. The marchers were mostly young, though there was a thin smattering of older people, but almost nobody from the middle generation, and everybody seemed to be dressed in costumes and masquerade hairdos. It was a fiesta — makeshift, ragged banners, baby strollers flying posters of Panthers with guns, blacks and browns moving like dancers, clapping out urgent, intense, incomprehensibly happy rhythms. A slim, polished black Negro girl with the voice of a clear, high trumpet, called out, "I'm talking about love," and the crowd around her responded, "Love."

"I'm talking about love for Bobby Seale."

"Love Bobby Seale," the crowd roared.

"I'm talking about love for the Panther Twenty-one."

"Love the Panther Twenty-one."

"I'm talking about freedom."

"Freedom."

"I'm talking about free the Panther Twenty-one."

"Free the Panther Twenty-one."

"I'm talking about love for the revolution."

"Revolution," the crowd yelled, and hurried and danced and smiled and called to the people on the sidewalk in their crazy, infectious happiness. Next to me a young woman in a short mink coat with two Gristede shopping bags made a tent of the bags, leaning each against her high suede boots, and returned a bewitched, half-dreamy smile to the passing marchers urging us to join them.

"What is it?" she said. "What's it all about? Aren't they *happy!* All that *energy!*" She passed a hand across her blond hair blowing across her face to restrain it, transfixed, poised on the edge of an enchantment that seemed to be carrying her off to join the march, leaving behind two stuffed shopping bags of dog food and boxes of Pampers. Joanna rushed up to me, saying, "What are *you* doing here?" I started to explain about Mary, and she pulled me along to rejoin her group that had moved on ahead. The young woman watched me go with pained regret. I waved to her without knowing why. She called, "Wait, what's it all about? What is it?" and an old man stepped off the curb and upbraided Joanna. "What are you dragging her in for with a bunch of murderers. Anti-Semites. You should be shot. You should all be shot." "We love you too, Gramps," a young man hooted at him, but another stepped up to him and explained and argued patiently while the old man railed on. Joanna was in a line of older people. They bunched up to let us in. Joanna looked pinched and driven by the wind, though the day was warm. Her face was squashed under an unbecoming ornate beretlike hat. It seemed impossible now, my notion about her and Bob. I told her about Mary over the roar of a slogan that seemed to be

Over the bridge
Into the jail
The people's power
Is the Panther's bail.

I liked it and found myself yelling it too. It had a good beat.
Next to me a very tall graying man in his fifties or sixties, well
dressed in tweed (hat and coat, very English), kept up a running dialogue with people on the sidelines, calling out to anyone who seemed slightly friendly to join us! Join us! Join us!
When we passed hecklers, he smiled broadly and mouthed an
epithet, "Fuck you" or "Cock-sucker," with a courtly smile
and inclination of the head. He would take my arm very po-
litely whenever we were ordered to run to close up the lines or
to lead me around an obstruction. We were on an avenue
lined with new luxury apartment houses, but the street was
broad enough to let the last of the dazzling sunshine in. The
crowd laughed and roared approval at a window high up in
one of the structures. Through the sun I caught a flashing
sight, before I passed it, of brilliantly yellow hair and a naked
chest with FREE BOBBY written across it in lipstick or red
paint. "It's Larry Eberle. It's Larry Eberle." The crowd
passed the information along. Nobody in our line knew who
he was, but the kids behind us told us he was a star of the
underground films. The TV cameras were thick at that point,
trying to get him on film, but the sun was making the work
tricky apparently. The cops stood impassively, their eyes flick-
ing over us without expression. We were coming to a bend
where the line bunched up and fed into a short tunnel under
an overpass, and then onto the bridge. We were slowed down,
close packed, funneling slowly down into the narrow opening.
Plainclothes men stood at the turn, working their movie

cameras, recording every face. The tall man turned to them, full face, and did his number — smile, epithet, courtly inclination of the head. The triumphant, ritual wailing of the crowd, echoing and magnified in the tunnel, floated back to us. I did it too as we went through, my tongue beating against the roof of my mouth, something glorious freeing itself in the act, something getting out of me that I thought didn't exist or was totally imprisoned. On the ramp leading up to the suspended part of the bridge, a young woman attached herself to me. She carried a mike. She said, "Can you tell me who your group represent? Would you like to tell our audience who your group represent?"

Her voice was very sweet and low. I could barely hear her over the shouts of the crowd and the noise of the bridge traffic beyond the pedestrian walk.

"I'm not with anybody," I said. "I'm just here as myself."

"That's very interesting," she said. "Do you mind answering a few questions? Would you say that this is a civil liberties issue with you?"

"Okay," I said.

Joanna said, "Don't talk to her."

I said, "Who are you?" and the young woman showed me the mike with letters on it, some little station that didn't mean anything to me. Maybe a Queens station.

She said, "Do you agree, then, as has been stated, that it's impossible for a Panther to get a fair trial in our courts?"

Joanna leaned across and yelled at her, "They've been in jail for more than a year, before the trial even started. Without bail. Is that fair?"

The young woman said to me, "Would you say that in general that is your own position?"

"Okay," I said, and then, from I didn't know where: "It's

the Panthers who are getting killed. We're killing them off, bit by bit."

"Do you agree with the Panther position on violence?" She would put the mike in front of me after she asked the question, just as they do on TV. It startled me. I said, "I don't like jails. I'm against jails."

That seemed to throw her for a minute. She recovered quickly. "Do you agree with the Panther's revolutionary rhetoric?"

"Do you believe in the patriotic rhetoric of the war?" I said. "Does it worry you?"

Joanna said, "That's good."

I said, "Is this going on the air right now?"

The interviewer said, "How would you describe yourself, typical housewife, secretary, single woman working in New York?"

"I'm the poetry editor of the *Scholarly Quarterly*," I said.

Her voice assumed a tinge of respect. "And your name?"

"Penelope Goodbody," I said.

She said, "Thank you very much," and moved aside.

Joanna said, "What did you do that for? You'll get that publication in trouble."

I laughed. "Does it exist? I just made it up." I felt wonderfully happy. We had come out on the open part of the bridge. I could see the water through the mesh floor on which we were walking and feel the play of the metal structure under the steady pushing action of the marchers and the rumbling traffic. It was like riding on something live. The tall man placed himself between me and Joanna and gave us each an arm to steady us, but I ran ahead to try and find Mary. Far below, I saw islands with buildings on them, jails or hospitals, unpleasant-looking places.

On the other side, at the square in front of the jail, the police were thicker. I skirted the crowd, searching for Mary. I got a quick glimpse of Paula and her boy friend through an opening in the crowd, but lost them immediately. There was a desultory speech being given from a truck that was the speakers' platform. The real show was obviously waiting for the whole march to assemble. I saw Mary suddenly, talking to a red-banded fellow who either was or looked a lot like the one in the heavy sweater at her meeting. I tried to get close to the truck but it was impossible. There were Young Lords in purple berets standing on the ground, and a phalanx of white kids in red headbands sitting thigh to thigh on the edge of the truck, swinging their heavy-booted feet, their eyes playing over the crowd in a mixture of nervousness, innocence and tough responsibility. I called out to them that I had to get a message to someone on the platform, and with the help of a thin young man with a long jaw Mary came to the edge of the platform. We yelled at each other across the crowd and the noise. She seemed to be telling me to come to the back of the truck. That wasn't easy. That end was closer to the jail, and the police were heavier there. They were the tactical police force, the ones in blue helmets. Across the street were police on horses and beyond them busloads of more policemen, lined up bumper to bumper and turning the corner. The area was desolate. Except for the solid structure of the jail, there seemed to be nothing but gas stations and the subway entrances and exits, squared off on the four corners. It had gotten much colder as the sun weakened. The cops had moved stanchions in such a way that it was impossible to approach the speakers' truck from the back. I retraced my way. It was almost a quarter of five and I made for a street telephone booth on the side where the cops were massed. I could feel them tense up as I ran toward them. Why not? We had become the kind of country where my big English leather handbag might as easily carry a bomb or gun as my driver's license and department store charge cards. A watchful eye was kept on me while I dialed. Miraculously, the phone was in working order. Terry answered. He had gone off to school as usual, and his voice now sounded cheerful and normal. I told him that I might be delayed but that I would definitely be home for supper.

He said, "Somebody sent you a big long box of flowers."

"Who?"

"I don't know. I put them in water."

"Maybe they weren't for me."

"They had your name on the box," he said. "They were outside the door when I came home. They're beautiful. I put them in water. And Viola left a message. She needs a new mophead and Spic and Span for next week."

He sounded sweet, like a little boy who only wanted to do right and be approved of — nothing to do with the stormy young man of last night. "And Bob called a couple of times. He said to call him at his office before five, without fail. And that's all, lady, from your friendly neighborhood messenger service. Get something good for supper. I'm starving. Don't forget Pepsi."

I found another dime and called Bob, but there was a busy signal. When I came out of the booth I realized that if I turned left and walked right through the line-up of cops I would be behind the stanchions and could make my way around them to the truck from the opposite end. I stopped at one point, making a show of looking lost, counting on my clothes and age and general straight look to make it convincing, and asked a neat little officer who seemed to be in charge if it were possible to get a cab anywhere in the vicinity. He

said he didn't think so and suggested that if I were going into
Manhattan I ought to use the subway before the rally broke
up. "It may get a little crowded," he said with an odd smile.
He looked more like a bank teller than a cop. He seemed to
be persuaded that I had gotten into the area of the rally by
mistake and he allowed me to circle the cops on foot, the cops
on horses and the reserve men in buses. The back of the truck
had another shoulder to shoulder line of red headbands. I told
my story over and over and it was moved along until Mary
appeared.

"The leaflets," she said. "Have you got the leaflets?"

I said, "I'm sorry. I had so much trouble with the car, it's a
wonder I remembered where the rally was."

She made an angry, impatient gesture. She had lost her chic
look. Her make-up was studded with city soot, her hair was
wildly blown about, her fake eyelashes looked insane, her
smart clothes had slipped and slid about on her so that they
looked like the phony rags of the rest of the demonstrators,
and she seemed exhausted and drawn out to a screeching point
of tension.

There was a tremendous roar from the crowd and a gorgeous slim black girl in an elegant pantsuit began to speak
from the mike on the truck. Mary had been halfway off the
truck, coming to me, but she clambered back. I yelled,
"Mary, Mary, I have to get home and I can't figure out how.
Please come with me."

She yelled something like "It's Yefrema," or some such
name. "After she speaks."

I couldn't make out what the speaker was saying except that
it was passionate and that she was gesturing toward the omi-
nously still and empty façade of the jail, and then her speech
seemed to be over. The crowd rhythmically chanted:

Nixon, Agnew,
Start shakin'
Today's pig
Is tomorrow's bacon.

That was a good beat too, but I wasn't happy anymore. I wasn't prepared to storm the jail, or to be arrested or beaten by a cop who thought I might be about to, or to see others beaten and arrested. I had been playing, but at least part of this crowd was for real, and whatever they had in mind was not for me to do. And I wanted Mary out of there.

Another speaker was at the mike, a slim, black man with a much stronger voice. But I couldn't hear him either, except for isolated end words, ". . . racist pig . . . fag judge . . . fascist fool . . ." The young guards didn't stop me from climbing on the truck after Mary. They even helped. I took Mary's face in my hands and made a still place between us. I said, "Please, let's go home." Her eyes swam toward recognition from a deep point of distraction. I couldn't believe it, but she said, "All right," and let me lead her off the truck and into the subway entrance, joining a straggling group of older people, leaving before the rally ended.

We met Stella Shaeffer on the subway platform and I put Mary and Stella in one cab when we got out on the Manhattan end and myself in another. I shoved a five-dollar bill into Stella's hand and told her to be sure to see Mary straight to the door. I picked up a steak and prepared macaroni in a package, some Pepsi, rolls and a chocolate cake for dessert. I had enough salad at home, and ice cream for the cake. The grocery bag was heavy and the separate pastry bags unwieldy, and struggling with the packages and the mailbox key and the elevator and front door, I felt too exasperated and exhausted to get through the evening. I wanted to go straight to bed.

But I felt better after dinner. I was doing the dishes and listening to the radio while the boys did their homework or pretended to. The news report in its garbled way mentioned trouble in the subway after the rally and I tried to catch the news on TV to see if they had anything on it, but it was too late. There was also mention of trouble in the jail. Prisoners had rioted and were holding guards hostage, until certain demands were met — speedier trials, lower bail, better conditions — but whether that had anything to do with the Panthers in the jail or with the rally wasn't said. By the next news report, the rioting had spread to jails in Manhattan and Brooklyn.

Terry came into the kitchen as I was returning from the incinerator room with the box the long-stemmed roses had come in. I was looking for a card and found one. In a round, girl's handwriting, it said, "As ever, Bob." His secretary? Or the girl at the florist shop? They should have noted, "Written and signed in his absence."

"Elliot's throwing up," Terry said.

I dashed out, hoping he had made it to the bathroom. Elliot was at the toilet bowl, retching convulsively. His eyes rolled at me, desperately. I held his head until he finished. I had no idea why except that my mother always had with me. Afterward I made him comfortable between the fresh sheets that Viola had put on the bed. His face was flushed but he looked contented against the clean white pillowcase. I took his temperature. It was 102. For his sick room, I brought him one of the roses cut down to fit a bud vase.

He said, "You're a wonderful mommie," as if he were about to cry.

I tapped him on the head. "What's the matter with you?

Getting sentimental because you're not feeling well? It's just a stomach upset."

I thought that he was laughing, but it was crying, his eyes squeezed shut and his mouth distended in a wide grin, his prominent teeth and gums exposed in an animal's grimace. I said, "Elliot, what's the matter, love?" and he flung himself at me, sobbing helplessly, burying his head in my body. When he stopped, he stayed as he was and with his face muffled, said, "I don't want you to give me away."

I said, "What are you talking about?"

"I don't want to be given away," he said again.

I shook him a little and said sharply, "Elliot, what in the world are you talking about?"

He looked up then. "Dad says he wants us and that you'll be glad to give us up."

I said, "Your dad is out of his everloving mind."

I must have seemed very angry, because he began to cry again. "Don't be mad at me."

To show him that I wasn't, I played cards with him, Casino and Go Fish, until he was sleepy. I went out and left a light for Paul to see by.

I rearranged the roses in a milk-glass pitcher while Terry stood by, riding me in a good-natured way for not approving of his choice of vase.

I said, "Elliot was all upset about being given away to Dad. What's that all about?"

Terry looked uncomfortable and Paul came in and began his open-mouthed fishy breathing. "Dad was talking to us," Terry said. "And Melody, too, about the future."

"Who's Melody?"

"That's not funny, Mom," he said. "They're getting married. I think she's great."

"Yeah," Paul said, "great," as if he didn't believe it.

I had forgotten Harry's Quaker girl. "He'll have to get a divorce first," I said. I was vibrating with rage, envy, depression, anxiety — I hardly knew what. Terry began to say something, but I cut him off. "Okay. Never mind," I said. "I get the picture." Paul watched me, with his old man's concern. I swept past them both into my own room.

Paul came after me. "I'm making something for you in shop, Mom. It's a surprise."

I said, "Not if you tell me about it."

"Not what it is," he said. "That's the surprise." His worried eyes spoke to me: *Don't be hurt, don't be sad.*

I went into my room and shut the door against them. They had siphoned off what they needed, my males, and were getting ready to clear off, one at a time or all in a bunch. Harry would glaze the operation with moral rightness. Terry would hang his pushing manliness on it. Paul would let me feel his pain, but he'd go anyway. Only Elliot would cling because he still needed the mysterious, powerful contact a little longer. Divine motherhood. How stupid it all was. Dumb-beast pregnancy, blind child rearing, ugly middle-aged meddling and messing around in their lives, and then — nothing, no feeling, just a pain in the ass to them in old age. Better to swim away from each other, now, while there was still time for me to salvage something of myself from that sea on which I had thrown myself as if it would bear me afloat forever and ever without effort on my part — a reward for having taken my proper place in life and no questions asked. Better to be alone, free to do what I wanted. But what did I want?

10 ———

I STAYED AT HOME with Elliot the next day, though I had
to go through an exhausting series of phone calls with Bob and
Joanna and Paula and Stella Shaeffer before it was satisfactor-
ily arranged. Stella brought Mary to my house first thing in
the morning. Mary accepted that because she thought it had
something to do with security. Stella's nephew had been
beaten in the subway and hospitalized with a mild concussion.
I kept thinking of him, clutching his head with delight the
day before. The cops had gone after kids with red headbands
or Lords in purple berets or Panthers in black ones. The trains
had been rerouted to run straight through to Times Square
without station stops and the cops were waiting for the kids
when the trains emptied. At least that was Stella's version of
Lulu's story. She called him by that unlikely name, though
Mary referred to him as Lou. He might easily have been doing
something illegal. The demonstrators had jumped turnstiles
and trashed whatever wasn't trash already in the subways and
out on the street. But the cops had beaten and not arrested
him, which Mary insisted would give the lawyers a legal
handle to get at the police. Mary explained all that rapidly
and with great excitement while the three of us had a second
cup of coffee. Then Stella left to meet her sister at a move-

ment lawyer's office and Mary settled back to wait out the day, under cover, until Stella returned with her report.

Entering into Mary's paranoid concept of the happenings cast a dreamlike quality over the day. Elliot was better, but listless, and Mary alternately boiled with energy and political talk, or sank into exhausted silences. She was sweet with Elliot and we played a lot of Go Fish with him, like idiots in an institution. I drifted through the day as I had drifted through most of my life, hooked up to other people's heartbeats, filling a great, internal emptiness with tidying and preparing meals and dishwashing until Stella came back for Mary, and first Terry and then Paul came home.

I spent the next two days with Mary at her house. They melted away in the same strange vapor, and when the kids left for the weekend and Saturday night rolled around I got ready for my date with Sadie's son as if I had been bewitched out of my will. Even when he materialized at the doorway, a real man — large, open-faced, clean, boyish, athletic, handsome — it was as if I were still held in the enchantment of Mary's visions and demons, as if I had mistakenly wandered into one of her dreams.

It was a good thing too, because if I had been in a normal state of mind I don't know how I would have managed. For two people who weren't making any real conversation, we were being wildly noisy. I knew he couldn't hear me no matter how loudly I spoke but I couldn't stop myself from getting louder and louder at each try. He, poor thing, didn't know what kind of noises he was making. If he pointed something out to me (on Broadway, a man and his wife, their baby strapped to the wife's back, all riding a motorbike together; on the expressway, the ice melting at the shores of the Hudson in the unexpected thaw), it was to chuckle, roar, exclaim, purr, point and choke in an explosive mixture that was more frightening than entertaining. It was a relief to get into the restaurant where we faced each other and I could mouth some nonsense while he read my lips. He obviously had money. The car was a big expensive one, the restaurant was a big expensive place with inferior food, and the ring on his pinky was a big expensive star sapphire. I decided to try to eat well, whatever else. I ordered drunken shrimp to start, and a broiled Maine lobster to keep me busy, and I urged him to start with an artichoke to keep him busy. I faced outward to the restaurant, acutely conscious of people watching us and turning their heads to see what all the strange noises meant. I told myself that they were tacky out-of-towners, nothing to worry about, but they worried me. I took to pantomiming and gesturing like a star of the silent screen and actually found myself selling him the artichoke by rubbing my stomach and smacking my lips.

In the middle of my lobster, decked out in that silly bib they supply, up to my wrists in butter sauce and shells, he commanded all my attention with a vivid description of his place at the shore. He carved a little house from the empty air between us with his incredibly expressive hands. He raised his fingers to his wide-open blue eyes, shaded their brightness from a more brilliant sun and gazed out into a glorious sea. He used his whole body to dive into the surf. He started an outboard motor and caught a fish. He built a fire in a fireplace. He basked in the sun. He ran with his dog along the shore, a big, long-haired dog who shook the water from his fur in great, spreading arcs of spray. He invited me to join him in these pleasures, in admiring the sea life, the pebbles, the shells, the wild roses that grew down to the shore. He pressed them upon me to show me their fragrance and warned me of their thorns. He urged me to pick wild berries and smacked his lips and rubbed his stomach, giving my idiom back to me, as he offered them up with heavy sweet cream. He assured me that the little house was tight against the wild sea storms. The performance was more than a marvel of communication: I responded as if he had created a work of art right there at the lobster-littered table. He finished with a burst of demonic laughter. If I had let myself go I think I would have applauded.

When he spoke again, I had more trouble following him, but he was on much more difficult ground, dealing with matters that couldn't be turned into simple pictures. Sometimes I lost him, and for some moments when I was sure that I understood his intent, I couldn't say how he had made his meaning plain, and couldn't entirely believe that he meant what I thought I was hearing.

He told me the story of his deafness, after I had finished my lobster and he his rib roast, and we were having coffee and brandy. He spoke of his wonderful mother, responsible for this wonderful son. He showed me his success, his business, his money, and told me of someone, a relative or partner or assistant he had trained to use sign language. He took my hand in his to show me how simple it was to learn, and shaped my fingers into a sign. His hand conveyed a dry, warm, wholesome love. I thought of crisp autumn leaves. He spoke of life, normal life, and of how he insisted on it. Therefore, he didn't need to spend his entire life among the deaf, did he? He brought the question into his eyes with great urgency.

I shrugged, but he pointed to his lips and then to me to say in words what I thought. I mouthed, "Of course not."

He was still and thoughtful for a long moment. When he began again he showed me the hospital, his mother in one bed and Mary in another and himself handing me the chocolates. He pantomimed love at first sight, seriously, but with a comic edge, as if to allow himself an exit if he were met with ridicule. And then, in a burst of confidence, gave me his age, thirty-five, counting it out on his fingers, told me that it was time that he married and had children, two, again on his fingers, and that it was me he wanted to do all this with.

I told him that I was married, but he seemed to know all about that. Mary must have told his mother that I was separated from Harry. Copying him, I held up my hands, the fingers outstretched, palms toward him, and throwing in an extra year and some, showed him my palms four times, mouthing, "Too old for you. Too old." And I wobbled three fingers at him, over and over, to stand for my three troublesome children. But he knew about them too and waved it away as of no consequence and then gathered them toward him as belonging to him, becoming part of what was his and joining the five fingers of his hand as the family of five we would eventually have. For a second, I thought, I'm misunderstanding all this. It can't be. Our waiter hovered about constantly, too fascinated to go very far off. I asked for more coffee to give him something to do. Again, Sadie's son made a dumb show of his love at first sight — one expressive hand, perfectly manicured, the star sapphire catching the light and tossing it off like a promise, extended toward me, then, the ring winking, his index finger to his right eye, then the palm of his hand over his heart, held still while he waited for the open love in his open blue eyes to be returned or rejected.

I didn't know what to do. I excused myself and went to the ladies' room, taking my bag and my fur-lined coat from the back of my chair, using my things as a protection against the walk through the length of the restaurant. People studied me with open curiosity as I went by and turned to look back at my strange companion, as if his being deaf made us both also blind. The ladies' room was wildly sumptuous, all done in red and pink. The individual cubicles were large L-shaped rooms with a toilet and washbasin and around the bend a make-up table and a little pink velvet-covered chair. On the table, a pink Princess phone, a red pen attached to the table by a golden chain, postcards of the restaurant, tissues, small pink cloth towels. I couldn't bear to go on with the evening. Maybe I could just stay in the ladies' room and write postcards to my friends. I could write one to him, give it to a waiter to deliver and run away from a painful scene. I would say that I had called home and that one of my kids had gotten sick. No, I had already told him they were with their father for the weekend. I would just write, "Please forgive me. I went home." What difference did it make what I did? I wouldn't ever see him again, anyway. I took a postcard and the red pen and wrote: "Dear . . ." I didn't know his name. Dear Sadie's Son? No name. Lots of notes were written that way. I took another card to begin again, but I was struck with the ugliness of what I was doing. I tore up the cards and freshened my make-up and accused my pleasant face of being unfeeling and cruel. But what I was feeling was fear, not hardness, and not fear of causing Sadie's son pain, but fear of my refusal bringing on his anger. Retouching my lips, in that idiotic pink and red fancy ladies' john, I had a terrific insight into myself. That I wasn't yielding and feminine and giving and all that crap with men because of my generous, womanly nature, but because I was scared to be straight with them. I was terrified of men's displeasure. From my father, and the strap he brandished more than he actually used to scare us into obedience, right down to Terry and his moods, and Elliot and his tears. I went back into the big room with its turning heads with my heart pounding.

Sadie's son was waiting for me, armored for rejection, but not pitifully and not menacingly. I felt foolish, casting myself as a heroine in a Victorian novel, but I was determined not to rob his proposal of a dignified response.

"You honor me," I said, "by putting your faith in me." He lit up with hope and I rushed on. "I could never live up to such expectations," I mouthed, "but in any case, I love somebody else. I'm sorry. And I thank you." Then I said that I would like to go home.

He was subdued on the way home, but not petulant or nasty, as some are at any kind of refusal. His depression came with a strong surface and a firm understructure. He knew this ground well and had been here before. He didn't get out of the car when we arrived at the apartment house. I rested my hand for a second on his solid shoulder — my apology — and went up to the apartment alone.

I watched television for a while, but it was some boring film about a slave revolt in Greece or Rome, and I found myself thinking of other things. Of how I was with men. I turned the TV off and tried to bring my ideas together the way Mary would. Had it all started with my father, in the classic way? My mother was very frightened of him and should have been. When he was angry with her, he hit her; when he was disappointed in himself, he hit her; when he was humiliated by his harsh world, he hit her. It was standard practice in his generation, brought over intact from the old country, along with his hopes for a good life. I could hear the *thwack* of the blows, my mother's miserable, self-indulgent crying and moaning that followed. Was I exaggerating? Had it happened once or twice and I remembered these isolated scenes as everyday events? My father was dead before I was nine, in everybody else's memory a sweet, good man who tried to do his best for his wife and two daughters. In mine, a terrifying threat. There was a Sunday when I was sick, left alone with him while Mama and my sister went to church. I was set up in a temporary bed on two upholstered chairs in the dining room to keep the infection out of the bed my sister and I shared, and my father was poring over his stamp collection at the table in the center. He left the table, and holding his body in an evil crouch, crossed in front of my bed, not glancing in my direction. He took a big knife from a drawer and moved back toward me in that evil crouch. His face and hands were as dark as the leather he worked in the shoe factory. His crumpled clothes and gaping fly hid an unfamiliar and dangerous body. This stranger locked up with me while I was weak and helpless surely meant to kill me. But he crossed before me without looking at me, as he had before. I pretended to shut my eyes but I watched him through the slits of my eyelids. He sat down at the table, took an orange from the bowl and with the broad kitchen knife peeled an unbroken length of bright skin which re-formed into the shape of the fruit as it dropped on the table. The smell of the orange penetrated the room.

Harry slapped me once early in our marriage, in the middle of a fight that I couldn't now remember anything about — except the slap. I ran to my bed and cried as Mama used to, but this ended differently, with Harry in my bed in a transport of hot, guilty, victor's sex. Maybe that was how Mama and Papa ended up too. I never fought with Harry in that way again. If you decide to stay, instead of walking out and closing the door, then you have to put a face on being chastised as if you were a child, a child's cunning face. Was that right? Wasn't it my business to shape my character? Why was I blaming my nature on men? On Papa, of all people, who had exercised as little power in the world as a tomcat on a back fence.

I didn't sleep much that night. I fell into a frenzy of thinking about the way I had lived my life, as if I were an onion, stuck in the ground, commanded by nature to grow until I wilted and died. I fell asleep as it grew light and woke to the ringing of the telephone. I meant to answer it, but it stopped before I had roused myself enough to reach out for it. While I was having breakfast, the phone rang again, but this time I didn't answer intentionally. I didn't want to talk to anybody — not to any of the singles, unmarried or widowed or divorced women, their kids off to their fathers for the weekend — not to anybody connected with Mary — not to any men on the loose from their regulars, hunting a fill-in for an empty day. It rang half a dozen times during that long day I spent thinking, working at it to hysterical exhaustion, as if I were digging myself out of a sandpit with my bare nails, getting nowhere. I let it ring until late in the day and the kids had not yet returned, when I thought it might be a call from them or from Harry about them, so I answered it.

It was Bob. "I've been trying to reach you all day," he said. "You did it. She's agreed to go in. I set it up for eleven, tomorrow morning."

I hardly knew what he was talking about and had to make an effort to push myself outward.

He said, "What's the matter? You sound funny," responding to the deadness in my voice, and remembering that we were supposed to be having a "relationship," he put on a tender, intimate tone. "Are you all right, baby?"

I said, "But Mary and I never even spoke again about her going into the hospital. You must have done it. Or Matt."

"Matt!" he said. "The best thing about getting her into a

hospital is that it will get her away from Matt. They'll end by killing each other."

"I can't go there now," I said. "I can't."

"That's all right," he said. "Joanna and I were with her all evening. I gave Mary a sedative. She'll spend a quiet night."

"What time is it?"

"After eight," he said. "Are you okay?"

"What do you want me to do?" I said.

"Get to Mary first thing in the morning and have her at the hospital just before eleven. Dr. Stone. They'll be expecting her at the private pavilion and Dr. Stone will be in charge."

"Does Matt know?"

"Of course Matt knows. He's at the apartment with her. He's promised to keep things quiet overnight no matter what she does. But she won't do anything. She let me give her a sedative by injection. Just get there as early as you can."

The next time the phone rang it was Harry with a long complicated tale which added up to his not being able to get the kids back that night.

I needed the kids to help me come back to myself, or out of myself, whichever it was. I was afraid to be without them. I said, "Can't you get them home somehow, even if they get here very late?"

He said, "I'll bring them in tomorrow. What's so terrible about that? Anyway, I'm sorry."

I said, "I don't like them to miss school."

He blew up. "Damn it, you can get away with murder. But I can't get away with a thing. You keep those boys on the most disorganized schedule day in and day out throughout the entire year, but one little slip-up by me and you're screaming your head off. This is a very important phase of my life, it just so happens, and I'm through putting myself into contortions for you. You're just going to take it or leave it." And he hung up.

I took it, crying against the kitchen wall phone, adding to my other troubles the worry that Harry might get mad enough to slough us all off, especially now when he was marrying someone else. If I wanted his help, I'd have to take his crap. I put away the food I had begun to prepare for supper and went straight to bed and slept like a laborer.

In the morning, life seemed barely possible again. I almost collided into Matt, coming out of their apartment as I was going in. Matt looked sullen, half-sleepy, well dressed, sensationally handsome. He rested one hand loosely on Mark's head. Mark looked up at me with his steady, thoughtful gaze.

I said, "I've missed you, Matt."

He returned me a strained smile. "She agreed to go," he whispered.

"I know. Bob told me."

"Good luck," he said. "She's wild. I don't envy you."

Mark shifted his serious gaze to his father, turning under his hand to do so.

I said, "Don't worry. It will be all right."

He said, "I have to run. I'll see you tonight," and he hurried Mark off.

Deciding to yield had cost Mary something. She was sitting in a chair, staring ahead, her fine face free of make-up, her eyes places of concentrated pain. Nothing had been done in the apartment, and I spent the time, after I had forced a cup of coffee on Mary, straightening beds, doing breakfast dishes, changing the baby and helping Bella dress. Stella Shaeffer arrived at ten, with a shopping bag of food and new information on her nephew. He had been released from the hospital in good shape and he didn't want any lawyers messing in.

" 'I don't accept the authority of the courts,' he keeps yelling at me and his mother, 'so why should I run to them to see if I can get them on my side?' Did you ever hear of such nonsense? You strike a blow wherever you can strike a blow. That's my philosophy. One small step in the right direction is better than a giant step in the wrong direction. Am I right? But you can't do anything with the kids today. They know everything." Stella said everything good-naturedly, as if she were proud of Lulu's arrogance.

When it was time to go, I thought Stella was going to wreck everything with a mawkish scene. Bella too insisted on a trembling farewell kiss, and we stood, bunched up in the narrow hallway, Stella with the baby in one arm and Bella clinging to the other, while Mary dramatically whispered, "I'm trusting you, Mama Shaeffer, with my baby and with my mother. I'm trusting you." Stella looked at me meaningfully, practically twirling her finger at her temple to indicate Mary's mental state. I led Mary out, and she let me, as if she were a lump, and stood by quietly while we waited for an empty cab. We rode in a silence that was better than any attempt to be light-hearted. Mary stared out of the window, but her eyes were turned inward. Just before the hospital attendant took her away from me, Mary tucked a folded paper in my hand. I read it in the corridor, near the elevators. There was a typed message:

He is a man whose tenderness frightens him as a manifestation of unmanliness, especially tenderness toward women. He becomes cruel — most of all to those women who seduce him into feeling love.

I read the note again when I got home, and then I put it away with the others she had written. In a burst of neatness, I hunted up a heavy envelope and placed all Mary's outpourings in it, and even typed on a white gummed label in caps, MARY'S PAPERS, and pasted it on. Then I tied its string and put the envelope on my night table.

I called Bob, but he was out on an emergency. I left a message with his secretary that Mrs. Schwartz had been admitted, that I had been told to leave and to check for visiting hours, and that I was at home if he wanted to speak with me.

Uneasy and restless, I tidied up the apartment. I had that feeling again of being hooked up to another's pulse. I ate some crackers and cheese and a cup of tea for lunch. I called Bob again. His girl said that he had been trying to get in touch with me.

"I've been here, right here," I said.

She said, "May I have your number again?"

I gave it to her and told her I'd be waiting for the call. Idly, I wandered into Terry's room and began to pick things up. His clothing closet was a tangle of sweaters, slacks, half-dirty shirts and socks hanging out of shoes and boots. How had he managed all this mess since Viola's last day? I started sorting things for the laundry and the cleaner, emptying pockets meanwhile. More crumpled bills turned up than could be accounted for by Terry's allowance. I ended going through all his things systematically and when I counted through the findings, there were forty-three dollars in single bills and a ten-dollar bill. I thought of gambling, selling pot or worse, some kind of extortion of his schoolmates, stealing. What? And why?

Bob called then, sadly disappointed in me. "For God's sake, what do you think you're doing? You don't seem to understand what's needed. Why didn't you stay with her?"

"They didn't allow it."

"You insist. You insist."

"What happened?"

"Nothing. Fortunately, I got there soon after you left and I quieted her. And Dr. Stone saw her too."

"You mean she knows? He's told her?"

"No, no. Not yet. She has to be prepared first."

"What do you want me to do, go back?"

"Absolutely. Grab a cab and stay right there until you hear from me again."

I took the car from the garage, counting on hospital parking. There was parking space, but it was metered. I put a dime in and walked two blocks north to a candy store where I bought a paper and wheedled a dollar's worth of dimes from the owner.

But I wasn't allowed to see Mary.

"I insist. I insist," I said. "Dr. Guerrero wants me with her. You can check it with him. Call his office."

The nurse was an officious, sullen young woman. "Mrs. Schwartz is *not* Dr. Guerrero's patient. She's Dr. Stone's patient. And she is not allowed visitors. I suggest that you get in touch with Mrs. Schwartz's doctor, Dr. Stone."

"I'll have Dr. Guerrero call you," I said, and went down the corridor to the phone booth. But all I got was Bob's answering service and they knew even less than his secretary had. They told me he could no longer be reached at his office but that they would get a message to him and that he would call me at the hospital. I stayed for hours, reading the papers, *Fortune, The New Yorker, Audubon, Life,* and running up and down to keep a violation off the meter, checking with the desk, feeling like a fool, but afraid to leave. I had the waiting room completely to myself, until visiting hours began and the floor came to life. I felt sick and glutted with the magazines.

It was a relief to watch real people. In a couple of hours, everybody left and the life of the floor died and sank into the dreary depression of night in an institution. Once again, I tried the desk. There was a new nurse in charge, distracted, rangy, informal, pleasant.

"You poor thing," she said. "They told me somebody was hanging around all day."

There wasn't any message from Bob and though she told it to me more pleasantly than the other nurse, it was still the same orders from Dr. Stone that were being repeated.

"Sorry. No visitors." She offered me part of a chocolate bar, which we ate together. "You couldn't really visit anyway, because she's under very heavy sedation. Why don't you go home? We'll take care of her."

I made one last try at the booth without success and then called the house to see if the boys were home. Terry answered. He said in a voice strangled with rage, "You haven't any right to come into my room that way. Search and destroy."

I said, "We'll talk about that later. I'm trying to reach Dr. Guerrero. Has he called?"

"He's been calling practically every five minutes. I'm supposed to tell you where to reach him." He gave me a number.

"Why couldn't he have told that to his answering service?"

"How should I know?" Terry said.

"I'll see you soon. I'm coming right home," I said, and started to hang up.

"Wait a minute. Wait a minute. We have to meet Dad and Melody at a restaurant at six-thirty. To meet her folks. The kids are getting dressed by themselves, but Elliot can't find a clean white shirt."

I tried to think if there were any in his drawer.

"Why does he need a white one? There must be some colored shirts in his drawer."

"Dad said white shirts. I keep trying to tell the idiot that Dad only meant a nice shirt, but you know how literal he is."

"I'll buy one on the way home," I said.

"We have to leave by six o'clock," he said.

I called the number Bob had given Terry. It was some kind of mobile health department tuberculosis unit and two voices answered the phone simultaneously, one saying in a Spanish Harlem accent, "Welcome to the people's liberated mobile health unit. Venceremos." I asked for Dr. Guerrero. There was some confusion between the two voices, but Bob came on the line. He was apparently speaking from the truck and I had difficulty hearing him. He apologized for the mix-up at the hospital and told me to go home. He sounded breathless and hysterically excited.

I said, "Are you all right?"

He said, "Never better. It's marvelous what's happened here. One of the most exciting things to happen in the public health field in years. I'll call you later, at home, sweetheart."

Because I was going against homecoming traffic, I got to my neighborhood pretty quickly. I parked the car in a garage near the house and I remembered to take the leaflets out of the back. I kept a couple for my folder and threw the rest in a trash basket. Then I bought Elliot's shirt.

Elliot grabbed the package as I walked in and Terry turned on me as if we had had no intervening conversation. "You haven't any right to go into my room like that."

"If you kept your room neat, I wouldn't have had any reason to go in," I said, helping Elliot remove the plastic packaging and pins. The shirt was badly creased, but it was too late to iron it.

"Bullshit," Terry said. "You went through all my pockets."
I said, "Would you like to explain where that money came from?"

"No, I wouldn't," he said.

"You're going to have to account for it," I said.

I was checking Paul out. There was something wrong with the way he looked, hopelessly crumpled and clownlike. It was his jacket-sweater on inside out. I pulled at it, to put it on right. He yanked away from me.

"It's inside out," I said.

"I'll do it. I'll do it. I'll do it myself," he said, looking from me to Terry in his worried way.

"You're the one who's going to have to account for coming into my room searching my pockets," Terry was yelling at me. "I have a right to privacy. To my privacy."

"You're setting your brothers a fine example," I said, before I could stop myself.

"Fuck it," Terry said. "I'm not taking them. You just figure out yourself how they're getting to that restaurant."

He picked up his outer coat and slammed out of the apartment.

Elliot burst into tears. "How am I going to meet Daddy?" I had bought too large a shirt for him and his thin neck wobbled in the starched ring of the collar. The cuffs hung out of the sleeves of his red blazer like ruffles.

Paul showed his fear as he tried to cover it up. "I can take him, Mom. We'll be okay."

I said, "Don't be silly," sharply, and Paul's eyes filled with tears. "I'll take you," I said. "Where are you meeting your father?"

There was a second of wild blankness.

Elliot wailed, "We're lost. We're lost."

Paul was making a desperate effort not to dissolve in real tears. "Dad only told Terry. I don't know where we're supposed to meet him. And he's probably already there, waiting."

The intercom buzzed furiously. I picked up the earphone and Terry's voice, cracked by the old wires, said, "Well, where are they? I'm waiting for them."

I wiped the tears from Elliot's face, zipped up his half-open fly and kissed him. Paul kissed my cheek. I gave him a five-dollar bill.

"Tell Terry to take a cab," I said, and thought I'd better give him a couple of more dollars and ran down the hall after them with five singles. "Don't lose the money in the elevator," I said.

That struck us all as excruciatingly funny. We laughed helplessly. "Have a good time," I yelled after them, and sent them into more convulsions, though I had meant it seriously.

The phone was ringing in the apartment. It was Stella Shaeffer, wanting to know when I was coming to relieve her with the children and Bella.

"I didn't know that I was supposed to," I said.

"But, darling, you know I always have a meeting at night. It's very rare that I shouldn't have a meeting. And where's supper for my Sam? He's a very understanding man, but understanding enough to broil his own lamb chop, he isn't."

I said, "Isn't Matt coming home?"

"That's what I was expecting," she said. "Exactly. But he called a few minutes ago that he had to stay in the office for an important conference."

I begged Stella to try to get someone else. "If you can't, call me, and I'll come. Try Joanna."

I hadn't finished creaming my face before she was back on the phone.

"Darling, I haven't accomplished a thing," she said. "Everybody seems to be somewhere else. I couldn't even reach them where they're supposed to be."

Stella left as soon as I arrived and I was busy for the next hour or so, bathing the baby and supervising Mark's bath and getting supper for Bella and Mark, then giving the baby her final feeding and settling Bella into bed. I took the edge off my own hunger by nibbling and ended up having no dinner at all. Shtrudel followed me about humbly, and after everything else was done, Mark helped me put together Shtrudel's dinner and we were watching him slop it down when Matt let himself in with his key. Matt's greeting was friendly and smooth, denying that we had ever gone through a bad scene. He gave Mark a little gadget he had bought — a round disk of a clown's face that you shook to put the clown's eyes in place — and Mark ran off to show it to Bella. Alone in the kitchen, Matt said to me, "What happened? I've been waiting for you in the lobby of your building for over an hour."

I said, "Was I expecting you?"

He said, "I told you this morning."

I felt a little crazy. "Haven't we been out of touch? Didn't we have a fight?"

He laughed. "Call that a fight? Hang around the champ. You'll learn."

"Are you the champ?"

"I'm not sure," he said. "Mary and I have a stiff competition going. But I'm a lot better than you, so watch out."

He shut the swinging door to the kitchen and pulled me to him, leaning against the door. In the embrace and kiss which he imposed on my body, there was an element of coldness and angry passion that depressed me. Mark interrupted, pounding on the other side of the door, yelling, "Daddy, Daddy, I got his eyes in." Matt led him off to his room to admire his new prowess, and to read him a book and tuck him into bed, while I finished tidying the kitchen. I was glad, I guessed, that Matt could act as if nothing had happened. Then why did it feel so bad — my gladness?

By the time I got into the living room, Matt was finishing tidying it. Either he and Mary shared the same mania for perfect neatness or she had imposed it on him. He had put the room to rights exactly as Mary would have.

He asked me if I would like some coffee.

"Instant?"

"What else?"

I refused but offered to make him some. He wanted to do it for himself. I waited in the living room. The little apartment smelt of restlessness and unhappiness. From Bella's room, I heard her radio, playing a loud insistent movement of a Shostakovich symphony, and from the other bedroom I could hear Mark, talking to himself and thrashing about or jumping on his bed. Shtrudel couldn't find a spot for himself. He stood uncertainly in the foyer, apparently trying to make up his mind which member of the household to throw in his lot with. It was Mary he usually stuck close to. When Matt came back, he padded after him and stretched out at Matt's feet, his long nose flattened against the carpet, his forehead wrinkled, and his sad eyes casting piteous glances at Matt's unconcerned face. Matt settled himself in an armchair close to me, busy with coffee, cigarette, ashtray.

"Did you visit Mary?" I said.

"No visitors," he said. "Dr. Stone will tell her tonight."

There was a short silence between us and then he said, with animation, "I've been wanting to talk to you about that night." I thought that he had gone back to our fight and I was unprepared for what followed. "What did you think of Mary's plan?"

"Which plan?"

"The communities."

I said, "You mean as part of her illness?"

"Illness?" he said. "I mean as a project, as an idea."

I said, "You mean as a serious political project?"

"It isn't a political project," Matt said. "It's a brilliant blueprint for implementing the new life style. It's completely workable. It knocked me on my ass. It's a marvel."

I was bewildered by his response. "Bob thinks it's a manifestation of illness, of madness."

"Which is more proof of Bob's general stupidity."

"Don't you think she's ill? What about those other papers?" I said.

"The things she sticks in my pockets?"

"I get one or two in the mail every day," I said. "How about that cure for cancer paper? That scared me. Doesn't it scare you?"

He said that he hadn't seen that one. He was silent for a minute, staring at the linoleum tile so intently that Shtrudel decided something was wrong and jumped and licked at his face comfortingly. Matt yelled at him and slapped him down.

"Do you think she's as sick as Bob says — mentally, I mean?"

"Yes," I said.

"I can't really feel that," he said. "She's the same to me, only more so."

"Maybe that's all madness is. Too much more so."

"What's mad about her? For you?"

"She's obsessed," I said. But I wasn't going to detail that, since she was obsessed mostly with him and I wasn't about to repeat my mistake and discuss Mary's view of his crimes. "Maybe it will all stop. Maybe after tonight, after he tells her, it will all go away."

"Okay," he said. "Let's say she is. Even if she is. What's crazy about her design for the communities? Bob is cutting her down if he thinks that. The communities are a great concept. We might even get one going before she dies. It would be doing something for her. A fulfillment. I'd work on that, if politics are kept out of it. Bob is diminishing her if he writes it all off as madness."

I said, "Are you serious?"

He put his empty coffee cup on the floor. Shtrudel gently tipped it over and licked the sugar from the bottom. Matt edged him away with the tip of his shoe.

"Why wouldn't I be serious?" he said angrily. "Wouldn't you work on it? Wouldn't Bob?"

"I don't think so," I said.

"Bob wouldn't work on it, implement it in any way? Does Mary know that?"

"I don't think so," I said.

"He's a political asshole," Matt said.

We heard Bella shuffling down the hall. She came toward us in her quivering helplessness, trailing a bathrobe she had been unable to put on but had crazily attached to her side, her white hair wildly disheveled, her blue eyes fired with a fierce will to make herself clear. She steadied herself against the doorjamb, and with her shaking hands extended in their endless dance, and her face working horribly, she sprayed and spat out a sentence. "Matt is right."

I led her back to bed and we kept our voices low then. Matt brought some papers from his study and asked me to sit at the kitchen table and go over the documents with him. He had supplemented Mary's long paper with a statistical chart and a sketch of buildings, his notes made at the reading, and another copy of the plan for the communities, one of the ones I had Xeroxed, which he had heavily annotated. Except about his own work I had never seen him like this. But he had barely organized the papers into the order he wanted when the phone rang.

Matt said, "Mary?" in a voice tight with terror, and then, rallying to a hollow heartiness, "Hey, baby, how are you?" but hardly giving her time to respond, talking a streak of nothings. "Everything here is great. Great shape. Jean's got everything in shape. The kids are asleep, Bella's in bed, everything's in order. Any messages for the crew? They didn't have that paperback you wanted, but I put in a special for it, and it should be in in a couple of days. And Andy Martin is here on a three-week lecture tour, then back to London and back here again in the summer. We had lunch before he left for the West Coast. He sends his love. All kinds of news from him. I'll have to tell you. But how are you, baby?"

He listened for a while, his eyes in a constant defensive movement against terror, as if blinking might blot it all out. "Carcinoma? Is that what the doctor said?" His voice was false and he had begun to sweat. "I really don't know what that is."

Another pause. "They say it's a form of cancer?" he said with polite noninterest, in the tone of one modestly trying not to judge in an area where he is ignorant. He was whitefaced and covered with sweat. "Would I really be allowed to visit you now?" and then in a rush of forced energy and enthusiasm, "Wait a minute, let me see what I can arrange with Jean." He put his hand over the mouthpiece but he didn't ask me anything. He stared ahead, breathing hard, and wiped his sleeve across his forehead. Drops of sweat dangled in his eyebrows.

I said, "Don't worry about me. I'll stay."

He turned away before he spoke again, his voice heavy with fake regret. "Baby, I'm so sorry. Jean absolutely has to go on home now. Her kids are alone. I'll get to you first thing tomorrow. Maybe I can look in on my way to work, if they'll allow that. Though I do have an early morning conference."

I touched his sleeve. He jogged me off. "I did *not* lie to you," he said. He sounded angry and agitated but genuine for the first time in the conversation. "Eventually everything with you ends up beating on me. I did not lie to you. I told you what the doctors told me. I don't know anything about this stuff. Am I responsible if they have a difference of opinion?"

Another pause. "Why ask me these questions? I'm not a doctor. I just don't know, baby, I don't know. I only know what the doctors tell me." He wiped his sleeve across his forehead. Automatically, I rolled some paper toweling off the rack and handed it to him. He took it and used it but he turned his back on me squarely. "I swear as far as I know you're perfect. Dr. Altman told me that. Said just what he said to you. 'She's clean.' Why should you believe this one? Stop worrying. You're all right. You're going to be all right. Especially if you follow up on the treatment. You'll be all right."

He was holding the phone away from his ear and I heard Mary's uncontrollable sobbing. I tried to get to the phone, but the sobbing stopped with a click. Matt listened for an instant, then he put the phone down.

I said, "Matt! What have you done! Why did you do that?"

He said, "Shut up, Jean. Just shut up."

He put his head against the sleeve of his upper arm, I thought to wipe the sweat again, but raising both arms around his head as if he were setting up a guard against a beating, he sobbed into his shelter.

11 ———

ALMOST IMMEDIATELY, while Matt was still crying and I sat by, suppressing my rage at him until rage became a depression so pervasive it lost all impact and turned solid as water, the hospital called to say that Mary had dressed and left and that they would not be responsible for her condition. And then she was at the door, letting herself in with her key, as I was putting away the papers that Matt had gathered and while we were still trying to think what to do. She cut away from us and went directly down the hallway to the bedroom. I followed, jabbering about the kids and Bella. She barely glanced at me, but I saw enough to catch the narrowed, dramatic un-Mary look of her eyes, strangely black, perhaps from the sedation.

She said, "Please get out. I don't want you here."

I said, "I was just leaving, anyway. Be good, Mary."

She turned fierce. "Are *you* good? Are *you* good?"

I said, "I guess I'm not much good, but I didn't mean anything. It's just a phrase."

She pushed me out. Her long slim fingers on my arm stung my flesh. Matt avoided my eyes. I didn't want to look at him either. I left as quickly as I could. I tried to call Bob from the street telephone, but it was out of order. I didn't try again, even after I got home. The hospital would let him know, and I had no relish for repeating to him Matt's part in our failure.

Broadway was a collective madhouse. Toward Columbus Avenue, a gang had built a fire of the junk in the trash basket. And waiting for a bus or cab, watching the live stream of ridiculous and pitiful humanity going by, I had to run and duck to avoid a whirling dervish of a man, spitting and spinning in some incomprehensible inner uncontrollable ecstasy. For the split seconds in which he stopped and rested, he was an ordinary man in good tweed pants and a handsome jacket. Then the whirling and spitting and wild ecstasy would begin again. Others avoided him automatically, scarcely looking at him. I took a cab, because it came first. I had met up with the driver before. He had a set spiel for his nuttiness. He was looking for a housekeeper companion, some nice little woman like me to live rent free in his luxury two-bedroom, two-bath apartment in Flatbush.

"No monkey business," he said, leering unreassuringly in the rearview mirror. "I need a little light housekeeping and someone to be with my two wolfhounds when I go on a little fishing trip. All the conveniences. Dishwasher, washing machines down the hall. Garbage disposal unit. Air-conditioned. I even have a portable hair dryer."

I said, as I had the other times, that I didn't know a soul who would fit the bill.

When he gave me the singles and change from the five-dollar bill I had used to pay and I thrust them in my coat pocket, an explanation clicked into place for the money I had found in Terry's room. Terry had taken it from my pockets. The ten-dollar bill was the clue. I remembered stuffing the bill in my jacket the night of the meeting when Sadie's friend had donated it. I was always sticking money in my pockets —

any time I shopped or ran down for a paper. He had been helping himself. It was a relief, in a way, because it was the least terrifying of the crimes I had been dreaming up for him. But I didn't face Terry with my theory when the kids got home, very late that night.

Terry was morose, Elliot was exhausted to a point of tears and Paul was inexpressibly happy about a tiny transistor radio Melody's folks had given him. Terry's present was a Swiss army knife and Elliot's an elaborate pencil case, to his disgust. I helped Elliot into bed. Harry had written excuse notes for for them and Terry came around glumly distributing one for each. I tried chatting with Terry about the evening he had spent, just because I wanted to know, but he was unresponsive, and in the morning it was snowing, and we all left the house together in a hassle about wearing boots and hats and gloves, which I only half won.

When I reached Mary's, Bella seemed to be alone, behind a locked door, helpless to convey anything or to open the door. I tried to reach Bob again but it was too early for his secretary to be in. I bought a *Times* and walked a few blocks through the quieting, white snow to a luncheonette and ordered coffee and an English muffin. The paper had news of the seizure of the mobile health unit, with a picture of Bob and a profile story on him inside. It made him sound terrific, though the facts were somewhat wrong. Bob wasn't Puerto Rican. He was Cuban, and Jewish on his mother's side. The profile presented Bob as the mastermind and organizer of the action, but the news story put its emphasis on a coalition of hospital workers and professionals, who wanted two Jewish doctors out and Bob in as head of both pediatrics and gynecology. I didn't know that Bob was qualified to hold either one, no less both. The Jewish doctors had already begun yelling anti-

Semitism and apparently nobody had thought to say that Bob was at least half Jewish.

When I finished eating I tried Bob's office again. This time the line was busy. I called Mary's. The phone rang for a long time and as I was about to hang up, Mary said, "Hello," breathlessly, as if she had just come in.

I said, "Are you all right?"

She was displeased to hear my voice. "I'm fine," she said, and nothing more.

I said, "I'm right nearby. Shall I come up? I'd like to."

She said, "I'd rather you didn't."

I didn't know what to do, so I went home. It was snowing steadily, hushing and coating with peace the dreadful city — the garbagy streets and unrelenting traffic, the crazy telephone lines, straggly trees and broken pavements. Even the people all turned beautiful, coated with white crystals, full of happy wonder. The city was a party at first.

By late afternoon, everything had pretty much come to a stop, except for the snow which kept falling, steadily, quietly, beautifully. I had managed to reach Bob's office, but not Bob. I kept the radio on, for storm news and because there were bulletins on the hospital uproar from time to time. An ambiguous statement from the Jewish university that governed the city hospital. In their view, there were no ethnic issues involved. A forthright statement from the Puerto Rican group. They wanted change, now. They wanted a doctor in charge with respect for the poor, for blacks and Puerto Ricans. They had gotten their shit together — with a beep in the middle — and weren't going to stand by while a policy of genocide was conducted against third world women and children. That time was past. There was some negotiation in process for the peaceful return of the TB mobile unit. Meanwhile it would remain in the barrio. The police commissioner issued a statement: "Contrary to some published reports, I want to make it clear that there were no guns employed in the seizure of the truck." The mayor said he was concentrating on getting the city out from under a bad snowstorm that hadn't even ended yet.

After the kids came home from school, Paul and I shopped at the supermarket two blocks away. We bundled up in scarves, heavy gloves, boots, and Paul dug up a woolen face mask he had been given as a Christmas present two winters earlier and had never used. His old man's eyes peered out of the slits like a stranger's. Underneath the deep snow, there was ice. I bought the fixings for Chinese pepper steak and lots of extras, as if we might be snowed in. We carried it home gingerly.

Bob had called while I was out. He was back at the truck and had told Terry that I should call him there. But the operator couldn't get through. The line had been disconnected or the storm had put it out. But he called again, while I was preparing the marinade for the meat. Even without my information, he blamed Matt for our failure.

"If he had supported her, it definitely would have worked. Maybe it will anyway. Dr. Stone says she needs time now to absorb it."

I asked him who had told him about Matt.

He said, "Mary told me that she begged Matt to come to the hospital so that she could talk to him and that he flatly refused, that he pleaded some business engagement. That's all she talks about. How Matt failed her."

"Well," I said, "that wasn't it exactly. But it doesn't matter."

He said, "She's very bitter against you too. For some reason. Not too clear to me."

I said, "Well."

He said briskly, "I guess we call it quits, baby. It was a
good try and I'm grateful to you." He was preoccupied with
other matters and wanted to put this behind him.

I said, "You're really where the action is, aren't you?"

He said, "What an experience. It's heavy, man, it's heavy.
I should have been here all those years. With my own
people. It's tremendous."

I said, "I have your car up here in a garage."

He said, "Don't worry about it. We'll get it all straightened
out." And then as if he were pushing himself to go through a
form he no longer believed in, "You might give it another try
with Mary tomorrow. See if you can stand by. In any case,
we'll continue your pay for two more weeks. It's only fair."

I said, "How does she sound to you?"

"She sounds better. Very calm and self-contained. I think
maybe she'll be all right." Someone interrupted him, and his
voice was tense with excitement when he came back to me. "I
have to run, sweetheart. I'll be in touch."

The six o'clock TV news showed him in a crazy knit hat,
shoveling snow to keep a clear path to the truck, surrounded
by cheering Latins, reporters, cameras, police. Into the mike
he said, "Doctors have lost sight of their obligations to the
people, if they ever had such sights. If I can serve my people
by shoveling snow, I'll shovel snow, and that's all I care to say
at the moment." He raised his fist, dropped the shovel and
ducked out of view to pick it up. The top of the knit hat
wobbled across the bottom of the screen.

Terry turned to another station with what looked like disgust on his face. He asked if he could take his dinner into his room, and I permitted that. After the kids were asleep, I braved his room. Terry was flung across his bed, a sprawling spread of despair, on his face a look of almost animated vacancy. The money was piled on the desk where I had left it, along with his dinner dishes and his school books.

I plunged in. "Do you want to tell me about the money now?"

He shut his eyes tight and compressed his lips. The silence was ugly. I said, "Shall I tell you where I think you got it?"

He said, "God damn it, do I have to keep my door latched all the time? For just a little fucking privacy?"

I said, "Do you want me not to care about where the money came from? Do you want me not to give a damn about you? Is that it? Because I can't do that yet, but if that's what you really want, I can try to learn."

He turned on his stomach and hid his face. Again, silence. I put my hand on his shoulder. "Terry," I said, as if I were waking him for school. "Terry."

He jumped up, sat down in his desk, crossed his legs. Superimposed on my not quite thirteen-year-old son, I saw the tall, graceful man he would become. He said, "Okay, supersleuth. What's your heavy theory?" He took from his drawer, with an elaborate show of bravado, a pack of cigarettes, and a lighter which he used with some difficulty. "As long as we're having the big moment of truth," he said between great puffs of smoke, "you may as well know that I happen to have quite a smoking habit."

I said, "If you don't want me to care about your killing yourself with cancer, I'll learn to do that too."

"Wow," he said. "That's some approach you've developed. If it wasn't such sickening bullshit, it would really get me."

He coughed, and rubbed his eyes. The room was comically full of smoke, but I didn't laugh. He flicked ashes in a miniature falling storm into a dime store ashtray he pulled out of the desk drawer. A label was stuck to its side. He must have bought the whole outfit that day; none of it had been in the desk the day before. He couldn't manage his anger and grown-up arrogance and the new habit all at once, because he savagely squashed the cigarette in the tray. I felt heartbroken for him, amused at him, at the same moment that I wanted to smash him over the head.

I worked my arm up and down through the smoke to thin it out. "I think you took the money from me," I said.

He looked frightened, but said brashly, like a little boy, "So what are you going to do about it?"

"I'd like to talk about it. About why you took it."

He searched my face, still frightened. "I have to have two hundred dollars. That will be just enough."

"For what?"

"You'll see," he said, "when I do it."

"But you don't think I'm going to let you keep it? Or let you go on taking more money from me?"

"Then I'll get it some other way," he said, between his teeth. He put his fingers to his mouth and worked at biting the skin around his nails. One long leg jumped convulsively, the knee jogging as if it were an exposed nerve.

"Terry," I said, "will you tell me just one thing? If all this has anything to do with drugs?"

He walked up and down the small room, flinging his arms wildly. "Listen, everybody smokes pot. It's no big deal. It's no problem. You don't need two hundred dollars to smoke pot. So stop being an asshole and showing your ignorance. God, don't you know anything?"

I said, "I'm not going to allow you to talk to me that way." I felt ashamed that I had never smoked pot. For a moment I was going to offer my apology — that I had nothing against pot, it was just that I hated to take smoke into my lungs. But he had begun to rail again.

"There you go. There it is. You don't give a fuck about me. And neither does Dad. You just want me to shine. That's all that interests you. Well, I'm through shining. I'm through being that good little boy you loved so much. I'm through doing things the way you like me to so you can rave to your friends about me."

"My friends!" I said.

"I don't care what you tell your friends about me. I'm not going through with that bar mitzvah, I don't care if Dad kills me. It would be a relief if he kills me. Or you can turn me over to the cops about the money. It would be a relief to go to jail. Anything would be a relief. Put me in a lunatic asylum. Whatever you decide. But I'm not going through with that bar mitzvah. I don't care what happens." He collapsed on the floor, his back against his bed, his flushed face hanging between his knees. He lifted his head, his eyes full of tears. "And I'm not getting any more haircuts either. You can tell that to Dad."

I said, "What does the money have to do with any of this?"

He put his head down again and spoke to his knees. "I've got friends going to Vermont. They're going to let me come. They don't know my age. They think I'm fifteen. They're older. One's eighteen. They're going to help me build a shack and live there. I can live on that money for years up there. You live different there — chop your own wood, grow your own food. You've got to help me, Mom. Because I'll go crazy. I'm going crazy. I told you. I warned you the other time."

I wanted to pull him toward me and comfort him with my body as I had when he was a child, but that time was over. We could only be to each other what any two human beings might be, close or far, quick or dull, yielding or hard.

I said, "If you don't want to be bar mitzvahed, it doesn't matter to me. I'll help you about that with Dad. If he cares about it. I don't know whether he does or not." And then, to lighten things, "You'll be doing yourself out of a load of gifts."

But he took me seriously. "I thought about that. Because just going through with it, and selling all that stuff would easily come to two hundred dollars. Maybe way over. What do you think?" But before I could answer, he had begun to fling his arms around again. "But that's just the thing I can't do. The bar mitzvah. I can't. I can't. And don't you think Dad doesn't mind. Don't you believe it. He minds. I bet after he marries Melody he'll make her become Jewish just like he made you. If that isn't hypocrisy, what is? What does he marry people for if he doesn't like what they are? Why doesn't he marry a real Jew if he thinks it's so important to be one?"

"I don't think Quakers can become Jews," I said. "Anyway, he wouldn't. He didn't make me. I did it to please him. Because of his family."

I did it so that he would marry me. I saw us sitting around the poolside at the home of one of his Great Neck friends. I was wearing a sensational white bathing suit and I had a great, dark tan. I was sipping a bloody mary and answering his friend's laughing question.

"What would you do for the man you love?"

"Anything to make him happy."

"Anything?" Laughing and leering.

"Anything."

"For Harry?"

"For Harry."

"Would you become a Jew?"

"Of course." Was that all? I had been imagining monstrous perversions. "I'd love to become a Jew for Harry."

And in the pool later, Harry so pleased that he came as close as he ever had to expressive love. "My beautiful, dumb shiksa cunt," he whispered, floating me around the pool in his arms, his eyes shining with generosity, "why don't we get married?"

"If that isn't hypocrisy," Terry was yelling, "what is? Who cares about being Jewish? Who cares about being Scandinavian or Eskimo? You people are sick, I tell you. You've got to be sick to go around changing yourself into something you aren't."

"Okay, okay," I said. "Calm down."

"I'm starving," was his remarkable response. "Let's go to the kitchen."

I watched him prepare one of his mad snacks — orange juice, peanut butter and cucumber sandwich on pumpernickel, Pepsi and pretzels. He popped a fistful of raisins into his mouth while fixing the sandwich. He had become totally loosened and flooded me with talk for over an hour. He filled me in on his new older friends who were planning the Vermont trek. He told me about surviving in the wilderness, curing illnesses with herbs, baking bread and living on vegetables, earning money by tapping sugar maples, and for no traceable reason went into a long digression on the history of the Soviet Union's participation in the world chess championship tournaments. He ended in a state of genial cheerfulness.

I thought we were good enough friends at the moment to warn him that it was dangerous for a thirteen-year-old to pick up and go off on his own. "Even if you weren't doing anything wrong yourself, if something happened to one of your friends or there was a drug bust and the cops picked you all up, you'd be in the worst trouble because of your age. I mean if you really don't want your parents to have anything to say about you."

He nodded and burst out with, "Mom, is there some way I could get my eyelashes removed? I can't live with these eyelashes."

I said I didn't think so. "Not without damaging your eyes."

I thought he was thinking that over, but what he said was, "If I went, would you put the cops on me, Mom?"

"Never," I said. "Never."

"Not even to get me back?"

"Not for any reason. I'd count on you to come back. It's not all that bad between us, is it, that you'd never come back?"

He said, "You don't know me. I could do anything."

"I don't believe that," I said. "You're not like that. You don't like to hurt people."

"Yes, I do," he said, gloomy again. "I like to beat people at chess, and get better marks, and be elected to everything. It's disgusting to want those things. A person like that could do anything."

The downstairs bell rang, insistently, in its cracked, hoarse voice. Terry lifted the intercom and asked, "Who is it?" It was eleven-thirty.

"It's Matt," the intercom said. "Matt Schwartz. Is Jean there?"

"Sure, Matt," Terry said. "She's here. Come up." He kept

his finger on the buzzer for a long time. The intercom was off the hook and we could hear the buzzer sounding below. "What's he coming so late for?" Terry said. "I'm going into my room. I don't want to see him." He kissed me awkwardly on the forehead. "Good night, Mom. You're okay sometimes. You really are." He rushed back in, before Matt reached the upstairs door. "Hey, have you looked out of the window? It's crazy. Everything's all covered with snow. The cars look like pound cakes."

Matt was a frightening sight, hatless, his eyes cutting black holes through a crystal coat of snow clinging to his hair and eyebrows. His coat was wrapped around him queerly. He had no boots. The snow melted around his shoes. I put some newspapers down and helped him out of his wet clothing. There was a bandage and a splint on his left hand, with the whole arm supported by a clean cream-colored muslin sling. He was shaking with the cold. I got him into bed at once, covered him and brought him brandy. He refused it.

"I'm nauseous," he said. He looked greenish blue and suffused with self-pity.

"How about tea? You need something hot."

He nodded and shut his eyes. His teeth chattered, so that I could hear it.

Terry came out of his room. "What's the matter with him?"

I said, "I don't know. He seems to have been in an accident. I'm making him some tea, then I'll ask him."

Terry said, "Why did he come here?" and then, "Can I do anything?"

I said, "I don't think so."

He said, "Call me if you need me. I'm not sleepy anyway." On my way back with the tea, he opened his door again.

"The schools are shut down tomorrow," he whispered, very excited. "The radio said. I'll turn off the alarm in the kids' room."

I fed Matt a spoonful of tea every few seconds. He sipped like a child, drawing the liquid between his lips in noisy intakes of breath. When it was almost gone, he said, "It's not sweet enough." I made him another cup, sweeter. Matt's trembling and teeth-chattering had stopped, but he was lying back with his eyes closed while slow tears rolled down the sides of his cheeks. I dried his face with a tissue and kissed him on the wet spots, and on his eyelids and mouth. The physical tenderness I had held back from Terry poured out for Matt. It seemed to do him some good. He stopped crying and I fed him the rest of the tea.

"If you're in pain," I said, "I have codeine."

"Aspirin," he said. "Mix it with a little water and sugar. That's the way my mother always does it."

I did as he asked and after he took it, he yawned a huge convulsive yawn. His lids dropped over his eyes. He seemed about to fall asleep.

"What happened?" I said. "Is your arm broken?"

He shook his head. "Only two fingers."

"Did you fall?" And why wasn't he at home?

He shook his head again, yawned and shuddered and closed his eyes. He was asleep.

I padded about the room, getting my nightgown and robe and slippers. Terry came out of his room when I went to the linen closet. He helped me make up the living room couch, furnishing a stream of storm information as we worked. When I went into the bedroom for a blanket, Matt woke.

"I have to pee," he said.

Did he mean that I should bring him a bedpan, or help him

to the bathroom? He got up himself, favoring his arm with a show of self-pity. Back in bed, he looked comfortable and awake.

"Don't you even want to know what happened?" he said, irritably.

"I've been trying not to bother you," I said. I sat down to hear but he was silent, staring ahead, looking inward at pictures he seemed to be finding inconceivable. He sighed and shuddered again.

As if he were a child, I tried to get him started. "Were you in an accident?"

"She locked me out," he said. "She changed the lock. Had a locksmith in. Mrs. Friend told me. Across the hall, after she broke my fingers."

"Who?" I said.

"You know that I could have lost those two fingers? And it could have been my right hand, my drawing hand?"

I didn't want to hear any more. I was riddled with guilt, and fear for Mary.

"I couldn't figure out what was happening when my key wouldn't work. Nobody answered the bell either, though I could hear Shtrudel barking. It was early — because of the storm. The office closed down soon after lunch. I kept trying and trying the key, like an idiot. Then I went to the corner and called the house. Mary answered, very cool, and told me that we were through, that my clothing and effects — effects! — would be sent to me wherever I said, et cetera, et cetera. At least it started cool. It ended in a horrible fight. I asked if you were with her. She went off on one of her demented sex things. Accused us of, I don't even know what she said, what she was accusing us of, some kind of perverted affair."

I laughed. "You say that as if it were an outrage."

He looked at me blankly. Ironies were not for him at the moment. "You haven't heard her," he said. "I tried to reach Bob, but I couldn't. He's all involved in that hospital fracas. I didn't want Mama or Papa Shaeffer. I called Joanna. She responded as if I were reporting an out-of-order telephone, but she promised to call Mary and to call me back. When she did, she told me that Mary sounded very good, better than she had in a long time, that she seemed very sure of herself and of what she was doing and that I shouldn't worry about her. That's what I got out of Joanna."

I said, "Why didn't you call me, Matt?"

"You couldn't have done anything. She wouldn't talk to you. I needed somebody who could get to her. I was terrified for the kids and for Bella too. I saw her wiping them all out in one sweep, cutting their throats and then turning the gas on herself." He sat up. "Help me light a cigarette."

I did, while he made a big thing of having only one useful hand. I said, "Can't you light a cigarette with one hand?" and added, "In case I'm not around, I mean."

"Do you want to hear?" he said, very irritated.

I nodded. "What about your fingers? How did that happen."

"That was later. I called Dr. Stone and hung around in that freezing, stinking telephone booth until he was traced from here to hell and back and finally got on the phone. He said that she needed time to absorb the shock of the truth he had told her. He suggested that I get a hotel room and let things ride for the moment. And that's what I got out of Dr. Stone." He put his cigarette out for me to take away, though it was only partly smoked. "I had twenty dollars on me, no hat, no rubbers or boots, no luggage, no credit cards because it goes against her fucking philosophy. I called Joanna back and told her she had to help me get into the house to get my check book and some clothing, and that if Mary wouldn't let me in then she would have to go in and get them for me. I got a little ugly about it. She agreed to meet me in an hour at the delicatessen. I called Mary again to tell her what I was arranging, but as soon as she heard my voice she hung up. I began to feel crazy, to see things, Mary dead, blood all over. I can't explain. It was horrible. I've never felt that way in my life.

"So I waited for Joanna. I hung around on the block, watching the house, freezing, everything burning inside. After a while Robin Mayhew came out with Shtrudel."

"Who's that?"

"You know her."

"I don't think so."

"Sure you do. You've seen her at our place lots of times. Very pretty. Southern girl. A little younger than Mary. A nut. She went to school with Mary. She keeps turning up all over. She's done a little of everything, Martha Graham, film, aesthetic realism, revolution, East Village, wild drug experiments. You remember, I think you were at the house the night her parents called from Texas to see if Mary could get her back from Leary's Milbrook commune."

"I don't remember her," I said.

"You know her," he said. "I'm sure you do."

"It doesn't matter," I said. "Go on with your story."

He flung his head back. "Why are you being so difficult?"

I said, "I'm upset. Forgive me."

It gentled him and he went on. "Robin Mayhew in the picture wasn't very reassuring. I went up to her and told her to tell Mary that I would be sending Joanna in to get my clothing and check book and to ask her what the hell was going on inside. She's very little, and she's looking up at me with her poncho fringe wiggling around, coming on with her big brown eyes and making with the wet, open mouth and the drawling vowels. She wouldn't have minded if I fucked her right on the snow in the middle of the street. Mary's idea of a friend in need."

He came to a dead stop. "I'm terribly nauseous," he said. "Don't you have anything for nausea?"

I searched the medicine cabinet, trying to figure out what was what from the prescription labels. I brought back water and a capsule of what I thought might be Thorazine or Librium. Terry's door was closed, but his light was on and the radio going. I tiptoed past, like a criminal.

Matt took the capsule and lay back, quiet and staring. "She's shitting all over my life," he said. "She's shitting on me, on everything I tried to do to be good, to live a good life. She's turning everything to garbage." He closed his eyes. "It's unbearable," he said. He opened them. "I keep seeing her face. How she looked. When I tried to force my way in. And I could feel how I looked. I could feel my lips frozen over my teeth in a snarl, like hers. And I didn't know which one of us was screaming. When she closed the door on my fingers and kept it closed. She kept it closed."

"I don't understand," I said. "Why did you try to force your way in?"

"I didn't plan to," he said. "I meant to wait in the hallway for Joanna. But Mrs. Friend came out of her apartment, all nosy helpfulness, what was the trouble, she had noticed the locksmith changing the lock, maybe we were robbed? Or something else might be the matter? I felt shamed. And then furious — furious. It was *my* apartment, *my* furniture, my kids, my wife and *my dog*, God damn it, I was the one who brought him from the pet shop vomiting all over me in the cab. I was going in to grab Shtrudel. I held the door as Joanna came out, held on with my hand. I should have put my foot against it. I should have braced my foot and my whole body against it. I should have protected my hand."

"Oh poor Matt," I said. "Don't talk about it anymore. Don't think about it."

He said, "I can't stop. I can't stop."

I said, "We'll watch television. It will put you to sleep."

"It's a good thing I didn't get him," Matt said. "What would I have done with him?"

I wheeled the portable from the living room and tuned in on a Katherine Hepburn–Spencer Tracy movie. She was a lady athlete with an emotional problem and he was her unintellectual but wise and great-hearted trainer. I had seen it many times. I pulled Matt's head against my shoulder and held his free hand in mine while we watched in a kind of stupor. He was asleep by the first commercial. I slipped myself out from under him. He turned freely on the side of the arm he had been favoring. I covered him, put out the light and went into the living room. Terry's light and radio were still on. I meant to fall right to sleep, but for a long time I lay awake, unable to control what my mind was seeing — Mary's face, snarling — Matt, pinned to the door, screaming — Terry, on a black country highway, alone, shivering.

12 ———

I WOKE to Terry shaking my shoulder gently and whispering, "Mom. Mom."

He frightened me and I spoke sharply. "What's the matter now? Put the light on if you want to talk." I needed to see his face, but I couldn't see anything in the sudden flood of light.

"I didn't know what to do," he said, "when I heard it."

"Haven't you been asleep at all?" I scolded automatically. "You're going to have to stop this staying up so late."

"Mom," he said, "come on. This is important."

"What is it? Will you please tell me? I'm exhausted."

He drew in his breath and said in a rush, "Bob died of a heart attack. The radio announced it. He was dead by the time he reached the hospital."

I felt an intense surprise as sharp as a pain.

Terry said, "Are you all right, Mom? I didn't know what to do when I heard it. I'm sorry. I should have let you sleep."

"No," I said. "You did the right thing."

He came close and patted my back rhythmically, lightly, as if I were a baby and he were burping me. "It's scary, isn't it?" he said. "One minute he's on the phone and the next thing you know he's dead. What's going on with your friends anyway — they're all dying like flies."

"Who?"

"Mary's dying. I know she is, whatever you say. And Matt broke his arm. And that woman who jumped out of the tenth floor window."

"She wasn't my friend. I just knew her to say hello to in the building."

"Anyway," he said. "Wow. It's weird."

"It's not his arm," I said. "Matt broke two fingers."

"Are you going to wake him up and tell him?"

I thought about that. He had been so exhausted. Better to let him sleep. And who knew how Matt would take the news? I didn't want to have to deal with him at that moment.

"We'll tell him in the morning," I said. "What time is it?"

"After two," he said.

I shocked him by announcing that I was going to take a pill and go back to sleep.

"How can you sleep?" he said.

I took a Librium and got back into bed. I asked Terry to put off the lamp. He stood near my couch, bathed in the milky muted glow of the streetlight shining through the still falling snow, patting my hand with the same light, rhythmic touch, as if I were a delicate infant.

I said, "Thanks, Terry. You'd better get some sleep, too."

He said, "Don't worry about me, Mom."

I felt an obligation to react, but I was only sleepy, terribly, terribly sleepy, almost sick with it. Even so, I didn't sleep at once. I closed my eyes and saw visions I couldn't control. Bob in the knit hat, falling through the milky snow, talking, talking, talking. The two of us in his office pull-out bed, our bodies and his breathless babbling, babbling. In a panic, I saw everybody learning about us, his death revealing all the secrets of his life. I got up to find and destroy the card that had come with the roses. I touched the black flowers in the filmy light. Their odor sickened me. I threw the card in the garbage and crept back into the uncomforting hollow of the couch.

I woke to an extraordinary hush and that strange new light. Snow was still falling. I padded about in my slippers and robe, to the kitchen where I put up a pot of coffee and made some frozen orange juice, and then to the bathroom. I looked old in the medicine cabinet mirror. At last, something had gotten through to my stupid face. My eyes were vacant inside, and creased with tiredness around the lids. I slipped into pants and a top, but I didn't bother with make-up.

In an unnatural inner and outer quiet, I poured coffee for myself and carried it to the living room window that overlooked Broadway. The street was changed as if by an enchantment. In a darling landscape, the little trees in the island had become exquisite dancers holding their difficult positions with perfect grace. A car crowned with icing went by soundlessly. Then a bright red truck, completely free of snow. Like an illustration for a children's book, each little storefront held a planting of a man shoveling snow, and each apartment house its super clearing a narrow path. In front of the supermarket, the snow clearers were young blacks. They had put aside their shovels and were fooling around, pummeling each other with snowballs, shrieking in high, shrill voices of big birds. The hushed atmosphere blotted up the sounds, sucking them away into its enormous silence. Two men were digging a car out of the snow. They had cleared the front wheels and the windshield and back window. One man was wearing a red plaid hunter's jacket and the other wore an army officer's long coat with a fur collar. I decided they were father and son. The older man in the red jacket opened the door of the car, sat with his booted feet hanging out, and tried to start the motor.

There was a weak, sick sound — then it died. Both men went around the back. The young man had long, bushy hair and he had set a sailor's knitted cap at the top of the heap, like a wobbly crown. Every few minutes, he would jump up and down and slap himself. An elderly woman, her head wrapped in a purple woolen stole, crept carefully down a narrow, cleared path, carrying a bright orange plastic shopping bag. She slid slightly, caught herself, stopped in her tracks, looked about helplessly, went on more slowly. I watched until she made it safely into the little grocery on the corner.

I could hear Matt moving around in the bedroom, walking to the bathroom. The phone rang. It's begun, I thought, this terrible day.

It was Paula White. "Brace yourself," she said. "Sit down."

"I know," I said.

"I have shocking news," she said, not listening.

"I know," I said.

"You know about Bob? Who told you?"

"I heard it on the radio. I mean my son did."

"He's dead," she said. "He died in the ambulance."

"I know," I said.

"Joanna's in little pieces," she said. "And listen. The Mary, adventure is into something awful. Mary and Matt. Wild."

"I know," I said.

"It makes you think, doesn't it, like how desperate life is — dangerous, scary? Because you think you're safe just because you're you but all the time you could just drop off, like Bob, into a hole, or your whole life be wrecked like Mary's."

I said, "Is there something I can do?"

"Wait a minute." When she returned, she whispered, "Joanna's like numb, poor baby." And then, louder, "We have to get together. We have to establish some kind of collective leadership with Bob gone. About Mary and all that. Stella Shaeffer's coming over too. And we're thinking about a memorial meeting, planning one, so we need to rap about all that."

"I'm no good at those things," I said.

"Wait a minute," she said, and when she came back she spoke decisively. "Joanna said we have to settle about Mary, about what to do. She says you have to come. So come."

"Are you at her place?"

"No, mine. Bring some fresh rolls and Danish from Babka's. To go with the coffee."

Matt walked into the kitchen a different man from the night before. He had discarded the sling and held his left arm normally.

"How are you?" I said.

He bounced his head up and down, winked, made an O with the thumb and forefinger of his good hand. He looked wonderfully young and fresh. "You look like a little girl without make-up," he said, and held me to his side with one arm, planting a kiss full on my lips, a friendly, clean, toothpaste, shaving-cream kiss. He gestured toward the phone. "Who was on your tail so early in the morning? Aren't you having enough trouble with me?"

"Paula," I said. "I'll tell you all about it after you've had coffee." I poured orange juice, split an English muffin and put it in the toaster, and started the coffee heating. He was at the phone, dialing. I asked him what he was doing.

"I want to reach Bob before he gets all tied up again today," he said.

So I told him that Bob was dead before he had his coffee after all. He sat down as if he had been struck. Then he asked me a lot of questions, over and over, that I couldn't answer because I didn't know any details, though Matt would repeat the question as if I were deliberately withholding information. He stopped finally and put his face in his right hand and rubbed it hard, the way he does when he's upset. I thought he had begun to cry, but it was laughter, theatrical, articulated, ha, ha, ha's, a cascade of them.

"Eat your breakfast" I said, putting it all before him.

He did, and asked for another muffin and a second cup of coffee. "He did it right," he said. "That's the way to die, on your feet, in action, no trouble to anybody. It's the best thing he's ever done. Promise to shoot me if I make a mess of it, the way Mary is."

"Glad to oblige," I said.

He said, "Does Mary know?"

"I don't know," I said. "They might have told her. Or she could have heard it on the radio, and it will be in the papers. Did you mean we should try to keep it from her?"

He shrugged. "What's the difference?"

"Do you think I should call her?"

"God knows." He stood up. "That really threw me," he said, "for a minute. I couldn't grasp it. But you know what I was really sitting here thinking? I was thinking, I'm going to live. I'm going to live. No matter what."

I nodded. I understood that.

Elliot ran into the kitchen in his pajamas, yelling, "Did you see it outside? Did you see it, Mom?" but stopped shyly when he saw Matt.

Matt said, "Hi," almost as shyly, and rubbed Elliot's mussed hair with his good hand. "Let's check it out," he said, and led Elliot off to the living room window. I listened and watched, conscious of the effort each was making — Matt to be winning, and Elliot not to disgrace himself before his mother's friend in that mysterious way that such things happened to him before he even knew they were happening and then were too late to stop. I wondered how they might do together. If it should come to pass. If Matt meant to marry me and live happily ever after after Mary died. And how would he and I do? And I? Wouldn't it be just going on in the same old way of all the marriages I knew, worrying about my looks to hold him from the younger competition, checking myself against his moods, meeting his needs, mixing aspirin with sugar and water the way his mother did, pretending to be more Yiddish than he was if that was what he wanted, or the simple Polish girl from the sticks, if he liked that image better, swinging with whatever scene was current, dressing up or down, playing smart or dumb, aping his taste and conversational gambits and political positions and shoptalk, or making a thing of being free and independent, going against his grain obtrusively, gratingly, wittily, but clearly at his expense — though in either case it came back to the same obsession with him, whether I would be buttering his balls or cutting them off — wearing long skirts and fussy sleeves while I served borscht or schav or pirozhki made from his mother's recipes at little dinners for friends who might push his career up a notch or two, managing beautifully his two and my three and the sixth child we would have to have — ours — even if it killed me — me, Jean, almost forty and with no more idea of what I was or what I wanted than a length of material lying on a shelf waiting to be cut and sewn into a Brooks Brothers suit.

But if he married me, Terry and Paul and Elliot and I would be safer, wouldn't we? And I would stop being eaten by the loneliness that made me do anything, take up with anybody, let anything happen. Maybe even some of that marvel that had existed at the beginning between me and Matt would come back and stay, forever and ever, until we were old and good friends and still sharing morning toothpaste shaving-soap kisses. Maybe there wasn't any more than that, and all the thrashing around for happiness was senseless expectation with no possible chance of delivery. Lasting happiness, that is. Forever and ever crap. I left them at the window, Matt deep in an explanation of the internal combustion engine and how it had altered the world of transportation, and Elliot so far out of his depth he was drowning, and I went to my make-up table to put my face on.

I left Matt at home with the kids, warning them not to wear him out, and enjoyed struggling through the snow to the bakery to pick up fresh rolls and jelly doughnuts and cocktail Danish pastries, seeing myself as a heroine in a Russian novel in my long black fur-lined coat and a tall white fur hat. Under the hat was a head full of nonsense. That's all I have in my head. Especially when I'm happy, I need trash to make it complete, a song or a piece of a movie to copy. Matt said, as I left the apartment for Paula's, "I don't know how I'd get through any of this without you," driving my depression away in one breath and blowing me up so that I floated through the streets. That's what comes of an entire education of trash.

And at Paula's the hours went by in a pleasant, drifting nothingness of cozy, gentle melancholy. We sat around in her cluttered apartment, drinking coffee, keeping the fire going in the fireplace, talking in subdued tones about what a wonderful person Bob had been, and Mary was, and about disasters like subway strikes and power blackouts and garbage strikes and school strikes and assassinations and sudden deaths and snow-storms and hurricanes and subway accidents and breakdowns and muggings and suicides and long wasting illnesses. Joanna did a lot of the talking, carrying on about general disasters as a substitute for the grief she couldn't discuss. She followed me to the bathroom and while I sat on the toilet she sobbed out the news that she and Bob were going to be married in the spring if his mother had continued to feel better. "Of course I can't say anything in front of Jennifer. Now, just when I could have begun to be happy out in the open like everybody else, I've lost everything." I couldn't help feeling she didn't believe it herself, but I didn't show her that. I just said, "I'm so sorry, Joanna," and tried to fix her hair a little.

Jennifer Torrington cried as much as Joanna, but Jennifer managed it beautifully — looking dignified and stoically tragic in her American bone-structured face and glorious red hair. Joanna was red eyed and swollen and blubbery. Jennifer came with a long-faced young girl. She had small, darting eyes and thin, very long straight brown hair pushed behind her tiny ears. She was Jennifer's daughter by her first marriage, in from some other life for a bit. After she said hello to everybody around the room, she didn't say another word until it was time to say good-bye.

Paula whispered to me, while we were in the kitchen preparing scrambled eggs with frozen chives and chicken livers and making another pot of coffee, that Jennifer had been Bob's mistress "since he was a child, practically. It's fantastic. She's over sixty, and she held on to him through everything. You remember, about five years ago, he was going to marry little Janey? She's a dancer — about twenty-two then — very thin, with an incredible long neck?"

I didn't remember.

"Well, anyway," Paula said. "Torrington visited her, just like a TV soap and told her that she had been Bob's mistress since he was seventeen and that she had no intention of ever letting go and that neither did he and that anybody who married him better understand that in advance. Janey practically went into shock and ran crying to Mama. Very old-fashioned little girl. You know her Mama, the musician? Big, loud woman, lots of black, black hair."

I didn't think so.

"Well, anyway, she called the whole thing off and whisked Janey off to Europe. Janey quit dancing, married that nice tall English boy who's living with my friend's sister since they were divorced."

I said, "Did Bob sleep with *everybody?*"

Paula shrugged and opened her palms — and her eyes — to me helplessly. "Well, *sleep* — screw, you mean? We're not talking about screw, we're talking about life-long relationships. I think he had like four serious relationships all going along at the same time, though I can really only document two and I guess I don't have to spell those out for you."

Stella Shaeffer came in to help and asked what we were talking about.

"Bob," Paula said.

Stella went into her litany. "He died in the struggle. He always thought about the good of the people, he always had time and patience no matter in how much of a rush he was. He loved people. He had a great love for people. Such human beings you don't find in this world every day."

After lunch, I couldn't stand any more talk and busied myself cleaning up odd corners of Paula's messy house. She kept the kind of place where even the soap was dirty. I carpet swept the Orientals. I washed the sugar bowl. I scrubbed the washbasin in the big bathroom and polished the brass faucets, shaped like geese. When I came out, I could hear that Joanna had erupted into a hysterical fit. She was sobbing uncontrollably, crying, "There's nothing left to look forward to. There's nothing to hope for." Paula was urging a tranquilizer on her and I stood by, trying to help. Stella Shaeffer was on the phone with Sam, getting some kind of report about Mary via Robin who was still at the house with her, apparently; and straight from the hysterics, Joanna went into a deep gossipy conversation about Robin. Jennifer stared out at her own grief, ignoring us. Paula tried to pull things together and make some constructive plans about Mary and about the memorial for Bob, but all talk wandered back into gosssip.

"Robin said," Stella began, "that when Mary heard about Bob, she laughed and ran around the room and threw herself on the floor."

Joanna said, "I wouldn't believe a word that girl said."

"If Mary did that," Stella said, "I say it's from the mental illness. *If* she did it."

"I doubt that very much," Joanna said.

"You doubt it's from the illness?" Stella said incredulously.

"I doubt that she did it," Joanna said. "I don't trust anything Robin says."

"By Robin, everything is beautiful," Stella said. "Everything is beautiful. I asked her about Bella, whether she was very broken up about Bob. You want to hear an answer? 'Bella's beautiful. That hair. Wow, it's beautiful.' If you ask me, she's not the proper person to be in charge there."

"The problem is," Paula said, "how do we get you back in?"

"Me?" I said, since she was looking at me.

Stella turned to me, "What does Mary have against you that suddenly she's so bitter?"

"Mary's obsessed with sex," Joanna said, before I could speak. "She thinks every man she meets is after her, and that every woman Matt meets is after him. I'll never understand why she thinks Matt is so attractive. He's a baby. He's not my idea of a man."

"Mary thinks Jean is having an affair with Matt," Paula said. I glanced at her, but she turned her head.

"She told *me* I was having an affair with him," Joanna said, "when I called to tell her that Matt had two fingers broken, after they took care of him at the emergency room."

"It's the mental illness," Stella said. "That's not my Mary. It's her illness talking."

" 'Where is he?' she kept asking me. 'What are you covering up?' " Joanna was a bad mimic at any time, but her attempt at that moment to reproduce Mary, a mad Mary, made me want to hit her. "As if I knew. Or cared, for that matter. God, what a night! Even the weather . . ." and she cried again.

"We've got to get organized," Paula said, and took a pad and pencil from the drawer of a hand-painted secretary and plumped herself down on the floor, using the coffee table as her desk. The gouache of herself looked up at her through the glass. We were drinking coffee in the big living room where we had had the meeting. I thought of Matt, squeezed behind the table that night, and of his coldness toward me. A sharp breeze jiggled the surface of my happiness.

"First we'll discuss Mary." Paula wrote on her pad in large, carefully formed letters, Mary. "And under Mary, there's Jean. Then Bob, and under that" — she was writing as she spoke — "memorial meeting." She paused, looked around at us with her open-eyed glance in which for me there always seemed to be something false pushing to be revealed.

"Funeral?" Jennifer Torrington said softly. Her eyes welled with tears.

"The family says no funeral," Paula said. "I've been in

touch with them. They're having a private funeral. I think maybe the mother's insisting on a religious Jewish service."

"That's not true," Joanna said hotly.

"Well, anyway," Paula said.

"You're always saying things like that," Joanna said. "Without cause. They just want a private funeral."

"Well, anyway, they have no objection to a memorial meeting. His mother's a little weird, you'll certainly admit that, Joanna, I hope, but we can work it out, I'm sure. So under memorial meeting, there's the hall, a people list, a speaker list" — she was writing throughout — "no guns — we're not letting any Lords or Panthers in with guns — and wow, I almost forgot obits, we've got to get on the phone about obits." She rose, her jumpsuit slithering around her hips. She seemed to be naked underneath. "You go ahead on the Mary-Jean discussion while I call some of the papers. They may as well get the facts straight."

I told them immediately, "Look, there's nothing to discuss. I'll do anything I can, but the arrangement, you know, all that stuff, I want that ended."

"That's not for you to say," Joanna said. "It's a collective decision. It has to be ended collectively."

I shook my head, silently but firmly.

Stella said, "Jean, darling, it's very important to learn to work with others."

Jennifer said, "We can't tell her to do something she doesn't want to."

"We don't even know what we want her to do yet," Joanna said. "It's a very undisciplined way to work. It should be discussed."

Cora and Chuck Spalding's arrival interrupted the discussion. They brought fresh, cold air in with them, and their good feeling at having walked fifteen blocks through the snow, but they quickly subdued themselves when they settled down in the living room, and everybody said once again what she had been saying all day, and cried again. I went into the kitchen to make more coffee. I could hear Paula on the phone in the entrance foyer.

"Cuban on his father's side, Jewish on his mother's. No, no, not Puerto Rican at all. No, no, born right here in New York City — Washington Heights. No wife or children, never married. He leaves only his mother and father. The vital fact to include is that he died in the barrio fighting for his people. In the very act of. Listen, Latinos are all the same people, you know. If you would just get the details right, and not worry about what I'm telling you. And, oh yes, that he was the kind of dedicated doctor who actually went to see his patients at home."

As soon as she finished with one, she'd dial another number and begin again. "You spell that G-u-e-r-r-e-r-o. Doctor Robert. Died in the very act of struggling for the right of the people in the barrio to have decent medical care. No, no, not a Puerto Rican. Not killed. Heart attack. Cuban on his father's side . . ."

She called the few big papers and then went on to local newspapers in New Jersey, Long Island and the other boroughs, and after them, the underground sheets.

Cora went to her and put a hand on her shoulder. "You'll wear yourself out," she said. "Can we help?"

Paula joined us, flopped herself on the floor, took up the pad and pencil again and started on the memorial. Jennifer Torrington drew names out of her head as if she were a computer — churches, meeting halls, speakers, people who would be very good at calling others. Chuck Spalding boomed discouragement in a bass accompaniment. Places were either too small or too big or would prove unavailable and people would certainly all prove disappointing. "You won't get a thing out of him," was his most frequent comment. But he got on the phone and started some of the calling. Cora listened. She was a beautiful listener, and I said as much to Paula on one of our trips to the kitchen to replenish the pastries.

"There's something lovely about her," I said. "Especially when she's listening. She really listens."

"Their son died. An only son. About a year ago." Paula was busy with a cheeseboard, fanning out crackers around a wedge of Brie. "Drugs. OD," and she whisked out.

I left soon after that. They already had a church meeting hall and a date set by that time.

When I kissed everybody good-bye, I felt best kissing Cora. Jennifer's daughter turned her cheek so far she presented me with an ear, as if head-on contact with me would have been foul. Cora kissed me on the lips and walked me to the door.

"Mary seems bad," she said. "Are you having a very rough time?"

"I'm not in that anymore," I said. "Like a job, I mean."

She listened, with her quiet indrawing eyes.

"I can't do anything for her," I said.

She nodded. "There are some things we can't do anything about," she said. "Don't grieve. You tried."

"I don't know what I did," I said. "I never should have gotten into it. I feel as if I did harm."

"I know," she said. "Short of saving her life, everything else is an insult."

"If they talk about me and Mary and the arrangement, will you tell them that? Because I'm not going on. There's nothing I can do for her."

She nodded and kissed me again and I left with the good feeling that I had found a friend.

The streets were no longer a party. The city was gripped by a desperately serious effort to get itself running again. The snow had stopped falling and the plows had come through, piling up immense blockades of instantly filthy snow, dotted with dog shit and garbage. I joined others, picking our way like refugees through narrow, slippery paths, and boarded a laboring, weaving, smelly bus that took forever to get me home through stricken streets, where a stunned population struggled to reclaim its territory — its city ground — brought to this amazing, gasping halt by a natural force. That power pleased me; I took a perverse satisfaction in it. We had been pushing and working at life like maniacs, and it was no more than we deserved to have been seized and shaken by a violence beyond us, to be belted with Bob's death and Mary's uncontrollable rage and a storm that stopped the whole city. It seemed right that they had all come together.

When I got into my own apartment, cold and tired, philosophy deserted me. Matt wasn't there. The kids didn't know where he had gone; only that he had left early in the day. And the boys had messed up the place so badly, particularly the kitchen, where they had been snacking all day, that it took me twenty minutes to tidy before I could even start supper. I wasn't very pleasant to them. And after supper, for all my talk, I couldn't keep myself from calling Mary.

Mary wouldn't speak to me, but Robin did. I think she thought I was Paula. She was hopelessly confused by the numbers and intimacy of Mary's friends. She stretched out

some preliminary nonsense until Mary went into the bathroom to bathe Mark and then told me in a conspiratorial
whisper that she had been talking to Matt and working things
out.

"How?" I said.

"We've figured out a way to get a doctor in, either tonight
or first thing in the morning."

"What will a doctor do?"

"I had this realization," she whispered, "that I really can't
handle it. You know. Like, she's beautiful and I'm not afraid
of her, but *for* her, you know? Like, I don't even know what.
What she might do. Like, anything. She smashed this big
mirror in her bedroom, with her fist, I didn't even know what
to put on it, though it wasn't as bad as it could have been. She
said she heard voices telling her to do it and people applauding
afterward, well, that's beautiful but I don't know if I'm the
right person to be into this with her because she's into something right now that could be very wonderful, very compelling
and mysterious, but that I can't relate to in that way because I
don't know where it's taking her and I'm not into that right
now." She cut off dramatically. "She's coming! So don't
worry, it's all in tune."

I tried to reach Stella or Sam at home, but there was no
answer, and I didn't want to search them out at Paula's where
they probably were, or even call there after declaring myself
out of it so strongly. I didn't know how to reach Matt. I
thought of Gloria but couldn't see any advantage in contact-
ing her. He couldn't have gotten out to Long Island. Anyway, a big fracas was on about Terry and the bar mitzvah that
had the phone tied up for the next few hours. Terry had
called Melody during the day and had told her to tell Harry of
his decision. It had apparently driven Harry mad, particularly

since he couldn't get in the car and come right in from Long Island to take Terry in hand physically. One of the conversations ended with Terry screaming loud enough to be heard all over the apartment, "Okay, sure you're my father and you'd do anything for me and I'm your son and I should do anything for you. Does that mean if you asked me to kill myself I'm supposed to kill myself? Does it? Does it?"

Harry called back, of course. I tried to talk to him about it all, but Terry got on the extension and yelled like a madman, "Get off the phone, Jean, stay out of this or I'll do something drastic. I'll kill myself if that will satisfy you," and I hung up, iced with fear that Terry really could go mad. The conversation and hysteria went on until I was ready to weep. I could hear the sounds of Paul and Elliot scrapping about something and I dashed into their bedroom to find them wrestling to kill. I gave them each a fierce whack and screamed at them to put their room in order or they'd be confined to their room for the entire weekend. My throat hurt and my hand stung for minutes afterward; but they were quiet and they straightened their room.

Looking very pale, Terry came into the kitchen and told me to pick up the phone, that Harry wanted to talk to me. He walked right out again and soon after I said, "Hello," very warily, I heard the click of the extension.

Harry said, "I suppose I owe that little crisis to you." His voice sounded weepy, not angry, and took the edge off his accusation. But I was cut anyway.

I said, "You can't mean that seriously. You think I want Terry so upset?"

Harry said, "Well you're not going to claim that you gave a damn about whether he went through with it or not?"

"No, I'm not. But that doesn't mean I started it."

"I'm going to get drunk for three days," he said.

I wondered how that would sit with the Quaker girl. "What does Melody say?" I was trying for an ally for Terry.

"She doesn't care any more than you do. Why should she?" He laughed bitterly. "Anyway the crisis is over. And I'm sure he'll put in a fine performance. Just try to keep things calm until the big day. You know what a fiasco like that could have done to me socially and professionally? All the invitations are out!"

I said, "I don't understand. Is he doing it then, going through with it?"

"Didn't he tell you?"

"He just said that you wanted to talk to me."

"He's going through with it for my sake and it's supposed to be the last thing that I ever ask him to do for me. I don't understand that boy. I don't understand what happened to him. He was such a sweet kid. What's come over him?"

"It's a bad age," I said. I couldn't believe that it was really settled, but I said, "I'm glad it's settled."

"God knows what's next on the horizon. I'm keeping out the storm warnings. He's upset about your not coming. Could you try and straighten that out with him? He thinks we're mistreating you."

"Aren't you?"

"Are you going to start a whole new brouhaha?" He sounded desperate. "You know you'd be uncomfortable. I'll be married by that time. I'm flying down for the divorce next week. You'd feel awful mingling in a crowd with Melody."

I laughed. "Don't worry about it. I was just thinking of Terry. I don't want him to think I don't care about something that's supposed to be so terribly important for him. After all, I'm his Jewish mother."

"Come on, Jean," Harry said. "Don't kid around."

Matt called soon after, complaining that he hadn't been able to get through. He was at Dr. Stone's office, conferring.

"I'll let you know what's happening. We're trying to get Stone and Altman in there."

"What for?"

"I'll be in touch," he said. "Stay off your phone, for God's sake. Read a book."

It wasn't until he had hung up that I realized I didn't know where he was staying. It might even be with me.

Sometime before we all settled down for the night I asked Terry, casually, "Is it true what Dad tells me, that you've agreed to go ahead with the bar mitzvah, for his sake?"

He howled as if I had touched a raw nerve. "Ma, please, could we not talk about it?"

I pulled back as from a dangerous substance that mishandled could blow up. But he went off to school cheerfully enough in the morning and came home even more so. School had been conducted in confusion because of the storm and the kids had made the most of it. But when Melody called to arrange to pick the boys up for the weekend in the early afternoon, Terry begged off. He told Melody that he had a lot of work to do, but he told me that he just didn't want to go, that he preferred to stay with me, if I didn't mind.

"Maybe we could do something. Eat at a Chinese restaurant and go to a movie." I had the sense that there was worry about me behind his offer, in the way that he hovered and patted me soothingly whenever he came within reach.

"That'll be great," I said, and spent the next fifteen minutes trying to connect with Matt who had called earlier to tell me to keep the evening open. When I told him that I would be busy, he didn't seem to understand.

"What do you mean? It's impossible. I've got it all lined up with Dr. Stone and Dr. Altman for tonight. They're committing her. They say it's the only thing to do. Robin's helped a lot. She got the doctors in and she'll get Dr. Stone in tonight so that he can sedate her. Then the ambulance and all that won't be too much of a shock."

I couldn't believe what he was saying. "Did the doctors say so?"

"Yes," he said. "It's a very dangerous situation. Not only for her. But for the children and Bella."

There was a silence in which I heard my own pulses clanging along my veins. I asked, "Did she let you in the apartment?"

"No."

"Where are you staying?"

"Gloria came in from the Island. She's staying with me at a hotel until we can get in and then she'll take the kids to her place. After they take Mary."

"What about Bella?"

"What about her?"

"I don't know," I said.

"She'll be all right," he said, and cleared his throat, almost gagging.

"How's your hand?" I said.

"It's okay. A little awkward to work with." And then, "Will you meet us and be with us until it's over?"

"I can't," I said. I didn't want to have anything to do with it. And with Gloria there. And I had promised Terry. "I have to be with Terry. Something's come up, that's why I was calling you, in case you were coming over."

"I don't believe it," he said.

"Please, Matt, call me later, afterward. I should be home about eleven."

"Call you? You mean I'm not going to see you at all?"

"I should be home by eleven," I said.

"Where are you going?"

"I have to take Terry to the movies."

"To the movies?" Then, in a lifeless voice, "I don't understand. I don't understand anything."

My attention kept sliding away from Terry's conversation during our dinner at the Chinese restaurant, but I would stop it from bumping headlong into what might be happening to Mary at that moment and turn my thoughts to nothing. To Terry my inattention meant something else.

"Am I boring you, Mom, with this school junk?"

I said, "No," though it was difficult to follow his complicated version of school politics and why the kid who was head of the student council was a fink fascist. I concentrated on listening, but I couldn't keep my mind tied to where we were. It floated free of the dreary ordinariness of me and Terry in a run-down, storefront eating place enjoying fried dumplings and barbecued spareribs and Chinese pepper steak, and froze immobilized in a soundless space where an unspeakable act I refused to recognize was occurring.

The movies were science fiction stuff, one about apes ruling a planet which turned out to be good old earth after we had blown it up with atomic weapons, and an old 1950s creepy thing about giant pea pods growing into facsimile people. Slouched in my broken-down seat, surrounded by the heavy odors of boots, stale wool, cigarettes, incense, pot — the mixed smell of the young crowd who poured in — I suspended myself in that heavy atmosphere, sharing Terry's popcorn and mint leaves and Pepsi, and his excitement and delight in the films. I had fun.

When we returned to the house, it was messy in a way that made it look unlike itself, the floor of the foyer covered with filthied newspapers to catch the dirty snow, a pile of boots, rubbers, gloves, odd hats and scarves and a shovel Elliot had borrowed from a friend, cluttering the narrow entranceway to the living room. I wandered about disconnectedly. I put the lamps on in the living room, picked up some of the papers and other junk, plumped up pillows, put the radio on, and waited for the phone to ring. Terry hung around, apparently concerned that he should be entertaining me, since we were alone, but he was suffering from movie hangover and closed himself away with a chess manual after a few desperate attempts at conversation. The phone didn't ring.

I wanted to call, but if it hadn't worked out according to plan and Mary was still there? Or if it had and she wasn't? Then Robin would be there, either way. Or somebody, even if the kids had gone with Gloria, to take care of Bella. So I called at midnight.

I woke Sam Shaeffer. He said, "Hello. Hello. What can I do for you at such an hour?"

I said, "Oh, Papa Shaeffer, I'm sorry I woke you. It's Jean. I was so worried. I had to call."

He said, "Darling, don't apologize. I don't expect to sleep much anyway. What a night we put in! We should none of us know from such a night again as long as we live."

I could hear Stella's voice behind him, and he called out to her, "It's Jean. You want I should tell her or you want to tell her?" Then, "Wait a minute, darling, Stella wants to talk a little."

Stella said, "Jean, Jeanie darling," and burst into tears. I could hear Papa Shaeffer. "That's the way you wanted to talk? Better I should talk." But Stella controlled herself and went on. "What's to talk? They took her away, that's all. Finished."

I said, "Were you there, Stella?"

"I saw it all from outside with Matt, me and my Sam standing across the street with him and Gloria. The cops, the ambulance, the strait jacket. I saw everything and I heard everything, including even how she screamed. That I should live to see such a thing. My wonderful girl. My wonderful Mary." She cried again.

Sam Shaeffer took the phone from her. "Darling, there's something we can do for you?"

I said, "No. I'm sorry. I was concerned. I couldn't be there because I had to be with Terry. Something came up."

He said, "And if you were here what could you have done? What could any of us do?"

I said, "But a strait jacket. And cops. Why did they do that? Wasn't she sedated?"

He said, "She fought like a lion. Like a lion. Sedation or no sedation."

"Where did they take her?"

"When they take them like that, my dear, there's only one place they take them. Only to Bellevue."

"Bellevue. Isn't that a terrible place?"

"Please," he said. "For God's sake. How much can a human being stand? Don't ask me anything else. To see such suffering. How can I bear it?" He broke into hoarse sobs.

"Forgive me," I said. "I shouldn't have called. Call me if you need me." I hung up. I hadn't asked where Matt was or if Bella was all right.

Terry was standing in the doorway. His face was greenish

pale and his eyes were very dark, fringed by the frivolous lashes he detested.

"What was that?" he said. "Did I hear right?"

I nodded. "Mary. The doctors committed her to Bellevue. It's a hospital for the mentally ill."

"I know what Bellevue is," he said. "I know all about Bellevue." He began to pace and fling his skinny arms. "That's not a hospital. It's a jail. You let them take your friend there? You were supposed to be taking care of her. You're supposed to love her. You were supposed to be keeping her from killing herself." He raised a quivering finger to my face. "I heard what you said. That you had to be with me. You're not getting away with that. You're not using me that way with your friends. I heard you say that about the cops and the strait jacket. You let that happen to your friend? You're not going to put that on me. You didn't have to be with me. Why didn't you tell me? I would have gone with you and stopped it."

I didn't answer him. He looked at me in silence, then turned and went to his room, latching the door.

13 ————

AT PAULA'S the following night, I was supposed to give a report of my visit to Bellevue, but I had a very confused recollection of my time with Mary. I had taken Bob's car because I wanted it off my hands, back in his garage. The streets were a mess and it was hell to park. The visitors' room was in the old part of a cavernous building, an enormous room, more like the indoor yard of an old elementary school, though there were hard vinyl benches and metal cigarette stands and tables. It was jammed with people. I didn't see anybody there to visit Mary, except myself. I wasn't nervous about seeing her. I don't know what I was — vague, empty, stupid. And I couldn't conceive what she would be like. The level of noise in the room was painful, bouncing and clanging off the hard walls and floors in a harsh metallic mix. I wrote Mary's name on a slip of paper and waited on a bench next to a man in a coat and hat who stared downward at the floor and picked at his lip. The young girl sitting at his side in a dark red corduroy bathrobe patted his hand and smiled into his eyes, but he didn't respond. I figured he must have been the visitor because he had the outer clothing on. I stood up and walked toward an ell where the patients were entering. Mary came around the corner in a vigorous stride, holding herself very erect. She was marvelously herself. The only crazy thing about her was her short robe, a wildly flowered puckered-nylon monstrosity.

She said, "Have you come to get me out?" in an imperious voice, and when I said nothing, she lifted her head and widened her eyes, luminous with anger, like an actress. "You're surely not here to visit, are you?"

I said, "Where'd that horrible thing come from?" pulling at her robe.

She pushed my hand away. "Gloria's idea of the right thing to wear in the nuthouse." She actually laughed. "She may be right, for once. She's a real thoughtful darling. She left me this and lots of other goodies for a long stay — changes of dainty underthings, hand lotion, deodorant, Tampax." She stopped suddenly and walked away, turning her back. She was wearing leather bedroom slippers and their hard heels clicked out her anger. Her beautiful legs moved like a dancer's. I called out after her. She turned and said in a very loud voice that dominated the room. "Don't come back, Jean. Don't come here to visit. Get me out. Tell that to Matt and all my friends. No visitors. *Just — get — me — out!* Nearby conversations had been stopped to listen to her. A young girl in a long skinny knit garment began to beat her hands together, laughing and roaring, "Tell them, sister. Right on, right on, right on!" and a middle-aged woman screamed at her visitors, "You hear her? You hear that? Me too. Me too. Take me out of here."

Mary disappeared around the bend, but the hubbub in the room continued. I thought I saw aides — guards or nurses moving toward the patients, but they were probably only other visitors or patients. There was nothing to do but leave.

At Bob's garage, they refused to take the car. I insisted on speaking to the manager, a round-faced young man in a business suit who blinked and stared out over my head while he said no. "It's a kind of special situation. You'll have to get in touch with his family."

I said that all I wanted to do was to return Dr. Guerrero's car to his garage. But he repeated, "You'd better get in touch with his family. I can't involve myself in these things. They get complicated."

"Listen," I said. "It's all right. I know he's dead. I just want to return his car."

His face registered shock at my coarseness, but he kept his gaze beyond my face. "I wish I could help you, lady, but there's nothing I can do."

"Just take it," I said desperately. "Isn't this his garage? You *have* to take it. Come *on. Please.*"

"I don't have to do anything," he said, his face getting a little red.

I gave up. What was it, some kind of special ritual, or new law of the land that I didn't know about? I maneuvered through the clotted streets in the thickening afternoon traffic looking for a garage that would accept the car. They were all full up. In despair, I wound up at an avenue near the piers and parked at a street phone. It was in order, and I called Paula.

"Come right over," she said. "You can have supper with me and Joanna. We got a pizza."

I explained about Bob's car. "I've got to get rid of it," I said. "I don't want it. Tell me what to do with it." I sounded hysterical, even to myself.

"What about Mary?" she said. "Did you see her?"

"Yes," I said, "but what am I going to do with the car? I feel like leaving it right here on the street."

"What's the matter with you?" Paula said. "Isn't your head working today? Take it to any garage and bring us the ticket. We'll take care of it."

"They're full," I said. "There's no room."

"Park it wherever you can. Don't worry about it. Just park where it's legal and remember where you parked it. I can't believe it's you. You sound absolutely irrational."

"But what will I do with the key? I don't want it."

She said, probably to Joanna, "I think Jean's flipped." And to me, "Bring it here. Listen, will you come right over?"

I said, "Okay. But I only have a few minutes."

I met Cora in the lobby of Paula's apartment house. There was so much sympathy in her being that I gave into my need to grab some. I let it show in my face when we kissed.

She said, "You look finished. Come and sit down a minute."

We sat on a marble bench in the fake Italian lobby. The apartment house was full of evening activity, the good smells of good dinners being cooked, men in good clothes coming home, their arms full of packages and mail just picked up in their letterboxes, arriving to the courtly, slightly mocking greeting of the black elevator operator.

"Was it awful?" Cora said.

"You ever been there?"

She said yes by nodding her head.

"Then you know," I said. "I have to get her out, Cora. How can I get her out?"

She said nothing.

"How come you're leaving?" I said. "Isn't there a meeting?"

"Later," she said. "I'll be back for it. I have to visit my grandchild."

"Grandchild?" She seemed much too young and I had assumed the only child Paula had told me about had been young when he died. "Where did he come from?"

"She," she said. "She came from what I thought was the worst thing that had happened to me. Only it turned out to be the best. Did you know I had a son who died?"

"Paula told me," I said. "Drugs, she said."

"Yeah," she said. "Except it wasn't that much. It was that he had something wrong with him, some kind of congenital deficiency. Even a little could kill him." Her voice was as usual, soft, conversational, comforting, but tears formed and rolled down her cheeks from the far corners of her eyes, welling up from a source over which she had no control. "We had had a lot of other trouble with him. He got a fourteen-year-old white girl pregnant when he was sixteen and they ran away and married because they thought they had to. We tried everything to get rid of that baby. We tried to annul the marriage. We tried to force her to have an abortion or to give the baby away. But that little girl was stubborn. They broke up before the baby was born. They kept trying to get together, but it couldn't work. He didn't know where he was at or where he was going, and I guess she didn't either, except about the baby. The last year, before he died, he became militantly antiwhite and refused to have anything to do with his wife and child because they were white. But he always sent her a little money, whatever he could."

"Is the baby white?" I said. "Whatever that is."

She wiped her wet face with a tissue, and searched in her bag for a wallet. She held out a picture. "There's Tessa," she said.

It was a formal color photograph of a much older child than I had expected to see. She must have been about Elliot's age.

She had tightly curled blond hair, a broad, high forehead, light chocolate skin, large blue eyes, Chuck Spalding's flattened nose with the distended nostrils, Cora's sweet cheeks and full, smiling mouth. She was a beauty, nose and all.

"She's beautiful," I said. "Is her mother blond?"

"No," Cora said. "I don't know where that hair comes from. But somewhere on her mother's side, I guess." She stood up. "I'd better go. Tessa's mommie has a dinner appointment."

I said, "You're friends then?"

"She's all right," she said. "She's been good to me. She lets me spend as much time as I want to with Tessa."

"Big deal," I said. "Why wouldn't she? It's great for Tessa and it gives her time off."

"No," Cora said. "She doesn't need me. She makes a lot of money and can buy all the help she needs. And she could have paid us back. We were rotten to her. She's all right." She smiled. "That's what I mean about life."

"What?"

"You know, how it goes, how it is. Surprising."

"Cora," I said. "What's this new meeting for?"

"For bullshit," she said. "To make us feel we're doing something, because we started years ago with Bella and Mary and we can't stop. As if meeting will do any good. It would be like meeting to talk about a hurricane."

I said, "I thought you were a real activist."

"Right," she said, in the softest voice. "Blow it all up and start again. That's my activism." She smiled. "Don't pay it any heed. I'm raving. I don't do a thing but write stories about women and go visit my grandchild."

I called Terry, after I used the bathroom to pee and fix my face and hair. With a bloody mary at the side of the telephone, I felt armed to take him on. But he was quiet and depressed. "Matt's been calling," he reported. "He left a message. There's a meeting at Paula White's tonight. He'll be there and he says you have to be."

"I'm there already," I said.

"Well then, Tony's coming over to play chess. Could we go out and eat? At a delicatessen? I'll pay?"

"Do you have money?"

"Yes, but you have to pay it back."

"Okay," I said. "Terry, about last night."

He interrupted. "Look, I don't understand you and your friends anyway so I never should have gotten into it. Forget everything I said. It was the part about me that burned me."

"I apologize for that part," I said.

He laughed. "You're always doing things or saying things and then apologizing. What a system!"

"But I wanted to say that what you said last night . . ."

He interrupted again, frantically, "Jean, could we not talk about it, please, please?"

I rang off.

Paula's apartment was warm, sumptuous in its messy way. Even the store-bought pizza smelled good. We ate it in the living room, having first moved piles of folded flyers and envelopes for a peace demonstration mailing Paula had been working on during the day. Joanna seemed better, more like herself, full of odd pieces of information and advice. They didn't ask me any details of my visit to Mary. I was supposed to save that for later. They got into a big gossipy thing about Cora and Chuck because I asked what Cora had meant when she said all she did was write stories about women.

"She just started to write, just like that," Paula said. "And she's very good, apparently. She sells everything she writes."

"Have you read them?"

"No," Paula said. "I don't know why. Just never got around to it."

"I don't care for them," Joanna said. "I didn't understand that last one about the old aunt. It had some beautiful things in it, but it wasn't very well organized."

"I'd like to read them," I said.

"I've got them around somewhere. I'll lend them to you," Joanna said.

"She just changed completely after Chucky died. All she cares about now is Tessa and her writing," Paula said. "It's a wonder she still shows up at meetings for Bella. You can't get her to do a thing anymore." She paused and began again, "Chuck's going to leave her one of these days. He'll have to. He needs a woman who knows how to meet his sensual needs."

"Chuck can get anybody he wants," Joanna said.

"The thing about Cora is that she comes on so soft and womanly but she's really very tough, a real emasculating female," Paula said.

"What does that mean?" I said.

"It means she's always cutting his balls off. But the thing about Chuck is that you just can't do it to him."

"Does she write about black women?" I asked.

"As far as I know," Joanna said. "I don't know what else she'd know about. Of course, Cora has a good education, but when it comes to life, I don't think she's led a very full life at all."

"How did she start to write? How do you do that? Don't you have to know how?"

"She always wanted to," Joanna said. "She was always a frustrated writer."

"I didn't know that," Paula said. "I thought she just took off out of nowhere and became a writer. I've been thinking about trying to do a couple of stories myself." She threw the paper plates in the fireplace. They flared up, and quieted into the small, steady fire that had been burning. A blackened city landscape had been carved in the logs, lit up and licked away at by the flames. "Chuck told me that she won't go down on him and when I tried to hint around with her once about it, to kind of open up the discussion and see what I could do, you know she didn't know what sixty-nine is? Never *heard* of it?"

To be by myself, I offered to do the dishes and prepare the coffee. Even after I could hear the sound of people arriving, I dawdled over the preparation of the coffee tray and by the time I carried it into the living room, the room was full. Jennifer Torrington was on the couch. Mama and Papa Shaeffer were in a corner with Matt. Robin was there too and a black girl holding an infant. Chuck had just come in. Matt hardly greeted me, but everybody's greetings were subdued. Matt looked closed in on himself. It was an attitude that added to his general air of downtown city elegance. He was in his working clothes — suit, oxblood shirt, wide striped tie — all handsome but without the outlandishly modish touches men had taken up. No mustache or sideburns for Matt either. His face was as smooth as the face of the younger man Mary kept in a small gold frame on her dresser, I had always thought as a joke, pictured in his cap and gown by an honest-to-God photographer, at his mother's insistence, when he graduated Phi Beta Kappa. Only his hair was longer, swept back behind his ears. If the rest of him was a stranger, his ear at least was a familiar. I could taste it, and feel at my tongue's tip the intricate pattern of its paths and feel along my body the convulsive movement of delight my mouth brought through it to his whole body. To insist on our intimacy, I touched his back as I walked by. He paid no attention.

I thought I had met the black girl before, but she said she didn't think so, when I asked her, and cracked the old joke, "Sure all us blacks look alike."

Robin said that I might be recognizing her from her pictures. "She's a fashion model," she said proudly. I was surprised to hear someone of Robin's generation brag about that kind of success.

"Come on," the girl said, "I haven't had only maybe eight assignments. And six of those were in *Ebony*."

"How about that *New York Times* spread?" Robin said. "You know how many millions of people saw that? Thousands."

Stella and Sam knew the black girl well. They drooled over the baby, kept handing him back and forth to each other, talking baby talk to him. He cooed back. He was very sweet, with his mother's polished skin, but a shade lighter. She had the long bony frame of a fashion model and a remarkable neck, like an animal's, on which her head swiveled proudly. She had a close-shaped Afro, big eyes, a small, thin nose and the pouting, forward structure of the lower part of the face of a tomcat. Her mouth was big, with wide lips and prominent teeth. She had a quick, breathless manner, and she laughed a lot.

"Emily's baby," Stella cooed, "little Mr. Gerard," bouncing the infant gently, holding him along the length of her arm.

"Well, no," Emily said. "He's young Mr. Swenson, in fact." She laughed.

"Your name isn't Gerard?" Stella asked. "So who was Sam packing up and mailing all Mary's baby clothing to?"

"Me," Emily said breathlessly, and laughed. "But that's

the cat I married because he needed an American wife. Gerard. You know."

"So who's Swenson?" Sam said.

"Swenson's my real old man," she said, and grinned widely. "That's why I'm back. They had him in jail in Denmark and then they took him back here and put him in again, but he's getting out and we're gonna settle down like old folks in Vermont."

"Drugs?" Chuck said.

Emily shrugged and laughed. "That's over," she said. "We're gonna be through with that."

"How are you going to live?" Chuck said. "Does he have any skill?"

Robin rushed in. "Peter's a math genius." Emily rapped her on the head with the knuckles of one polished black hand, laughing a lot. "He can earn more bread than he'd know what to do with. He was like one of IBM's geniuses."

"Is he Negro?" Chuck said. "Black?"

"Danish-American," Emily said. "Bright as the morning sun, with a black, black soul." She laughed, put her hands together in a praying gesture and closed her eyes, as if the thought of him was too much.

"So if you're married to one, and the other is the father, how are you going to resolve the problem?" Stella asked, but Cora came in at that moment and Papa Shaeffer insisted that the meeting start.

"No more special caucuses. Everybody come to the main meeting and speak, and no side shows."

Joanna took charge. She was uncomfortable and halting in her speech. "I guess we all know why we're here, so we can forgo any preliminaries or introductions or general discussion. Umm. Maybe the first thing to do I guess would be to hear from Robin and Emily who asked to please be allowed to come to speak to us to make their views known. They have a few questions to raise. Umm. I believe that they understand that they are then supposed to leave because of not being members of this committee, and . . . umm . . ." She trailed off, then began again, vigorously, just as Chuck was about to say something. "Shall we hear from Robin first? Robin?"

Robin looked up, startled, and pulled her hands out from under her poncho. She had a sharp, pretty face with the simpering mouth and little chin favored by cameo artists. She kept her lips open a lot and wet them with her tongue. I thought of Matt's description and glanced at him, but he wasn't looking at anyone. He was looking at his crossed knee and at some imperfection in the cloth that he was working at with his fingernail.

"Uh," Robin said, "uh," and pushed her hands out further and moved them around in front of her as if she were pulling something toward her in the empty air. "Uh, wow, like I don't know how to begin," she said. "Because we all know what there is to know, but what about the things we don't know, what about what's inside?" She spoke in rushes of words and small pauses, grasping at the air when she paused. "The private things, right? Like what about the inside part of Mary? What are we doing to that? That's what Emily made me see. If only she'd gotten here sooner. Wow. That could have changed the whole rhythm. Because they have that, Mary and Emily, they have that thing together going for them that makes them groove together. So Emily knows. Like we don't have the right to say to Mary, live this way and not your way, have this experience and not that experience, do what we want you to do, we don't want you to have your kind of

strength and your kind of, you know, whatever it is that she's
made up of, her chemistry, her destiny, her secret knowledge
and adventures and insides and outsides, like her own hair or
her own body smells that belong just to her and shouldn't be
violated by anybody even if we think we're doing it out of
love. Because" — she was rushing along now — "what is
love? Is it dependence, is it guilt, is it just weakness and sickness, how do we know?" She opened her little, nervous hands
to us, brought them back to her open, moist lips, gazed at us in
an agonized way.

Papa Shaeffer groaned. "Somebody knows what she's talking about maybe?"

Emily burst out. "Shit. I don't care about all that stuff."
She held the baby close to her body. Under cover of the
loose, vestlike, fringed top she was wearing, she nursed him.
"I know Bellevue. I know state hospitals for what they call
the insane. My mother's been in one for fifteen years. Just get
Mary out of there. If you aren't crazy when you go in you sure
are when you come out. If you come out. Get her out. That's
the only thing I came here to say and I'm saying it flat out
loud, just as flat out loud as I know how, and I don't care who
I'm stepping on. You just better get her out, man, just get her
out of there." Matt watched her with a steady look that
showed nothing. She took a deep breath. "Listen, I know
Mary since we were in high school together. She doesn't belong there. Nobody belongs there. If those doors are opening
up to let anybody out any minute, Mary has to be the first
one." She waved one sinuous arm like a silken whip. "Okay, I
haven't seen her since she's gotten sick, so-called sick. I've
been away. Okay, you say I don't know anything about it.
But I don't have to see her. I don't care *what* she's supposed
to have done, broke your finger, broke your arm, broke your

head, man, you just don't know what you're doing, putting someone in that place." She burst into tears. She stood up, controlling them quickly. "Come on, Robin, we had our say."

Robin scrambled up, threw her hands out at us helplessly, said, "Matt, I guess you'll explain about all the rest, what the doctors said and all, right?"

Matt fixed her with the same steady look. He was holding the bandaged hand in his other hand and he looked down at it, studying it. Robin followed Emily, fluttering her hands at us in farewell as she went.

Joanna had trouble with the silence that followed. She murmured something senseless about thanking the girls for coming and turned to Matt. "I guess the best thing to do now is to get Matt's report on what the doctors said. Matt, could we have that report next?"

Matt didn't speak. He continued to study the arrangement of his hands and shook his head from side to side signifying no. The silence lengthened.

"Umm," Joanna said, and anchored her heavy glasses more securely behind her ears. "Umm."

Papa Shaeffer rushed in. "What is this? What are we doing here? What is this meeting for altogether?" He stroked his beautiful white hair back from his forehead with an unsteady hand. "Hasn't this young man suffered enough? What? We called a meeting to torture Matt?"

Mama Shaeffer said, "Please, Sam, give a little thought to what you're saying. What are you saying?"

Papa Shaeffer mimicked her tone. "Please, Stella, I'm saying we should use a little bit common sense. We have to have a meeting that Matt should tell us the doctors told us that Mary must be sent away? We all know that very well. It's totally unnecessary. We need a medical report that we're not qualified to pass judgment on in any case? Who needs it? With all due respect to Mary's young friends and their feelings."

Joanna said, "Comrades, it's taking a great effort for me to chair this meeting. I know I should be criticized for not, you know, organizing it better. Under the circumstances . . . under the circumstances . . . with Bob no longer . . . no longer . . . we have to make an effort . . ." She paused, began again. "I want to criticize myself for not starting with an agenda. The reason for this meeting is the question of . . . the question of . . ." She tried a fresh start. "I think we should decide on an agenda. I think we should have suggestions for an agenda."

Chuck Spalding took over, in his deep, commanding voice. "That's a very good idea. How about Jean getting a pencil and paper and keeping notes."

I said, "Forgive me. I really don't want to complicate things, but I shouldn't be here either. Any more than the girls. I'm not a member. And I certainly don't want to become recording secretary or something."

Mama Shaeffer said, "Don't talk that way, darling. You're one of us."

Paula said, "Well that part's not complicated. We hired Jean to do a certain job. We have to decide whether we want her to go on with it or not. Just a simple practical matter, no wheels within wheels at all."

"There's nothing to decide," I said. "I'm not going on. And there's nothing for me to go on with."

Joanna said, "I definitely feel that the question pertaining to Jean is unfinished business and should be wound up here tonight one way or another. Umm. Umm. I think she should sum up for us, and also give us her report on her visit to Mary today at the hospital. I think that Jean . . . umm . . . umm . . . isn't as familiar as we are with collective work and collective decisions and that . . . umm . . . umm . . ."

Cora said, "Joanna, shouldn't we get back to that idea of putting down a suggested agenda? I'll take notes if nobody else will."

Matt stood up. "I'm not a member of this group either. I would very much like to be excused." His manner was formal to absurdity.

"This is ridiculous," Jennifer Torrington said. With her carriage and her clipped speech and the way she pursed her mouth with distaste, she put a distance between herself, her breeding and her background, and the fumbling incompetents in the room. She put up a hand as if to stop Matt. He withdrew from it. "My understanding of this meeting was that we were getting together to be of help to you, Matt. To make decisions about Mary, and about Bella and Jean if necessary, to see to it that you were given the means to do what has to be done, that is, to speak bluntly, money from Committee funds. Am I wrong?" She smiled at Matt, a professional smile that flashed and vanished without feeling, and motioned to him to sit down again.

He stood. "And may I suggest" — his voice hardened — "that you proceed with your meeting and let me know what your decisions are? Then I'll let you know whether I intend to follow them." His control barely covered his anger.

Cora said, "If we have any purpose here at all, Matt, it's to help you with Bella and Mary."

"Tell you what," he said. "Let's make a deal. The Committee money is all yours. You take care of Bella. I'll worry about Mary."

"You can't leave, Matt," Paula said, "before any decisions have been made. What if we decide she should be taken out of Bellevue?" She gave him her open, false stare.

"Right now?" Matt said. His eyes were like black stones. "Would you like me to run right down and bring her home tonight?"

Joanna said, "You're being ridiculous, Paula. We can't make a decision like that. We're in no position to. That's a medical finding. The psychiatrists will determine that."

"The major issue," Jennifer Torrington said, "is danger, danger to herself or to the children and to Bella, of course. That's the reason she was committed, and that would be the only reason to keep her there."

"A danger to the children!" Stella began to cry. "A more wonderful mother to those children, you'll never see, believe me."

"There she goes," Sam Shaeffer said, but he leaned over and patted her back.

Cora said, "Why are we keeping Jean or Matt here against their wishes? Jean feels she can't do any more."

"And maybe we don't want her to," Paula said.

"Okay," Cora said. "Fine. And Matt's doing the best he can in a terrible situation. He knows we're here to help him if he wants us. He knows there's money available. He can call on us whenever he wants to."

"Oh, no," Paula said. "What good is that to him? He needs us, he needs people at his side."

"I don't think that's what Bob would have wanted," Joanna said.

"What?" Paula said to her in irritation. And then to me, "And that's not fair. You saw Mary. You have to report on that."

"There's nothing. There's no point," I said.

Chuck said, "We need a little order here. Jean, could you very briefly tell us whatever you think we need to know. Just practical details. Do we owe you any money? A quick report on Mary's condition. You understand. That will simplify matters enormously."

I said, "You don't owe me anything. I've returned Bob's car. Paula knows about that. There are no other details."

"And Mary?" he said.

"I don't know what you want to know," I said, standing, meaning to show that I was half out of the room. "It was a very short visit."

"Well, just describe it," Paula said. "We purposely didn't ask you earlier and now you're not even going to describe it?"

"Physically, she seemed fine," I said. I spoke to Cora's listening face, so as not to look at Matt. "She was very angry. She asked me not to visit her and she left the visiting room almost immediately. She said to me to get her out. She said to tell Matt and to tell her friends. Then she left. That's all."

"That's normal," Paula said. "They all do that. They all say that they're not sick and that they shouldn't be in the hospital. That's normal."

"That's perfectly untrue," Jennifer said indignantly. "There's absolutely no value to treatment if the patient doesn't recognize illness."

"I'm going now," I said. "I have to get home."

Matt said, "So am I."

"One minute." Sam Shaeffer, raised his hand. "We have another problem. The problem is with Bella. First, it's physical because she needs someone to take care of her. Second, it's psychological, because since she saw the cops and the strait jacket, her trust in us flew out the window. Robin, altogether, mustn't set foot in that house. Her, she really despises. She insists she's an FBI agent."

"That's no problem," Joanna said. "I'm sure we all agree that we can do without Robin."

"Bella's not too happy about Matt, either, but she's not sure."

"I'm not planning to stay there," Matt said. "My sister took the children and the dog. I'll be staying with a friend. If I can count on your managing for Bella, I'd appreciate it."

Jennifer Torrington leaned toward him. "It's our whole reason for being, Matt."

"Let's pull a little organization out of this crazy hat," Chuck said. "First things first. One." He held up a large, pink, brown-edged palm and folded down one finger. "Two people who aren't part of our committee are asking to leave the meeting. I say, permission granted." He extended the next finger, folded it. "Two. Jean is asking to be released from her paid assignment. I say, permission granted." Same business with the finger. "Three. Matt is asking for concrete help with Bella. I say that we should take on this responsibility, subject to our working out the details, and report to Matt regularly as to her situation. Four. Matt quite understandably finds it painful to discuss Mary and the tragedy of her condition. Nobody sympathizes more than I with that. I say we give Matt the clear promise of money and help available to him from Committee resources and Committee funds, no questions asked, whenever he wishes. Five. That we excuse Jean and Matt, go on with any other Committee business after they leave, and I hope to God we conduct ourselves in a more orderly fashion than we have been."

Paula said, "You're terrific, Chuck."

He gave her a dazzling smile.

Joanna said, "Do we have to vote on what Chuck proposed, or can we just assume that we're all in agreement?"

"Let's just say," Jennifer said, "that we're in accord with the spirit of Chuck's resolution."

We were in the foyer, Matt leaning against the wall, watching me struggle into my boots when Stella came to the open doorway from the living room. In a timid, pleading voice that shook slightly, she said, "You're a good boy, Matt. I know you'll do everything possible for my little girl."

"Sure," he said, not looking up.

I kissed her and told her not to worry.

14 ———

JUST BEFORE I LEFT the house to meet Matt, I picked up
the envelope of Mary's papers and carried it along, in case the
doctors would want to see them. I bought a *New York Times*
to study the want-ad section on the subway trip. I needed a
job. The columns held two possibilities. The less attractive
one was downtown. The other was in the patient library at
the medical center. By the time I met Matt I had imagined
myself into a pleasant, quiet, undemanding job that I could
stay with indefinitely. And if I lied about a college degree,
that would get me twenty-five dollars a week more. We went
into a coffee shop before taking a crosstown to the hospital.
Matt ordered coffee and a toasted corn muffin. I didn't want
anything, but I ordered a small glass of tomato juice. The
waitress wrote out our checks before she brought the order.
My juice was forty-five cents. I was outraged and carried on
about it. Matt was annoyed with that, in his new contained
manner. He was wearing his business clothes again and looking strikingly handsome. He lifted the arm with the broken
fingers and rested it on the table. I leaned over and kissed
his fingers, one by one, ending with the splint.

"I don't understand you," he said.

"I don't understand myself," I said.

"I hate that," he said. "I hate when you do that."

The waitress set down our food and I said nothing until she left. She flirted with Matt and he responded automatically. She was a hard-faced blonde. I knew he didn't like her. He followed the action of her behind under the tight, knit mini skirt as she walked away. I said, "What do you hate?"

He straightened himself and blew a sigh through his nose before he spoke. "When you turn something serious away by putting yourself down. It's your way of copping out of a scene you want to avoid. And building yourself up. Coming on honest and humble."

"I'm sorry," I said.

"That's no good. It's part of the same thing. Do anything, say anything and then apologize."

"That's what Terry says."

He didn't like that, but I hadn't meant he was acting like a child. I knew from the night before that he wasn't interested in Terry. I had tried to explain to Matt why he couldn't come home with me and why I couldn't go to his hotel with him and leave Terry alone. I only told him about the bar mitzvah. I left the scene about Mary out. Was I protecting him or me? He might think my statement about not understanding myself an affectation, but that was only because he couldn't see into my head.

"When I can't sleep," he said, "I think about you. I thought a lot about the night you had to take Terry to the movies. That wasn't it. Terry has nothing to do with it. You want to keep yourself clean, out of it, what's being done to Mary."

I said, "If you know that, you know more than I do. I don't know what I'm doing."

"That's it," he said. "That's your system."

"My system?"

"Your way of making yourself look pure to yourself. You know where that ends up? With Mary? If I had taken your attitude? Dying, demented, in the streets, or in the kitchen killing her kids and then herself. But you blame me. For this."

"You sound like Bob," I said. "I don't blame you. Do you think I'd be going with you now if I thought you were to blame?" And then I made an offering, tapping the envelope on the table. "I brought those things she wrote. I thought it might help the doctors. Somehow."

He nodded and put the envelope under his arm when we left the luncheonette.

The room in which we met with the doctors was worse than the visitors' hall. It was a big room, but all its furniture, a couple of desks and five or six straight-backed decrepit chairs, huddled in one corner, and we sat in a mean, dirty, small area, like a cleaning closet. One of the psychiatrists had a little boy's face — round, continually smiling; the other doctor was older — slim, glum and quick. They asked to speak to Matt alone. I went out into the narrow hall. The door clicked shut behind me, locking automatically. There was no place to sit, nothing to do, nothing to look at but grime. I stood in the center of the corridor, avoiding leaning against the peeling walls. Plague, madness, seven-year itch could be communicated through their touch. I wandered down the corridor, turned a corner into a wider one, at the end of which was another locked door. I paced, back and forth, dreading a long wait. But Matt was out quickly. The two doctors were bunched behind him in the doorway, the round-faced one holding the big envelope of Mary's papers and a collection of folders. They came toward me in single file. The quick, glum doctor looked at me.

"What about her?" he said. "Is she her sister? Doesn't she want to take her home?"

"She's not related, doctor," Matt said, in a strangled voice. He didn't respond to my searching look. The doctor was looking at me.

I shook my head no. "I'm not related. I'm a very close friend," I said. "Is she staying, then?"

The smiling one answered. "We were strong for releasing her, but now we're reviewing the data."

"Could I have those papers back now?" I said, putting out my hand for the envelope.

"We haven't really looked at these yet," he said. "We'll add these to the history."

We were all walking along the corridor now in that rushing walk of doctors, their white coats waving behind their legs.

"What about a private hospital?" Matt hurried to keep up with the older doctor. "Are they better?"

"Spend your money, if you like," he said, as if he didn't give a damn. He opened the door at the end of the corridor with a key hanging alongside a bunch of others on a metal ring attached to a chain. He held the door for me to pass through, but stayed ahead of me.

"Is it all right for me to visit her?" I said.

"Do whatever you please," he said. "It doesn't make a bit of difference." Without a glance at us, he waved a brisk hand in farewell and strode away from us with his rapid, gliding walk. Round-Face hung around for a few seconds, mumbling some meaningless drivel, shook our hands, and walked away.

Matt and I walked out of the building and into the street. There was a strong, unpleasant wind blowing.

"I have to go to the office," Matt said.

"Wait," I said. "Tell me what happened."

"I'm not sure that I know what happened." His voice was thin and strangled, and his cheeks were stained with a red flush. "It was all so God damned fast. First, they . . . not they . . . he, the tall, thin doctor, the older one, said that she had talked to him very freely, that they had had a very decent talk, whatever he meant by that, and that she knew that she had cancer, she knew that she might die of it and she knew that she had had a breast removed. Was I under the impression that her mental condition was mostly comprised of an inability to face this reality? I said, 'I guess so.' How then could I account for this discrepancy between our evaluation, mine and the committing physician's, and his present findings that Mary did indeed have a clear and realistic view of her situation? I felt like a kid at an exam. What was the right answer supposed to be? I said, 'I don't know.' Then he said, 'Mr. Schwartz, your wife is very, very ill. She may have only a short time to live. Whatever mental problems she may be having, don't you want to take her home?' and I — I" — he gasped, to control his breath — "I busted out crying like a freaking kid." He took a cigarette from a pack in his pocket, lit it with difficulty in the wind, and took a puff before he began again. "They asked me what the problems were and I told them how she's been and the kinds of things she's been doing, changing the lock and my hand, but very fast, and I showed them the papers which they glanced at, very fast, and suddenly they had reversed themselves and were going to review the case."

I said, "But why did he ask that about me?"

He didn't answer. He yelled, "I can't stand any more. I can't take it. I have to go to the office," and he cut away from me and crossed the street.

I went in the other direction, uptown, to see about that job. I got it — a real dumb, pleasant job in a two-room library perched at the top of the medical center with a great view of the Hudson from the room on the right and the Harlem from the one on the left. The library existed in a well-warmed, sunny, sleepy atmosphere that I thought would be restful. In fact, I was bored and restless. I did the garbage work, whatever the librarian told me, step by step, down to dusting the shelves and getting containers of coffee. I kept the cards in order and typed letters thanking the volunteers and the book donors and that kind of thing. The librarian was a slow-talking, drab midwesterner, about twenty-five years old, dazzled by working and living in New York. She had immediately involved herself in a "relationship" with an older married man and mostly my job consisted of listening to tales of the "relationship." Her affair was a lot more interesting than the job, so I didn't mind. She had taken a trip on an Israeli boat before settling into her life's work as a librarian and had let the chief engineer hop into her bed on board and later whenever he arrived at the port of New York. He did, every two months or so, pledging undying love, a quick divorce and marriage, but always taking off with his vessel — back to his wife and kids in Tel Aviv. Honey had his picture on her desk — an 8½ x 11 color photograph of a full-faced, blond man in a naval uniform, gazing heroically, and slightly cross-eyed, into the distance. He managed to come up with something that demanded his immediate return when it came time to leave. His garage had burned down, one of his children had swallowed a plastic button, his wife had threatened suicide, his mother was at death's door with an acute attack of shingles. Honey reported everything to me, including extracts from his letters, sometimes tearfully, but more often with great bursts of laughter. He came into New York soon after I started on the job. Honey was transformed during his stay; as if she had shed an old skin, she emerged new and glowing, with her hair rinsed to golden red and burst of gorgeous clothes I had never seen. He left because his dog died and his son broke a foot playing soccer. She told me all about it, laughing and groaning, shaking his picture and ending by knocking it face down on her desk.

I wasted a lot of the time Matt and I spent together keeping him up to date on her stories. He listened with a little smile, in a distraction in which he was now constantly enclosed. I mostly talked nonsense with him. All the rest was too awful to talk about.

Bella? Bella seemed to be managing. The Shaeffers kept Matt informed about her, though they were having their troubles staying close to her. She had decided that Matt was trustworthy, after all, and asked for him, and he went to see her once a week or so. But he didn't like to talk about it. She had some little old lady in there doing for her. She went under the grand title of practical nurse, but she was really one cut above a cleaning woman. Matt was staying on at the residence hotel on the upper west side, and spent his weekends at Gloria's with the children and Shtrudel, who was turning out to be the biggest problem of all because he seemed to be spending all his time vomiting and whining and trying to chew his way through Gloria's imitation Colonial wooden doors.

Nobody was seeing Mary. News of her came by way of doctors, lawyers, social workers, as if she were a beloved country from which we were exiled, whose agony was communicated through radio and television bulletins. Every report was garbled, strange, impossible. A young movement lawyer had called Matt to warn him that she was suing for release and for incarceration without cause, and then a few days later that she had dropped the suit. The doctor's early reports were bad: she was violent; there would be no visitors allowed. Then, very hopeful: she was to be sent home rather than passed on to another hospital. Then a dramatic shift. She had been moved to a violent section. Then, nothing. Then, a terse report that she was to be transferred to the state hospital in Brooklyn and that visitors were not yet permitted. Matt would be informed when.

And I — I was happier than I had ever been in my life. That was monstrous. But I couldn't push my happiness away in the name of some moral abstract which I couldn't work out anyway, though I felt it hovering out there somewhere. Even Terry and his silences couldn't disturb the still place where I knew joy; I wouldn't give it up for anything.

The thing with me is that my ideas about life were shaped by all those big realization movies and books of the fifties. You know — wham! — everything comes clear to the hero in a single blow to the gut; and fadeout — he's changed for life. But what it had taken me until I was almost forty to learn is what happens after the fadeout. Nothing. The hero goes back to whatever he was doing before — typing, quarreling, bombing, making money, screwing without love.

After all the big scenes, Terry was going along, finishing school, dressing up for Harry and Melody's wedding, and going through with his bar mitzvah without a hitch, leaving no visible scars. What was left was a clutter of radios, cameras, tape recorders, a small TV, electrical machines that brushed and irrigated his teeth and trimmed his hair and shined his shoes, chess sets, books, gloves, scarves, shirts, sweaters, boots, knives, pens, typewriters, fishing rods, paint sets, easels, even a new Monopoly set, from someone who insisted that he was still a child. We had a lot of fun going through the stuff on a rainy Sunday. Harry had brought it all into the city in his station wagon, at Terry's request. Harry had argued for leaving it all out on the Island, but Terry wanted his loot where his body was most of the time. He wanted to give some of it to his brothers anyway. He gave Paul a globe of the world with a set of lights that illuminated the free world, the communist world, the Arab world, the world of the Alliance for Progress — inaccurately, as Terry pointed out. What gadget could keep up with our world? The three boys spent the afternoon taping original commercials, dramas, rock songs. They were startlingly funny. The kids were so excited by the results and by my laughter that they were seriously considering the formation of a media corporation, but they lost interest the next day and Terry erased the tapes to make room for a new Rolling Stones album he had borrowed from a friend.

He had more than fifteen hundred dollars of money gifts stashed away in a bank account, held in trust for him by Harry. But there was no mention of Vermont. Though Terry seemed back on the track, there was something unreachable about him, something explosive. He didn't bathe or change his clothes and the mess in his room was unbelievable — a welter of electronic wonders covered by dirty shirts and sweat-dried socks, coated with the ashes of his new habit and overlaid with the sickly odor of burning incense. Once every two weeks, Viola went in and cleaned. He didn't object because Viola was one of the underprivileged, and under cover of her action, I would steal his clothes when he was asleep and put

them in the hamper so that he was forced to change them.
Both of us were afraid to touch certain things. He was writing poetry on the new typewriters. In the Olivetti:

> *Bright, bright day.*
> *I run and leap and shout*
> *For no reason.*
>
> *Now I am tired.*
> *I lean against the school wall.*
> *Will I die?*

In the large Smith-Corona portable:

> *Come out with me, my brothers,*
> *Come out into the streets*
> *Come out crying*
> *Freedom*
> *Brotherhood*
> *Equality*
>
> *Come out with me, my brothers,*
> *Come out into the streets*
> *Come out yelling*
> *Fuck war*
> *Fuck starvation*
> *Fuck man's inhumanity to man*
> *Fuck life*
> *When death is nobler.*

On his desk, on top of a pile of sweaters, a large white sheet,
printed in carefully done block lettering:

I HEREBY DECLARE MYSELF A MENTAL INCOMPETENT.

signed with his changing, scrawling self-important signature.
For a long time, the forty-odd dollars stayed on his desk

where I had left them. One evening when I came home from work I found the money on my dresser. We said nothing about it. He didn't seem to be taking any more, but I was careful to keep my money out of sight and reach.

It was easy working uptown near the apartment in that nothing job, except for the weariness of boredom, of feeling myself foolish and useless for so much of the day. And it was easy to lie away my evenings with Matt. I was taking a course in cataloguing to upgrade me in my new job.

And I was happy. There should be a project study on human happiness. I don't mean social happiness, or what is meant by happiness in the life-liberty sense of making a living, but the mystery of individual happiness. Happiness, love, joy — whatever it is. Aren't there elements common to all of us in a state of joy that might be broken down, isolated, named and understood? Even if, like a cloud, love and joy are ephemeral, fleeting, subject to unrecognizable alteration by a shift of wind or a temperature drop into hatred and anger, isn't there some hard information to extract from such a study which could be useful to us?

I tried to work that idea out with Matt and babbled away at him sitting at the desk, studying some plans while I lounged on the double bed in his small old-fashioned room at the hotel.

His response was dismay. "I drive my women crazy," he said. "Don't talk anymore. Read the *New York Times*. I have to work."

He was in trouble with his work, partly because of Mary and all the interruptions. More because he was dissatisfied with what he saw as a steady degeneration into more salesmanship and more business than anything else in the firm he was moving up in. But he had a real assignment at the moment. He was part of a group designing a model village to be built outside Washington. A rich model village, but he was excited by the possibility anyway, since doing something unusual here could set an example. He had the shopping area to play with and he was trying to come up with something useful and efficient, but charming and individualized, knocking out the usual supermarkets for the little separate shops of the past century, and to stay within limitations that would make the design acceptable to his bosses and to the builders and moneymen, so that he could save his energy to fight for the concept. He often worked when we were together, between times in bed. Perhaps he really needed to use every little space of time he had. But I think it was a ritual that he fed on. He liked it best if I fell asleep while he worked. He liked to come back to the bed and wake me, maybe because I was so glad to be waked.

We didn't speak of Mary, but I knew he was writing to her because I had seen the letters, on his desk and in his hand, stamped, ready to be mailed, addressed to the hospital in Brooklyn.

"Does she answer?" I asked him.

"No," he said.

But one day she did. That's all he said about it. He told me that the doctors said she was ready to have her friends visit, and that Paula and Joanna and Cora were going the next day if I wanted to go along and if I could get the time off.

"How about you?" I said.

"I'm not visiting yet," he said.

I arranged for time off easily with Honey. We went separately, agreeing to meet outside before we went in, Joanna and

Paula in one car and Cora and I in her little bug which she asked me to drive. She didn't enjoy driving. We didn't talk much on the long trip from highway to speedway to tunnel to beltway, skirting rivers and bays covered by a thick smog held down by a sudden thaw. I asked her about her writing, but she wasn't a talkative writer.

"What I write about?" She laughed. "I don't know how to tell you. I try to write about the life I know that I don't find in anybody else's books."

"Does it take a lot of discipline?"

"I don't know," she said. "It's crazy. I'm hooked on what I'm doing now. I keep getting up earlier and earlier every day to get to work. This morning it was five-thirty."

She didn't offer any more. I tried to think myself into her position, to translate what she was saying into terms of Matt's concentration on his work and then back into something for myself. What activity could bring me that happy, avid, selfish interest in my own work?

We met the others in the parking lot and joined a mass of visitors clustered in front of a huge, grilled, locked gate, waiting for it to be opened. We were conspicuous in that collection of misery, especially Paula in her cape, and I in my leopard-trimmed winter suit, a leftover from the old, great wardrobe I used to have, though its seat lining was completely shot. Paula's conversation, loud and clear, relating her boy friend's activities on the West Coast, where he had been organizing some kind of reparations for the black and Indian movements, had everybody listening, until the gates opened and we all pushed and pressed and surged forward to be first, even here where to be first meant to be first to confront misery most directly. Everybody seemed to be carrying a parcel or shopping bag of food.

"We should have brought something," Joanna said. "But I didn't know what was allowed."

"Wasn't that stupid!" Paula said. "We could have brought some goody she's longing to have. Like bagels and cream cheese and lox. Or Malomars."

"There's a cafeteria where they can buy things," Cora said. "You sound as if you expect it to be like Girl Scout camp."

Mary's response was very like Cora's when Joanna apologized for no food. "Forgot your CARE package for Mary, girl nut? I forgive you, as long as you have matches. Do you have matches?"

But that was the chief directive we had been given, before the last door was unlocked and we were allowed into the section where Mary waited for us in a kind of hallway lined with wooden benches, jammed with patients and visitors in an extraordinary confusion and noise. No matches to be given to the patients. She looked stormy at the refusal, but she stayed friendly. She was dressed in her own clothes, striped pants and a ribbed sweater, not some ghastly uniform which was what I had been half expecting. Her eyes were heavily made up and brilliantly liquid — perhaps from medication.

She said, "Come see the quarters," and hurried us along a passage toward a large open ward at the end, but stopped on the way to push open a half-closed door. She watched us as we peered into the large, dim room, thick with metal crib beds. In the nearest crib I saw a very old woman, dried and blanched the pearly gray of driftwood. She barely breathed. Next to her was another, and beyond her another, and then I stopped looking.

"You're not in *here?*" I said.

She shook her head. "Bella's department. If they have their way."

She pulled me ahead and waved to the others to stay apart. "What do they say about me?" she said. "What do they tell you?"

"Who?" I said.

"About getting out," she said impatiently.

"I'm sure you'll be out soon," I said.

"Promise," she said. "Promise."

I nodded.

"Say it," she said.

"I promise," I said.

She came even closer, whispering directly into my ear. "Give me some matches. I must have matches. It's torment."

I said, "I don't have any. I don't smoke."

She turned away from me and hurried back to the others, waiting, sitting on a wooden bench. When I got there, she was laughing and half crying on Joanna's shoulder, whispering in her ear, rolling her head and flinging out her arms like a bad actress. Joanna looked stiff and uncomprehending under a suede beret that made her into an absurdity. She started, and pulled away angrily at something Mary was saying and Mary moved on to Paula, flinging her head in Paula's lap, giggling and thrashing about like an adolescent. At the far end of the bench, an obese adolescent rubbed her crotch rhythmically with the palm of her hand while an older woman steadily fed her from a container of cottage cheese. The girl's cheeks were streaked scarlet and her eyes were glazed. From the big, open ward, sounds of a variety of radio stations blared unbearably.

"Isn't there someplace better than this to visit?" Cora shook Mary loose from Paula. "Come on, there has to be a better place than this, Mary."

"I have cafeteria privileges. I'll take you there." She was

all energy at the prospect. "First, come see my quarters. And my guerrilla band."

She led us into a huge room too cluttered with beds, radios, clothing, girls and women to get any clear idea of what it was, though there was some kind of nutty orderliness. She called ahead, "Chickee, chickee, visitors coming, hide your stuff, sisters." She led us to a sheltered side, formed by a break in the wall, closets or elevators built into the room from the corridor. There were three beds in this little island with a narrow window between Mary's bed and the next patient's. Barred and sooty, the window looked out on a high wall. Mary's bed was covered with newspapers and periodicals. She flung herself on it, screwing her head like a spastic. "I see sky," she said. "Here, try it," she offered. But she was already on to the next thing. "Come meet my roomies." She introduced us to the woman sitting on the next bed, her ear glued to a radio blasting rock. She was knitting furiously. She looked up, nodded brightly at the introduction without ceasing to listen or to knit. She was a stuffed doll tied at the neck and waist, the puff of her face topped with bunched curls, the puffs of her upper and lower body wadded into a knitted green garment. Her legs hung from the chair, skinny and shapeless and inert in tiny, spike-heeled pumps. The woman on the next bed was up and ready to greet us. She could have been anywhere from thirty to fifty — flowing golden hair, thin plucked eyebrows, wide light blue eyes, a huge lipsticked mouth.

"I can't tell you what a pleasure it is to meet friends of Mary. That girl is my absolute favorite girl of all time. I love her. I just love her. I'd do anything for her. I want to add her picture to my collection."

She swept open her narrow locker door. Among the tacked snapshots, I saw a man in uniform, two children in different poses and at different ages, herself perhaps — younger, in a big hat on a beach, laughing — Cary Grant, the Kennedys gathered at one of the funerals, Johnny Cash.

"Do any of you have a picture of Mary? Could you mail me one right here at the hospital?" She whispered, "While you're at it, slip some matches in the envelope." She broke up laughing, but launched again into a babbling conversation.

Around us spread the grotesquely ordinary life of the enormous room. Women fixing their hair, sewing, chatting, listening to individual radios, writing letters, some sitting and staring. It was easy to imagine Mary living here, at the same time that it was horrifying and unimaginable.

"That's weakness," Mary's roomie was saying to Cora. "That's my nerves. I never had strong nerves. But then I'm cheerful. I keep cheerful. Mary's a little moody. She has to watch that. I keep myself busy, changing my pictures around, fixing my clothes, making my little corner here look nice . . ."

"We have to go, Sylvia," Mary interrupted. "I'm taking my guests to the cafeteria."

"The tunnel, oh boy!" Explosive laughter from both. "Don't eat the tuna fish," Sylvia said, when she recovered. "And don't touch the hamburgers. You're paying for it; why pay for poison? Stick to ham or egg salad, but watch out for the mayonnaise."

"I'm lucky," Mary said. "They're pretty good buddies."

"Is that girl who was on the bench in your ward? The one who was being fed?" I asked Mary.

"I didn't notice," she said. "But she probably is."

She cuddled against me as we walked, and whispered, "I hope I don't have to stay until the baby is born."

"What?" I said.

She palmed her flat stomach as if it bulged. "Don't tell anybody. It's Bob's. Matt will be so angry. And just when he's having the right feelings again."

She worked a letter out of her pants pocket, much folded, teared on or coffee spattered, unfolded it along its worn creases and showed me:

Dearest, dearest Mary,
How good, how good to get your letter . . .

in Matt's familiar writing, and snatched the letter away, laughing like a silly kid.

"No, you can't see it. It's my love letter," she said, tamping it back into her flat pocket.

She rounded us up at the elevator. "Now we have to stick together," she said. "This is tricky. It's your basic madhouse trip and I don't want it to be a bummer." And she darted away from me to Cora's side, cuddling against her and whispering in her ear.

The scenes through which we were moving assaulted me like bad weather. I felt cold. My throat and head hurt. I had no sense of having seen anything clearly in the crowds of people we had passed except one young man, just out of childhood, railing against a woman. His mother? Wife? She listened quietly, answering nothing. His hands made short, darting, jabbing motions at her as if he were stabbing her. Then he spit full in her face. She wiped it off with a tissue that he took from a supply on his lap, even helping her get a bit she hadn't reached. When she was clean, he started his tirade again. He spoke in Spanish. I wanted to know what he was saying, to come to her defense, but my high school Spanish wasn't good enough for that rapid, violent speech.

Mary called out, "Oh, shit, I left my pass. Wait a minute," and she darted away from us.

Paula said, "Like, you know, in a way, she seems happy here. Isn't that crazy?"

Cora said, "Did she tell you she believes she's having Bob's baby?"

"Well, sure," Paula said. "I get your drift. But I didn't mean happy-happy, just crazy-happy."

Joanna said, "She said something so horrible to me, so horrible."

Paula said, "Now, you're not taking that talk about Bob for real? That's a delusion."

"Not about Bob," Joanna said. "About me. I'll never forget it. As long as I live."

"What did she say?" Paula said.

"What difference does it make?" Cora said, sharply, to Paula — and to Joanna, gently, "Forget it, Jo, she doesn't know what she's saying."

"Come on," Paula said. "It will make you feel better."

"What will?" I said.

"To tell us," Paula said.

"I couldn't bring myself to repeat it," Joanna said.

"It's always better to get anger out," Paula said.

"I'm not angry," Joanna said.

"Don't think about it," I said. "She's not herself."

Mary returned and we went down the elevator to the basement to enter the tunnel — a narrow, tile-lined, long, straight passage with a curved roof and a hard floor, harshly lit by exposed white lighting. Something happened to noise in there. The most ordinary sounds became violent and menacing — our clicking heels, our laughter, the voices of others far ahead — and we were surrounded by whirrings, purrings, grindings, as if we were penetrating to the heart of an infernal machine. The air of the tunnel was cold and lifeless. Mary was walking ahead with Cora. Paula and Joanna were next and I followed alone. The space wasn't wide enough for three. The passage seemed to go on forever.

"How do you like it, Jean?" Mary called back to me in a distorted voice.

"I hate it," I said. "Doesn't it ever end? Is that the trick?"

"Wait," she said. "If we're lucky, we'll get the full treatment. If the kids see ladies walking, they put on a show."

"What's the point of this tunnel anyway?" Cora said.

"It's the way we have to go to the cafeteria."

"You've got to be kidding," Paula said.

"It's true," Mary said. "Couldn't it make you crazy?"

An incredible racket started up. Mary jumped, clapped her hands and ran ahead. "Here it comes. Here it comes. They're doing a number. Run. Run. Follow me."

We ran after her. The noise reverberated intolerably, bouncing off the hard surfaces, bounding ahead, rushing up from behind, entering my body like a seizure. She herded the others into an opening in the wall. For a second I thought that Mary had brought me to this spot to have me killed by some weird means. I screamed and she came back for me. Laughing and running, pulling me by my hand, she made for another opening, thrusting me in.

"Hold your head. Hold your ears," she screamed into my face. She put her arms around my head, covering my ears. "Like that. Like that. Do mine."

I held her head, protecting her ears, thrilling with fear, while the noise swelled in intensity and came to a head in the shape of a two-tiered hospital food cart stacked with metal trays, dirty dishes and metal covers being ridden at top speed by two white-jacketed youngsters, roaring at the top of their lungs in Spanish. The apparition racketed past and whizzed down the endless corridor ahead, the noise rolling back to us in waves of shock. We collapsed on each other, laughing helplessly. "There it is," Mary said. "The whole bit."

15 ———

I EXPECTED MARY TO BE OUT soon after our visit. But it
dragged on and she got worse. She was put into a violent section, visitors weren't permitted and Matt told me that she had
agreed to have shock treatment. Without discussing it with
Matt I thrashed around trying to find help for her. I spoke to
every doctor who entered the library, looking for advice. One
of the young surgeons had heard of something going on at the
psychiatric institute and he brought along a friend to talk to
me the next day. We went to the cafeteria and over coffee
and oily doughnuts they outlined a procedure that I didn't
understand. The theory was that removal of the glandular
system would control the mental thing and the cancer simultaneously. It sounded like one of Mary's creations, but the
method was receiving very serious attention at the institute,
and they would be eager to admit her. They were ready to
request her transfer immediately if Matt granted permission.
They would operate at once. They presented the matter as if
there were no choice. She would die anyway and this might
save her life. I ran off to Matt's hotel room after work on the
day I was given all the details as if I were carrying a reprieve.
But I waited to tell him until late in the evening.

It mixed him up. He had struggled to a plateau in his feelings that would allow him to get through this time in his way. The possibility of her being made completely well shook that up. He got out of bed and fully dressed. He couldn't discuss it with me, naked, in the bed where we had forgotten her existence. I dressed, too, and we ended talking about it in the coffee shop downstairs. He said that he would meet with the doctors at the institute and then check it out with Dr. Altman and Dr. Stone.

"If she lives," he said, "I guess we'll go on, in our way."

I hadn't thought about that.

"Whatever's wrong between us, I'm committed to her. I guess I'll always love her."

"I know," I said.

"I seem to be all wrong for this time. I believe in one wife, one family." He laughed. "Even one dog."

"Weren't you having affairs?"

He shook his head. "You're my affair." He looked down at his hands. He spent a lot of time studying his healed fingers, since the splint had been taken off. They did look strange, weak and sickeningly white. "I wanted you to know how I feel," he said, rubbing the fingers.

A week later when it was all set he wanted me to know more. It was going to be the last time we would meet for a while. We were going to part after dinner and that would bring our "affair" to an end. He was telling me this at a restaurant on the upper west side that had been converted from two stores. The wall between hadn't been broken through, and there were two long narrow sections with tables lined up with their backs to the wall. It was impossible to talk without being overheard on either side. The students on our right were much more concerned with themselves, but on our left an older couple with nothing to say to each other gave us all their attention. He told me that Mary was being transferred the following day. She would be operated on immediately. It would either be successful or not, and if it did no good she'd be no worse off than now.

"How do they know?" I said. "Can one live without glands?"

"Cortisone," Matt said.

"But how long can anyone take that?"

"That was one of Altman's objections, among many others," Matt said.

"He's opposed?"

"You know how he is," Matt said. "He never seems to be giving a shit. For him, I'd say he had a strong reaction. He doesn't like the institute. He says they experiment. He's for leaving her alone. So were the doctors at the state hospital."

"Who's in favor?" I said.

"Dr. Stone. And the people at the institute, of course. And me. Because if I didn't try everything to save her, I'd feel . . ." He didn't finish. "And you. You brought this plan to me." He finished his salad, picking the whole bowl up in one hand and getting every bit out. "They say there's a good chance for her to live and to be normal."

"Why won't we be seeing one another anymore?" I said, returning him to the beginning of our conversation. The woman of the older couple listened with great interest.

"I can't," he said. "I can't do this unless I concentrate everything on it. I'm bringing the kids home to be there when she gets out of the hospital. They told me that whatever happens she'll be feeling very well after the operation. I'm keeping the woman who comes in to clean and help with Bella. I want everything to be good and smooth — as good as possible. I saw her today." I thought he meant Bella, but he meant

Mary. "It was the first time she wanted to see me. She's so weak and thin. Gentle. Beautiful. And funny." He smiled, listening to something that had happened between them, but not telling it to me. "She had pictures of me and the kids next to her bed. She had had them in her bag all the time. There was something heartbreaking about her."

I laughed. "We do our best to break her heart and find it astonishing that it worked."

"I don't need that kind of talk," he said. "I can't use it."

I didn't say what I was feeling. He had cheated me. It was all right if he wanted to end it but not at the beginning of our evening. I couldn't even remember what our last time together had been like. I didn't want to stay through dinner, and I told him I was leaving.

"You haven't had dessert," he said.

I looked back, just before I went through the outer door to the street, and he was watching me. So were the older couple. I waved. He raised his hand slowly, as if he were taking an oath. I went out onto Broadway, a step which can feel like a descent into hell in the mood I was in. Matt would probably stay to eat both our desserts. They were on the dinner and he was always hungry, no matter what.

He called me a few days later. Mary was at the institute. Would I go see her? She was wild because she had been expecting to go home. He wanted to keep himself out of it. Did I understand how important it was that Mary feel he had nothing to do with this new move? I said, "Yes, of course," and walked through the buildings from the library to the psychiatric hospital. Demons must design these buildings. The structure was built down the stone wall of the Palisades over the river and when you entered the lobby floor, it was really the eighth. I took the elevator down to the sixth floor where Mary was. They told me that I couldn't see her. I tried the next day, with the same response. The third time Matt was at the entrance. I had walked out on the street, to get the air which had come up miraculously spring that morning, and met him on the steps of the institute with a doctor I had never seen before. He was blond, square faced, young, with a mid-westerner's relaxed speech, so that the unhappiness nakedly expressed in his blue eyes was all the more remarkable. Matt grabbed my arm.

"Jean, Dr. Walkers says . . . it's not . . . it's not . . ." His face was gray, and his hands were shaking on my arm.

"You people close to her," the doctor said, "have to understand that she was a very, very sick girl before we touched her. She was all . . ." He crisscrossed his arms to cover his body in a swooping gesture and with a grimace of distaste. "It's all over her," he said, moving his arms that way again.

I said, "But didn't you know that in advance?"

He said, "She was a very, very sick girl before we touched her."

I turned to Matt. "He said that already. What is it, have they made her worse?"

"That's the kind of talk that doesn't do any good," the doctor said. "There wasn't any way to make her worse. If I were close to her I wouldn't talk that way. I'd just stay by her side now and give her all the support in the world."

He looked so miserably unhappy that I said, "How? How would you do that?"

"I'd go right up there and sit by her side and hold her hand."

"I can't," Matt said. "I can't stand it."

"Can I do that?"

"You sure can," he said. "Just sit right there and hold her hand. I'll take you up myself and tell the nurses."

"Is she dying?" I said.

"Right now?" Dr. Walkers said. "No, you don't understand. She's going to feel much better; she's going to feel all well for a while, after she recovers from the operation. After that . . ." He made a downward gesture with his arm.

Mary was in an immaculate, narrow room overlooking the river. There was just the bed, a table and a room full of equipment. They brought in a chair for me and put it alongside the bed. She was the only patient in the room, with so many nurses and doctors in attendance that I never got them straight in my mind. The room was dimmed against the sunlight and she was high in the bed — tubes, bottles, recording attachments flowing from every opening of her body. One hand and her forehead and eyes alone were free. I took her hand in mine; it was dry, hot, crisp yet limp. I kissed her hot forehead and she opened her eyes and looked straight into my face. There was total recognition, a kind of welcome, and an appeal to make it all stop. I said, "I'm here, Mary. I'm going to stay with you." I thought she pressed my hand in response.

I didn't speak again, not to her, nor to the nurses who tried to keep me comfortable while I stayed with her. They all wanted me there. That puzzled me. For the sake of their collective conscience? To make her more cooperative? Mary obviously hated them all. Whenever anyone approached her, she glared loathing and refusal with all her helpless strength. They needed me, they, the machine people, the technologists, needed genuine human compassion because it hadn't yet been bottled for intravenous feeding. Had they mistreated her? Not likely. They had done this operation for themselves;

it was too important to them to let anything happen to Mary. That reassured me about the immediate things, the things they seemed to be torturing her with. They needed to learn something from this technique, from its successful result, and perhaps they would and in time save others. That was their business and their calling. But why had I meddled and fussed and dragged her into still another useless agony?

The nurses and doctors called me Sister. I didn't correct them. If they had called me Mary and stuck me with their gadgets in her place, I wouldn't have set them straight. I don't know how long I stayed. At one point, a nurse loosened my hand and led me away and Matt came in as I went out. We didn't speak. I called Honey at the library and explained. She was good about it and said not to worry about coming back that day. I called Viola and told her to write a note for the kids, saying I would be home late.

I was bilious and nauseous and my vision was blurred from a painful headache. I went to the ladies' room. I had started to menstruate. Hadn't I finished menstruating only a few days earlier? I was probably going into my menopause. Old, old. I smelled foul to myself. My body had absorbed the hospital smells of Mary's room. I walked to one of the hospital cafeterias and had tea and a couple of aspirins. When I came back up, Matt had left. The nurses greeted me effusively. "Good girl. You came back. She still needs Sister," and they led me to my post as if I were another attachment, a life line through her thin, hot hand.

I had no watch and no sense of the passage of time. The day darkened and they lit up the room, too brightly. From time to time, the nurses gave me juice and tea, when I refused to be relieved to eat. I wasn't hungry. At one point there was a fuss. Mary became very agitated, clawing at my hand, desperately trying to communicate with her eyes. I called a nurse and doctors ran in. They put me out for a few minutes and when I returned, she was peaceful. She slept more now, but when I changed hands, she stirred and clung to the new one I gave her. Parts of my body fell asleep and tingling painfully would slowly come back to life. In the early evening I thought I heard Mama and Papa Shaeffer's voices outside, but if I did, they were turned away, because nobody came in. I heard the light conversation of the nurses and doctors, beamed from another planet, in an incomprehensible language. What life or meaning existed was in my hand held by Mary's weak, hot, thin fingers.

A different set of nurses sent me away, after midnight, with hearty reassurances that I wouldn't know her in the morning. "She'll be a new person. She's got it licked. You'll see, Sister. She'll be as good as new. You go home and get a good rest now. You earned it."

Harry was at the apartment. Elliot had gotten sick and the boys had panicked and called him. His anger dissipated when he saw me. He made a cup of tea for me and sat with me in the kitchen asking me about Mary. But I couldn't really speak of it.

He called Melody, explaining where I had been. "No sense making that trip home now, darling," he said. "I'd have to practically turn around and come straight back to the city by the time I got there."

She said something. "I'll stay here at the apartment." He laughed in a sexy way and said, "Not very likely." He switched to a funereal, solemn voice to tell her about Mary.

He was being very good to me. He rinsed the tea things and offered to sleep in Elliot's room so that I could get a good rest.

He had had the doctor, who thought Elliot was brewing something contagious. Harry had put Paul in the living room, just in case. He enjoyed being kind to me, I could see. We could have been slipped back into the time when the kids were younger and we were living in the house in Forest Hills. Presently we would go to bed together and our old life would continue as if nothing had happened. I thought about that, in my bed, alone, before I fell asleep. What had happened to those people, Harry and Jean, who had loved one another, or thought they did, and to their flesh that had joined to make three children? Was it this same flesh that lived on in a disconnected present? I saw myself when I was twelve climbing a steep downtown street in Altoona. It was a raw, windy day, my stocking was twisted around my leg and falling down, I had failed a test in algebra, a boy had called me skinny, and a group of men in the window of a cruddy barber shop on the corner laughed at my slipping stocking. I swallowed, again, the accumulation of humiliations of that long-ago day. Where was that girl — myself at twelve? Where was the body? Where were they buried, the bodies of myself in my lives and deaths?

But nothing had ever happened to me. I had spent every night of my life safe in bed — mine or somebody else's. I had never been bombed or flooded or frozen or seized or imprisoned or degraded or beaten or starved or arrested or burnt or shot or even stopped and questioned by the police. I had never been in a hospital except to have my babies. I had led a charmed life. I was to be congratulated.

Elliot's illness was measles. He was very sick, in spite of a gg shot. He had hallucinations. There were bottles strung across the windows, fragmenting the light and smashing into themselves and into his eyes. There was a monster in the TV. He was a mass of pain — bones, ears, head, eyes. He didn't always recognize me and shrank from me, his eyes filled with the horrified vision I had become. But he wanted me near him. Or Paul. "I can't stand your smell," he told Terry. "You move too fast," he told Harry. "You're breathing so that I can hear you," he yelled at Joanna. "Go away." I stayed at home to tend him. I told Honey that I would understand if she had to get someone else. She said that she would, but that she was planning to get somebody who wasn't any good. That way, she could fire her when I was ready to come back. Harry said not to worry. If the money he was giving me wasn't enough, he'd see to it that we were taken care of adequately. What did I think he was anyway? What I thought was that he was happy to have his new wife and his old family and that at a sign from me he would have taken over his former place and worked it both ways.

I didn't go anywhere near Mary because of the danger of infection, but my phone rang incessantly with news of her from the Shaeffers and Joanna and Paula. She was healing quickly. By the time Elliot was better and happy to have anyone at all stay with him to play the marathon Monopoly game we were in the middle of, Mary was due to go home. Joanna came to be with Elliot while I ran up to the hospital to see Mary. I heard voices — Matt's and a stranger's. I stood outside listening. The strange voice was reading something and Matt and Mary were laughing and interrupting the reading and one another with their outraged reactions. I heard Cora's voice saying something I couldn't follow, then the strange voice again.

"He did a good book, *The New Brutalism*, or some such title. Don't put him down."

"Well, he's the king of gibberish," Cora said, "in that piece."

"You ought to answer it, Andy," Mary said.

"The whole concept works out without a passing thought for the class nature of the city grid," the strange voice said.

"Come on, now," Matt said. "Are we taking your concept as a given element?"

I wasn't going to be able to keep up with that kind of conversation. I wanted to go away, but one of the nurses from the other night saw me. "Here's Sister," she called out, and ushered me in to Mary.

Mary looked incredibly well. Her face was rounded, the skin translucently clear. She wore no make-up and her own calm intelligent eyes had been returned to her. She took my face in her hands and kissed me full on the lips. She was in a different room from the one where I had sat by her side. This was flooded with sunlight. She could see the river from her bed. Everything in the room was covered with books and magazines and papers or massed with flowers and plants. The strange voice belonged to a short young man with flaming red hair and a face that made you feel good to look at, it was so full of energy and humor. I kissed Cora and avoided kissing Matt by making a big thing of being introduced to Andrew Martin, visiting from London.

"You sound American," I said.

"That must be because I am," he said. "I've been living in England for five years."

"My oldest friend," Matt said. "We started in grade school together.

"*Slouching Toward Bethlehem*," Cora said, returning the conversation to where it had been. "That's another thing I'm sick of. She flipped the paperback over, face up on Mary's table on wheels. "What would the literary marketplace do without that poem?"

Mary laughed. "Right. Get a couple of those lines under your belt and you've got it made. Instant literary know-how. 'Things fall apart; the center cannot hold.' "

" 'Mere anarchy is loosed upon the world,' " Matt said.

" 'The best lack all conviction, while the worst/Are full of passionate intensity,' " Andy said.

" 'And what rough beast . . .' " Cora said, prowling around the room. She stopped, "You look lost, Jean."

I said, "I don't know that poem. Am I allowed to stay?"

"You're kidding," Andy said.

Cora tossed the book to me. "It's the epigraph," she said.

I didn't know what that was.

Matt said, "It's right at the beginning," when I opened the book in the middle. He found it for me and read over my shoulder.

I said, "It's a wonderful poem," unable to understand their derision.

Andy looked unbelieving. "You've never read Yeats? How could you get through college without reading Yeats?"

"I didn't go," I said, bristling in my ignorance. But I was unhappy and used Elliot as an excuse to leave. Matt apparently found one also, because he ran to catch up with me on the street.

He asked me to walk down the drive with him. "It's important," he said. "I must talk to you."

I called Joanna at a street booth, after losing a couple of dimes in the attempt. She told me to stay out, the air would do me good. It was a mild spring day, almost clear for New York. For most of the walk, he talked about things that didn't seem important, mostly about Andy Martin and the life they had led as kids. He told me that Bella was doing very well, that the kids were fine, that Shtrudel had become a hopeless neurotic. He was a vigorous walker, but I wasn't, and my shoes weren't right for a long walk. He wanted to get to the esplanade in the upper eighties to see the cherry trees in bloom. I insisted on taking the bus after we had walked awhile. In the exposed arrangement of the seating, we hardly spoke. Under the flowering trees, on the paths above the river, in the late afternoon sunlight, with not much garbage strewn around and not too many people — a preoccupied tramp on the bench next to us studiously going through a shopping bag of trash, and a young girl sitting on the grass, breast-feeding an infant while an older woman stood nearby looking painfully self-conscious — we became imprisoned in silence. It pressed down, a suffocating fog. Matt smoked two cigarettes, staring ahead at the broad river and up at the budding blossoms. He didn't look at me. It was intolerable to me that I should weigh so heavily on him.

"I think I'd better go, Matt," I said, forcing myself to break the silence. "I shouldn't be away too long."

"No," he said. "You can't go like that again." He stood up, and partly lifting me by the elbow, made for the parapet on the other side of the broad esplanade, carrying me along. He leaned on the stone wall. Even here, the rich pink blossoms flowered above the fumes of the thick, moving stream of highway traffic, and below that the wide, placid river.

"There's no place to talk in this whole fucking city," he said. A troop of youngsters stopped nearby. They slipped the leashes from the dogs they were airing. The dogs ran free down the narrow sidewalks and the broad island of new grass in between. There were two big, smooth, fawn-colored dogs as high as small ponies. They ran with amazing speed. A little dog with a flirty tail stayed nearby and sniffed at my shoes.

"Doesn't she looked wonderful?" Matt said. "She's herself."

I nodded.

"I'm going to be able to do it," Matt said. "It's going to be all right. No more of that horror."

"You don't owe me any explanation," I said.

"In that restaurant, with those people listening, I couldn't say what I wanted to."

I didn't say anything. A sick silence engulfed us again. When he didn't seem able to say anything else and I couldn't stand the silence any longer, I said, "Don't worry about it. This isn't the first thing that came to an end in my life."

He looked up from his study of the scene below the parapet. He fixed a stray hair blowing across my cheek. I put my arms up to tuck it into my bun. "It's just until . . . until afterward," he said.

I shook my head. "That doesn't make any sense. You're just using that as an excuse to end it. You've found out how dumb I am and you know it won't work out."

He said, "You don't understand. I can't do it any other way. Afterward, all that will be gone."

I said, "That's not the way it will turn out. You'll see."

He put his arms around me, pulled me to him and kissed me hard on the mouth. The boys moved up the wall a bit, hooting and smacking their lips together.

"You'll see," Matt said. "That's the way it's going to be. You'll see."

16 ———

ELLIOT WAS IN SUCH BAD SHAPE that I got permission to take the kids out of school early. Paula had offered her beach house. She was going out to the West Coast, and wouldn't be using it until August. She offered it to me and to Joanna, jointly. That was all right. We went out late in June, leaving Terry in the city, spending weeknights with his friend Tony and weekends with Harry until his last weeks of school were completed. He would join us as soon as he could, or stay with Harry, whatever he chose.

We were stocked to the rim of the freezer with food brought out from the city, and the one store on the island was open for milk and butter and wood for the fireplace if we couldn't pick up enough driftwood. There was a little red wagon to haul groceries. There were four bedrooms and a great modern kitchen and huge pantry, and a living room full of wicker furniture and round tables and a big fireplace. There was a sun deck for Elliot to sit on, wrapped in blankets in a reclining chair, a nineteenth-century tubercular. In a week, he was strong enough to make it to the beach to sun on the fine sand and watch the sea. In a few more days he was testing the "burning cold" water and then he was completely well, tagging after Paul in his active wanderings.

Joanna was good company for the kids, and she didn't bother me. In the morning, against Elliot's chatter and Paul's exaltation with life at the shore — the house, the deck, the wagon, the bikes, the stretch of sandy road leading in one direction to the high dunes of the beach and in the other to the working life of the bay, with its ferry slip and fishing boats and its endlessly fascinating low-tide sea life — Joanna and I moved in a glum sisterhood of silence, each taking a cup of coffee to a spot to be alone in, away from each other and from the boys. We got friendlier as the day went on, and almost chummy about planning dinner. She was a rotten cook so I cooked and she washed up with some help from the boys. In the evening a fireplace coziness joined us, but never to the point of any real talk. She had returned to her sealed self.

She was happy. She liked to give the boys a lot of information and they liked to receive it. She loved sun and soaking it up on the beach and didn't mind about the water being too cold because she didn't swim. There was a potter's wheel and kiln and all the necessary stuff in a beautifully finished shed attached to the house where she spent some time every day, bent over the wheel, her coarse hair unmanageably wild from the sea and wind, her eyes peering conscientiously from behind her thick glasses at the unpromising mess before her. The shelves in the shed were lined with Paula's products, mostly lumpy, coarse objects. On the wicker coffee table in the living room, there was a pretty teapot and sugar bowl with a finer glaze than the others that Joanna had done on a previous visit. Joanna had taken a course in pottery.

I thought about courses in pottery, in my thinking sessions, lying on the beach, wondering what I could do to make my life better — make pottery, open a knitting shop, become an interior decorator or a make-up expert. But these were all things unlearned, to be added to my long list. I had never studied yoga or the dance or been analyzed or attended an encounter group, but then neither had I ever had an abortion, or been raped, mugged or killed in an elevator. Mixed congratulations.

When the weather got hotter, Paul braved a real swim and emerged pronouncing it the greatest sensation in his whole life. I followed and fell in love with the feel of the sea and lived for my three swims a day. I stopped using junk on my skin. I left the eyeliner off and faced my tired, crinkled eyes for what they were. I had good, thick, curly lashes and a pretty face. I was going to live with it plain from now on. But I worked at getting a perfect tan anyway. I slept nine and ten hours a night. I seemed to be consciously enjoying being asleep even while I was soundly sleeping. I thought about sleeping when I was awake. I looked forward to it, gossiping with Joanna before the fireplace, as if sleep were a thrilling assignation. Sometimes I couldn't wait and fell asleep while she was listening to the eleven o'clock news. Listening was a three times a day ritual with her, the news made even more nightmarish in the repetition: the war, the official statements, the enemy's denial, the traffic deaths, conspiracy charges, abortion reform fights, kidnapings, terrorism, peace talks, negotiations of all kinds, hijackings, charges and countercharges of anti-Semitism, Panther trials, civilian massacre trials, murder trials, riots, demonstrations, flaring wars between nations in corners of the world that didn't seem to really exist, the nonsense item they always found to end each broadcast with — and then the weather, reported as if every dip of the wind was a judgment day warning. Joanna said she had to keep in touch. She kept up a running comment. "It's fascism. It's open fascism." Or, "Did you hear that? Did you hear that? I've never heard anything so ridiculous in my life." Or, "Well, that's encouraging." Or, "It's too depressing." And about a lot of the items, "Will we never learn? It's Bella's case all over again. It's a return to McCarthyism."

I didn't want to hear the news. I wanted to be still, to locate the spot of my emptiness and examine it. I didn't want to rush out and fill it. I wanted to hold emptiness up against the hot sun and the icy sea until it was clearly revealed. It was easy to swill around and think life was filled to the brim. But I wasn't going to do that anymore. I didn't say any of that to Joanna. I did my thinking privately, and tried to do it systematically, during certain hours of the day, the hours I spent lying on the beach. Elliot and Paul let me alone. They had all that space and one another and Joanna to bother. I tried to think one thing through, and not indulge my usual aimless dipping and darting. I started with myself when I was little and went on to my sister and mother and father and tried to push myself beyond the old stale memories. But I didn't have any others. I saw my mother as I always had, the ignorant, timid, wretched woman I had fled as from a contagion. I saw her in the closetlike toilet at the end of the hall, on the seat, the door wide open, wiping herself from the front, instead of from the back, which I considered the properly genteel manner. Worse than that, I heard her speak, "You'll never amount to anything. You'll never be any good." *There* was a reason for hatred and flight, better than questions of bathroom finesse. But there must have been more than that. That couldn't have been all there was to my mother, and all there was to our feelings for each other. And my father's image needed more than the knife and the stooping back and the peeled orange and the *thwack* of his blows. But I was stuck with these rotten little bits that told me nothing. About my sister, nothing, as if she had never existed — not a memory, except of a body in the way, in the space I needed for myself. It was bad enough to have wiped them out, but in the process I had erased myself.

In the afternoon we walked along the shore or on the bay side or in the sunken forest, a bowl of greenness, a miniature blossoming valley beyond the high dunes, protected from sea and bay, crisscrossed with charming little paths. In the enchanted forest, everything flowered, even the vines creeping along the ground and the fuzz that clung to the rocks. Joanna named flowers, shrubs, vines, grasses for the boys; she even knew the names of birds that flew by so quickly I saw no more than a flash of color. I felt my ignorance, but it was too late to try to learn anything from her. There was too much to learn to take on the natural world too.

I forced myself to think about that next session. My embattled ignorance. I really valued ignorance, counting it a higher knowledge, since it contained all my priorities — how to look good, how to win a man, how to have babies, how to gossip, how to cook, how to alter the air in a room so that it became a lovely place, how to respond to sun and sea and another body. Enough to fill the empty spot? Not without Matt. If he came back, his presence would rush in and fill me up. And if he didn't?

There had to be a different answer from the right man. That old answer. There had to be another way of connecting with what was beyond me. But I gave it up for that day, because a storm was blowing up and I had to leave the beach.

It stormed for two days. We enjoyed it, snug in the house, the living room warmed by a constant fire in the fireplace and the kitchen toasty with cooking and baking and the rest of the house kept comfortable with electric heaters, running up a huge bill for Paula. The sound of the wind and the sea outside made us feel giddy with security. We had a Monopoly game going for four; and Paul and Joanna alternated with chess in the evenings. Elliot had found a complete "Peanuts" collection in Paula's library. Joanna had her wheel. I had the cooking and baking. Paul did all the manly things, the trash and the wood and the fire and hauling groceries from the store in the little red wagon. His old man's worried eyes were deeply peaceful. He held his body differently, with his well-formed chest jutting out as if he were expanding his lungs for the first time. "Why can't we live like this all the time?" he asked me. "I could get odd jobs around here after school. Then I could become a fisherman or maybe drive the ferry. You'd see. We'd be all right." I told him that I had been thinking about things like that too.

When the storm cleared, it left a crystal-clean world and a glorious, steady wind that drove the clouds across the sky like the fake ones in the old movie palaces I had gone to as a kid. It was cold but brilliantly sunny and we went off to the beach in sweat shirts with hoods. The sea was no playground for humans. It was a purple, slate blue with deep streaks of green toward the shore, and had waves that rose like Park Avenue glass buildings to crash in a roar of foaming white. We dabbled at the very edge, respectfully. The swirling rush of water dug our feet deep into the wet sand. The others gave up at once and went back to the house but I stayed on, letting the wind use me. Gritty with sand, I followed, and found them on the deck, huddled over a project.

"Try and find a box," Joanna called to Paul, hunting around in the shed. "Try the store; they'll have a carton."

He whipped away down the walk toward the store, yelling to me as he raced by, "Go see what I found. Over there." His face was a blaze of happiness. In the flat, white landscape under the intensely blue and white sky, his orange sweat shirt was a banner of his joy. He had found three baby birds, washed up under the one lone bush on Paula's sandy space behind her house. Joanna said they were quail. They were beautifully soft colored and fluffy. They were rigid with fright and held their eyes frozen, not blinking. We watched them, fascinated, speaking in whispers. Paul came back, racing up to the house, but slowing as he approached the birds on tiptoe. He had a cardboard carton in his hand. "This should do it," he whispered.

"What are you doing? Are you going to use that as a shelter?" I whispered.

Elliot couldn't keep his voice down. "Hey, Paul, that's boss. That's great." The birds blinked at the noise, but held their rigidity.

"We'll have to cut it down a little," Joanna whispered.

"You go gather some grass and leaves and twigs," Paul whispered to Elliot.

"We ought to give them some water," Joanna said.

"Water?" I said. "They just escaped drowning."

"Fresh water," Joanna said, and went into a kind of baby talk. "You're safe with us, little birdies. Don't be afraid, we're going to help you."

I thought she was kidding, and I laughed, but she shot me a hurt look, so I stopped.

"What do they eat, Joanna?" Paul said.

"Insects," she said. "Maybe milk would be better than water," she added uncertainly. "They're just little babies. Aren't you?" The birds glared out of the sides of their beady eyes, prisoners refusing to answer.

"Maybe we should put them in a sheltered spot and let their parent birds find them," I said.

"Their parents must have been killed in the storm," Joanna said. "Or they'd be safe in their nest. Wouldn't you?" she said in that voice she had worked up for them.

"The storm blew them to us to take care of," Paul said. He stooped over the birds with his hands clasped before him as if he were praying.

They almost immediately began to sicken. Paul had cut down the box and lined the bottom with grass and twigs and leaves, whatever Elliot could find on the sandy area right around us. Joanna put the box under an exposed light bulb. She said that would keep the birds warm. The light was on day and night. It worried me that the birds might not be sleeping — or even sitting down for that matter. I tried to catch them at it and even got up and came down the stairs in the middle of the night to check, but I never saw them do anything but stand stiffly on their poor little threads of legs and glare out of their lidless eyes. The first day one of the birds tilted the water dish and sloshed it all over the bottom of the box, so Paul redid the box. Elliot brought in a sad collection of sand beetles and snails and put them out on another dish, but the beetle was only playing dead and crawled away, and the other stuff lay in the dish untouched until it began to stink, or so it seemed, and I made Paul throw it away. Joanna was all for giving them milk and took everything else out of the box and put some milk in a larger, firmer dish that couldn't be tilted, but one of the birds fell into the dish. The bird looked repulsive with its bony, frail frame exposed under the flattened, sticky feathers. Paul became frightened and desperate and his tone to Joanna turned bitter and argumentative. He wasn't letting anybody go near the birds now. He tried to wipe the bird clean, but the bird trembled violently and glared and backed away on its twig legs. The next morning, the bird who had fallen in the milk was bloodied, and when I suggested that his companions had attacked him, Paul screamed at me, "That's crazy. You're crazy. Something got at him. Something else got in the box. A mouse, maybe. We ought to fix some sort of cover." He made an attempt to wipe the blood away, gave up and stood at the box, gazing beyond it, with the tears streaking down his cheeks.

I spoke to Joanna, asking her to help me persuade him to put the birds out. "They're going to die," I said. "Or at least one is."

She, too, cried. "No, no, don't say that. We'll keep them alive until they're a little stronger and then we'll put them out."

The following day when the boys were out of the house, hunting bird food, Joanna and I tried to tend the wounded bird. The kids had bought wild birdseed at the store; it was strewn over the floor of the box where it remained untouched. A big, bloody wound had been reopened on the sticky bird. I was sick of this hopeless mess. It had ruined my peace.

"I don't give a shit about these birds," I said. "I don't care whether they live or die as long as it isn't right under my eyes, and as long as it doesn't break Paul's heart."

Joanna looked horrified.

"Millions of birds die," I said. "Nature provides enough of them so that they can die like flies. And what are they going to grow up for anyway? Some hunter is just as likely to come along and shoot them. Maybe the quail population is too big or something and that storm was just the thing to even things out. Who are we to interfere? We're torturing them. And we're torturing Paul. We ought to put them out, right now."

Paul was standing in the doorway, a glass jar of insect goodies in his hand. "No," he said, extending his arms as if he would strike me down. "Stay out of this. Don't touch my birds. I don't want to hear what you say. I don't want to talk to you. I don't ever want to talk to you."

He tried to stay up and watch over them, to forestall the others attacking the wound. He fell asleep, of course, and the wound was enlarged. I came down at four in the morning for the third time and he let me take over for him while he went to bed. I promised to watch faithfully and to do only what he would want me to. He walked away, a little old man again, stooped and sad eyed, and was down by eight, huddling over the box, on guard. Joanna came up with a last-ditch saving action of feeding the bird with an eyedropper, but that didn't work. Elliot had turned his back on the entire operation as soon as the wound had appeared. It was too terrible; he wasn't going to watch. I packed a lunch for myself and Elliot, and we fled, spending the day at the beach. I lay on my stomach, pressed against the hot sand, sifting its varied-colored grains through my fingers, doped by the sun and air and my own depression. I couldn't attempt to think, but I ached with amorphous longing for a new life, for a way to live differently.

I unstuck Paul from the box long enough for him to have his supper, while Joanna took over his watch. The birds all looked worse, and the bloodied one was hanging on by fierce instinct. I cornered Joanna in her room.

"They're dying," I said. "It's making Paul queer to watch it. It's bad for him."

She began to cry, "What about me? Nobody thinks about me."

"Well, stay out of it," I said. "Leave it all to me."

"What are you going to do?" She threw herself down on the bed and sobbed. "Why is life so cruel? Why is my nose always being pushed into the cruelty of life? It's too much to bear." Her voice had risen with her hysteria and Paul came pounding up the stairs.

"What are you doing, Mom? What are you doing to her?"

"Oh for Christ's sake," I said. "About the birds," I began, facing him.

"No," he said, sticking his arms straight out in front of me to hold me off. "No. Let them alone."

I said, "*I'm* not harming them."

He said, "You said you didn't care if they lived or died."

"I was just talking," I said. "You know I care. But I'm not going to be a fool and make things worse out of ignorance and sentimentality."

He said, "I don't know what you're talking about."

But Joanna did. She sat up. She had removed her glasses and her bulging, naked eyes were reproachful and accusing.

"They can't live in a paper carton under a light bulb in a living room," I said to Paul. "Outside they stand a chance. Maybe birds have a way of helping one another."

"How do you know?" Paul said.

"I don't," I said. "I don't know anything about it. I just feel that it's better for them outside. We could put the box out under the bush where you found them. We could cut away a part for them to walk out if they want to. We could keep an eye on them there."

"Tonight?" Paul said, huge tears forming in his eyes.

I wanted the birds out before the first one died. I didn't expect the wounded bird to make it through the night. Paul must have shared my dread, because he was listening.

"It's warm tonight," I said. "No wind or anything." I started out of the room. "We'll do it together." Miraculously, he followed me. "Coming, Joanna?" I stopped for her. But she wasn't talking to me. She went to the window. I could see the trembling of her hand, fingering the filmy white curtain.

Paul took forever to settle on just the right spot. I let him take his time. The evening was beautifully soft and clear, melting into the tender colors of the sunset. He rearranged the bush endlessly, carefully measuring the box to determine how much space was needed and separating and bunching branches until he felt he had the area just right. We carried the box together. He cut away one side of the box with a hunting knife he had found on a shelf in the house. "These knives are real good, Mom. I'd like to get one. You know, for emergencies like this." He was concerned about the birds getting cold, later in the night, and he gathered more brush and junk to protect the base of the box and went on worrying the spot. I backed off, telling him to come in when he was finished. He stayed too long and I went out to the sun deck and called, "Paul? Paul?" He came in a zigzag run, holding his head as if it might split, howling, "Why couldn't they have lived and gotten strong? That's the way it's supposed to happen," and rushed into the room he shared with Elliot, and slammed the door.

I covered the naked light bulb with its proper shade and tidied up the spot where the box had been disarranging the living room. It was a relief to have the room restored. Joanna came down the stairs and went into the kitchen. She had changed her clothes and looked forbidding and formal in black pants and a black blazer. She had struggled with her hair and flattened it neatly if unbecomingly. I followed her into the kitchen. She was making herself a cup of tea.

"That's what I want too," I said.

She turned away, took her tea and started to walk out of the room. I went into something like a fit. I grabbed her arm and whispered fiercely, "If you think I'm going to get into a situation now where you stop talking to me, damn it —" But I stopped because of the hatred in her face.

"You think you can have everything, don't you? You think everything you want will just fall into your lap." It sounded like a curse coming from her. I let her walk out with her tea.

Paul and I were down before six to check the box. I knelt with him to push aside the branches. The ground had a wonderful, sharp smell. Everything looked natural and quiet. The box was exactly where we had put it. All three birds were gone. Paul searched the bush with care, but he didn't turn up any sign of them. They were gone clean. There were no corpses, there was no blood, no indications of struggle; they had walked away to live or die someplace else. I couldn't have asked for more.

17 ————

THE LIBRARY JOB WAS GONE. There wasn't any angle that Honey could play to get me back in, but she steered me to another on a research project. What was really being produced out of that project was a mountain of paper. Our study was tied to the National Institutes of Health. That meant everything had to be typed in seven copies and Xeroxed in the hundreds. The head was a maniac perfectionist woman doctor and I was constantly returning work to be redone by the girls I supervised because a word had been broken incorrectly or the salutation improperly spaced. The only good thing about the job was that it was nearby. Honey kept me clued in on her love life at luncheons at an air-conditioned delicatessen. Over thick corned beef and pastrami sandwiches she described her new lover, a distinguished teaching doctor, old enough to be her father. His wife was a very busy pediatrician, so that gave him a lot of leeway to see Honey often. She never looked drab anymore. She made time for the Israeli boatman, too, whenever he arrived.

August in the city was unbearably hot. The kids were spending the last six weeks of vacation with Harry and Melody. I had a sensational tan and could have had my pick of the married men free for the summer. Though my loneliness was so intense it felt like an illness, I didn't want someone or something. I wanted Matt. I didn't want to be lonely, but I didn't want to be "busy" either. I wanted my corrupt happiness back, whatever it didn't have and wherever it was going.

I worked all day and went home at night, and weekends I read the Sunday *Times* and went to the movies, where it was cool and dark. I thought about what I wanted to do, and I began to feel that I knew what it was though I didn't know how to go about doing it. Mary was the one I wanted to talk it over with, but when I got back from the shore she was in the hospital again. She had had two good months. I knew that from Paula and Cora and from Terry who had seen her at a peace demonstration in Central Park and reported to me when he joined us at the shore that she was great, the greatest, and I shouldn't worry about her anymore.

Mary was in the cancer hospital, a part of the medical complex, but set off by itself a few blocks away. It was a smallish, human-looking building from the front at least. The back slid down the rocks the way they all did. Mary was sharing a room with a talkative, pleasant girl who didn't seem to be very sick. Mary looked well, too, but she couldn't sit up. She lay flat on her back, her eyes smiling out of a face that had become round and soft-looking. She was in pain and we didn't talk much. Soon Paula walked in, and Stella and Sam Shaeffer right after her. They said that others were waiting, so I left. There was a crowd in the visitors' room down the hall. I knew some of them, Joanna, Robin, Cora and Chuck, and others who looked familiar. The room was apparently the ambulant patients' recreation room. Men and women in bathrobes, hauling bottles and rubber contraptions that were attached by tubes that disappeared under their robes, sat around looking at the TV news or watching Mary's visitors.

Joanna rushed up and kissed me. I was surprised, but I returned it. "How is she?" she said.

"I don't know," I said.

"Let's forget all that nonsense," Joanna said. Her glasses misted over, and she kissed me again.

"Sure," I said, and gave her a hug.

"This is it," she said. "We'll never see her out again."

I dropped in to see Mary during my lunch hours and after work. Now that we were speaking again Joanna sometimes came home with me or we'd go to a movie together or she'd drag me to a meeting. She had become active in Women's Lib. An oldie's group. I met her leaving one evening, as I was arriving. Mary was alone in the room. There was only Mary's bed, close to the window, and an empty space where the other bed should have been. Mary felt feverish and looked uncomfortable. There was an overpowering smell of cologne.

"What happened to your buddy?" I said.

Mary waved her hand and frowned slightly, as if annoyed. "She died." And then, "Will you wash this junk off me, Jean? I'm suffocating."

I soaped her washcloth and asked her where it had spilled.

"It didn't spill." She was exhausted and spoke with effort. An uncontrolled smile pulled her lips apart. "Joanna thought it would be cooling. Wash my face and neck and arms."

Her face had stayed so round from the cortisone that it was a shock to feel how her arms were nothing. Her body burned.

"I tried to wash myself and spilled water on my gown." She plucked the coarse cloth away from her body with long, trembling, skinny fingers. "Could you?" She fell asleep between sentences. I could hear her breathing in little shallow gasps. I tended her body as if it were already a thing, washing and

changing her as I might clean a table top. It hardly mattered
that she was scarred and deformed now. There wasn't any
body there anyway. What was left of her was in her round
face and burning head. When I finished, there was still a
strong smell of cologne.

"I can't seem to get rid of it," I said.

She opened her eyes. "It's better," she said. "Throw it
away. I'll tell her I used it all up."

I dropped a bottle of 4711 in her wastebasket and palmed
the sheets to see if they were wet. "It must have spilled in the
bed," I said.

"It's in my hair. That's what you're smelling." Her talk
came on breathless gusts of sound with long pauses between
words.

I soaped the cloth again and wiped her hair away from her
cleanly defined hairline. Her broad, domed, pure forehead,
swept clean of the bangs, gleamed with sweat. The room was
unbearably hot and close. I struggled to open the wide, heavy
window, coated with soot, and moved it a little beyond the
slanting glass ventilator. I took another cloth soaked in plain
warm water and wiped away the soap. She opened her eyes
and smiled at me.

"You should have told Joanna to stop," I said.

"I didn't want to hurt her feelings," she said.

Her eyes rolled shut and she seemed to be asleep. I was
smoothing her sheet when she opened her eyes and thrust her
lips forward in a pouting request to be kissed. I never could
stand anybody doing that. But I bent down to kiss her.
When our lips touched she opened her mouth and took mine
in hers, sucking and thirsting at my lips and tongue. I tried to
draw back, but I thought I felt her body arching toward me,

and I was afraid she might hurt herself. I stayed at her mouth past the recoil of horror at entering the body of her death and went on to a response of love throughout my body and down my limbs that melted me. Afterward I stood at her bedside in a daze of disbelief, understanding nothing, and myself least of all. Mary was asleep.

A nurse walked in, scolding, about my being there at that time, about the smell and about the window, and I left while she was closing it. Out in the air, weighted with moist, windy heat and with loneliness dragging at me, I walked slowly along Broadway and saw Matt coming out of an Italian restaurant. He had his arm around a small blond girl. Her tan was more sensational than mine, and she was dressed in a white crocheted mini. I pulled back against the side of the building. Matt and his girl were kidding around. As they walked, she put one short, sturdy, bare, tanned leg between his long ones, bringing him to a helplessly laughing halt. And did it again as soon as he began to walk. Her voice reached me clearly. "Mattie, you forgot how to do it!" She spoke with the affected open vowels that girls put on now, no matter where they come from. They stopped at a car parked near a meter. She stood him against the meter post, play-acted blindfolding and tying him and then gunned him down. He responded in a death throes exaggeration. They clung together before she got into the car, and he went around to the traffic side as she started the motor. She rolled her window open and they put their foreheads together. He crossed back to the curb and watched her pull out, raising his hand in the oath-taking gesture of farewell that I knew. Matt stood still for a second, glanced at his watch, took a pack of cigarettes and a mutilated matchbook from the chest pocket of his white, openwork knit shirt and moved forward in my direction. He stopped almost directly in front of me to light the cigarette. His hair was longer. He was thin and very pale and ugly. I hated everything about him, but most of all his mouth as he drew in the smoke. I wanted him dead. Or myself. Both. I felt demeaned beyond the possibility of going on living. He saw me at that moment. His face lit with surprise and joy. He jumped up on both feet, a basket-shooting leap, and ran forward, smiling. "Hey, Jean," he said. "You're here. Isn't that great."

With a smile that must have looked crazy, I said, in a rush, "I was at the hospital, you son of a bitch."

His face went still. "What's the matter?"

"What's the matter?" I mimicked his tone, as if I were Elliot fighting with Paul. "Nothing's the matter with you, that's for sure."

He put his arm out, defensively. "Is she dead? What is it? Let's get back there." He took my arm and ran toward the hospital, carrying me along, but I pulled away and stopped. He stopped too.

I yelled, "Who's your darling little blonde?"

"What blonde?" he said.

I felt I would go mad on the spot if he lied. "I saw you," I screamed. "I saw you. I stood and watched, like a demented forty-year-old slob in love with a lying kid. I saw you come out of the restaurant. I saw the whole bit. I saw your touching farewell hand movement. You and your sexy little playmate." I was crying uncontrollably.

He came very close. I thought that he was going to hit me. "You're gathering a crowd. Stop yelling." There were a couple of people back at the corner standing and watching us.

Matt moved his arm. I was sure that he meant to hit me, and I did it first, striking him in the face with the side of my arm. He gripped my arm, very hard. "Are you crazy? You're unbelievable. That's my kid sister. She came in from the Coast to be here until it was all over. Her little boy got very sick and she has to go right back." He shook my arm and dropped it with a flinging gesture.

A cop was moving casually in our direction along the gutter. He came near, but stayed in the gutter. "What's the trouble here?" He held an insistently neutral expression on his young smooth face.

"No trouble, Officer," Matt said.

The cop didn't look at him. "How about you, lady? You having any trouble?"

"No," I said. "It's personal."

"Do you have to do it on the street, then, where people call it to my attention?"

"We're on our way home," Matt said, and took my arm. We walked away.

"I'm sorry," I said, and began to laugh and cry.

He had changed. Either it fired him up for me to be a fool, or he had learnt something about his own sensuality during the months we had been apart. We separated on Broadway, but we were to meet at my apartment after his visit to the hospital. I had a sandwich at a luncheonette filled with med students gobbling waffles and ice cream. I wasn't happy and I wanted to be. Matt was back, wasn't he? When I got into my stifling apartment, I began to cry and tear my clothes off and rant and wail aloud about what an idiot I had been. If it was demeaning to have thought that Matt was betraying me, it was worse to have betrayed myself — to have instantly lost what I was promising myself to be, at the sight of Matt with another girl. And she wasn't even. I lay in the bed and wept and couldn't stop when Matt arrived.

He liked my state. He spoke tenderly and moved aggressively. "My friend and I are going to make you all better," he promised. He dominated and controlled everything we did in a different way. And later, while I was fixing something cold to drink, he followed me into the kitchen, fooling around with me as if I were a toy — lifting me high in the air and forcing me to plead to be let down, grabbing my head in a wrestler's lock, feeding me bits of cheese and cracker when I repeated the words he insisted I say, and back in the bedroom, pinning me down on the bed and smothering me with pillows until I burst into more tears and his friend and he had to make me better again. This time he lost himself and his deliberate method and we moved together into an exquisite territory where nothing mattered but this sensation, this bodily love, this perfect happiness without striving.

It was the first time that we had spent a whole night together. We played and talked and snacked until it was light and then he was talking about "later." He told me that there was a good possibility of a teaching job in England for him. Andy was working on it. "I'd have to make a commitment for at least two years." Matt was fussing with a cigarette and matches and an ashtray and scattering old ashes all over the bed. "Your husband wouldn't object, would he?"

"Don't call him my husband. We're divorced and he's remarried."

"You never mentioned that," he said.

"Object to what?"

"If you went to England," Matt said, and before I could savor the proposal, added, "I can take care of you, but I don't know if I'll be earning enough to support your kids and mine."

"I can take care of myself," I said.

"There could be trouble about finding work there. Rules on non-nationals. Won't Harry take care of the boys?"

"Have I agreed to go?" I said. "It seems to be a big worry to you already."

He grabbed my head and fake-punched me in the nose. "She's off," he said. "There's a blonde waiting for me in a London flat."

I freed myself and placed myself at the opposite end of the bed, facing him, crouched on my knees. "I've been thinking a lot, Matt, about changing all this." I raised my arms to indicate everything — my life, the city. "For the boys too."

He wasn't listening. He was more interested in my body, naked before him. He reached out and grasped my waist, kneading his hands across my ribs, ending at my breasts, making the nipples sing under his palms. I took his hands and held them in mine. "Listen to me," I said.

"Sure," he said. "What were you thinking?"

I felt vulnerable and stupid and my shining solutions to the emptiness of life came out nonsense. "I was thinking of working among the kind of people I come from. Girls, especially. In those Pennsylvania cities that are all alike. One of them, not necessarily the one I came from."

"Like doing what?" he said.

"I don't know," I said. "I was thinking about the Church. I could join one of their groups. The good ones."

He burst out laughing. "You gotta be kidding," he said. "Look at you." He grabbed me again. "You're going to waste this in Wilkes Barre or Scranton?"

We slept a few hours, and then it was time to get up and go to work. Matt woke morning-sour. He was different again that evening at the hospital, masked in controlled anger and reserves of guilt and depression or plain exhaustion. I didn't know what he was feeling. He hardly greeted me. Well, he had warned me that he couldn't manage more than one emotion at a time, and at the hospital too many things demanded his response. Outside the door of her room, he could go on to something else. I didn't understand him and was repelled, but I knew that revulsion wouldn't live past his first touch. "That's the way it's going to be," I told myself. "Stop thinking about it."

They must have been pouring stuff into Mary. She was some drunken-idiot replica of herself, her head propped, the eyes rolling uncontrollably, a helpless smile pulling at her lips. She slept intermittently, with her mouth fallen open like an old woman's. Between naps, she made a fiercely concentrated effort to greet the stream of visitors, to remember names and to ask after kids, or about work projects or political actions or to comment on a new dress or hairdo or beard. But she had trouble with her thick tongue and what she said was altered into absurd little legends. "She called me her dear, her little squash," Joanna said, when what I had heard was, "Your head's a little squashed." Stella Shaeffer had her story. Mary had greeted her with, "I've never seen you in that hat," but Stella had heard, "I'll ever see you in my heart," and that's the way it went. Papa Shaeffer was outside, directing the flow with the help of Robin's odd ideas of organization. He urged visitors to stay just a minute, not to talk unless Mary spoke first, insisting that these were instructions straight from Mary herself. He said to each visitor, "Mary told me, 'Now I'm tired. Now I want to say good-bye to my friends. Now I'm ready to die.'" I could hear her saying that only in his Russian-Yiddish accent, if at all, but when I arrived early one evening, before the visitors had started, she woke as I entered the room, thrashing about and shouting, "Call a meeting. Call a meeting. No more of this shit. I have to be made better."

A young doctor strolled in behind me. He had adorned his small dark face with a dashing handlebar mustache. "What's all the commotion?" he said in amusement. He sat on Mary's bed and took her flailing hands in his.

"Hi," she said, and transformed herself into a child. She tried to produce a winning smile but it slipped out of control into a leer.

He winked at me. "Don't look so upset," he said. "The stuff we're pouring into her, she feels fine. Don't you, Mary?"

She nodded. Her eyes rolled back in her head.

"You remember me," he said to her, and winked at me again.

"Certainly," she said thickly. "Of course I remember you."

"Sure you do," he said. "Who am I?"

"You're a doctor. You're Doctor . . . Dr. Howe." She nodded wisely.

"No," he said. "Try again." He had propped himself on his elbows and was sprawled across her board of a body, his face so close to hers that their lips almost touched.

She smiled, bewildered, trying to please. "Doctor . . . Dr. Eberhardt," she said.

"No-o-o," he drawled, as one would tease and encourage a child.

"Oh, I know who you are," she said. "Dr. Walkers," and as he shook his head, ". . . Stone," and with desperation, "Freeman, Hartke." In an attempt to charm, she slurred, "Who cares about your name, anyway?" and pushed out her lips to be kissed.

He gave me a sly look, patted her on the head and stood up. "These new drugs are terrific," he said, and ambled out, smoothing his short, white starched coat over his flaring hips.

Mary pulled her lips back into a crooked smile. She whispered fiercely, "Jean, help me. Call a meeting. They have to listen. Tell Matt. No more mistakes. Altman . . . Bluestein . . . whatever his name is. Get Bob. And Bella. They're wasting time. It's taking too long. Hurry up. Hurry up."

I rubbed her wrist, saying, "Yes, yes, yes." She fell asleep. I pointed out the young doctor to Matt. "Who's that one?"

"He's nobody," Matt said. "Some little intern. Or technician. I forget."

The visitors came in an unending file, even after she went into coma and lay, diminished, sunken, without any life but the shallow breaths taken through a mouth changed into a little black hole. They came two by two to stand for a few seconds at the foot of her bed in silence and then made way for the next pilgrims. Most were young people who had read her essays in a paperback compilation of movement writings that had become a best seller. But almost anybody who had ever had anything to do with her came by during the two weeks we were waiting for her to die. Robin showed up every evening with new groups of followers. And one evening Bella came, using a walker, flanked by a circle of middle-aged helpers, and when word was passed around the crowd massed outside the hospital, it turned into a demonstration. Someone softly sang, "I dreamed I saw Joe Hill again." The crowd took it up and others stood with raised fists while Stella, with the tears streaming down her jolly, sweet face, helped Bella raise a violently trembling arm in response. The hospital administration didn't care for what had happened and spoke to Matt. Matt let them know that he'd be happy if they cut the flow, but they were reluctant to do so. Stories about Mary were appearing in all the papers, and in the newsweeklies. Joanna read one to me, in the waiting room, in a properly hushed voice.

In a city hospital room, a young woman who promises to become a saint of the radical movement, is dying of cancer, while hundreds of her followers silently file past her bedside to receive an unspoken blessing. Mary Moody Schwartz, only child of Elizabeth Vance Moody, convicted atom bomb spy, recently released by special pardon, has been hailed as the prime mover and innovator of a vast new commune movement, as well as one of the chief ideologues of the mushrooming women's lib movement. Hospital authorities, confronted by the unusual situation, have hesitated to forbid the continuation of the show of grief for the dying twenty-six-year-old young woman.

"They have her age wrong," Joanna said, and read on.

The demonstration is being conducted in a well-organized and orderly fashion, apparently spontaneous, and more religious in character than political, it has been stated. Long lines snake around the hospital complex in upper Manhattan, and two by two, visitors are ushered through the doors by young volunteers . . .

I cut her off. I had seen Sadie, leaning heavily on the arm of her son, waiting her turn in line. I ducked into a ladies' room and stayed for twenty minutes, to avoid them. When I came out, Matt was in the visitors' room with Gloria and a much tanned older woman, his mother. His mother studied me closely when he introduced us.

"What did she think?" I asked Matt. We were at supper the following night in the hospital's good restaurant, a wood-paneled, subdued room that smelled like a ship's dining room.

"You'll hate what she said," he said. "You'll hate her forever."

I insisted.

"I guess it was a kind of blessing. She said that in a couple of years when your age really begins to show, you'll get a face lift and look twenty-eight again."

"I see," I said.

"And she said if you really loved me, you'd give up your three boys. Andy says that too."

I didn't respond.

"Doesn't Harry want them?" Matt said.

"I want them," I said.

"They could spend vacations with us," he said. "It could be a rough situation. You'll have to be at home until Katy's big enough for nursery school, and I'll be the only one earning money." For a second, I couldn't think who Katy was. "Unless Harry means to do a real share of . . . you know. It's very tough to support five kids."

I didn't say anything.

"How much money would Harry be willing to give you?"

"How much would you like?" I said. "And did you discuss with your mother and with Andy how much time off I get? And which old age home I'm to be placed in when no longer useful?"

He looked at me with sharp dismay and put his hands over his eyes. What was he doing behind his hands — laughing at me again? He dropped his hands. His eyes were hard and self-condemning. "It's useless," he said. "I don't know how to live. It doesn't matter what I feel, it never comes out right. I didn't know how to live with Mary, and I won't know how with you."

"Didn't," I said in a rage. "She's not dead yet."

He shook his head and pushed his food away. "It's impossible," he said. He stood up.

"Where are you going?" I said. "You haven't finished your dinner." Misery rose in my throat like bile. "Sit down, Matt, please," I said. "Please. Let's not talk about these things yet. It's too soon. Sit down and have dessert. Please."

The waitress approached to clear the table. She looked at Matt inquiringly. He sat down.

"I'm sorry," I said. "But that was Paul and Elliot and Terry you were talking about, not three things."

He stared down at the table and moved a bread crumb in circles with the tip of a finger. "I thought we weren't talking about it," he said.

"I just wanted to explain," I said. And in a rush, "You hurt me when you laughed at me the other night. Why is it funny that I want life to be more . . . more . . . to add up to something more . . . to be good . . ." I didn't finish.

He looked up with a studying, cold glance. "You sound like a stammering Mary," he said.

"Well, I'm dumber," I said.

"Okay," he said briskly. "You want to talk about what you said the other night? You want to know what I really think? I think it's romantic crap."

"Because it's me?"

"You — anybody — me. I've lived with it. I don't want it. I thought we wanted the same things, you and I. But maybe we don't."

"Like what?" I said.

"I don't know. Do we have to put it in words? A private life. Private joys. The state can't wither away fast enough, as far as I'm concerned, but I don't see any sign of it, under any system. Mary's communities. I almost fell in love with them.

Then I thought about it more deeply later. I could have plunged into that, all that chaos and stultifying organization, nobody allowed to pee without a collective judgment on the color and quantity. I don't want it. There must be a better way. I don't want to end my life a Sam Shaeffer."

"Oh, poor Papa Shaeffer," I said.

"Poor Papa Shaeffer!" he said. "He thinks he's terriffic. He thinks he did his part to change the world. That's poor Papa Shaeffer's version of the good life."

"You're using him to keep yourself aloof. That's what I do. It's not true what we say, in the way we use it."

"What does that mean?" he said. "That was certainly a bit of confusion."

"It won't be different in England," I said.

"I don't expect it to be," Matt said. "Andy was telling me about the London School of Economics."

"I don't know anything about that," I said.

"I don't know what we're talking about," Matt said. "I thought we loved each other. That's different enough for me."

"I went to a wild demonstration with Mary — when I acted as her guard, remember? I never felt that way before." I stopped. How could I convey that glorious surge of communal happiness?

He waited, puzzled, and returned to where he had been. "You know what's important," he said. "What I learned with you. The way we're happy."

"Maybe there's a way of putting them together," I said.

"What?" he said. But I couldn't explain.

We walked through the buildings to the Broadway exit. Matt wanted to get a carton of cigarettes and some magazines to read while we waited. Mary would probably not last the night. He had asked me to stay with him. Broadway was suspended in a haze of smelly heat and a yellow, menacing light of early evening. The gutter's edge ran flush to the curb with filth: newspapers, dog shit, empty packages and wrappings, ends of hot dogs and pizzas from the open counters of the food joints, a melting ice-cream cone, leaflets of all kinds — supermarket flyers, primary election appeals, scrawled peace leaflets in four garish colors, US OUT OF CAMBODIA, THAILAND, VIETNAM, LAOS, a splotch of color for each country — and on the tipsy, broken sidewalks an extraordinarily varied collection of people in all sizes, shapes, colors, passing by in their extraordinarily varied ways of walking, dressing, speaking, gesturing, an army in disarray, each unit moving in a tunnel of hope along the edge of death toward a mysterious victory or defeat. Was it all for Matt's bursting instant of private joy? For the private joy of an old woman coming toward me, teetering on her high-heeled pumps, her hair dyed to a used-up hideous red, restraining her tiny dog attached to her by a red leash, and for its joy, rushing after bits of garbage with quivering intensity? Yes, and for the mixed joys of another group, a child howling with exhaustion, hung on the narrow, skinny hip of a dark little mother screeching in Spanish to her fat woman companion, naked under a loose cotton dress, directing an older black child to pee in the gutter, between a Cadillac and a Saab.

We walked back toward the hospital. Before we reached the room, Matt's face closed in on the anguish of entering that place. The last of the line for that evening was passing through. Visiting hours were over. We took our stations and waited.